Edge of Summer

An Anna Ghere Mystery - Book One

Patra Ann Taylor

Hope & Nova Creative

Library of Congress Control Number: 2025911073

Paperback ISBN: 979-8-9920703-2-3

E-Book ISBN: 979-8-9920703-3-0

Dedication

To Stephen Bucher, my one and only.

Walk Slowly
by Adelaide Love

If you should go before me, dear, walk slowly
Down the ways of death, well-worn and wide,
For I would want to overtake you quickly
And seek the journey's ending by your side.

I would be so forlorn not to descry you
Down some shining highroad when I came;
Walk slowly, dear, and often look behind you
And pause to hear if someone calls your name.

Let brotherly love continue.

Be not forgetful to entertain strangers:

for thereby some have entertained

angels unawares.

Hebrews 13:2 (KJV)

Forward

Consider the lily-of-the-valley. Over the course of my eight decades on this earth, I have done so hundreds of times, each deliberation of their beauty a genuine delight to my senses.

I remember the spring day in 1928 when I first discovered the white bell-shaped flowers in a neglected bed behind our small barn on South Street. With the temperature a perfect seventy degrees, my brothers and sister had tossed their hats, gloves and sweaters onto a pile on our kitchen table before heading off to school, their souls finally freed from the months of oppressive Indiana winter.

After Mother washed the breakfast dishes, she took my hand and led me into the green room. "It's time," she announced, her face lit by a sunbeam streaming in through the front window. "Let's get to work."

I looked around the narrow green room that extended along the west side of our house. Through the bank of windows, the tree branches dotted with the first evidence of green buds, I glimpsed Prairie Creek beyond.

Small clay pots containing Mother's spring sprouts—an assortment of flowers and vegetables—lined the windowsills, two deep, around three walls of the room. Since bringing up her new plantings from the basement a few weeks ago, she had tended her fledgling sprouts, turning and shifting them regularly to be certain each received its full share of sunlight.

Mother also kept jars of seed in our cellar that she would later plant directly into the rich black Indiana soil. But that day she focused on getting her "up-starts" into the ground.

"Carry these, Anna," she instructed, placing a pot in each of my hands. "Be careful not to drop them."

Mother loaded her sprouts, a dozen or so at a time, onto a tray and carried them to the backyard. She and my brothers had spent several chilly days preparing her garden beds, hand-tilling the soil while working the last of the fallen leaves and her winter compost into the dirt. Throughout the winter, Old Barney had contributed considerably to her compost pile. My father liked to tease that planting season was the only time of year in which Mother appreciated our horse.

With the preparation behind her, Mother began the joyous work of planting her sprouts, humming a pleasant tune as she worked her way up and down neat rows.

While she worked, I danced and played in the sunlight, chasing shadows with the shifting morning light. I breathed in the fragrance of the freshly turned soil, as I twirled and fell, twirled and fell, in the still-brown grass. When I grew tired, I turned my attention to exploring the flower beds along our back fence, imagining Mother's special light blue delphiniums blooming there later in the spring. She adored the quaint qualities of the flowers that inspired memories of her own childhood on the family farm outside Mulberry. My sister Gem told me that Mother's delphiniums were the most beautiful flowers in the whole town, maybe even in the world.

"Anna. Anna! Where are you?"

I heard her voice, then the rustle of her dress skirt as she approached. "There you are. Remember, don't go near that creek without me."

"I won't."

I lay on my belly, facing a narrow flower bed that stretched along the back of our small barn, my head propped up on my hands. Mother stooped next to me. The bed was dotted with a clutter of dark green sprouts in various stages of growth.

"Look, Mother," I proclaimed, pointing to a cluster of tiny white blooms. "Bells."

"Lily-of-the-valley," she muttered. "I'd forgotten about these."

I sat up next to her. "Aren't they beautiful?"

"Magnificent in their simplicity." Her head nodded in appreciation as she gazed at the flowers.

"Can we grow some in your garden with your other flowers? Please, Mother! Can we?"

"They wouldn't grow there, Anna. They thrive in the coolness of the shade. That's why they love it here. But you and Gem can enjoy summer picnics next to the lily-of-the-valley. You can spread an old blanket on the ground right here. I'll make you sandwiches and cookies to eat while you enjoy their company."

Over time, I discovered more about the white-bell flowers behind our old barn, hidden away from our day-to-day lives. It's difficult for me to separate that first discovery of Lily-of-the-Valley from what I learned about the flowers through my many decades on this earth. Even now, portrayals of their special place in the cultures of the English, the Romanians, and especially the French, plot their escape from my pencil tip to re-live their victories across the plane of my story-telling. I've promised to set them free before I go.

The stories from my childhood flow through my mind gathering depth, color, texture, and understanding through the gentle passing of time. Bits of evolving perspective and pieces of historical context add to their splendor, thriving in the coolness of the shade of my mind. The details I've picked up along the road of life demand their inclusion in my brief history of The Bygone Era.

I dare not leave them out.

The memories of a seven-year-old now inseparable from those of a feeble elder, I boldly color my recollections of a lifetime for the sake of my storytelling.

With love,

Anna Ghere

Prologue

To hear Aunt LoRetta tell it, Pauline and I almost drowned when we fell through the ice on Prairie Creek last winter. My aunt's version of the incident didn't quite match up with Pauline's or my first-hand recollections, but facts seemed irrelevant in the shadow of an epic tale.

"What happened out there today, Annie?" Popo sat on a wooden stool he'd pulled next to the feather bed I shared with my sister, Gem. Mother had tucked me and my friend into the bed after she'd dried us off and slipped us into flannel nightgowns. Pauline and I sat draped in blankets playing with a deck of cards Gem had slipped us while we waited until Doc Becker came by to pronounce us still among the living.

Unlike Mother's outburst of hysteria, which helped fuel Aunt Lo's already-vivid imagination, Popo's calm questioning put me at ease.

"Well," I began slowly, not wanting to stir up a frenzy all over again, "Pauline and I walked Helen home after school. Her mother wasn't there, so Helen said we couldn't stay, not even long enough to warm up." I pursed my lips and shook my head.

"That explains why Helen wasn't part of your shenanigans today."

"When Helen got home, she didn't want to come here with Pauline and me to play Rook. Helen doesn't like cold weather. When it's cold outside, she stays in her house all weekend, until her mother drags her out to go to church on Sunday." I wriggled and rolled my eyes to make Popo smile.

He nodded as if he was taking it all in. "I can't say I blame her, but let's talk about what happened with you and Pauline."

"Popo, Helen stays in bed all day and *reads*," I added. "She even reads schoolbooks!" I couldn't hide my astonishment.

"You like Charlie to read to you."

"That's different."

"You and Pauline could learn a thing or two from Helen."

"Why do people always say that?"

"Because it's true." Popo drummed his fingers on the headboard. "Can we get back to how you ended up in Prairie Creek this after-noon?"

"Popo, it was so cold outside today! Since we were freezing to death, we ran up the alley on this side of Washington Street, then ran through the trees along the creek. Instead of going up to South Street and crossing over the bridge by our house, we took a shortcut." I paused, hoping the story made sense to my father. "That's when we fell through the ice," I added under my breath.

I gave Popo my best "end of story" face. He wasn't buying it.

"You know your mother doesn't want you wandering through the woods on the other side of the creek. With good reason!"

We were running, not wandering, but I didn't think pointing that out would help me end this conversation any faster. "Mother doesn't want us on the other side of the creek because she'll get a telephone call from Aunt Iris about us being in her yard," I stated matter-of-factly.

"Your mother is not concerned about your Aunt Iris. She's concerned about your safety."

"We go through those woods all the time with Blinn and Cory. The trees aren't even thick there near our house. When they're bare, we can see across the creek to Aunt Lo's painting shed from the windows in the green room."

Popo shook his head. "That is beside the point, young lady. Do what your mother tells you. If you'd listened to her, you wouldn't be in the situation you're in now."

I wondered what situation my father was referring to, but didn't dare ask.

The sternness had slipped from his voice when Popo continued. "Besides, the twins are older, and I hope they have a little more sense than two seven-year-olds. Where did you get the idea that the ice was solid enough to hold you? Did one of your brothers tell you that?"

I sat looking at my hands.

"Did Blinn or Cory or Gus tell you the ice was safe to cross?"

"No."

"Angel?"

"No one told us it was safe, but last week when Pauline and I went out to the barn to tell Gus that Mother needed him, the twins were out there sharpening those old ice blades... you know, the ones that hang on the wall next to Old Barney's Christmas bells."

"Go on."

"Cory told Blinn he heard the ice might freeze solid in the next few days. Blinn got real excited. He said that if it did, they could skate all the way to the Barner's Woods on those ice blades. That was a whole week ago, Popo."

"Those old blades belonged to Karl and me when we were young." Popo paused a moment, his eyes cast upward, searching his childhood memories of that bygone era when he and his only brother were still close. In a soft voice, he told us that during their youths, he and Karl loved to ice skate up Prairie Creek during winter. "We'd skate all the way to the edge of town," he recalled, contentment on his face. "The thick stand of trees along both sides of the creek was bare that time of year, yet beautiful against a translucent azure sky. We used to bet who could spot the first cardinal perched on a limb high above the icy creek. I always let my younger brother win."

Lost in his memories, Popo sat for a moment longer before continuing. "I hope you know the temperature needs to stay below freezing for several days before the creek is solid enough for ice skating... or cutting across on foot. Haven't you noticed the snow melting off the last couple of days? When the snow is melting, doesn't it make sense that the ice on the creek is melting too?"

"I suppose. We're sorry."

"I don't want you to be sorry, Angel." Popo tapped my forehead with his index finger. "I want you to use your head before you do impulsive things that could cause tragic consequences. That goes for you, too, Pauline."

"Yes, sir."

Despite his gentleness, Popo's scolding hurt my feelings. I looked up into his face. He placed his palm on my cheek and used his thumb to wipe away a tear that had slipped from my eye.

Popo continued his questioning in a gentler tone. "What happened after you two silly girls ran onto the ice and it gave way?"

"Pauline was ahead of me..."

"Why am I not surprised?"

I rolled my eyes over to my friend, who was staying quiet. I felt Popo's hand on my knee, which prompted me to continue.

"Pauline was ahead of me when the ice broke. She went down into the water up to her chin and started screaming. I was only in waist-deep, so I reached out to pull her up. I had just gotten her back on her feet when a man stepped into the creek, grabbed me under one arm and Pauline under his other, lifted us out of the water, and set us back on the bank.

Popo jumped to his feet, his eyes wide with surprise. "What? A man pulled you out of the creek? Are you sure about that?"

My father's reaction confused me. I nudged Pauline with my elbow. "Right?" I prompted her.

My friend nodded.

Concern spread over Popo's face. "Did you tell your mother this?"

I thought about it for a moment. "I don't think so. She already had us dead from drowning.

"And exposure," Pauline whispered.

"And exposure, so we were busy trying to convince her we were still alive."

"Then what happened, Annie?" Popo's voice had dropped an octave, and taken on a cool, controlled tone.

"The man set us on the bank, like I said, and then shouted, 'Run, Annie, run! Don't stop until you're home.'"

Popo stepped back, a hand clutching his chest. "The man called you by name?"

I looked at Pauline. She nodded once.

"Yes," I confirmed. "He called me Annie."

"But you didn't know who he was? Did you get a good look at him?" Popo's agitation took over as he paced back and forth in the small room.

"No, he didn't look familiar. When we got up on the bridge, I looked back through the woods, but there was no sign of him any-where."

Popo thought for a moment. "Maybe he was under the bridge or down the street by that time."

I shrugged. "Maybe."

Popo stood in my bedroom doorway, deep in thought. "The worst part is," I said, invading his thoughts. "I lost my boots."

"Your boots?" My father looked puzzled.

"My red rubber boots," I reminded him. "The ones Aunt Lo found at the rummage sale a couple of years ago. They fit Gem when she brought them home, but this year, Gem had out-grown them and passed them on to me. They were a little too big, so when the man pulled me out of the creek, he lifted me out of them." I sighed. "I loved those boots. No one in my class has red boots except me."

"I'll walk over to the other side of the creek and see if I can find them, Angel. Since they're red, I might be able to spot them and fish them out of the water before the ice freezes again. I want to go look around, anyway."

Popo stepped back into the room and kissed me on the head. "Your sister will be up soon with some chicken soup. You girls stay put."

As he turned to leave, I said the obvious. "He was an angel. We're certain of it.

The gentleness disappeared from my father's voice.

"He damn well better have been."

Act I

Chapter 1

Aunt LoRetta referred to the illusive interlude between late August and late September as "the edge of summer." To linger too long in summer, or rush too eagerly into autumn, was to miss the many delights that defined this special time of year. Aunt Lo often reminded me that God's plan for summer's beginning and end was His alone, that He delighted in challenging our made-up notions about His perfect timetable.

"Be vigilant, Annie," my aunt urged me. "Pay attention or you'll miss the moment of its coming."

"But how will I know, Aunt Lo?"

"You'll just know," she assured me. "When you sense the first wisp of a breeze kissing the fringe of autumn, you'll know our beloved season within a season is upon us."

Oh, the many wonderful pleasures that arrived at the edge of summer: picking the last of Mother's green beans for supper, the singing of the cicada choir in the evening, catching lightning bugs in Mason jars past dark, the rising white mist off Prairie Creek at dawn, and sleeping late into the cool of the morning.

It's the time of year when the pace at the Ghere-Douglass Company, the wholesale dairy business owned by my father and his brother, returned to its normal rhythm after a hectic summer, and when Mother's attention turned from growing and canning to sewing and mending to prepare her children for the new school year.

I loved being tucked under Aunt Lo's arm as she whispered to me about the stealth approach of our favorite time of year. "Just another day or two, a week at most, before the music begins," she whispered, her sweet breath tickling my ear.

I nodded, hopeful that my ears would not fail me.

I watched when she pointed skyward at the undulating ribbons of grackles or starlings or red-winged blackbirds, making their way south. She always watched intently until each flock was out of sight.

"There's only one thing more glorious than the edge of summer."

I awaited her answer, knowing Aunt Lo would tell me in her own time. Finally she sighed and closed her eyes again, imagining. "Heaven," she breathed.

I giggled. "How do you know, Aunt Lo? You've never been to heaven."

"Not yet, but I believe it's wondrous... so beautiful that we can't describe it with mere words."

I stood at her side as I imagined such a place.

"We're on its doorstep." Aunt Lo's face shined. "If you listen closely, you might hear summer preparing its encore, even as autumn rehearses its sonata."

My aunt paused, looking upward. I slipped her arm around me, my eyes following her gaze, hoping it would help me see what she saw. She continued in a whisper, "To witness the moment those two full symphonies commingle is to wait breathlessly for the moment they collide in a jarring cacophony of past and future. In the meantime, we stand in the breach, living in the tension, that incredible place where the present stalls, if but for a moment, our attention fully on what was and what will be, before it all disappears into the mundane rut of autumn, while the dreaded winter closes in at its heels."

We waited patiently for our beloved season within a season to be upon us. It seemed we lived our best lives... at the edge of summer.

***

On the first Saturday of August 1931, I stood on the platform of the Wanatah Railroad Depot, holding my father's hand. Gem fidgeted beside me, a finger twirling her wavy blond hair as she shifted from one foot to the other, watching Aunt Lo as she prepared to take her leave, her hand on the arm of the conductor as if he were her date to the prom. Aunt Lo turned with a swish of her skirt, pulling Oscar to a stop before delivering her instructions to the porter, who straggled along behind them.

"Would you look at that," my father whispered to Gem and me. "Your aunt's new skirt gives her usual sashay a bit of added flair."

My sister and I laughed. Popo enjoyed poking fun at his sister.

I admired my aunt, dazzled by the elegance in her new traveling clothes. Her gored, calf-length skirt with a deep yoke fit her trim body like a glove. The colorful summer print skirt paired perfectly with her simple creamed-colored blouse of silk *crepe de chine*.

Several months ago, Aunt Lo saw a similar ensemble in the spring issue of *Gazette du Bon Ton* she'd received secondhand from her cousin Louisa Rousseau, whom she was off to visit for two weeks.

Aunt Lo couldn't read the articles written in French, but enjoyed the photographs immensely. The moment she discovered *"les dernières nouvelles de France,"* the only French phrase her cousin had taught her, my aunt insisted she must have the outfit. With some cajoling, she convinced my mother to make it for her.

The crowning glory of the skirt were four gold and royal blue metal buttons she'd asked Mother to stitch vertically in a row onto the front of the yoke.

"Where in the world did you get these?" questioned Mother after Aunt Lo had placed them in her hand. Mother pushed away from her sewing machine to give her sister-in-law's reply her full attention.

"Genuine Lalafina," Aunt Lo answered. "I'd swear to it. I took them off of one of PaPaw's old blazers."

"One of PaPaw's old blazers?" Mother asked. "I'm surprised you didn't take them off of Karl's blazer while he was wearing it."

"Of course not, Maggie. My brother hasn't an ounce of fashion sense, or any sense at all, for that matter."

Mother and I chuckled.

Aunt Lo continued, "I found PaPaw's old blazer in a dusty box in the attic. Aren't the button's divine?"

"Are they real gold?" I asked as I peered into Mother's hand at the Aunt Lo's prized buttons.

Aunt Lo knelt in front of me and leaned her nose within an inch of mine. "I believe they're brass," she whispered. "But if people mistaken them for gold, who are we to argue?" Then she placed a finger on my lips. "Mum's the word, Annie."

I frowned. "Is it a secret, Aunt Lo?"

Aunt Lo pulled me into a hug. "Oh, no, dear child. Secrets are burdens far too heavy for seven-year-olds to bear."

I looked up at Mother, but her eyes wouldn't meet mine. I thought about the two cards of beautiful buttons she had shown me in early spring. She'd called them enameled openwork floral buttons before hiding them away in her bureau drawer. I wondered if they were still there, but I hadn't gotten up the nerve to peek.

***

As we watched her on the Wanatah platform, I thought Aunt Lo was every bit the fashion plate as the models she'd shown me in her French magazines, especially compared to the wholesomeness of the young farm women who lived around our town.

"Be careful, Jacob," Aunt Lo's sweetness disguised her emphatic orders. "Nothing damaged, nothing lost between here and Chicago, if you please. I need every article in pristine condition for my stay."

"Yes, ma'am."

Gem snickered at the sight of poor Jacob struggling under the load as he made his way along the tracks to the baggage car.

"Be careful with my hat boxes, dear," she called to the porter's back.

He nodded once, his black bobbin cap now askew on his head. "Yes, ma'am."

"Come along, now, Miss Ghere." Oscar patted her hand that still clung to his arm. "It's time to get you settled aboard the train. It's scheduled to depart soon."

"Of course, Oscar. A moment, please. It's a long sit between here and Chicago."

"It is that, Miss Ghere."

I took Gem's hand with my free one and pulled her close to me. We looked at each other, holding our words for our carriage ride home.

My eyes followed hers to the single strip of sunlight that had fought its way onto the platform where Aunt Lo now stood.

As she turned her head for a look around, I glimpsed Aunt Lo's soft gray eyes, the gentle slope of her up-turned nose, and her rosy lips, extraordinary features that had somehow come together on an ordinary face. Yet my father's only sister personified elegance. Poised and confident, witty and charming, my aunt was like no one else I knew except maybe my father.

As we waited, I replayed the words Aunt Lo had whispered to Gem and me during our brief carriage ride to the Wanatah Depot. "Expect the mysteries we solve during the heat of summer to yield a harvest of truth at its edge." I couldn't wait to ask Gem what Aunt Lo meant.

"Are there mysteries to solve awaiting you in Chicago, Aunt Lo?" Gem asked her.

She sounded sad and serious. "I hope so."

"Oh, tell us, Aunt Lo. Please tell us," my sister urged.

"Let's hope there's nothing to tell." Then she turned to the conductor. "It's time, Oscar." She kissed Gem's cheek and then mine. Popo returned his sister's hug, then kissed her on the forehead.

"Have a wonderful trip, Sister. Say hello to Louisa and Jean-Claude for me."

"I will, Brother." Then she winked at me and Gem. "Stay here, girls. I'll wave to you from the passenger car."

That was Oscar's cue to help her aboard the train.

I turned and glimpsed at the place where Aunt Lo had stood in the single beam of sunlight. It had faded. Even the sunlight shone brighter when she stood in it.

When the train whistle signaled its departure, we spied our beloved aunt leaning from a passenger car window, waving her hankie with a white-gloved hand. "Toodle-oo," she called, as the steel wheels of the train screeched against the rails. "I'll be back before the cicadas sing."

Chapter 2

After breakfast, I ran upstairs to collect a stack of old blankets while Gem wrestled our old baby carriage from the porch. With the blankets in the carriage, Gem placed Thea on top of them and pulled the canopy into place. Then, I followed my older sister down the front walk, and we took a left turn onto the sidewalk that ran along South Street, the first leg of our usual summer morning strolls. When we reached the corner, we crossed over and started back on the other side of the street.

"How many more days?" I asked my sister.

"How many did I tell you yesterday?" Gem's voice was calm and breathy as she pushed the carriage up the slight incline onto the bridge over Prairie Creek.

"Eight."

Gem's head bobbed up and down. "That means Charlie will be back in seven days. That's next Saturday... one week from today. Gus, Blinn and Cory will be back, too. You can wait that long."

"I suppose."

The first autumn he came to live with us for the school year, Charlie preferred playing with my brothers, especially Blinn and Cory. I tagged along whenever they'd let me, which wasn't that often. When school started, I'd watch at the window every afternoon for the boys to come home, yearning to start school myself so I could walk back and forth with them. Charlie loved to read, something the twins viewed as a chore. I loved to sit in the window seat next to Charlie, engrossed in whatever book demanded his attention. By the time I started first grade, I could read, thanks to Charlie.

When we walked Thea, Gem and I liked to pause atop the bridge to have a look around. Looking south down the creek, we often saw the Interurban rattling its way along the shoreline for a short distance before crossing over the bridge that bears its special tracks. Mother forbade us from setting foot on that bridge, but I knew my brothers sometimes crossed over it. I'd seen them do it with my own eyes.

Today, it was quiet on the south creek, so we continued our journey another two blocks before crossing back to our side of the street at the corner next to Mrs. Parlett's house, and then heading for home. I wanted to be there to kiss Popo goodbye before he left for work.

"When will Aunt Lo be back from Chicago, Gem?"

"She'll be back a week from Friday, six days after the boys' return. Gus will be back in time to pick up Aunt Lo from the Wanatah Depot when she arrives on the afternoon train." Gem took a deep breath as she bounced the baby carriage along. "Maybe we can go with him!

I wrinkled my nose. "It was crowded in the carriage when we took her to the Wanatah Depot. Aunt Lo takes a lot of baggage when she travels to Chicago." I recalled how Popo had struggled to get it all into the carriage for the trip to the train depot. He'd suggested that Gem and I stay home, but Aunt Lo wouldn't hear of it.

"I think she takes everything she owns for a two-week visit." Gem chuckled. Aunt Lo's ways tickled Gem.

"Tell me again who she visits in Chicago?"

"She stays with her cousin, Louisa Rousseau, in a little town outside of Chicago called Wheaton. There's a college there."

"Is Louisa our cousin, too?"

"I suppose she is." Gem lifted the canopy of the carriage to check on Thea, who seemed content sucking on the edge of her rag doll.

"Louisa is married to Jean-Claude," added Gem. "Aunt Lo told me he's French and very handsome."

We strolled along in silence for a bit, both of us deep in thought. Finally, Gem continued her story about our aunt's trip. "Louisa also invites two other friends to visit during the first week Aunt Lo is there. They're librarians, too. They also stay with Louisa and Jean-Claude, to catch up, whatever that means. Popo said he doesn't know how Jean-Claude survives the week." Gem shrugged and rolled her eyes.

As we approached the bridge, I ran ahead. I stepped up on the bottom rung of the wooden railing to get a better view north toward Barner's Woods. Popo told me that where we live used to be part of Barner's Woods, a vast expanse of thick woods in all directions. He said the trees along this stretch of Prairie Creek are all that's left of those woods this far down the creek, but a couple miles up the creek a portion of the woods remains on Barner land, with the massive Barner Farm beyond that. Popo and Uncle Karl's company does business with Barner Farm so Popo often travels there to visit Joshua Barner, the farm's current proprietor.

The view from the bridge differs completely from any seen from the windows of our green room that extended along the entire west side of our house. During the summer, the sound of meandering water over stones and the patches of blue sky filtering through the branches overhead are the only assurances that the creek still exists beyond the dirt path that runs between our house and the thicket of trees and bushes that hug the creek bank.

Up the north creek, the people who live there have cleared most of the trees on either side, carving a sculpted view from the wilderness for as far as the eye can see. (In all seasons, I loved leaning over the railing and breathing in the beauty.) Even with my eyes completely engaged, I caught a whiff of the last of the musk melons still in the rich soil around our town, awaiting the light touch of the field hands to separate them from their vines. The aroma of tomatoes from earlier in the summer now gone—Mother put up the last from her garden weeks ago—its absence giving way to that delicious musky aroma that made my taste buds tingle. Though faint, I knew that as the sun climbed in the sky, the smell would grow in intensity and drift for miles. The musk melons in their final stage of ripening are a sign that the edge of summer will soon be upon us.

I also knew that Mrs. Barner's abandoned cottage was tucked into the woods at a place where the creek widens next to a clearing in the native woods. Popo says there's been talk for years that Joshua Barner planned to tear it down, but the nostalgia of his carefree days growing up there always stops him.

***

Some summers, the hot August temperatures lowered the water level to where it wasn't much more than calf-deep in places. During the hottest days, Mother often rousted the boys out of their beds at day-break to wade into the creek where the water was deepest to carry out buckets-full to water her garden.

This summer had been kinder. The spring rains had filled the creek to overflowing, and the occasional summer downpour had kept its level high and active. Because of all the rain, the leaves on the trees on either side of the creek were still spring green.

Now in full bloom, Mother's flower beds burst with the color and fragrance from her favorite perennials that she'd begun coaxing out of the ground on the first warm day of spring. Along our back fence and far edge of our property opposite the stand of trees along Prairie Creek, Mother had lined her narrow beds with her favorite light blue delphiniums, accented by the occasional patch of tulips, so eager to grow, to show off their beauty.

But as we approached the edge of summer, Mother's flower bed in the center of our backyard stole the show. Unlike her vegetable garden, with its straight even rows, Mother's perennials seem to grow wild. Her assortment of bee balm, catmint, daylily, clematis, coreopsis, and lavender attracted a multitude of butterflies and hummingbirds, while her bee balm, catmint, and lavender, along with the salvia, were also fragrant. The result seemed to be Mother's seasonal foray into chaos, but Gem and I knew better. Mother's hidden hand orchestrated her flower garden's spectacular display. We were certain of it.

The days since my brothers left for Uncle Madison and Aunt Rachel's farm turned out to be the driest of the summer. Since Popo's work at Ghere-Douglass became more demanding since the stock market crashed in 1929, the chore of watering the vegetable and perennial gardens in the boys' absence fell to Mother, Gem and me. Gem loved wading barefoot into the flowing creek and scooping up buckets-full of water for the thirsty plants. Then I placed the filled buckets in a wagon we'd rolled close to the creek bank. When I had four full buckets, Gem would climb out of the creek and pull while I pushed the wagon along the narrow path through the trees to the garden, where Mother helped us pour the cool water on the plants that were still vital.

During the past week, Mother had removed the dried tomato stalks and piled them on the compost heap, but her corn, peas, green beans, turnips, and potatoes were still producing, though not as robustly as earlier in the summer. After a quick rest before heading back to the creek with the wagon, I watched as she bent down and ran her hand lightly across the tops of a few succulent baby spinach leaves. After a moment of thought, she announced, "These will be ready to pick in three or four days." Mother's large patch of spinach and two rows of herbs had thrived throughout the summer under Mother's loving guidance. Nothing got dry as a bone behind her back.

"I think it's going to be a scorcher," Mother announced one particularly hot early August morning. She examined the leaves on her remaining crops, concern on her face.

With tiny Thea sitting in a basket under the foliage of our sweet cherry tree, Mother began pacing through her neat rows of vegetables. When she finally stopped, she turned to me.

"Annie, go across the street and ask Bernard if he can help us haul water to the garden this morning. Between the four of us, we'll have it done in no time."

As I started up the dirt path beside our house, Mother called out, "Don't dawdle, Annie. I want to get these plants watered before the sun is overhead, and I still have canning to do before the house gets too warm."

When I returned with Bernard in tow, Gem had already dragged the wagon and four buckets out of the barn and waded into Prairie Creek. Mother was there on the bank, lifting out the first bucket Gem had filled.

"Let me lend a hand, ma'am, if ya please."

"Thank you, Bernard." Mother had a special affection for the boy, who was a friend of Charlie's and my twin brothers, Blinn and Cory.

"Annie, help your sister."

For a moment, I stood on the bank, watching as Gem waded further into Prairie Creek, where she stopped and turned.

"Grab a bucket and come on in," she called, waving an arm as an invitation to join the fun. "It isn't as cold as it was last winter." My sister tilted her head back and laughed.

Standing thigh-deep in the water, she laid her palms on its surface, as if to get a sense of the creek at the height of its glory. I watched as she stood there in the shadows where the depth of the water seemed darkest against the mud and stones on the bottom. She looked up suddenly, her eyes meeting mine. Was it an illusion? Staring into Gem's liquid blue eyes was as if I were gazing into a reflection of the water that flowed around her. In that moment, it occurred to me that my sister's nickname was befitting of such a soul as hers—brilliant and sparkling. Gem fit into the landscape as a red rose fits into a wedding bouquet.

"I forgot my bucket," she called. I kicked off my shoes, lifted a bucket from the wagon, and waded in.

***

As I climbed up on the wooden railing and looked up Prairie Creek, I thought about that day we'd turned the chore of watering Mother's garden into a fun adventure. It was this summer's most perfect day, despite the heat and the absence of our brothers and Charlie. I couldn't wait to find out what the edge of summer held for us in the coming days when my family was back together again.

From my elevated advantage, I looked down on the last remnants of the old stone crossing that had eroded since the town of Jeffries built the bridge. We'd dubbed that place where the water swirled around those stones just beneath the surface "the rapids."

I leaned over for a better view. "Gem, Gem!" I screamed, pointing. "Look!"

"What in the world is the matter with you, Annie?" Gem stepped up on the bottom rung of the railing beside me.

"Down there!"

"Oh, dear God! Run, Annie! Go get Popo."

I jumped off the railing, ran down the bridge and across our yard. "Popo!" I screamed. I took the porch steps two at a time. "Popo!"

My father met me at the door.

"Angel, I'm here." I heard the panic in my father's voice as I fell into his arms.

"You're okay now. Where are your sisters?"

I pointed to the bridge and huffed in a breath. My voice weak, I sobbed, "Oh, Popo. There's a man in the creek. I think he's dead."

"Stay with your mother." Popo bolted through the open door.

The oddest thing struck me as I watched my father go. He never left the house unless he looked his best, but there he went, his thick brown hair tousled, his face covered in shadow, his feet bare. He wore an old pair of pants and undershirt not fit for the public eye, out to take command of the situation... to make everything better.

With Mother's arm draped around my shoulders, we stood on the porch watching as he waded into the creek, grabbed the man by the back by his clothing and pulled him to dry ground. I spied Gem, still on the bridge, looking down at the scene, calm as a cucumber as she bounced Thea's carriage with one hand and held her position on the railing with the other.

Mother and I watched as Popo rolled the man over, then stood over him for a good look. "Maggie, ring up Sheriff Boggs and tell him we have a situation on our hands," he instructed. "Don't say it's a dead man, or Sally will have the news spread all over town before he gets here. Let's keep this close to the breast until it's in Sheriff Boggs' hands. But Maggie, please tell him to hurry."

Without replying, Mother turned and went inside.

I ran to Popo's side. He took a step back from the body and seemed deep in thought.

"Oh, Popo," I whispered. My father put his arm around me and pulled me to his side.

"Have you seen this man before, Angel?"

"No."

"Are you sure?"

Before I could answer, Bernard ran up to us. He stopped a few feet away.

"I ain't never seen a dead man afore." Bernard took a deep breath and stared at the body.

"Is he familiar to you, Bernard?" my father asked.

The boy dropped to his knees next to the man and gave him a closer looking-over.

"No, sir, Mr. Ghere. I ain't never laid eyes on him 'til just now." Then more to himself, Bernard continued, "I've prayed a whole heap o' birds up to heaven, an' a couple o' squirrels, an' one o' Mrs. Parlett's outside cats, but prayin' a man through them pearly gates sure seems a heap different kind o' job." Bernard shook his head back and forth, as if evaluating whether he was up to the task.

"Now's not the time to doubt yourself, Bernard. Give it your best shot." Popo patted his shoulder. "I'm sure you'll do just fine."

Then my father looked up and waved Gem over. She pushed the carriage down off the bridge and into the yard next to us.

"Gem, have you seen this man before?"

Gem stepped closer to the body and leaned down to get a good look at his face. "No, Popo, I've never seen him before." She walked around him again. "Annie, is this the man who pulled you and Pauline out of the creek last winter?" she asked.

Popo's eyebrows shot up.

I shook my head. "I didn't see that man's face, but he didn't wear fancy clothes like this man, that's for sure."

I looked over at the creek and tried to remember something, anything, more about the man. I fixed in my mind the moment he'd stepped out of the creek, his pants wet to his knees. The image of his boots flashed across my memory... old, brown leather, heavy string laces, a stitched seam across the toes. I circled around the dead man and looked at his feet. His shoes were two-toned saddle oxfords. I looked up at my father.

Popo gave my shoulder a knowing squeeze. "They're something, aren't they? I don't know anyone around here with shoes like that."

"Do you think someone killed him and threw him in the creek?" Gem asked Popo.

I gasped.

"Sheriff Boggs should be here soon. That's a question for him."

Gem pointed at the creek. "See there, Popo. I think that's his hat."

Popo sniffed, then waded back into the creek, retrieved the hat, and placed it on the man's chest.

"Gem, take Thea inside and see if you can get her to eat an egg. I want your mother out here to watch over things while I make myself presentable."

"Can I stay here with Mother?"

"I'm sure she'd appreciate your company, Angel."

As Gem wheeled the carriage past me toward the porch, she whispered, "What's Bernard doing?"

"Praying the man into heaven."

"People don't need to be prayed into heaven. They're going, or they're not."

"Who told you that, Gem?"

"Aunt Lo." Gem looked back at Bernard. "But I admit, Bernard's good with birds."

After Gem lifted our sister out of the carriage and disappeared inside, I sat down on the bottom step of the porch. With my eyes glued to the dead man, I waited for Mother. Bernard walked over and plopped down beside me.

"How'd it go?" I asked him somberly.

"He didn't budge."

Chapter 3

Sheriff Boggs scraped the last of the generous piece of blackberry pie off his plate and shoved his fork into his mouth. After the morning's hubbub in our front yard died down, the sheriff seemed genuinely grateful for Mother's offer of pie and coffee.

It had been a while since the Clinton County Sheriff had joined us at our kitchen table. Despite months of his absence, he seemed as comfortable as an old shoe, always the wayward adventurer eager to share his antics with his rapt admirers.

Still twitching from the excitement of discovering a dead man in the creek, I sat across from Sheriff Boggs, my eyes fixed on his face. But for the bit of blackberry that clung to his lower lip, he took charge of the situation with calm certainty. I remembered Mother's friend, Alma Mae Butler, once describing the demands of being the sheriff here in Jeffries required the ability of sitting with one's feet up for extended periods of time. That, and holding the Widow Winslow's hand through her never-ending stream of predicaments.

"Maggie, that was mighty fine pie. Blackberry has got to be my favorite."

"Boggy, it seems your favorite is whatever I'm serving." Mother grinned, grateful for the compliment.

"That's a fact, Maggie." The sheriff placed his napkin on the table and pushed away his plate. "That was quite a circus we had going on out front."

Mother put a hand on her hip. "I didn't tell Sally a thing, other than I needed to speak to you. That's when she tracked you down at your house."

"Someone got wind of Annie's little discovery before the sheriff got here." Popo looked at Mother.

Mother turned back to the breakfast dishes still in her sink. She'd have words with Popo when our company left.

"Now, now, Augie, it had nothing to do with Maggie. I can assure you of that. She didn't say a word about a dead man on the telephone. She just asked that I hurry."

"Sally figured something was up," Popo huffed.

"I'm sure she had some help." Sheriff Boggs' head bobbed up and down. "I smell a rat, and my number one suspect for head rat and town gossip is my beloved wife."

"Sweet Martha?" Mother dried her hands on her apron and walked back to the table. "She doesn't seem the type to spread gossip."

"You don't know Martha the way I do. I have a feeling she was yakking to that old biddy on the switchboard about your call before I had my pants buckled and my badge pinned to my shirt. I'll be sorting my suspicions into facts as soon as I get home. I'll forgive and forget over one of Martha's special Sunday rump roasts covered in onion gravy. The only roast I've had in months, I got over at the Blue and White Café."

"Speaking of the Blue and White, how are things going with Roxy and her new husband?" Mother enjoyed drawing the good sheriff into a little gossip session of her own.

"This Paul Lockwood is a winner." Sheriff Boggs gave an approving nod. "He works as hard as Roxy, which is saying something. I've never seen a woman work like her... no offense, Maggie."

"No offense taken."

"I hope this marriage sticks because if she shuts down for another one of her honeymoons... how many has it been?"

"We've all lost count," piped up Popo, sounding exasperated.

"Now, now, gentlemen." Mother crossed her arms over her chest. "Roxy had to get rid of a few grifters. No one can blame her for that."

"As I was saying..." Sheriff Boggs paused until all eyes were on him again. "If she shuts down for another one of her honeymoons... the one last spring lasted ten days... I'm sure I'd have another commotion on my hands from those rowdy railroaders. When they saw that closed sign on her door, I thought the lot was going to throw stones through her front window. Hungry railroaders... they're a breed all their own. I sent them down to the Little Palmer House, but that extra business didn't make the manager one bit happy." Sheriff Boggs laughed.

"Arnold Grayson can be mighty persnickety about his clientele." Mother topped off Sheriff Boggs's coffee cup.

"After that second hissy fit he threw in my office," continued the sheriff, "I started sending those boys to the Airport Diner out by the fairgrounds. I've never eaten there myself, but I hear they serve pickled eggs out of a barrel left over from the Great War."

Popo cleared his throat. I slipped out of my chair and stepped over to my father, pressing my back against his side, the *tink, tink, tink* of his spoon on the inside of Mother's old china cup, signaling his desire to end the gossip session and get back to the business at hand.

Mother continued, "I understand there was quite a ruckus when Roxy re-opened the Blue and White."

"There certainly was." Sheriff Boggs said that two of the boys from the Nickel Plate told anyone who would listen about Roxy's inconsiderate act of closing the diner for ten days. When she reopened, they stormed in like a couple of rutting boars, taking up twice as much space with their fog of fury, blasting the proprietor because of her thoughtless absence.

"Roxy asked in her sweetest tone, 'How may I help you, fellas?'"

Sheriff Boggs' parroting of Miss Roxy made Gem and Mother laugh, but Popo and I didn't weren't amused.

The sheriff said when one railroader insinuated something unflattering about Roxy's honor, Paul Lockwood came busting out of the kitchen waving a hot skillet still dripping with bacon grease and chased those two rascals down to the square and around the corner to the front of the Little Palmer House. "Mr. Grayson witnessed the men's arrival through the hotel's front window, and he..."

"Boggy?"

The sheriff turned to his friend.

"Do you mind if we return our attention back to the dead man my daughter discovered floating in the creek just outside my front door this morning?"

I nodded, feeling my knees wobble and a sense of gloom gathering in my chest. That morning, I'd awakened with a sense of joy and anticipation for the coming of the edge of summer and the return of Charlie and my brothers. All that had changed in an instant. I pressed harder against my father's side, knowing that what he wanted to discuss mirrored what I wanted—to identify the man and find out how he died.

"Sure thing, Augie." The sheriff's smile vanished.

Despite his effort at injecting a bit of levity into the situation, the mood in the room made a sudden U-turn back toward the somber.

After taking a long look at me, Mother scooped me under her arm and pulled me from the table. "This is getting to be too much for our young daughter." Mother walked me to the sink and dabbed my forehead with a cool rag. "Maybe you should go upstairs and lie down, Anna."

"I want to stay."

"Angel, your mother is..."

"Please Popo, let me stay."

Finally, Popo nodded. "It's her business as much as anyone's."

"Augie." Mother's voice was calm. "She's seven years old."

My father's head bobbed in agreement. "The world has gotten to be a much uglier place these last few months. We can't protect her from that, and we can't protect her from this."

Popo sat across from the sheriff, his legs crossed, his body hunched over the table, stirring his coffee. Folded into himself... that's how Popo did his best thinking. Finally, he placed his spoon on his saucer, looked up at his old friend, and asked, "What do you think, Boggy? Was the man murdered?"

"Augie, I've been the sheriff here in Clinton County for nearly fifteen years. If my experience has told me anything, it's that people around here aren't the murdering kind. That should put everyone in this room at ease. It's true, I got folks stomping into my office demanding I do something about a spat with a neighbor they should settle over the back-forty fence. 'It's your job... that's what we pay ya for,' they insist. They aren't paying me all that much, especially since the county cut its budget, so I'm not inclined to get my boots dirty settling feuds between old friends."

The sheriff paused to take a sip of his coffee.

Shaking his head slowly, he continued, "Then these same folks sit in their church pews twice on Sunday and again on Wednesday night listening to their pastor preaching about how they should love thy neighbor as thyself. Somehow, the Word gets lost on them. I'm telling you... Jesus doesn't like it. But what do I know? I'm just the sheriff in this town. To my earlier point, folks 'round here might be squabblers who want to goad me into finishing their petty arguments, but they aren't murderers. That's what my gut tells me."

Popo straightened up as he nodded. He seemed satisfied with the sheriff's answer, relieved that a murder hadn't taken place right outside his front door.

Sheriff Boggs took a deep breath, then stood up. "My gut says no, but for the sake of a proper investigation, I'm going to ask Doc Becker what he thinks, just to put everyone's mind at ease, including Annie's. I will say this though... the man has a goose egg on the side of his bean..." Sheriff Boggs rubbed the side of his own head in sympathy. "...right about here. I suppose someone could have hit him with something, but it just doesn't feel like that. I'll get my feelings sorted into facts soon enough."

Popo stood and smoothed his clothes.

"I know you will, Boggy. Thank you."

"The fact remains, I got a mystery on my hands. I don't have a clue who this fellow is or what he was doing in Jeffries, but you can believe I'll get to the bottom of it. I better get on over to the office where I can get a handle on the rumor mill running overtime before that mayor of ours has the whole town in an uproar. Whatever this is, it doesn't come to Jeffries often, so he'll have to make hay while he can, especially since there's an election coming up in November." Sheriff Boggs pulled his watch from his pocket. "Is it that late? I need to stop by the butcher to pick up my Sunday dinner... the shop closes early on Saturday. I'll be seeing you folks later."

Mother followed him to the front door with me right behind her. "Enjoy that rump roast," Boggy.

"You can bet your bottom dollar I will. Then on Monday I'll spread the rumor that it was a wee bit dry. That will get the hens around town clucking... and give my beloved a taste of her own medicine."

"Hens?" my mother huffed as she closed the door. "He should hear what we hens call the gossipy men in this town."

I looked up at my mother.

"It's not fit for polite conversation. That's all I'll say."

***

"Do you have any work to do over at the office today?" We'd eaten our lunch in silence, all of us caught up in our own thoughts of the morning chaos. I could think of nothing else but the dead man I'd discovered in Prairie Creek. I kept going over in my head how they loaded him into the undertaker's wagon and hauled him off to the town morgue. Bernard rode out to the ice plant with his father to get a load to haul over there. Sheriff Boggs said the morgue was going to need it on a hot day like this.

"A few orders to finish up... a couple of calls to make." Popo seemed in no big hurry to get across town to the Ghere-Douglass Company. "I planned on getting over to the office earlier but..."

"I'm sure Iris got word to Karl about your whereabouts this morning," Mother assured him.

My uncle's irascible wife, Iris, always has her nose in our business. But since she lives on the other side of the creek where I found a dead body, I understood how this was her business, too.

After taking the last sip of coffee, my father pushed back from the table. "Things are tightening up since the stock market crash, so Karl insists I stay on top of sales. He's right, of course, even if we must work on Saturdays. I'd better get over there. I'll try to be home by six for supper."

Mother nodded as she wiped Thea's mouth with her dishrag. Thea squalled.

After Popo left for his office, we lingered around the table.

"He was a handsome man, well-dressed, about Popo's age, I think," Gem muttered.

My sister's observations surprised Mother. "Gem, you don't need to worry about that man another minute. You heard what Sheriff Boggs said. He'll handle things from here on."

"But Mother, aren't you curious about who the man was... about his life? I wandered through the crowd that gathered out front this morning and listened to what they were saying. No one has any idea who he was or where he came from. I'm going to write everything down in my diary."

"I'm surprised you haven't filled that diary up by now," Mother teased. "You got it for your birthday at the end of June and you haven't stopped writing since."

Gem shrugged. "I like writing everything down."

Mother changed the subject. "I'll clean up in here. I want you girls to go out and check on Old Barney."

Gem nodded. "That horse just isn't right without Cory around. He got real agitated this morning with all those people milling about. They had the chickens stirred up, too."

"Did someone feed the horse and the chickens this morning?" Mother was particular about taking care of her chickens.

"Popo gathered the eggs, but with all the excitement, I don't know if he fed them."

"You girls see to it."

Gem sighed. "Thank goodness our brothers will be home soon."

"And Charlie," I added.

Seven days.

Chapter 4

I burst through the door of my parent's bedroom, crawled up between Popo and Mother, and crossed my arms over my chest. I wasn't going anywhere until my father and I talked.

Thea was fast asleep in the cradle Mother had pushed against the bed next to her. My baby sister had had a rough beginning in life—born weeks too soon—so she was rarely far from Mother's sight. After urging from Popo, Mother had finally allowed Gem and me to push Thea in her baby carriage along South Street, although Mother was emphatic about how far we were allowed to go.

"Do not cross Harrison Street with that carriage under any circumstance," she'd instructed us each morning as we prepared to take our walk. "You can go down as far as Mrs. Parlett's house the other way, but then turn back toward home. Do you both understand?"

"Yes, Mother," we'd replied in unison.

After my intrusion into my parents' bed, Mother continued reading the *Motion Picture* magazine Aunt Lo had brought her from the library. My aunt was the head librarian and her position allowed her the occasional benefit of pilfering back issues of certain magazines that weren't in demand by her patrons any more. The cover of the January 1931 issue of *Motion Picture* that my mother thumbed through for the hundredth time featured a photograph of actress Laura La Plante, her apple cheeks daubed with red rouge. The day Aunt Lo brought Mother the magazine, Popo swooned dramatically when he saw Miss La Plante's photograph.

Mother had rolled her eyes. "Are we all to suffer through that old gag again, Augie?"

Popo's face had lit up with his smile. "Yes, you are." Then off he'd go, telling us a tale from his youth—a tall tale, according to Mother.

***

My brothers weren't much interested in another telling of my father's youthful shenanigans, but Gem and I were certainly up for it, hoping Popo would slip in a detail or two he'd left out of his past telling's... some new tidbit for Gem's diary.

"Boggy, Thomas Barner and I used to take the Interurban to Indianapolis on Saturday night." Popo seemed serene as he relived his happy days running with his friends. "We'd go to the silent movies at the Ritz Theater on Illinois Street. Thomas liked the Rivoli better, but for me and Boggy, there was something special about the Ritz."

"She was something, all right." When Mother stayed for the telling, she'd often add her acrid comments.

"When Thomas didn't have to work late on the farm, we'd get there early to get seats near the front next to the piano player. That woman never missed a note. It always amazed me how she learned the music for a new feature film every week or two."

Popo often paused there in his story, looking up to scroll his memories.

"She had this beautiful daughter."

"We are all aware of her beautiful daughter, Augie."

Despite Mother's comments, Popo continued, "The piano player's daughter sat next to her on the piano bench and turned the pages of the music for her. She had apple cheeks just like Laura La Plante's. When the house lights went up for intermission, her rouged cheeks sparkled. I told my pals that was something I'd only ever seen on the Silver Screen. So we'd go back the next Saturday night, and sure enough, her cheeks sparkled under those house lights. It was a phenomenon we never saw at the Rivoli."

Popo smiled at the memory.

"I had the biggest crush on her," Popo added, again reliving the emotions of first love. "She never so much as spoke to me, but I'll never forget the first time she spoke to Boggy. She said, 'Excuse me, sir.' When Boggy stepped aside in the aisle so she could pass, she swished the full skirt of her dress against his legs. We thought he was going to faint and fall back right there in the aisle. Later, of course, Thomas and I elbowed and hee-hawed him about the girl's use of 'sir,' as if he was an old man. Compared to her youth, we were all old men."

"A girl knows what she wants," Mother muttered.

"Popo, what did she want?" I only asked him that question once.

"I'm going out to the barn to check on our sons while you explain to our daughters what girls want. It's still a mystery to me."

We could hear Popo chuckling until the backdoor slammed with a bang.

***

"Tell me, Angel, what do we owe the pleasure of your company this fine evening?" Popo had rolled over on his side and propped himself up on one elbow.

I looked at my father's smiling face. "Popo, did you talk to Sheriff Boggs this afternoon?"

"Why would I talk to the sheriff this afternoon?"

It occurred to me my father was using his formal tone for this conversation, so I played along. "Well, Popo, you might want to know if he found out any more about that dead man you pulled out of Prairie Creek this past Saturday morning."

"As your father, I think it best we put any further talk about that dead man to bed, which is exactly where you should to be right now. In bed."

"Popo!"

My mother nudged me with her elbow. "*Shhh*. You'll wake your sister."

"Angel, you need to put this behind you. Seeing dead people is something you need to save until you're much older. Your mother and I don't want you having nightmares or worrying your pretty head about such things now. I want you to enjoy your childhood as best you can. You can worry about dead people when you're older."

I thought about what Popo said. The only other dead person I'd ever seen was PaPaw Ghere, Popo's father, who was the founder of the Ghere-Douglass Company. I was only two when PaPaw died, so I don't remember the funeral, but Gem does. She tells me about it sometimes.

"Besides, Angel, that man was a stranger in town. Nobody knows who he was, or where he came from. That's what I heard when I was out making calls this afternoon. I'm sure Sheriff Boggs' investigation will turn up more facts in time, but you don't need to worry about any of that anymore."

"But Popo, I need to know! What's his name? Where's he from? Does he have children at home who love him? What if it were you, Popo? He matters to someone."

"Yes, I'm sure he does, but that doesn't involve you."

"Popo, I need to know that if it were you, someone would find out who you were and where you came from... that you didn't just leave us. What if he has a daughter who believes her father didn't come home because he didn't love her anymore?"

My father took a deep breath. "Tell you what, Annie. I'll leave the office a little early tomorrow afternoon and stop by Sheriff Boggs' office on my way home to see how his investigation is going. I'll do that even though I'm sure there will be another write up in the *Morning Times* tomorrow."

"Sheriff Boggs is your friend. He'll tell you what he knows."

"If I promise to do that, will you go to bed now?"

I tightened my crossed arms and stewed.

"I want to go with you."

"What? No, Annie, you're not going to the sheriff's office with me."

"Then I'm staying right here." Was this a situation in which an unstoppable force meets an immovable object that my Aunt Lo often refers to? I'll have to remember to ask her when she gets home a week from Wednesday.

"Take your daughter with you, Augie."

My mother's support surprised me.

"Is that what you want, Maggie?"

"You were right on Saturday. We cannot protect her *pretty little head* from life forever. I doubt there's anything we can do to stop her from fretting about that poor man, but getting the answers she needs may help her get beyond it. Besides, I want answers just as much as Anna does."

"Fine. If you can get to my office by four o'clock, we'll walk over to the sheriff's office together and see if there's anything he can tell us. Will that make the two of you happy?"

Mother and I nodded.

"There's one condition." Popo sat up in bed to give Mother a full view of his face. "I don't want my seven-year-old daughter walking that far alone." By the look on his face, he had just become that immovable object. "Until we know more about the circumstances of this man's..."

"Gem can take me."

"I have a better idea." Mother rested her magazine on her lap. "Let's ask Bernard if he'll walk you to Ghere-Douglass. When you get back, he can stay for supper."

"That sounds perfect. I'll remind him to bring his Bible, just in case."

"I don't think you need to worry about reminding him, Annie." My father's eyes sparkled as one corner of his mouth turned up.

"If his father is back from his ice route, we can ride Cooter!"

"You can walk."

"If Gus was here, he'd carry me when my feet hurt."

"You and those feet of yours." Popo tickled me. "The day you were born, your mother said to me, 'Isn't she the most beautiful baby you've ever seen?' Then I said, 'Would you look at those feet of hers... they're enormous.'"

I giggled. "No, you didn't say that, Popo."

"I most certainly did."

I wiggled my toes, which made Popo laugh out loud.

Chapter 5

"What are you doing, little sister?"

"Gem, you scared me." My sister sat down on the floor next to me, where I watched the Thompson house through the bottom of our parlor window.

"You didn't tell me what you were doing, Annie."

"Mr. Thompson just pulled away in his ice cart. I'm waiting for Mrs. Thompson to go to her job at the Little Palmer House. Then I'm going over to ask Bernard if he'll walk me to Popo's office this afternoon."

"Why in the world would you go to Popo's office?"

"We're going to go visit Sheriff Boggs to find out if he knows anything new about our dead man."

"He's *our* dead man, huh?" Gem turned from the window and leaned her back against the wall. "There was a big item on the front page of the *Morning Times* on Sunday about his death. Did you read it?"

"No." I liked to read the funny pages in the newspaper, but that was all.

"There's a lot of words, but it doesn't say anything we don't already know."

"What did it say, Gem?"

"Annie, you can read it yourself. The newspaper is still on the table next to Popo's chair in the green room. You better get to it before Mother shreds it for the chicken coop."

"I'll have Bernard read to me later."

"Do you want me to read it to you now?"

"No, Bernard reads better than you do."

"He does not!"

As I continued my vigil, Gem stayed next to me. "The last couple of days, I can't think about anything other than that dead man," she said.

"Do you want to go with us to visit Sheriff Boggs?"

"I do, but I promised to go to Evelyn's house this afternoon to play Rook. Her father brought her a new pack of cards from Chicago. But promise you'll remember every detail Sheriff Boggs tells you so you can tell me later. I want to write it down in my diary. Promise."

"I promise, Gem."

"I hope Bernard can walk you to Popo's office this afternoon, or Mother might not let you go."

"Oh, he will walk me. Mother said I could invite him for supper. She's making chicken and dumplings, Bernard's favorite."

***

When Popo, Bernard and I arrived at the sheriff's office, his secretary, Biddy Ann Blout, told us Sheriff Boggs had just stepped out for a piece of pie.

"I don't know about you two, but I could use some pie myself."

"What, Mr. Ghere?" Bernard's eyes were as big as saucers. "Pie before supper? Why, I ain't never heard tell of such a thing."

"We have pie before supper all the time, don't we, Popo?"

Popo smiled. "Every chance we get, Angel." My father patted Bernard's back. "Pie is good anytime, Bernard. That's an important life lesson."

The sheriff's office was in the ground floor of the Clinton County Courthouse, which dominated the center of our public square. Popo told us that the three-story limestone building cast the shadow of justice over every inch of the square during the sun's daily transit.

"God casts the shadow o' grace over every corner o' the earth, all the time, don't ya know," Bernard added.

He didn't have to open his Bible for that bit of wisdom. His observations often rolled off his tongue, even when no one was paying attention. I was only interested in getting over to the Blue and White Café for a piece of pie, and a talk with Sheriff Boggs. I couldn't recollect ever being in the courthouse before our brief visit with Miss Biddy Ann, but I had been in the Blue and White Café plenty of times and was always eager to go back.

My father wasn't a tall man, but his stride was long and confident. I had to hurry to keep up. When I reached his side, I took hold of his hand. He gave mine a little squeeze and looked down at me. I noticed a piece of his wavy brown hair had escaped his morning application of pomade and rested on his forehead. That wasn't unusual at this time of day, especially in the summer heat.

As we approached the restaurant, Bernard pushed ahead of us and opened the door. The gesture seemed to confuse Popo for a moment, then he turned to the boy and smiled. "Thank you, Bernard."

I followed Popo into the diner, offering Bernard the exact display of gratitude.

"The calm before the storm." Popo muttered the words as he looked around the small establishment.

"What's the calm before the storm, Popo?"

"Angel, it's that time of day when Roxy serves the pie leftover from the mid-day rush. When Roxy prepares for the supper crowd, she offers fresh selections. It's a whole new beginning, at least in terms of pie."

"Oh," Bernard said, his face open in wonder. "I thought that meant somethin' else, I did."

Popo laughed heartily. "Perhaps it does, when the taste buds aren't craving pie."

Rather than take our usual seats at the counter that stretched down most of one wall of the establishment, Popo waited for a word from Miss Roxy.

"Take a seat anywhere, Augie. I'll be with you after I check in with Paul about supper. Can I bring you a cup of coffee?"

"Not today, thanks. I've had my fill."

Popo made a show of looking over the row of open tables that lined the wall opposite the counter. Sheriff Boggs sat at a table nearest the front window, his mostly uneaten piece of pie in front of him as he fielded questions from three other customers.

Popo pointed us toward a table at the back of the diner. As we passed the table where Sheriff Boggs sat trying to eat, my father rapped on his table with his knuckles. "A moment of your time, please. I need to report a crime."

With all eyes now on my father, we settled into chairs around the table in the back, the one that sat in perpetual shadow, receiving little light from either the front window or the line of bare bulbs on the ceiling.

When the sheriff shooed away the folks who had pinned him down at the front table, he picked up his pie plate and cup of coffee and joined us.

"What other crime, Augie? My hands are full trying to unravel the mystery surrounding the dead man Annie found in the creek, not to mention trying to find the hoodlum who threw a rotten tomato at the Widow Winslow's window yesterday. Crime of the century, to hear her tell it."

I scrunched up my face. As often as Popo told me that every person mattered and deserved kindness, I just couldn't see it when it came to the Widow Winslow. I don't know why I wanted to stick my tongue out at her every time I saw her. Most of the men in town fawned over the Widow Winslow, yet she reminded me of the old witch in "Hansel and Gretel." Charlie brought a volume of Grimm's Fairy Tales home from the library last winter, and set out to read me the entire book, story by story. I liked Rapunzel's hair, but that was the only thing I liked about the Grimm Brothers' stories. Not a comforting notion about any of them. I told Charlie I didn't want to hear anymore, which hurt his feelings, but he asked Aunt Lo to take the book back to the library the next day.

Thinking about "Hansel and Gretel" reminded me of something I saw a few weeks after Pauline and I fell through the ice on Prairie Creek last winter. I'd gone out to the barn to take dried apples from our cellar to Old Barney. As I stood outside looking up the north creek, Gus appeared next to me.

"What 'cha looking at, little sister?"

"Look." I pointed to the sky with my empty hand. "Smoke coming from that abandoned cottage in Barner's Woods."

He stared toward the gray plume billowing into the crystal blue sky in the distance. I could see Gus's breath as he inhaled the cold air, and blew out the air warmed by his body. "It looks like it's coming from that abandoned cottage. More likely, it's coming from the house at Barner Farm. No one has lived in that old cottage for years."

Gus's explanation seemed reasonable.

***

"Boggy, my daughter who discovered the Corpse in the Creek—in the words of that *Morning Times'* reporter—would like a first-hand report from her sheriff regarding the progress of his investigation. It would be a great favor to me if you'd set her mind at ease knowing that you're doing everything possible to identify that poor fellow and what caused his demise."

The sheriff laughed. "How many times did you read that item in the *Morning Times*, my friend?"

"More than I care to admit."

I looked across the table at my father's face. His lips turned up as if responding to his friend's attempt at levity, but his eyes serious, penetrating.

"That story is jam-packed with details, none of them very satisfying," Popo added.

Sheriff Boggs turned away from Popo's glare. "So, you want the inside scoop? Is that right, Annie?"

"Yes, sir."

"If I tell you, will you promise to keep it to yourself?"

"Oh, no, Sheriff. I already promised to tell Gem every detail."

"Will you tell little Thea, too?"

"I will, but she won't remember."

"And what about you?" Sheriff Boggs turned to Bernard, giving him his full attention. "Holy cow, it's little Bernard Thompson! I didn't recognize you. You've grown into quite the young man."

"Yessir. That's jest what happens over time."

"Let me tell you something else that happens over time." Sheriff Boggs grabbed ahold of a little roll of fat on his waistline. "This comes from knowing where I can get the best pie in town."

Miss Roxy arrived at the table just in time to put an end to the banter between Sheriff Boggs and Bernard, a conversation I had hoped would take us into suppertime and the fresh pie selections.

"Sorry for the delay, folks. I had to get my meatloaf in the oven for supper. I'm serving it this evening with mashed potatoes covered in onion gravy, with a side of green beans, and fresh biscuits with homemade jam."

"I think you just gave me a reason to work late again, Roxy..." The sheriff caught the look from my father and added, "...if the case of the dead man isn't reason enough."

Popo piped up and told Roxy we'd stopped by for a piece of pie and a conversation.

"You've come to the right place for both. What kind of pie does everyone want?"

"I'll have cherry, if ya please," said Bernard.

"Me, too."

"What about you, Augie?"

"I'd kill for a piece of your sugar cream pie about now."

Sheriff Boggs clinked the end of his fork on his plate next to his half-eaten pie.

"I think the choices this afternoon are Dutch apple and Dutch apple." The sheriff scooped up a bite with his fork and shoved it into his mouth.

"Dutch apple it is. Sounds delicious, doesn't it?" My father nodded once at me, as if to say, "I told you so."

Bernard and I nodded.

When Miss Roxy returned with our pie, Popo and Sheriff Boggs were deep in conversation about the story that appeared in the Sunday edition of the *Morning Times*.

"I don't know how that reporter filled up the front page and much of a second page with what I told him."

"Journalism seems a creative process." Popo sighed. "What did you tell him, Boggy?"

"Mostly 'no comment.' I thought you said you read it."

"I did," Popo assured him.

"When that reporter talked to me, I had two young girls who knew more about my case than I did. That reporter beat me to the scene, thanks to my beloved, so I should have been questioning him, though considering my line of work, that would have been a might embarrassing." The sheriff took another bite of his pie, then stirred his coffee. "I need a little warm-up on this, if someone can get Roxy's attention."

Without prompting from Popo, Sheriff Boggs picked up the story where he'd left off.

"While the deceased's clothing was still dripping wet, that reporter demanded full disclosure of an investigation I was a full eight minutes into. So, I gave it to him. I wanted to give him this..." The good sheriff held up his fist. "...but being a public servant and all, I thought better of it."

"He took up most of the front page with that photograph." Popo rested his fork on his pie plate and shook his head. "It looked pretty gruesome, but the man didn't look like that when I pulled him out of the water."

"You're right, Augie. He looked pretty good, except for that nasty bump on the side of his head. Makes me think he hadn't been dead for long when your girls found him."

The sheriff tapped the table in front of me. "That's a detail you can convey to Gem... that he hadn't been dead long."

I leaned close to Bernard and whispered, "Will you help me remember the details so Gem can write them in her diary? Oh, and will you read that item from the *Morning Times* to me when we get home?" I thought I better ask before Bernard was full of dumplings and ready for a nap. Dumplings can do that to a person.

"Shore. The *Mornin' Times* don't use hard words like the Bible does," answered Bernard.

Sheriff Boggs said the reporter used up three paragraphs speculating on whether Doc Becker would examine the body. "He was standing there when I gave the order for the wagon master to take the body to the morgue, and then go directly to Doc Becker's office to inform him of its arrival."

"You're sure they did that?"

The sheriff rolled his eyes. "The driver has tied one on a time or two at the Sleepy Owl Saloon, and I've seen him home safely with his wife none the wiser. I'm sure."

Popo glanced at me, but I was careful not to react. I knew what "tied one on" meant.

"Besides," added Sheriff Boggs, "I spoke to Doc Becker briefly this morning."

"Did you find out anything that wasn't in the *Morning Times*?"

"Just that the man likely died due to head trauma, likely from a fall, although he couldn't rule out that someone hit him. People fall, hit their heads, and die in their homes every day. Doc Becker said he found a couple of minor scraps conducive of a fall. Not much else worth mentioning other than he found no defensive wounds."

The sheriff also told us that Biddy Ann sent telegrams to the sheriffs in the surrounding counties to check for any reports of missing people. "If we don't get any responses in the next few days, we'll expand our circle of inquiry."

Sheriff Boggs said he also also checked with the boarding house but came up empty-handed.

"I'm going to check with Mr. Grayson over at the Little Palmer House. By the look of the man's clothing, he could afford to stay there."

"My ma works there," piped up Bernard.

"I seem to recall that, now that you mention it, Bernard. How does she like working for Mr. Grayson?"

"She gits on fine with him, I reckon. She never complains none."

"He's been none too nice to me since I failed to arrest Paul Lockwood and those two railroaders over their little showdown that ended in front of his hotel's front window. That man knows how to carry a grudge. He hasn't offered me a brownie since, but he hasn't eaten a bite of Roxy's pie since either." Sheriff Boggs raised a clutched fist, a satisfied grin on his face.

"Anything else you can tell us about the case?" I could tell Popo wanted to get home for supper.

"There are a couple more people I want to talk to." Sheriff Boggs rubbed his chin as if he'd given the idea some deep thought. "One of them is sitting right here."

The sheriff turned to me.

My eyes widened, and I could feel the heat in my face. "Me?"

"Annie, I want you to tell me again everything you remember about that walk you took on Saturday morning with Gem and baby Thea."

I took a deep breath. "Well, after Gem pulled the carriage off the front porch, we loaded up Thea and walked down to the corner at Harrison Street. Mother doesn't want us crossing Harrison Street." I shrugged my shoulders at Mother's rule. "So we crossed over South Street and came up the other side. When we got on the bridge, we stopped because I like to watch for the Interurban, but we didn't see it."

"Annie, think about that for a minute. Does anything else come to mind?"

I closed my eyes and focused on that moment. "I heard the rattle of the Interurban tracks in the distance because I remembered Mother telling us not to play on that special bridge with the tracks on it. Cory said it was a silly rule because if the Interurban came along, they jump into the creek to avoid getting run over." I looked at Popo, hoping I hadn't given away my brothers' secret.

"Anything else? Anything you remember that might be a clue to figuring out the identity of that man?"

"There was rustling down there. I always look because we some-times see a red fox running through the trees. Gem thinks it wanders down the creek from Barner's Woods. On Saturday, we saw nothing like that, just squirrels playing in the undergrowth."

Sheriff Boggs nodded. "Go on, Annie."

"I already told you the last part... how we walked down to the corner past Mrs. Parlett's, then crossed over and came back up the other side of the street, the side our house is on."

After I recounted the part where I spotted the dead man in the creek, the sheriff patted my hand. For the first time since Saturday morning, tears welled up in my eyes. The sheriff and Popo sat in silence, allowing me to let all that had happened flow out of me.

"Annie, because of what you just told me, I'm going to talk to Hector, the engineer on the southbound Interurban. He might have seen something."

"Will you let us know if you learn anything new?"

"I will."

"I want you two to finish up so we can get home for supper." My father pushed back from the table and stood up. "Old Man Gregory just came in, and I want to have a word with him before we leave."

Popo took a couple of steps up the aisle, then turned and pointed at Bernard. "Be sure you save room for supper, Bernard. Maggie is serving chicken and dumplings this evening. Your favorite. Maggie's dumplings are the best in the county."

"I knows all about Mrs. Ghere's dumplin's, sir." Bernard rubbed his belly.

Chapter 6

After Popo stepped away to speak to Old Man Gregory, I put my elbows on the table, my chin in my hands and stewed about the dead man, distressed that Sheriff Boggs had discovered nothing about who he was and why he was in Jeffries. Was his family worried? Did the man have a son or daughter who couldn't sleep for worrying, not knowing why he had not returned home to them?

Sheriff Boggs looked at me. "Now might be as good a time as any to finish my story about what happened between Mr. Lockwood and the two railroaders who caused that big ruckus here after the Lockwoods returned from their honeymoon. Now where was I?"

I suspected the sheriff was distracting us with the telling of one of his tales, but I listened so I could repeat it to Gem for her diary. "You were at the part where Mr. Lockwood grabbed up his skillet with hot bacon grease still in it and chased the rascals out of here," I grumbled.

I looked up the aisle to see that Popo had settled into the chair next to his old friend. They were deep in conversation, probably about the Corpse in the Creek.

"It really had hot bacon grease in it?" Bernard asked.

Sheriff Boggs pursed his lips and gave Bernard and me one firm nod. "It was hotter than... let's just say that bacon grease was hot. I was sitting over there..." He pointed at a table near the front. "...when Paul grabbed up that skillet and came thundering out of the kitchen like a wild animal. When those two railroaders..."

"Nickel Plate, right?" I was filling in the details for Bernard's benefit.

"Right. When those two railroaders from the Nickel Plate got a load of Paul Lockwood and his skillet, they made a break for the door. From what I'm told, when they got outside, they paused on the sidewalk to congratulate themselves for putting Roxy in her place and slipping out without paying their bills to boot. But here came ole Paul, a bear with a burr up its backside. Those boys got a load of him and started running full on up to the corner and turned onto Main Street. They had a pretty good lead on Paul until one of 'um tripped over something and sprawled across the sidewalk there in front of the Little Palmer House."

Bernard looked confused. "I think I missed somethin'."

"I'll catch you up later," I said, nudging him in the ribs with my elbow.

Before the sheriff pickup his story to carry it to its conclusion, Miss Roxy walked up the aisle with the coffeepot.

"Are you telling that old story again, Sheriff?"

"Yep, but if you'd like to take over, go ahead."

"No, Paul likes your version better. He comes out the hero in your telling. In mine, I'm more focused on those bad grease burns on his arm that took me a month of doctoring to get healed up."

With an upturned palm toward Miss Roxy, the sheriff quipped, "I present the heroine of the story." With Roxy's official go ahead, Sheriff Boggs wasted no time continuing.

"One fella was sprawled out on the sidewalk in front of Little Palmer House, so the other one stoped to help his buddy up just as Paul came barreling around the corner, that skillet held up like a baseball bat. Paul might be wiry, but he sure is strong from lifting and touting iron skillets all day. Anyway, a second later, he's standing over the men, calling them everything in the book but civilized. Of course, I knew this because I had followed the three of them out of the Blue and White, although I admit I kept some distance between me and the impending brawl because of my aversion to flying bacon grease."

Bernard chuckled.

Sheriff Boggs took a sip of his cold coffee, then held it out to Miss Roxy. "Top me off, if you please."

He set his cup on its saucer. "Paul's standing over these two fellas with a hot iron skillet, cussing like a sailor."

"He was in the Army," noted Miss Roxy.

"My apologies, Roxy, and my apologies to the U.S. Navy." Then, turning back to Bernard and me, he resumed his story. "He was string-ing together curse words in a fashion I've never heard before... or since."

Bernard's mouth hung open. I didn't think he was breathing.

"I strolled up to the scene, making a wide circle around Paul so he could see it was me, as he was still holding his weapon at high alert. That's when I spotted Arnold Grayson, his face pressed against the glass in the front window of the Little Palmer House. His eyes were about to pop out of his skull."

"Paul looked at me and said in the calmest voice, 'Good evening, Sheriff. What can I do for you?'"

Bernard laughed full out, holding his side.

"I said to him in my calmest sheriffing voice, 'Roxy wants you to get on back to the Blue and White. She needs you. The customers are getting restless waiting for their supper.'"

"Right there..." Roxy pointed at the sheriff. "That's my favorite part of this entire work of fiction."

The sheriff ignored her. "I took ahold of Paul's arm—the one not holding the weapon—and turned him around and started walking him back the way we came. The whole time he's yelling over his shoulder to those boys who had never been happier to see the sheriff show up in their entire lives. Paul yelled, 'Don't you ever come back, do you hear me?' That added to their misery. The icing on the cake was him reminding them of all the food they'd never eat again, yelling them over his shoulder as Roxy's delicious menu items popped into his head."

"'Roxy's delicious menu items,'" Roxy mimicked. "Where do you get such hogwash?"

The sheriff looked at her and shrugged. "'No more pot roast with roasted carrots!' yelled Paul. 'No more chicken and dumpling! No more pork chops with baked apples! No more beef stew with home-made biscuits! No more meatloaf with mashed potatoes and onion gravy!'"

"Yum," Bernard muttered to himself.

"In between his yelling, he'd talk to me, cool as a cucumber. 'Is the diner still busy, Sheriff?' he asked. 'The same way you left things, Paul,' I replied."

"'No more strawberry-rhubarb pie! No more Dutch apple pie with hand-churned vanilla bean ice cream!'"

I looked down at my plate that was absent the hand-churched vanilla bean ice cream and sighed.

"I patted Paul's arm to calm him, but that didn't stop him from yelling. 'No more cherry pie with butter crust! No more sugar-cream pie warm out of the oven! NO MORE CONEY DOGS WITH MY WIFE'S SECRET SAUCE!' Then, civilized as a king at the royal ball, he said to me, 'How's the lovely Martha doing these days? I haven't seen her in ages.'"

Sheriff Boggs took another a sip of his coffee, his story nearing its climatic end.

"Paul loves my pie. I think that's why he married me," Roxy added matter-of-factly.

"I married Martha for her rump roast, so I'm not in any position to be pointing fingers at a man for his motives."

Roxy rolled her eyes and gave the sheriff a nudge on his back with her elbow. "Everyone knows why you married Martha, and it had nothing to do with her cooking."

"Where was I? Oh, yeah... once those boys cleared out, Arnold Grayson burst out of the hotel, yelling up the street at me. 'Hey Sheriff, aren't you going to arrest these three rabble-rousers and throw them in jail?'"

"When I said no, that didn't make Arnold too happy."

"Did they stay away like Mr. Paul told 'em?" Bernard asked.

"Nah." Roxy stepped up to finish the story. "After they got their fill of pickled eggs at the Airport Diner, they showed up here a week or two later with a box of chocolates in hand and begged me to take them back. I had an ex-husband do that once, but I thought better of it."

"An act of bravery on their part, I'd say," quipped the sheriff.

"Now I have those two boys wrapped around my little finger." Miss Roxy held up her little finger and gave it a twirl. "There hasn't been a moment of tension from those two since. They seem as content as two pigs in Shinola."

Sheriff Boggs leaned across the table toward me and Bernard and said, "I think Paul Lockwood sealed the deal with his new bride that evening."

"For as long as he'll have me."

"What about Mr. Grayson?" I asked. I knew he was sweet on my Aunt Lo.

"Arnold stomped across the square and into my office every day for weeks, demanding restitution for the grease spots he had to clean off his front walk. I refused every request. He hasn't invited me in for a warm brownie since."

"Talk about overrated," added Miss Roxy. "Those things aren't fit to eat, if you ask me."

The clank of a plate caught Miss Roxy's attention. She glanced toward the serving window where Paul had placed a piece of pie, Dutch apple, no doubt. "Order up," he called.

"Sheriff, you left out the part of us losing our pie business over at the Little Palmer House."

"So I did, but I figured that part was yours to tell, Roxy."

"They haven't served a decent piece of pie in their fancy-schmancy restaurant since," she continued. "Paul was concerned when I cut Arnold off from the pies I sold there (for a whole nickel more a pie than anyplace else) so Paul built a sandwich board and placed it on the sidewalk of an evening when people were attending movies at the Clinton Theater. The sandwich board offers coffee and pie afterward. We've gotten so busy we opened the basement room for the overflow and hired on Mrs. Flud to wait tables at night." Miss Roxy swiped the back of her hand across her forehead. "Arnold can serve his copycat brownies all he wants, but what folks really want is pie."

Finally, Miss Roxy looked toward the kitchen. "Speaking of pie, I've got some to deliver to a customer, and my supper gravy to tend. It was a little off earlier."

"Salt." Sheriff Boggs suggested.

"You know what they say, more salt and butter fixes everything. Can I get you anything else before I get back to it?"

"Nope. I better get back to my office. Thanks to little Annie here, I have a new potential witness to track down."

"In the Corpse in the Creek case?" she asked.

"It's not the Widow Winslow's rotten tomato case, that's for sure," replied the sheriff. I take it you've read the item in the Sunday *Morning Times*."

"That and listened to my customers talk about it all day Saturday and all day today. Who else are you going to talk to?" Roxy placed her free hand on her hip. It appeared the pie and the gravy could wait another moment or two.

"Hector Toops."

"Nice fellow." Without hesitation, she added, "I've got one more potential witness for you, Sheriff."

He turned around in his chair and looked up at the diner's proprietor. "Pray tell, who might that be?"

"Jimbo."

Chapter 7

I found the Sunday *Morning Times* folded in half on the table next to Popo's favorite chair in the green room, just where Gem said it would be. This time of year, the thick swath of trees and shrubs hides the view of the creek outside the windows, though the sound of the water rushing toward the Ohio River remained ever-present through the open windows.

When the weather permitted—Mother closed off the room in winter because it was difficult to heat—we loved gathering in the green room to listen to Father Blinn's old Zenith radio while playing games on the floor. Since Charlie came to live with us during the school year, he'd often climb onto the window seat, me next to him, to read. With Charlie's return for the coming school year still four days away, Bernard sat next to me in the window seat, unfolded the newspaper, and read from the front page.

***

MAN FOUND DEAD IN PRAIRIE CREEK

Unidentified corpse discovered by children outside South Street home

A corpse was found floating in the Prairie Creek near the South Street bridge early Saturday morning by the daughters of Augustus and Margaret Ghere. Upon the gruesome discovery, Mr. Ghere pulled the man, who has yet to be identified, to shore before alerting the Clinton County Sheriff's Office.

According to Sheriff Clyde Boggs, the Corpse in the Creek exhibited no evidence of foul play, although this reporter personally bore witness to the sheriff's detection of a large lump on the side of the deceased man's head near his left ear. When asked if a lump on the head could result in death, the sheriff replied, "Not usually," a comment that leaves open the possibility that the man was murdered by a blow to the side of the head and tossed into Prairie Creek.

The dead man has dark brown hair worn in a tapered fade cut, parted on the left. He has hazel eyes. He is approximately five-foot eight inches in height, and of average weight. He appears to be in his mid- to late-thirties.

As witnessed by the large crowd that gathered near the Ghere home prior to the sheriff's arrival, the Corpse in the Creek wore a brown patterned suit with a matching double-breasted vest, a pointed collar shirt, a silk green and gold geometric tie, and two-toned shoes, an outfit that might be considered unusual for an early morning jaunt in a town such as Jeffries. Also on the scene was a high-crown fedora, which Mr. Ghere claims he retrieved from the creek. No wedding band or other jewelry were present on the man or his attire.

One witness at the scene, who asked to remain unidentified, said of the dead man, "He appears to be living high on the hog when the rest of us is really startin' to suffer from this dang-gone Depression."

When asked if he had any idea of the identity of this stranger in town, the esteemed sheriff responded, "No comment." When asked if he knew the cause of death, the sheriff responded, "No comment." When asked to describe his next steps in his investigation, the sheriff responded, "No comment." When asked if there was anything he could tell the good citizens of Jeffries about the Corpse in the Creek, the sheriff replied, "Listen, buddy, I'm ten minutes into my investigation, now get out of my way or I'll arrest you and throw you in the clink. Trust me, the food ain't too good there." When asked if I could quote him on that, he responded, "Please do."

The Corpse in the Creek was removed from the scene in the death wagon by two men from Goodman Mortuary. They were instructed by the sheriff to deliver the dead body to the Clinton County morgue. This reporter speculates that Dr. Henry Becker will examine the body to determine the cause of death and to find any other information that might assist the sheriff as to the decedent's identity.

From the top step of the porch to the Ghere home, Sheriff Boggs asked the crowd to report any information about the dead man directly to him or Biddy Ann Blout over at the sheriff's office. Then he told the crowd to disburse, saying, "Now go on home, this isn't a carnival."

When asked if the good citizens of Jeffries should stay inside behind locked doors in case there's a murderer at large on the streets of Jeffries, the sheriff replied, "No comment."

Chapter 8

In the summertime, we sleep with the windows open. Even then, on a handful of nights, the heat drives my family downstairs to the green room to escape the stifling air. It's not unusual to find our brothers sleeping on our front porch, which catches whatever bit of breeze blows out of the southwest.

The first sign of the edge of summer arrives in the cover of night, veiled in the sweet haze of relief from the sweltering days, a cool breath of fresh air wicking the moisture from our dewy skin. Gem and I go to bed uncovered, but awaken snuggled under a blanket, not remembering the moment we drew it to our chins and sought the warmth of each other. So pleasant are the dreams on those late summer nights that we refuse to acknowledge even the simple betrayals of this world that might chase them away too soon.

On the Wednesday after I discovered a dead man floating in Prairie Creek, I awoke gently. My first thought wasn't about the death of the stranger outside our door, but my concern that perhaps the edge of summer had decided to arrive early this year. Oh, how disappointed Aunt Lo would be to miss its beginning here with us.

Gem was next to me, on her knees, gazing out the window above our bed. "Look there, Annie," she whispered.

I didn't want to move from the furrow my body had made in the old feather mattress Mother once shared with her sister, Rachel. I felt safe lodged there in the doorway of my subconscious, half awake, half asleep. My sister leaned down and nudged me. At her insistence, I climbed out from the warmth of our bed and sat up.

"Annie, look." Gem's voice sounded more urgent.

I rubbed the sleep from my eyes and climbed up next to my older sister, following her finger where she pointed. "Do you see it... the sparrow sitting on the branch of our cherry tree?"

Sparrows were busy birds, but the one that lingered on the cherry tree branch seemed oblivious to the character of its fellow birds. It was bigger than most, its belly full of its breakfast. A sunbeam reflected off it, making its breast appear whiter than usual, its wing feathers dappled with various shades of gold and brown. The sparrow sat motionless, majestic as an eagle.

"Do you see it, Annie?" Gem asked.

I nodded, breathless at its sight.

"Good." My sister slipped away from the window. "I wanted to make sure it was real."

***

The trees along Prairie Creek were home to a variety of birds... cardinals, bluejays, tree swallows, goldfinches, woodpeckers, purple martins. Charlie loved to peer through the windows in the green room and identify the birds he'd learned about from his father on their farm. One day, as we stood together watching the birds, Popo joined us at the window. A beautiful cardinal sat perched on the ledge right outside. But for the glass, we could have reached out and touched it.

When it flew away, I groaned.

"What do you see now?" asked Popo.

After a moment of searching the ground and the tree limbs, Charlie answered, "Mostly sparrows."

"Sparrows aren't as pretty as the cardinals and purple martins," I complained. "They're brown and ordinary." I searched the tree limbs, hoping to catch sight of the cardinal again.

"Annie, the sparrows eat the bugs," Charlie insisted. "Without them, the bugs would destroy Aunt Maggie's garden. Then what would we eat?"

"Charlie's right, Angel." Popo nodded. "We all have our place in this world."

***

"You girls are awake." Mother looked up from where she stood in front of the kitchen sink, drying dishes. Baby Thea sat perched under the window in a large wicker basket, a pillow cushioning the bottom. Mother had draped an old soft towel over the dried prickly plant stalks, stiff and unwoven by time. Amidst her chores, Mother looked over at her infant and smiled.

"She'll walk soon." Mother's words nudged reality, pushing fate aside.

"Thea's still tiny, Mother. It might be a year before she's strong enough to walk." That's what Doc Becker told Mother, but Mother was having none of what Gem—or the good doctor—suggested.

Thea peered over the side of her basket, clutching her doll made from fabric scraps, watching Mother work.

"She'll be toddling around underfoot before we know it." Then turning to Gem and me, "I was about to wake you. Sheriff Boggs is coming for breakfast. He called last evening and said he wanted to talk to you, Gem. Popo wants to get that out of the way before he goes to work."

"Fine, but Annie already told him everything."

"He's just doing his job, talking to everyone who might give him a clue to the identity of that poor man."

Mother pulled her iron skillet to the front burner and used the end of her spatula to scoop out a glob of bacon grease from a coffee tin she kept next to her stove.

"Boggy wants to jump on the Interurban in the public square and ride it out to the edge of town, so he has plenty of time to talk to Hector Toops without interfering with the man's schedule. Annie, I understand you gave the sheriff the idea to talk to him."

"I suppose." I yawned, torn between wanting to learn what Sheriff Boggs had to say about his investigation and wanting to get back into bed before the day's heat set in.

Mother pulled five plates from the kitchen shelf and placed them on the counter next to her stove. "I need you girls to go out to the chicken coop, collect the eggs, and feed the chickens and Old Barney. Be sure to open that barn door, so he gets some fresh air. Then go upstairs and make yourselves presentable. Gem, you'll have to comb the rat's nest out of Annie's hair."

Mother patted the back of my head as if emphasizing the toughest of Gem's morning tasks. "By the time you finish your chores, your father will be out of the bathroom. After breakfast, he's going to walk to the Interurban stop in the square with Boggy, then go to work. This Depression is affecting everyone, and your father and Uncle Karl have to work twice as hard to keep the business going. They're both missing PaPaw Ghere and Mr. Douglass these days."

"I miss PaPaw, too." Gem's brow furrowed and her full lips turned down. "He'd know what to do."

Mother nodded in agreement. "You two need to get moving." She turned to look at the clock on the kitchen wall. "Sheriff Boggs will be here in twenty minutes. You have a lot to do before he arrives, and I've got to get my biscuits in the oven.

***

"Martha sure appreciates you feeding me this morning." Sheriff Boggs slathered more of Mother's homemade blackberry jam on a biscuit atop a thick pat of butter.

"One of these days, I'll send Augie her way for breakfast, and we can call it even. How does that sound?"

"That sounds just fine," replied the sheriff, his mouth full of biscuit. "Just fine."

Popo was fond of Mother's cooking, so I doubted he'd cooperate with her scheme to pawn him off on Mrs. Boggs.

The sheriff helped himself to another biscuit Mother had placed in a bowl in the center of the table and covered with a piece of her finest embroidered linen. She only used her linens for holidays and when someone special paid a visit. "I just can't decide if your biscuits are better with jam or that gravy of yours." With that, he tore off a piece of biscuit and used it to chase the last bit of gravy around his plate.

Mother smiled. "Why choose when you can have both?"

Finally, Sheriff Boggs placed his knife and fork across his plate and pushed it away. "That was mighty fine. Thank you again, Maggie."

"Anytime."

Now that his stomach was full, Sheriff Boggs wasted no time getting down to business. "Gem, I was wondering if you'd tell me what you remember about Saturday morning?"

"Annie told you everything there was to tell."

"Tell me anyway, Gem," he urged, his voice soft and comforting. "You might have a detail that Annie didn't pick up on."

"Okay." After a moment, my sister began. "After breakfast last Saturday, Mother suggested we take Thea out for a morning walk. The sun hadn't burned off the cool air yet so I sent Annie upstairs to get a blanket to wrap Thea in. I was holding Thea and tugging on the carriage to drag it off the porch, but one wheel got stuck on something. Tugging on that carriage caused quite the ruckus."

"What kind of ruckus?"

"The loud squeaking of the rusty wheels disturbed the sparrows."

At Gem's mention of sparrows, my eye got as big as saucers.

"Where, Gem? Where were the sparrows?" Sheriff Boggs leaned over the table toward my sister, his eyes fixed on her face.

"They were over in the trees by the creek, squawking, and a flock of them..."

"How many birds, Gem?"

"Oh, I'd say more than a dozen. More than usual for this time of year. They flew out from underneath the bridge, kind of frantic, as if a cat was prowling around looking for a meal. Sparrows can get themselves in a tizzy, but it seemed odd to me. I've never seen them boil out from under that bridge like that. The bridge isn't high off the water, so..."

Gem's voice trailed off as if she was still trying to figure out the behavior of the birds that morning. "I'm going to ask Uncle Madison when he comes on Saturday. He knows a lot about birds."

"Go on with your story, Gem."

"I was curious about the birds, so I walked down the porch steps for a better look and saw a mist—or maybe I should say, a hint of mist rising off the creek. Aunt Lo says the early morning mist on the creek is a sign that the edge of summer is approaching."

"Your Aunt LoRetta is quite a gal."

Gem picked up her story without prompting from the sheriff. "The edge of summer is Aunt Lo's favorite time of the year. She loves to point out the stark differences between the hot days and the cool evenings as the summer pushes up against autumn. She loves the sights, sounds, and smells of the edge of summer. I love them, too. I guess I was thinking about that when I noticed the sparrows."

My sister paused again, collecting her thoughts. "The edge of summer is my favorite season, too. That's something I share with my aunt and my sister. Aunt Lo says the bird songs change with the onset of the edge of summer. I've been listening closely to try to distinguish the difference."

"Think carefully, Gem. When you were standing on the porch steps watching the sparrows, did you see anyone around? Anyone at all?"

My sister bit on the end of her finger. "No, I didn't see anyone."

My sister's recollection of how we walked up to the corner at Harrison Street, crossed over and came back down to the bridge matched my telling.

"When we got to the middle of the bridge, Annie peered over the rail, hoping to spot the Interurban down the way. It had already passed."

"It had passed, but could you still hear it?"

Gem looked up, searching her memories, then closed her eye and dropped her head forward. "Yes. Yes, I could... but barely. The squirrels get frantic when the train car goes through, and it seemed they were settling back in."

My sister told the sheriff that once we got to the corner, she saw Mrs. Parlett pull back the curtain on her front window and peek out. "I waved at her..." Gem held up her usual full-hand wave. "...and she waved back." Gem closed her hand but for two fingers, which she moved up and down, mimicking her memory of Mrs. Parlett. I spotted the knowing in Sheriff Boggs' eyes.

The sheriff listened intently to Gem's recount of when we returned to the bridge.

"When Annie pointed out the man in the creek to me, I told her to run and get Popo."

"Did you follow her off the bridge with the carriage?"

"No."

"Why not, Gem?"

My sister's behavior seemed odd when it happened. Now it seemed odd again with Gem's telling of things, but I held my tongue.

"I wanted to know where the sparrows had gone." Gem took a breath and seemed to change directions. "The first moment I thought the sun was up to its old tricks, burning off the cool air before we were ready. I felt its rays warm my skin and caught a whiff of wisteria." Gem raised her nose, reliving the moment. "Then I caught the subtle fragrance of ripe musk melons." Gem licked her lips. "I couldn't help wonder where the sparrows had gone. Usually, I can see them popping around on the ground like popcorn, hunting for bugs, squawking... making a fuss. They weren't there, so I started searching the trees. There he was."

"There who was, Gem?" The sheriff leaned closer to my sister.

"The sparrow. He was sitting on the limb that reaches halfway across the creek from Uncle Karl's yard. He didn't move for the longest time. It was the oddest thing." Gem paused, the sheriff motionless until Gem continued. "He seemed so peaceful. Then I looked down at the man in the creek. He was wearing a suit with a brown pattern. In the sunlight, his suit seemed a perfect reflection of the sparrow's dappled feathers. When Popo ran out, pulled the man from the water, and rolled him over, I saw his white shirt."

Gem placed her hand on her breastbone just under her throat. She didn't say so, but I knew what she was thinking. The sparrows had a white breast.

"Anything else you can tell me? Did you hear anything when the crowd gathered out front?"

"Oh, I heard plenty, but it was just people yakking. It occurred to me that he was a rich, handsome man. I couldn't imagine what he was doing in this neighborhood."

"Anything else you can think to tell me?"

"No, Sheriff. That's it."

I knew my sister had written everything in her diary, but she didn't say so. Perhaps she didn't want Sheriff Boggs to ask to read it.

"Gem, if anything else comes to mind later, please let me know. I better get down to the public square to catch the Interurban. Hector Toops runs a tight ship. He can't tolerate being late."

"Boggy, I'm sorry if Gem didn't give you anything new. I hope this wasn't a waste of your time," offered my father.

"Never a waste of my time when Maggie's cooking is involved, Augie. Besides, Gem gave me a new lead."

Mrs. Parlett.

***

I sat in silence, the pieces of the Corpse in the Creek's puzzle churning in my head, lifting the edges of the known, hoping to discover a clue that would help solve the mystery of his identity. For me, it was much more than that.

I thought about the man's sudden departure from this life, and how his death would change the lives of those who loved him. While I didn't love him, his passing certainly changed my life. I resolved I wouldn't get over his death, because I didn't want to. I wanted to hold him in my heart forever, just as Gem holds PaPaw in hers. In finding the man, part of me had grown up. I felt an unrelenting desire to know the truth I'd never known before. I became determined to know everything about the man who died on my doorstep. Popo referred to that adult trait as "a dog with a bone." I was now that, if I was anything.

The need to get on with the day finally shook us all from our reverie.

"Popo, can Gem and I walk downtown with you and Sheriff Boggs? Please, Popo, please."

Mother piped up. "Girls, I don't want you walking home alone." Especially not now. She didn't say that, but I knew what she was thinking.

"I'll tell you what, Maggie. If the girls want to walk down to the public square with us, they can come back this way with me on the Interurban. I'm planning on getting off a couple blocks up, so it won't be a problem for me to walk them the rest of the way."

Gem and I jumped up and down.

"Okay, then. Get your shoes on, girls. Don't keep Sheriff Boggs and your father waiting. I'll get the coins for the Interurban."

"Don't worry about that, Maggie. The ride won't cost us a penny. This is official county business."

After Gem and I buckled our shoes, we ran out the front door and fell in behind Sheriff Boggs and Popo. As we turned onto the sidewalk toward town, I put my hand up and waved to Bernard, who sat on the front step of his house across from ours. "Good morning, Bernard. Charlie and my brothers will be back in three days." I held up three fingers.

"Thank the good Lord," he called back.

"Hey, Bernard, do you want to take a ride on the Interurban?" Sheriff Boggs shouted.

Bernard stood up. "I shore would!"

"Come on then. Time's a wasting."

Chapter 9

Gem, Bernard, and I sat on the bench at the Interurban stop on the edge of our town's public square, the three-story courthouse rising in front of us. Gem said our grandfather used to tell her stories about its construction.

"PaPaw always called it an architectural marvel," Gem reminded me as we sat in the building's shadow. "He said it was so marvelous that officials across the state duplicated the design in many other counties until the architecture became ordinary. I suppose our courthouse is still an architectural marvel to folks who don't go anywhere."

"We don't go anywhere, except to Mulberry now and again to visit Aunt Rachel and Uncle Madison on the farm. Popo took us to Indianapolis a while back."

Sheriff Boggs paced back and forth in front of us. Popo planted his feet about midway along the sheriff's path so he could converse with the sheriff coming and going.

"I wouldn't have a bit of trouble convincing folks around here that someone murdered this fella, even if I can't put my finger on a perpetrator." The sheriff paused and shook his head before continuing his long walk along his short path. "Augie, it boggles my mind that folks just don't want to consider his death was an accident. Either way, I need to find out this his name and why he was in Jeffries."

I saw the pressure building on our sheriff, who seemed out of sorts, a condition contrary to his jovial nature. It was as if he'd taken the stage in a dramatic play, cloaked in the role as sheriff, and Popo's friend had disappeared before our eyes. Figuring out the identity of the Corpse in the Creek was currently his sole mission in life, the only reason he breathed. I felt comforted by his display of determination.

I remembered the sheriff being this tense one other time. Last winter, Popo enlisted his friend's help to find out who pulled Pauline and me out of creek when we fell through the ice. The man helped us, and done us no harm, so I didn't understand why Popo dragged Sheriff Boggs into it.

Two weeks later, Sheriff Boggs showed up at our house late one night. I awoke to the faint rap on our front door and held my breath as Popo slipped quietly down the stairs. The two men spoke in hushed tones. It was difficult to force myself out of the warmth of my bed, but I finally crept into the wide hallway, lit only by a nightlight in our bathroom. The two men were in the parlor. I listened through the cold air register right above their heads.

"Augie, you need to put this behind you. You wanted assurance that your girls are safe, and I'm telling you they are."

"Fine." Popo didn't sound convinced.

"I think you're imaging things that aren't there."

"I've heard that before."

"You need to let this thing go, my friend." After a lingering silence, the sheriff said, "I better get home before Martha realizes I'm missing in action again."

I heard the front door open. "Thanks for your help, Boggy. I owe you one."

"No problem. Now get some sleep."

I tip-toed back into my room and crawled back into bed next to Gem. I lay there for a while mulling that day Pauline and I had fallen through the ice, remembering every detail I could about the man who pulled us out of the freezing water and sent us running for home. Now I wondered if the sheriff discovered who he was. I also wondered if Popo knew, and would make a dramatic announcement over breakfast the next morning... relieving me of the secret I shared with Mother. That announcement never came.

***

I looked up and studied the sheriff's handsome face. A year ahead of Popo in school, he looked more youthful than my father. He had taken the job as sheriff at a young age when no one else wanted it, mainly because the throng of raucous railroaders who rolled through our town daily caused distress, often exaggerated, among the town folks. When the Great War began skimming off the county's finest, the sheriff remained behind to keep the peace, as the rail industry geared up to transport soldiers to military bases to prepare for war, and move needed supplies to factories to build the nation's implements of war. The government considered the men who worked on the railroad essential to the war effort. Sheriff Boggs considered them a nuisance.

I remember Sheriff Boggs telling a piece of his life story at the Blue and White Café one afternoon. "I spent my first year on the job with one hand on the throats of a few instigators who hopped off the railroad looking for trouble, and the other holding the hands of a few vociferous townies who loved to complain about those boys." The sheriff shook his head, exasperated. "Once the war got serious, the townsfolk had other things to think about so things settled down."

***

"The man's family deserves to know what happened to him." Popo patted his friend on the shoulder. "You'll figure it out, my friend."

Sheriff Boggs nodded. "You can bet on it."

"I should get over to Ghere-Douglass before Karl misses me. You take good care of my girls."

"Don't you worry about your girls, Augie. With Bernard here to help me, they'll be just fine."

Sheriff Boggs stepped aside to allow paying passengers to board the Interurban ahead of us. Then he pulled himself up the three metal steps, his body filling the doorway.

"Morning, Sheriff." The kindly engineer settled into his seat, ready to continue his daily journey to Indianapolis.

"Good morning, Hector."

"What can I do for you this fine morning?"

"To tell the truth, my deputies here..." he moved aside as Gem, Bernard and I scrambled into the single train car. "...and I are investigating the death of a stranger in town. Perhaps you can give us some insight."

"Don't know nothing about a death, but I'll be happy to talk to you."

The sheriff pointed to an empty seat in the first row. Gem and Bernard sat down, me on top of them, as the Interurban lurched forward. The sheriff remained standing, balancing himself in the doorway of the single rail car.

"Can you let us off there near Columbus Street? I expect our conversation won't take long."

"Sure thing, Sheriff."

Sheriff Boggs wasted no time getting to the questions he wanted to ask Hector Toops. He reached into the breast pocket of his shirt, pulled out the article he'd clipped from the Sunday newspaper, and unfolded it. "To your recollection, has this fellow ever been a passenger on your route?"

"No, sir." Hector Toops shook his head back and forth. "He has not."

The sheriff took in a breath and sighed loudly.

"But I have seen him before."

"Is that a fact?" Sheriff Boggs refolded the newspaper clipping and slipped it back into his shirt pocket. "Do tell, Hector."

"On Saturday morning, just after I made my turn along the creek before crossing over, I spotted a man—that man—sitting on a rock just inside the tree line. Children like to sit there and watch me go by. I always wave at them."

"Tell me about the man, Hector."

"He was sitting there, his head in his hands, so I stopped, opened the door, and called out to him. 'Hey, mister, are you okay?' He raised his head slowly, and looked over at me. He seemed disoriented, as if he'd been on an all-night bender, or something. I asked him again, 'You okay?' I don't like to get behind on my route, but it didn't seem right to leave him sitting there if he was ailing."

By this point in Hector Toops' recollection of Saturday morning, I had wriggled away from Gem and Bernard to go stand next to Sheriff Boggs. His hand on my shoulder acknowledged my presence and steadied me as the Interurban rattled its way along its route.

"You're a good man, Hector. Did he say anything to you?"

"It was more of a groan. 'Hit my head, hit my head,' is what I think he said." Hector put his hand to the back of his head and rubbed. "No, come to think of it, he was rubbing the left side, as I recall."

Hector Toops paused, focused on the curve in the track where it entered the woods.

"I pointed behind the man and told him Doc Becker's house was up that way, just a few yards. 'You should pay him a visit to see if he can help you. He's a good doctor.'"

Mr. Toops lifted a hand toward Doc Becker's as he considered his encounter with the man. I felt the sheriff's hand grip my shoulder gently, a signal for me to remain quiet.

"Doc Becker rides with me to Indianapolis from time to time," continued Hector. "We've gotten acquainted. Anyway, the man stands up—seemed unsteady on his feet, so I'm still wondering if he tied one on the evening before at the Sleepy Owl Salon."

"Good, Hector. That's real good. Don't leave out any details."

Hector stared at the track ahead of him. "After he steadied himself a bit, he drew the back of his hand across his nose, like you'd do if you had a cold. I thought it odd because a gentleman dressed like that would have a proper handkerchief." Hector nodded knowingly. "Then he looked over his shoulder and pointed. I assured him that was the way to Doc Becker's office and went on my way."

"What else do you remember about the man?"

"Well, Sheriff, he was a good-looking fellow. Well-groomed, slick haircut and all. Expensive suit, not that I'm any judge of such things. Not much else I can recall."

"Hector, you've been quite helpful. Could you let us out there just before Columbus Street?"

"I could let you out where I saw him, if you like."

"Do you children know where that rock is?"

"Shore do." Bernard's voice sounded strong and confident.

"Let us off at Columbus Street, Hector. We've got another stop to make, don't we, Annie?"

"Yes, Sheriff Boggs. We do."

I stepped back to where Gem and Bernard were sitting and sat down on their laps.

"Did you get all of that?" I asked.

Both nodded.

"Where are we going next?" asked my sister.

I leaned my head back between theirs and whispered, "Mrs. Parlett's house."

Chapter 10

Mrs. Parlett pulled back the curtain on her front window. After seeing Gem and me waving, she unlocked and opened her door. With her arms outstretched, she gushed, "My favorite girls." Gem and I fell into her arms for a long hug.

"Won't you come in? I have the teakettle on." Mrs. Parlett stepped aside as Gem, Bernard, and I filed in ahead of Sheriff Boggs.

"Nice to see you this morning, Mrs. Parlett."

"Nice to see you, too, Sheriff."

"Bernard, you've grown two inches since the last time I laid eyes on you. Where, pray tell, is your Bible?"

Bernard smiled. "I skedaddled right quick the smornin' an' plumb forgot to bring it along with me."

Mrs. Parlett offered Bernard a tight-lipped smile. "The Boy with the Bible is without his Bible... doesn't seem right."

"No, ma'am."

"I'll tell you what... if the occasion arises, I've got one you can borrow."

Bernard placed a finger on his forehead. "I got a few verses here, jest in case."

"I'm sure you do, my boy."

Without questioning the purpose of our visit, Mrs. Parlett led us into her parlor, where we took seats around her coffee table. "It's a bit late in the morning, but I had a hankering for a spot of Earl Grey. My oldest son sent it to me from New York. I usually save it for special occasions, but at my age, everyday I'm on this side of the grave seems a special occasion. If you'll give me a moment, I'll make enough for everyone."

***

I loved Mrs. Parlett. A sweet widow who lost her husband during the early days of the Great War, Mrs. Parlett had four adult sons, but not one grandchild, a fact she often brought up in casual conversation. Fortunately, she'd inherited "a bundle" (Aunt Lo's words) from her deceased husband, which kept her in good stead financially. In the first few years after her husband's unfortunate death, Mrs. Parlett entertained a string of gentlemen callers. (She used to invite her lady-friends to tea to discuss the slim pickings available in our little town due to the war.) As Mrs. Parlett drifted into old age, her suiters drifted away.

The bane of Mrs. Parlett's existence, other than her lack of grandchildren, was the quince tree in her front yard. She hated quince. Every year in early autumn she'd send a note to Mother asking if the boys would come pick the quince before they fell and rotted in her yard.

Mother insisted the boys help with any other chores in our neighbor's yard (Mrs. Parlett always had a list) in exchange for the bushel or more of the pear-shaped fruit they picked. By the end of the day, Mrs.

Parlett's flower and vegetable beds were ready for the spring planting, but for the many leaves that would fall throughout the winter.

Few women in town knew how to get the best out of a bushel of quince the way Mother did, not even Miss Roxy at the Blue and White Café, whose cooking was praised by railroaders from all three lines that crossed our town. Mother would go to work making delicious pie filling and tasty marmalade she'd put up for the winter. That's when the word went out across Jeffries that Mother was "deep in the quince."

"How much quince did Mrs. Parlett's tree yield this year?" our neighbors asked.

"Is Maggie's honey-poached quince pie as good as last year's?"

"Has Old Man Gregory shown up at her door, hoping for a little hospitality that included a piece of her pie?"

The talk went on about Mother and the quince until folks in town found something else to talk about. I think Mother enjoyed being the talk of the town for a few days or weeks every autumn.

***

After she poured our tea and offered us cream and sugar, Mrs. Parlett sat down on the couch next to Gem and got down to the business at hand. "I assume you're investigating the case of the Corpse in the Creek."

"Yes, we are... me and my deputies here. But I prefer not calling it that. It gets folks all roiled up, though that's exactly what that *Morning Time's* reporter was up to."

"This Depression's got newspaper sales down, like everything else. You can't blame the young man for trying to sell a few extra papers with a sensational headline, can we?" Mrs. Parlett stirred her tea, the steam rising in a cloud around her face.

"There's nothing like a dead man floating in a creek to boost sales." Sheriff Boggs quipped, but changed his tone when he got to the questions he'd come to ask. "Mrs. Parlett, did you see this man..." Sheriff Boggs tapped the picture from the newspaper article he'd spread out on Mrs. Parlett's kitchen table. "...walking around in this neighborhood on Saturday morning?"

"No, sir, I did not."

"Did you see anyone else in this neighborhood on Saturday morning before the circus came to town down on the Ghere's front yard?"

Mrs. Parlett hesitated a long moment, considering her answer. "Yes, sir, I did. I saw a good friend of mine."

"Please tell me the name of your friend, Mrs. Parlett?"

The old woman hesitated again, looking down at her hands that lay folded in her lap.

"The name, please, Mrs. Parlett." Sheriff Boggs urged.

"I know the gentleman as Jimbo."

Sheriff Boggs shifted in his chair and scraped the fingers of one hand through his thick, brown hair. I glanced at Gem, whose eyes were fixed on the sheriff's face rather than the woman's.

"Mrs. Parlett," the sheriff's voice now low and controlled, "It's not a good idea to entertain the town's hobos in your home."

I nudged Gem. She ignored me.

"Is that what you believe I was doing?"

The corner of his mouth turned up. "I'd bet a rump roast smothered in onion gravy on it, ma'am."

Mrs. Parlett looked down at her hands again. We remained silent for another awkward moment.

"Now Sheriff," she finally retorted, "In my opinion, it's not a good idea for you to poke your nose into the town folks' business. Seems to me you wouldn't get a thing done if you spent your days chasing after people's decisions you don't approve of."

Sheriff Boggs took a deep breath, as if drawing back the lecture he was about to give our neighbor, taking the proverbial step back from Mrs. Parlett's business.

"I feed Jimbo now and again," she continued, "three or four times during the summer and fall before he heads south—Alabama is where he holes up for the winter," Mrs. Parlett offered. "He doesn't much like spring around here, either. Too wet, too mercurial, as he calls it. Jimbo says the sunsets in Alabama are the most beautiful he's ever seen. He loves those sunsets almost as much as he loves apple season in Indiana." Mrs. Parlett paused, her eyes searching upward, perhaps imaging the Alabama sunsets she would never see. "I'd like to spend my winters in Alabama, if I were a few years younger. What about you, Sheriff?"

Gem, Bernard, and I sat motionless, our breathing shallow, our eyes fixed on the now downcast face of our hostess. Was Mrs. Parlett about to drop a piece of the puzzle into place? We waited, daring not to move for fear we would miss a soft utterance from the old woman.

"Upon occasion, he comes and stands on my front walk, in the shadow of my elm trees, and waits for me to open the door. He never knocks. During the summer, I often peek out, wondering if this will be the day, praying that it will be. I must look hard, or chances are I'll miss him there." Mrs. Parlett's face lit up at the thought of her special visitor.

"'How are you this fine evening?' he asks me. 'I am well. And how are you, my friend?' I reply. 'Madam, I have never been better.'"

With that, I'll give a subtle gesture with my hand, and he'll bow, just enough that I know he accepted my invitation. Then he'll go around back and sit on that old bench under my sugar maples and wait for me.

"I share what I've got. Sometimes it isn't much, but he's always appreciative whatever I serve him. After he eats, we sit until the last of the day's sun fades away. We talk about our lives, Jimbo telling me about the characters he meets during his day's journey through life, me reminiscing about my life when my husband was still with me, and our boys were young. Then he thanks me and slips into the night, leaving me wondering when he'll visit again. Sometimes I sit outside until the mosquitos bite, not wanting to let go of how it feels to be alive again."

Sheriff Boggs allowed Mrs. Parlett a moment with her thoughts.

"When was he here last?"

"Oh, it's been three weeks, perhaps a month ago. I'm sorry. At my age, one day seems like the next. But I'm certain it was him on the street on Saturday morning. I was looking out my bedroom window and, lo and behold, there he was, rushing down South Street toward the creek. I waited awhile at the window, but never saw him return."

"What time was that?"

"Umm." She tapped an index finger to her lips. "First light. Six-ish, I'd say, but I didn't look at my clock."

"Enough light to be certain it was Jimbo?"

She nodded. "I'm certain."

Another long silence made me squirm in my chair. Finally, Mrs. Parlett pushed back from the table and stood up.

"Sheriff, are you going to arrest my friend?"

He shook his head. "Can I tell you a little secret, ma'am?" Gem, Bernard, and I leaned forward in unison. "My working theory on this case is that the man found dead in Prairie Creek on Saturday morning fell and hit his head. At the moment, I have no reason to think otherwise. My problem is that so many folks in Jeffries have a heart for murder. They're grabbing at straws to keep their minds off the sad state this nation and their lives are in. We can't blame them for that, can we?"

Mrs. Parlett shook her head slowly. "No, we cannot. Jimbo knows so much about the state of our nation. He's fascinating to listen to, and always surprises me."

Sheriff Boggs looked deep in thought, as if pieces of the puzzle were sliding into place. Then he looked up at Mrs. Parlett again. "I have one responsibility and that is to find out the identity of the man Annie found dead in Prairie Creek. His family deserves to know his plight—why he hasn't gone home. If accomplishing that means I talk to Jimbo, along with every other man at the hobo camp, that's what I'll do."

"Understood, Sheriff."

"Good." Sheriff Boggs stood up. "I need to get my deputies on home before their mother thinks I lost them."

We trailed Mrs. Parlett and the sheriff to the front door. Then he paused. "Mrs. Parlett, I'd be remiss in my duties if I didn't state again that you should not mix with hobos."

"Nonsense. Jimbo's a gentleman. He wouldn't hurt a fly. Besides, you wouldn't deny an old woman a day with a purpose, that purpose being to lend a hand to a fellow human being. And... and... getting in return what is always a delightful evening of conversation."

Mrs. Parlett followed us out to the porch. "Sheriff, my husband was a good man. He left me a nest egg, so I can get by if I watch my pennies. Most of my days spent in my garden are enjoyable, but one day seems like the next. We make memories with other people, not alone." The woman closed her eye and took a breath. "I don't get many visitors these days," she continued. "My sons come when they can, but they're busy trying to keep food on their tables. The only other regular visitor I get is Gus Ghere."

Gem grabbed my arm. What? It shocked us both to learn our oldest brother visited Mrs. Parlett regularly.

"That boy stops by every week or two and asks me if there's anything I need. I hesitated at first to impose, but he kept stopping and kept asking. So now he runs the occasional errand for me. Just before spring takes hold, he'll come by to till dead leaves and manure into my flower and garden beds ahead of my spring planting. I never asked him to do that. He just does it. He's a good boy, just not much of a conversationalist."

"Thank you for your time." Sheriff Boggs stepped off the porch and onto the front walk. I imagined Jimbo standing there in the shade of the elm trees, waiting for his friend to open her front door.

"Oh, and Sheriff," Mrs. Parlett called from the porch.

Sheriff Boggs turned around, giving the old woman his full attention.

"You come back... anytime."

"Yes, ma'am."

We walked home in silence. After Gem, Bernard, and I climbed the steps to the porch, I turned to Sheriff Boggs. He was leaning on the handrail, one foot on the bottom step.

"Doesn't that just go to show you?" he mumbled.

"What's that?" I asked.

"Always listen to Roxy Lockwood."

Chapter 11

After breakfast the next day, Gem collected Thea in her basket while I ran across the street to invite Bernard over to discuss our visit with Mrs. Parlett. With Mother busy in her sewing room, we retreated to the stone bench in our backyard. The bench was a leftover from Mother's Uncle Frank, who built the house. He had positioned the bench to allow visitors to gaze at the perennial bed or turn around to face the other way to see everything else—the vegetable garden, the small apple orchard, the side of the barn and chicken coop, and even a hint of Prairie Creek that flowed beyond the thick stand of trees.

Gem and I sat down on the bench facing the trees as Bernard stretched out on the patch of grass in front of us. Gem placed Thea's basket where it caught the soft rays of the late morning sun through the trees. Our baby sister held her rag doll in one hand and gripped the edge of the basket with the other, peering at us with great interest.

"We're in for 'nother hot one." Bernard offered the casual comment as a lead-up to the real reason we'd retreated out of Mother's earshot.

Gem leaned forward and tugged her diary and pencil out from underneath the old towel in Thea's basket. She opened it, touched the tip of her pencil to her tongue, and jotted a note.

"So far, what do we know about the Corpse in the Creek?" she asked.

I elbowed my sister. "We're not supposed to call it that."

Gem grinned. "That's what everyone else calls it."

"The sheriff don't like it none so we need to git in a row behind 'im."

Gem rolled her eyes at Bernard, then continued, "Yesterday, Popo questioned us about every detail that happened after he left us with Sheriff Boggs, so it's good that I wrote everything down while we still remembered it. Is there anything new?" Gem jiggled her pencil between her two fingers as she thought.

"It seems like days since we got on the Interurban with Sheriff Boggs, but that was just yesterday. It also seems like forever until Charlie and our brothers get home." I sighed. "How many more days until they get back?"

"Two," said Gem and Bernard in unison.

Two whole days. As we sat in the garden thinking about how upside down our lives had gotten since Saturday, I realized Thea had her rag doll, Gem had her diary, and Bernard had his Bible. Charlie anchored me. He'd been gone since school let out for the summer, leaving me more out of sorts with each passing day, and especially since the discovery of the Corpse in the Creek. I wondered if working all summer on his family farm changed Charlie. What if he no longer wants to read to me, or walk to school with me, or watch birds with me? What if he's outgrown his younger cousin and now prefers the company of my brothers and their friends?

All the talk about the Corpse in the Creek and being privy to Sheriff Bogg's investigation distracted me during these final days without

Charlie, but late last night, when it seemed the only light in my life was that of the moon shining through my bedroom window, I was scared. For the whole of my seven years of life, death had kept its distance. A few days ago, I'd looked death in the face right outside my family's front door. The experience set so many emotions roiling around in my mind, emotions that nudged me awake in the dead of night. I wanted to scream. I wanted to let it all out. If only I could put my hand on Charlie's arm to ground me.

"Things will get better, Annie."

I wriggled my bare toes in the dirt. "Things haven't gotten better at Popo's business."

"I know."

"Two more days." I uttered the words just loud enough for Gem and Bernard to hear.

My sister put her arm around my shoulder and squeezed. "That's not long, little sister. Charlie and our brothers will be back, and Aunt Lo won't be long behind them. Everything will be back to normal soon. I promise."

I wriggled my toes some more, hoping that the normal state of my life would return in two days. But I couldn't imagine ever returning to my life as it was on Saturday morning before finding the Corpse in the Creek.

"That-air was my furst ride on that-there Interurban keer." Bernard took a deep breath and rolled over on his back. "Ef I'd had a pock'ful a nickels, I'd git on one day an' ride 'til I war broke."

Gem smiled. "I think I would, too. What about you, Annie?"

"Only if you, Charlie, Gus, and the twins... and Aunt Lo went with us."

"Mother is going to call us soon. So let's talk about what we remember about our visits with Hector Toops and Mrs. Parlett." Gem looked over a few pages of her diary. "I want to make sure it's all written here so we don't forget a single thing to tell the boys when they get home."

I jumped up. "Gem, I told Sheriff Boggs we would take him to the rock where Mr. Toops spotted the man before he died! We went by Mrs. Parlett's and never made it to the rock."

Gem pulled back her pencil from her fresh diary page. "After we eat, and Thea goes down for her nap, we can go there." Bernard and I nodded. "But we can't tell Mother, or she'll forbid it. Do you understand, Bernard?"

"I hain't gonna tell no fib."

"No one is going to lie. Keeping your mouth shut is something else entirely."

"Hain't so, Gem."

Gem touched her forefinger to her thumb and drew them across her lips. Bernard got the message.

***

After drying and putting away the last of the dishes from our lunch—an egg sandwich and applesauce—Gem announced to Mother we were going out for a walk.

"Where are you going?" Mother kept track of her charges.

Bernard spoke up, causing Gem and me to hold our breath. "T'other day, I he'ped Mister Lockwood clean out that-air ol' shed ahind the Blue and White Café. He gin me this."

Bernard turned his pants pocket inside out to reveal a shiny silver dime. "I'm a-buyin' candy. The way I figger it, suckin' on jaw breakers is jes' as good a way as any to pass the time 'til the boys get back an' to keep our minds off'n that dead folk."

If Bernard said it, it was true.

"You and Old Barney aren't the only ones missing those boys." Mother sighed. After the events of the last few days, she seemed as eager as the rest of us to have her brood back at home under her watch.

"I want to look in the window at Thrashers," Gem added. "Maybe I'll get an idea for a dress to start school in."

"It is about that time of year." Mother thought for a long moment. "Fine, but stay together. And don't be gone too long."

"I'll be back t' he'p settle in Cooter fer the day. This-here heat takes it outen Pops, so he needs me."

Bernard loved that horse... and his Pops, too.

After saying our goodbyes to Mother, we crossed the South Street bridge, strolling along, fighting the urge to run.

"Does your mother know where you girls are going?" Aunt Iris stood on her porch, one hand on her hip, the other wagging a finger at us. "You shouldn't be out alone with a killer on the loose."

I stopped on the sidewalk and turned to face her. "Aunt Iris, after a lot of investigating, Sheriff Boggs believes the man fell and hit his head, and died from it."

"What? Are you sure about that?"

"He told us that yesterday morning."

"You spoke to Sheriff Boggs yesterday?"

"Yes, we're helping him with his investigation. He calls us his deputies. Isn't that right, Bernard?"

Our friend nodded his head. That settled the matter.

"I have a dish of horehound drops. I'd be happy to share them with you children if you want to come in. You can tell me all about it."

"Thank you, Aunt Iris, but horehound drops break Bernard out in hives." Gem smiled sweetly at our aunt. Bernard's eyes widened to the size of saucers. "Annie and I will have to pass on your kind offer because we don't want to eat in front of him. We'll talk to you later, Aunt Iris... tell you everything we know."

Gem took a hold of my arm and pulled me away. "Let's go," she whispered. "And don't look back."

We'd walked a half a block before Bernard found his voice. "Lordy me!" What words'll I be spoutin' when some feller comes a-pesterin' 'bout them horehound drops an' whether they'll set my skin a-raisin' up in sech a fretful rash!"

Gem laughed. "First, no one is going to ask you, and second, if someone does, say 'Gem was mistaken.'"

"Gem was tellin' tales taller'n a cornstalk, that's fer sure." Bernard walked along another moment before changing the subject away from the moral quandary he found himself in, thanks to my big sister. "Now, ain't it peculiar how yer aunty's eyes must've been a-playin' tricks on 'er? Here we was, strollin' past with Sheriff Boggs an' ol' Popo, bold as brass in broad daylight, an' later on, when the sheriff was a-seein' us home, safe an' sound. Yet yer aunty, bless 'er heart, she didn't catch nary a glimpse of us? It's right puzzlin', I reckon, like them goblins done snatcher 'er eyesight whe we wasn't lookin'."

"Our beloved Aunt Iris doesn't get out of bed before the crack of noon. She says she needs her beauty sleep."

"Why, ef ye don't take no offense to my sayin' so, hit ain't workin' one blessed bit. Sich a thing as this here plan is plumb broke down, like a wagon wheel in a muddy lane—an' that's the honest trugh, sure as preachin'."

Gem stopped in her tracks. A grin crossed her face. "And that, Bernard, is no lie."

We walked up to Columbus Street, where we crossed over South Street and past Mrs. Parlett's house on the corner. A block down, we turned left on Armstrong, which took us back toward the creek.

Bernard took the lead just before the Armstrong Street bridge, leading us down along a well-worn path into the trees that lined the creek. It wasn't far... just a few feet... but the trees and undergrowth were much denser here than by our house. I wondered how a man who had hit his head found his way to the rock where Hector Toops spotted him sitting.

When Bernard arrived at the rock a few feet from the Interurban tracks, he turned and pointed behind us. "Well, I'll be! That there li'l trail winds right up to ol' Dock Becker's place, sure as shootin'. An' let me tell ya, if'n Gem hadn't been leadin' us 'round that big ol' barn like a cat chasin' its tail, why, we could been there quicker'n a jackrabbit on a hot griddle. Ain't that jest the way of things?"

"Maybe the man was looking for Doc Becker's place and got lost. Then Mr. Toops saw him sitting on the rock and pointed out where to find Doc Becker."

"Annie, that makes sense, but how do we know for sure?"

Gem and I sat down on the rock to think as Bernard paced around us. "What do you do when you come here with our brothers?" Gem asked.

Bernard continued as he looked here and there, for what I didn't know. "We jaw, we do, an' like it here right fine, 'cause it feels far off from all that's known. But Gus an' them twins, they hear yer matcher holler, an' I catch ol' Cooter's step a-comin' up the lane, so's I kin scamper off to help my Pops."

"What if it's the milk wagon coming up the street?" Gem sometimes asks odd questions.

"That sounds right strange-like, I'll tell ye."

I wondered if Gem would make a note of that in her diary.

Bernard wandered near where the Interurban tracks turned parallel to the creek bed before crossing the narrow bridge. Only wide enough for the Interurban car, it had no path for pedestrians. Popo said during the Interurban's early days, several men had stumbled over the edge of the bridge and into the creek... at night... on their way home from the Sleepy Owl Saloon. We referred to those times in Popo's story as "back in the olden days."

"I know Hector Toops reported to Sheriff Boggs a few times that boys were playing on the tracks right here." Gem pointed to the bridge a few yards away. "Mother chewed out Gus and the twins about such shenanigans when she'd gotten wind of the engineer's complaints. She says Hector has to pay special attention when he passes through this area when the boys are around."

"'Tain't jest yer brothers an' me what comes 'round here." If Bernard had mentioned any names, I'm sure they would have ended up in Gem's diary.

"Look, Gem! Is that your sparrow?" I pointed at a bird perched on a low-hanging tree branch a few feet beyond Bernard's head. The sparrow looked straight at us.

Gem's hand touched my arm, a signal to be still. "Maybe," she whispered, almost too faint for me to hear.

Bernard, Gem, and I gazed at the bird.

"I'm not sure..."

"*Shhhh*. Don't talk, Annie."

The sparrow fluffed its feathers a moment, then flitted down to the ground and hopped around the roots of the tree, pecking in the dirt for an insect or a seed to eat. As Bernard shifted his weight, the sparrow hopped further away from him, then flew up through the trees and out of sight.

"Bernard," groaned my sister. She frowned and shook her head side-to-side.

Our friend mimicked my sister's dower face. "'Twuz nuthin' but a lil' sparrer, I'll tell he."

That's when my eye glimpsed something white at the base of the tree.

"What's that?"

I ran over to the tree and fell to my knees. Gem and Bernard were soon at my sides.

"What is it, Annie?"

I rubbed my hand over the rough bark, my eyes following the trunk upwards until its branches touched the sky.

"Black waller-nut," muttered Bernard.

At the base of the tree, the tops of root exposed from decades of flooding formed a tangle of nooks and crannies, some filled with dead leaves or pieces of walnut shells discarded by squirrels that had enjoyed the fruit of the tree. I pointed to the edge of something that appeared to be a white paper sticking out from a narrow crevice. I looked over my shoulder at Gem, who nodded her head as if to say, "Go ahead, do it."

As I tugged the corner of the paper, a gentle gust of wind rattled the branches high above us, reminding me of a sigh of relief. I felt I had freed the ancient tree of its burden.

"Whut in tarnation is it?" Bernard asked, turning his ear toward the crevice. "It tinkled, like a little bell, it did."

I continued my task, inching the paper from its hiding place. A moment later, I cradled an envelope in my hand and fell back on my heels.

Gem reached out and rubbed a corner of the envelope between her thumb and forefinger. "It hasn't been here long, or it would be damp and dirty."

Inscribed with a few words hand-written in elegant script with a fountain pen, I held the envelope a little closer to Gem's face. "What does it say?"

My sister brushed a smudge away with her finger.

"It reads, 'Do you still love me?'"

"Should we open it?" I asked.

"I think we should take it to Sheriff Boggs right this minute. The man who was sitting here early Saturday morning probably hid this note in the tree."

"We should go now."

Gem and I stood up, leaving Bernard on his knees, still looking at the crevice.

"Hol' yer hosses fer a minit." Bernard pulled a pocketknife from his pants pocket, opened the blade, and slide it into the narrow opening. Out rolled two coins.

After placing his knife back in his pocket, Bernard picked up the coins and examined them. Then he held them out to us. "Them's Walkin' Liberty half-dollars, sure as shootin'!" His eyes were bigger than saucers. He caught his breath, then using the reverent voice he uses for bird funerals, he read the words inscribed on the coins.

"In God We Trust."

Chapter 12

"Sheriff, you have company." Biddy Ann Blout walked to the front counter of the sheriff's office and peered over it at Gem and me. Exhausted from our run from the rock on Prairie Creek, we arrived there doubled over from side stitches and panting, sweat beads dotting our foreheads.

"Well, well, well, what do we have here, Biddy?" He leaned over the counter to see for himself.

"I've been toying with keeping that door locked, and this settles it." The sheriff's secretary went to her desk, leaving her boss to deal with us.

Sheriff Boggs walked around and pulled the bench near the door closer to the counter. "Sit," he instructed as he turned the fan that sat on the counter towards us. The *whap, whap, whap* of the fan blades forced air into our wet faces, blowing back our hair.

"Hey, what about me?"

"You hush now, Biddy." Then turning to us he said, "To what do I owe this unexpected pleasure... oh, and where's your trusty sidekick?"

I pointed to the door, which the sheriff had propped open with a wedge of wood, scarred by a thousand kicks. Still panting heavily, I attempted to explain Bernard's whereabout. "He's... he's..."

Gem rescued me. Taking a deep breath to settle herself, and running the fingers of both hands through her damp wavy hair at her temples, lifting it away from her face, then moistening her lips with her tongue, she explained. "We were coming to talk to you, but as soon as we got to the public square, Bernard heard Cooter neighing... then saw him and his father's ice cart out front of the Sleepy Owl Saloon. He took off running to his horse, but we came straight here."

"Okay, that explains Bernard's absence." The sheriff paced back and forth along the counter twice before stopping in front of us. "Ladies, my theory about the cause of death of our mystery man seems to be the hot topic on this afternoon's grapevine."

My eyes widened. Aunt Iris.

"I'm guessing I have you girls to thank for the unexpected respite from the usual tittle-tattle. Folks aren't talking murder at the moment, so they're mostly minding their business."

"You're welcome, Sheriff." Leave it to Gem to take credit where credit is due.

"Which brings me to the latest question on my mind... what are you two doing here? Again? Not that I don't love seeing my favorite girls, but I'm trying my best to solve the mystery thrown at me three days ago."

"Five."

"I stand corrected... five days ago. Thank you, Annie, for pointing out the length of my incompetence."

I tipped my head back and grinned. "You're welcome."

Gem drew the letter out of her pocket and held it out to Sheriff Boggs. He looked Gem in the face, then shifted his eyes to me. "What's this?"

"We found it in a crevice of a tree near the rock down by the Interurban tracks, but we didn't open it." I spit the words out fast, hoping he'd focus on the part where we didn't open it. No such luck.

"Does your mother know you were prowling around down by the creek near the Interurban tracks?"

Gem and I shook our heads solemnly.

"I'm getting a clear picture of what you two... make that three... have been up to since yesterday morning."

"After we stopped by Mrs. Parlett's, you forgot to take us to the rock," I offered politely.

"Oh, so your afternoon shenanigans are my fault?"

I smiled weakly, happy that he had come around to the truth on his own.

Finally, the sheriff sighed, and took the envelope from Gem's hand. We watched as his eyes followed the handwriting across its face.

"Do you still love me?" Gem whispered.

"This adds an interesting twist to our investigation, doesn't it, deputies?"

"One more thing, Sheriff," Gem offered.

"There's more?"

"We found two silver half dollars with the letter. They're in Bernard's pocket for safe-keeping."

"I can't think of a safer place," sighed the man. With that, the sheriff walked back behind the counter, entered his office, and closed the door.

I watched the minutes tick by on the clock that sat on the counter near the wall. Five minutes, ten minutes, fifteen minutes since the sheriff left us sitting on the bench in front of the fan. I finally stood up and walked over to examine its face up close. Besides the large, black numbers, the words in the center of the face read, WAKE ALL. Right below that in slightly smaller letters read, ONE SPRING. An alarm clock seemed out of place in a sheriff's office. While the face of the clock fit the office's otherwise black and white and somewhat dreary decor, the casing was another story. Peachy-orange, the color of my favorite orange sherbet, the clock casing was too pleasant for its surroundings... one vibrant flower against a plowed field.

"The sheriff should spring for a proper wall clock." Biddy Ann stood up and walked over to the counter. "If I forget to wind that thing, we're both here until Martha calls, wondering if she should feed the sheriff's supper to the cats. He often says yes, so he has an excuse to eat at the Blue and White Café again."

Staring at the clock, I could detect the big hand move, minute by minute. When the clock read eight minutes until two o'clock, I turned to my sister, who still sat on the bench with her hands folded in her lap. "Gem, let's go home. If we're gone much longer, Mother will worry."

Before she could reply, the sheriff's office door flew open. A moment later, he was standing in front of the counter, the letter open in his hand. He looked at us as he straightened to his full height. "Well, deputies," he said with a wry smile, "you may have found an important clue."

"Any names?" asked Gem.

The sheriff pursed his lips and shook his head. "Nicknames, but none I can connect to anyone." Then he explained that if the letter we found belonged to the dead man, and he had every reason to believe that it did, he had come to town in search of the woman he loved. And wound up dead for his efforts. "That means he knew someone here in Jeffries. I do not know why he left the letter there near the rock, but maybe he wasn't thinking straight after he hit his head." The sheriff paused, considering his explanation. "Later on this afternoon, I'm going to meet up with Doc Becker again to find out if he has any further insight into the man's cause of death. The body is still on ice over at the county morgue." The sheriff pulled a red handkerchief from his pants pocket and dabbed his forehead. "In the meantime," he said, shoving his hankie back into his pocket, "I'm going to do what I've tried to avoid doing."

"What's that?" asked Gem.

"I'm gonna head over to the hobo camp and see if I can track down Jimbo. I've been on the lookout for him popping up around town, as he's wont to do now and again, but I haven't seen hide nor hair of him since Annie found the dead man."

"Do you think he's involved?" Gem stood up and stepped closer to the sheriff.

"Not exactly, but I have a niggling in my head telling me he knows something that might be helpful to my investigation. That's the only reason I can come up with as to why he'd be over on South Street on Saturday morning since we know he wasn't there to grift off Mrs. Parlett."

"Mrs. Parlett seems fond of Jimbo,"

"You're right, Gem," stated the sheriff. "She does. While I still don't think an old woman should keep company with a hobo, Mrs. Parlett knows him well enough to believe he wouldn't hurt a fly. I'll trust her on that. Jimbo may be harmless, but there's a reason he's been avoiding me. So I'm going to pay a visit to the hobo camp out at the edge of town before the sun goes down on another day of my investigation without the answers I'm looking for."

"Is it right smart to be a-goin' out there all by yer lonesome?" All eyes shot to the doorway where Bernard now stood. A contemporary with my twin brothers, Blinn and Cory, our neighbor stood an inch or two shorter than my brothers. His lanky body only barely blocked the light... and the heat... coming in through the doorway.

Rather than acknowledge Bernard's sudden reappearance, Gem blurted out, "Are you going to take your gun?"

"Nope. No guns. I'm going to go you one better than that. I'm going to ask your father to join me. That old boy owes me a favor or two. Besides, thanks to you girls, he's in this up to his kneecaps, like it or not."

"Sheriff, do you even have a gun?"

"I do, indeed."

I heard Biddy Ann mumble, "Oh, no. Not that old story, again."

Sheriff Boggs ignored her. "My Uncle Spunks... his real name was Lester Boggs, but after he made it out of the Great War in once piece, my grandfather nicknamed him Spunky, which seemed an awful lot to say in my family, so he shortened it to Spunks." Sheriff Boggs paused, enjoying the memory of this piece of his family history. "During the Great War, Uncle Spunks was a member of the American Expeditionary Forces, and fought alongside the British Army on the Western Front when..."

"Sheriff."

He turned and looked at Biddy Ann. She held up her index finger and twirled it in the air.

"To make a long story short..." The sheriff turned back to Bernard, who remained in the doorway. "Uncle Spunks got the service weapon off a German soldier he'd killed. The way my uncle tells it, the Kraut had slipped into the Allied trenches on a moonless night and happened upon a Tommie, sound asleep in a funk hole."

Sheriff Boggs' eyes looked upward, imagining the horrific scene. "After joining the AEF, Spunks developed the habit of keeping his hand on the grip of his M1911. When the Kraut came out of nowhere, dropped on top of the sleeper, and drew his combat knife to slit his throat, that instant caught up with reality in Spunks' foggy brain. In that single eternal moment, he raised his service weapon and fired a 9mm bullet point-blank into the head of the enemy.

"Once Spunks heard the blast, the ensuing chaos returned him to real time when he fell to the ground sobbing, distraught over his miserable failure to act in time to save the Tommie. But in fact, the Tommie lived to fight another day. In hindsight, Spunks says he wished he'd knocked the Kraut upside the head with the barrel of his M1917 Enfield, or stabbed him with his Mark I trench knife, for all the trouble the gun blast caused. When things finally settled down, his buddies presented Spunks with the Luger self-loading pistol they'd taken off the Kraut, telling him they hoped he'd have their backs in the future. Spunks always did."

The sheriff nodded his head in appreciation of his uncle's character under fire. He continued, "Spunks brought the gun back to the states when he returned home, and gave it to me when I became sheriff. He reminded me that its reputation proceeded it, that it would be there to save me or someone else if ever needed. When I pinned on this badge..." The sheriff tapped the badge on his shirt. "...I decided I'd probably never need it, but I keep it close, just in case. Of course, Spunks still carries an M1911 on his hip, his hand is jumpy when he's not holding its grip." The sheriff sighed. "My aunt says he spills a lot of coffee."

Turning back to Biddy Ann, he asked, "Short enough for you?"

She shrugged.

"It's time to go before the sun sets on the day, along with my enthusiasm to question a bunch of unpredictable hobos on their turf. Roxy's got beef and noodles on the Blue and White's supper menu... I can't miss that."

"Sheriff, I'll tell ye what... I'll haul ye out to Ghere-Douglass in Pop's ice cart. Ye'll meet up with Mr. Ghere, slick as a whistle. Why, it's hotter'n blue blazes outside, an' the back end's still cold as a witch's kiss from all that ice. Ye'll git there faster'n greased lightnin', I reckon, an' cool as a cucumber to boot."

"Doesn't your father have more deliveries to make this afternoon, Bernard?"

"Nah. The ice done melted quick as lightnin' this mornin', an when he come a-trudgin' back to the ice plant fer more, the boss-man hollered out from a frown so tight, sayin' they'd got themselves a right pesky trouble with one o' them ice-making' contraptions, an' he'd best skedaddle on home an' come a-callin' ag'in come tomorrow."

"Bernard, I think you should take the girls on home instead."

"Ghere-Douglass is a sight closer'n home," pointed out Bernard. "I'll tell ye true, te'd be doin' me an' my ol' hoss a kindness. Ol' Cooter kin git his fill from th' trough out yonder, an' I kin tug 'im under th' roof o'er th' loadin' dock fer a heap o' shade, too, don't ye know. Th' hobo camp's jest a hop, skip, an' a jump from there. So what d'ye say?"

After a moment, the sheriff looked at his secretary.

"Biddy, give us about a ten-minute head start, then call over to the Ghere's and let Maggie know the girls are with me. If she asks for more information, tell her we're going for a Blood Orange to chase away the heat."

Bernard rubbed his hands together and muttered, "O, I'm plumb crazy fer Blood Orange sody-pop."

"Don't say more than that," the sheriff continued. "I don't want the grapevine lit up again any sooner than it has to be, if you know what I mean."

Biddy leaned on the counter and gave the sheriff an amused look. "The men in this town certainly are vicious gossips. Seems to me the

Widower Pastor Burke needs to give them a good talking to about the evils of gossip." One corner of Biddy Ann's lip turned up.

"I was referring to my beloved."

"I know who you were referring to, Sheriff. I'm just attempting to straighten out your thinking a bit."

"Where would I be without you, Biddy?" The sheriff pursed his lips and shook his head.

"Is Mr. Ghere aware that you're on your way?"

"I believe so," replied the sheriff. "Of course, we talked around the barn a bit and threw around some colorful words to keep the listening ears off the scent, but he got my message, although he hasn't a clue I'll be arriving in an ice cart surrounded by my favorite deputies."

"You're making it sound like a picnic now, Sheriff."

"Do you want to come along for the ride?"

"No, I think I'll stay put and get some proper work done, if you don't mind."

"Suit yourself, Biddy. Remember, ten minutes."

"I'll remember."

I turned to wave goodbye to the sheriff's secretary, but she didn't see me. She was readjusting the fan on the counter toward her desk.

Sheriff Boggs stood in the street and took a long look at Cooter and the ice cart.

"Let's get this show on the road before I change my mind."

Chapter 13

Mr. Thompson's ice cart was little more than a covered wagon, with two small wooden wheels in the front and two large ones in the back. Bernard told me that as a boy his father started out with an ice cart that he pushed around the streets of downtown Terre Haute, calling out, "Yoo-hoo. I-C-I-C-ice. Get your I-C-I-C-ice," to provide a small income for his widowed mother and five sisters. Because of his hard work, his employer, Consolidated Ice Company, soon rewarded the young Thompson with a larger cart.

Soon after he moved with his mother and new wife into their small house on South Street—a house with a horse Bernard's mother had inherited from her parents—he took on an ice wagon to accommodate the largest route in Jeffries. He just never adjusted his words to his new circumstance.

Mr. Thompson's ice cart had a bench seat tucked under the overhang of the wagon's roof to provide the driver with a bit of shade on hot days. The bench seat behind Cooter, the Thompson's third horse since the family's relocation to Jeffries, held a driver, his tongs and pick, but not much else. During ice season, Mr. Thompson walked alongside his horse for most of his route, Cooter stopping instinctively in front of the homes of Mr. Thompson's regular customers without prompting. (During the winter, Mr. Thompson took part-time employment delivering coal from an old horse-drawn wagon.)

"Bernard, where's your father?"

"He's bellied-up pretty good to the bar." Bernard turned and pointed at the saloon Mr. Thompson patronized.

"Have you ever driven this thing?"

"Lawzy, yes, Mister! I been a-doin' this here thing sence I war jest a leetle feller o' eight. You ain't got nary a care in the world, I'll tell ye."

Uninvited, Gem squeezed up next to Bernard on the bench. That left the sheriff and me to sit on the back of the cart, our feet dangling. Bernard slapped the reins on Cooter's back and the horse sauntered forward. Nothing moved fast on hot humid days in Jeffries, Indiana.

"If this doesn't get the tongues a-wagging again in full glory, nothing will." The sheriff raised a hand and waved at the folks on the street, who stopped to gawk at the spectacle of their sheriff hitching a ride on the back of an ice cart.

***

None too happy when we pulled the ice wagon up to Ghere-Douglass, Uncle Karl paced the length of the loading dock, frowning and shaking his head. Popo stood with his arms crossed against his brother's barrage of nonsense. My father often said Karl was the master of making a mountain out of a molehill.

Sheriff Boggs slid off the back of the ice cart and strode up the wooden steps toward Popo, with Gem, Bernard, and me at his heels.

"What have you brought upon this fine business this time, Augustus? Our dearly departed father would roll over in his grave if you brought the long arm of the law to our doorstep."

Gem and I giggled. Bernard looked terrified.

The sheriff walked toward Uncle Karl and stood in his path, interrupting his methodical pace.

"What do you know about the poor fellow found dead in the creek just a few feet from your house? Where were you on Saturday morning?"

"Sheriff, I-I-I had nothing to do with that man's death, I swear."

"Is that a fact?"

"Sheriff, I never stick my nose in where it doesn't belong. I have enough to do to mind my own business."

"Speaking of minding one's business, it's come to my attention that your wife is spreading gossip all over Jeffries regarding my theories on this matter."

"You know how women talk."

"I do indeed." The sheriff shook his head, as if trying to get an image of his beloved out of his head. "Karl, I am here on official business. Unless you know something about the man your niece found dead in Prairie Creek on Saturday, I'd appreciate it if you'd get back to minding your own business inside. Augie and I have things to discuss that I'd prefer not set the grapevine ablaze before I get back into town."

My uncle sniffed and walked back into the building.

"Now that you've dragged my girls out here, can you tell me what's going on, Boggy?"

"Gem and Annie might not like it, but I'm going to lay it out straight. Your daughters and Bernard found an envelope by that rock near the Interurban tracks."

Popo looked at Gem and me, disappointment in his eyes.

Softening the blow of our actions, Sheriff Boggs explained to Popo that we'd done the right thing by bringing the envelope to him. "He came here looking for the love of his life. I suspect he fell and hit his head and died before he found her. The cause of death may be more clear after I speak with Doc Becker again this afternoon. Problem is, my investigation keeps pointing me to Jimbo. It's time I put in the effort to have a talk with him. Augie, I thought walking into the hobo camp with you might make me seem a little less official... and a little more vulnerable." One corner of the sheriff's mouth turned up.

My father pursed his lips. "I'm not sure if that's a compliment or an insult. Before I agree to go, I'd like you to answer one question."

"Sure, old friend. Ask away."

"Did you bring your gun?"

"What is it with your family's obsession with my gun?"

Popo looked confused. "No gun then. You're taking me along for protection?"

"I'm taking you along because two men have twice the sway as one in situations such as the one we're walking in to."

"Since I'm not the protection, are you taking any, Clyde?" Popo rarely called his friend by his real first name. It seemed odd coming from his lips.

Sheriff Boggs looked my father straight in the face and pointed toward the sky. "I've got my connections. That's the only reason I'm still standing after all this time."

"They better be good ones," Popo said. "Let's get moving." Popo began giving orders. "Bernard, there's a watering trough right along the side of the building, if you're interested."

"You've done gone an' peeked right into ol' Cooter's noggin."

"Once the horse gets his fill, I want you right back here looking after my daughters. We're not expecting another delivery until morning, so you can stay here on the loading dock until we get back. No going out looking for any more clues under any circumstances. Is that clear?"

"Yes, Popo," Gem and I said in unison.

"One more thing." Sheriff Boggs turned to face us, a hand on his hip where his gun should have been. "If we're not back in an hour, go straight into your father's office and call Biddy. Tell her we're missing in the most urgent tone you can muster."

"What then?" I heard the panic rising in Gem's voice. "What will Miss Biddy Ann do then?"

"Gem, I'll be honest with you." The sheriff turned and walked toward the loading dock steps. We could barely hear his parting words. "I have no idea. But she'll think of something."

***

"Has it been an hour yet?"

"No, Annie, not even close."

I wiped sweat from my eyes with the back of my hands. The cover of shade provided little defense from the sweltering late-summer heat.

Since Popo and Sheriff Boggs left, following the railroad tracks into the woods, Gem, Bernard, and I had little to say to each other. Bernard found a broom, jumped off the loading dock, and swept out the ice cart. Gem leaned against the wall near the door and retreated into her own thoughts. I fidgeted. I wished I was passing the time until Charlie and my brothers got home listening to our big Zenith radio in the green room... or playing Rook with my friends, Pauline and Helen... or eating pie at the Blue and White Cafe with Popo while listening to the town gossip. Being Popo's shadow was one of my favorite things to be.

Every few minutes, I darted down the steps of the dock and ran out to where I had a better view of the railroad tracks.

"I think I see them!" I yelled. "Look!"

Popo and Sheriff Boggs strode in the center of the tracks toward Ghere-Douglass. My relief at seeing them overwhelmed me.

Bernard and I joined Gem on the loading dock. When the two men climbed the steps, I saw they weren't happy.

"Did you talk to him? Did you find Jimbo?" Gem asked.

"No." The word lingered in the air. We'd come here for nothing.

My father changed the subject. "Does your mother know where you are?"

Sheriff Boggs stepped in to rescue us.

"I told Biddy to call Maggie and tell her the girls were with me. As for Gem and Annie's trip to the rock with Bernard this afternoon, well, I'm staying out of that one."

"Mother told us not to play on the tracks," I insisted. "She never forbid us from going to the rock. We didn't get anywhere near the tracks, did we Gem?"

"The three of you can work that out with Maggie on your own time. I want to get back into town. I owe my deputies a bottle of Blood Orange."

"And Bernard owes us candy. Isn't that right, Bernard?"

"I'll allow as how hit's gospel-truth, seein' as I done give my solemn word."

"Let's get on with it, then. I've got to check in with Biddy to make sure no one else has found a dead body lying around Jeffries. Then I've got to pay Doc Becker a visit before I stop by to do a little hand-holding with the Widow Winslow."

I cringed.

Bernard climbed up on the bench of the ice cart with Gem right behind him. "I guess we get the back again, Annie. Are you going with us, Augie?"

Popo climbed up next to me. "I could use a bottle of pop myself after our encounter in the hobo camp. I'm just sorry it didn't get you any closer to the answers you need."

Sheriff Boggs looked over my head at his friend. "I think Jimbo got my message loud and clear."

Popo seemed confused. "How's that, Boggy?"

"He was there."

***

Popo told us all that had happened on their visit to the hobo camp over supper that night.

When the two men walked into the center of the camp, it seemed like a ghost town, but they felt eyes on them. Boggy and Augie stood back to back to keep watch in all directions. Augie spotted a lean-to sheds the 'bos had built into a thick stand of shrubbery. He nudged the sheriff just as the lawman pointed to movement in another direction.

The flap on the lean-to opened, and a man crawled out and stood up. Two others followed at his flanks. None looked too intimidating until Augie caught the glint of sunlight flicker off the blade held against the thigh of the right flank.

"Good afternoon, Sheriff. To what do we owe the pleasure of your visit?"

"I'm looking for Jimbo. Is he around?"

"Is he in some sort of trouble?"

"I just have a few questions for him. I suppose you heard about the man found dead in Prairie Creek on Saturday morning. Someone spotted Jimbo down near the creek early that morning."

"The dead man... was he murdered?"

"No, sir, I don't believe he was. I'm trying to identify the man so we can inform his family of his unfortunate demise. I thought maybe Jimbo ran into him somewhere along the line."

The eyes the two men felt on them when they entered the hobo camp now revealed their owners. Men hidden behind the trees and makeshift shanties slipped out of the shadows and formed a broad circle around the intruders. The one holding the blade had circled around and now looked from Augie's eyes to the back of the sheriff's head.

Sheriff Boggs planted his boots in the dirt, straightened his body to its fullest height, and said the oddest thing. "Jimbo has friends in town."

The wall of tension that greeted the arrival of the intruders dissipated with the casualness of the sheriff's demeanor, the angry faces surrounding the two relaxing into neutral curiosity. Popo resisted the urge to shake the tension out of his arms as he fixed his eyes on Blade Man, who maintained his defensive posture as he slowly moved, step by step, around the circle. As he drummed his fingers on the blade he held against his side, the irregular twitching of his left eye seemed to signal his insanity was about to break through his façade at any moment. What was Augie thinking when he readily agreed to come out here with the sheriff unarmed? He had no doubt that Blade Man could take out them both out in a flash, and with a little help from his 'bos, have their bodies buried deep in the woods and a nice squirrel stew simmering on the camp fire long before Biddy Ann and her posse arrived to rescue them.

"What's your name, fella?" Boggy asked one of the man.

"My friends call me Skeeter."

"Nice to meet you, Skeeter." The sheriff used his friendliest tone. "Can you tell me the whereabouts of Jimbo? I don't see him around."

"Jimbo's gone."

"Gone where?" asked the sheriff.

"Last I saw that 'bo, he was carrying a bindle stick and headed that way..." Skeeter pointed back the way the two had entered the camp. "...outta this here jungle. Said he'd flopped here long enough and was catching the first cannonball he came across going south. Ain't seen hide nor hair of Jimbo since."

"South, you say? Headed to New Orleans?"

"Could be." Skeeter sniffed, then dragged his forearm across his nose.

Blade Man spoke up, startling Augie. "Maybe it was Charleston, Skeeter. Jimbo liked the sunsets in Charleston."

Other cities were called out from the crowd of men. "Memphis. Natchez. Bristol. Savannah. San Antonio," the names a jumble of worn pieces of their faded lives, all tossed into the same trash heap.

The sheriff knew they were stirring up confusion, but he let it ride.

"If you or your boys happen upon him in the next few days, I'd be mighty grateful, Skeeter, if you'd pass along word to Jimbo that I'd like to talk with him. Having the sheriff owing you a favor might come in handy one day."

"Yes indeed, Sheriff. It might."

"Now, my friend and I will be on our way."

The circle parted, allowing the two men to leave on the path they'd come in on. Just as they'd passed the outer edge of the circle, a man called out, "Thanks for stopping by, Sheriff."

Without missing a stride, his eyes straight ahead, the sheriff whispered three words to his old friend. "Don't look back."

When the two men were out of hearing range, Augie broke the silence that enveloped the two men on their walk back from the hobo camp."Boggy," he said, "I smell a rat."

"Well, my friend, you and I both know there's never only one rat in the barn."

Chapter 14

Where do sparrows go at night? The fate of the sparrows haunted me as I ran barefoot along the winding path lit only by the full face of the summer moon casting its golden beams through the copse of trees. A lingering remnant of Barner's Woods. I shivered. My skin, rough with goosebumps, felt cold to the touch. A breeze out of the north caused a persistent swaying in the treetops above my head, a quivering of the shadows at my feet. My nightgown swirled around my legs, making each step more difficult than the last. But I didn't stop until the path emerged from the trees where it mimicked the twists and turns of creek bank for a few yards. I loved that place in the path. It reminded me of God, though I didn't know why.

I faced the creek, mesmerized by its intricate dance in the moonlight, the sound of trickling water meandering toward its greater destination. Suddenly, the flap of an owl's wings drew my eyes upward. The raptor glided out over the creek, its wings fully extended, beautiful in the moment as it relaxed on the updraft of the breeze and lay there without effort. Then its wings came down and broke away from its comfort, the mighty bird now focused on the hunt. I prayed Gem's sparrow was well-hidden.

I stepped closer to the creek, to the flowing water. Then someone called out my name.

"Annie!"

My blood ran cold as I looked across the creek toward the sound of the voice. That's when I spotted the man standing on the other side, his hand raised in a motionless wave, his eyes fixed on me. "Stay away from the creek, Annie. You might fall through the ice."

Consumed by fear, I turned and ran back along the path, then into the cover of trees. The moonlight seemed dimmer now, my way obscured, but I kept moving, overcome by the stranger's presence. The man called out again, "Run, Annie, run. Don't stop until you're home."

As I climbed the wooden steps to our back porch and pulled open the door, I paused there panting, less afraid. "Hey, mister," I called out. "I thought you were an angel."

"I am an angel."

***

I awoke with a start, sitting up in bed, disoriented. I wrapped my arms around my body, shivering. Gem lay next to me, snuggled into her feather trench, covered with a blanket against the welcome chill of the late summer night.

I took a deep breath, thinking about the man who pulled Pauline and me out of Prairie Creek last winter... remembering Mother's secret.

It was a day I'll never forget, the first day all the townsfolk knew that the winter that had began in the waning days of 1931 was not long for this world, that the Creator's song had at last gone forth commanding rebirth from the barren earth.

Spring had teased us for some weeks, alluding to glorious sunshine but delivering pelting rain and chilling winds out of the north instead, dampening our hopes of a premature end to the brutal winter. But on that first real spring day, talk at the Blue and White Café undoubtedly shifted from our discomfort to the first spotting of the blade-shaped leaves of daffodils as they raised their yellow heads to the music. With spring finally unambiguous as to its intentions, the local farmers became steadfast to their task ahead.

The excitement at school that morning was palpable, as the children shed their heavy coats and ran around the playground like wild animals freed from their circus cages. When the bell rang, the teachers herded us into our classrooms after chasing the stragglers back into the fold. With all eyes on the windows, we jiggled and vibrated through our reading, writing and arithmetic lessons, the teachers unenthusiastic and listless with their confinement every bit as much as the children. After our lunch break, oh, those all-too-short moments of spring's freedom, set the bear-in-the-trap tone for our afternoon school session, our instincts to plot our escape fueled by the open windows in our classrooms. The teachers finally gave up, releasing us to the playground. Classroom by classroom, the children joined the growing riot that occurs whenever the human spirit escapes its bonds and is left to its own devices. Teacher after teacher found a seat on an outside bench, hands folded in their laps in resignation, eyes closed, heads tilted back to absorb the warm rays of the life that had spent the last several months confined and yearning for rebirth.

In the revelry of freedom, I found Charlie whooping it up with his classmates. My Charlie, who seemed content curled up with a book, gave me a glimpse of his pedestrian colors at long last. He told me he wanted to join the after-school kickball game about to begin on the field behind Old Stoney. With a wave of a hand from my teacher, which I took as permission, and Charlie's promise to save me a spot on his team, I ran to tell Mother we would be late coming home.

I crossed over Prairie Creek at the Washington Street bridge, pausing only for a moment to notice the thin wisp of smoke from a chimney somewhere up the creek. Then I took the well-worn path through the trees. I'd stayed out of the woods since that wintry day in January when Pauline and I fell through the ice, but the freedom of spring renewed my courage, sending me into the stand of bare trees along the west side of our house. I was in a hurry.

Just ahead, I neared the corner of our barn. The clucking of Mother's liberated chickens filled the spring air. When the day showed itself, Mother must have opened the chicken coop and shooed her sedentary birds into the pen for their feed. She knew everything thrived in the sunlight. Just as I was about to emerge from the trees, the door on our enclosed back porch opened.

"Mother!" The word caught in my throat. I froze, my eyes glued to the form of a man emerging from our house. After he walked down the old wooden steps of our enclosed porch, the man turned back to the door, held up his hand and said, "Nice to see you again, Maggie."

"It was my pleasure," she replied. I couldn't see her face, but imagined it lit with a smile.

Instead of walking up the wagon path between our house and trees to South Street, the man slipped onto the path through the trees toward Washington Street. An old leather satchel in one hand, he adjusted his worn felt fedora with the other. When he finally looked ahead, there I stood, my back to a tree just off the path.

He stopped right in front of me. "Well, hello, Annie. Lovely spring day, isn't it?"

I looked him up and down, wanting to remember everything about him. His deep blue eyes sparked in the sunlight that filtered through the limbs not yet burdened with leaves, his face unfamiliar, yet somehow known to me.

I figured him to be ordinary in his looks, his brown hair trimmed and neat around his ears, his face bearing the slightest wrinkles of survival, not age. He was average in build, though taller than my father. His overcoat was threadbare from wear, his old laced-up boots spotted with water stains.

After he walked past me, I stepped on the path to watch him go. "Hey, mister," I yelled. "Thanks for pulling me and Pauline out of the creek!" He raised a hand but kept walking.

I moved through the trees toward the creek bank and watched long enough to see the man emerge and cross over the Washington Street Bridge toward town. When he was out of sight, I ran back toward the house.

"Mother!" I panted.

"Good heavens, Anna. You startled me."

Mother stood in front of the kitchen sink, Thea in her arms, two teacups on the table, Mother's old cups, the ones she used for family, not the ones she used for company. Her teapot sat in the middle of the table, her tea ball now resting on a saucer.

"Who was that man?" I turned and pointed toward the back porch.

She hesitated. "He's a... a friend." Mother had chosen the word carefully. Friend. "The man sells sewing notions... fabric, thread, buttons... that sort of thing. He stops by once in a while to ask if I need anything."

"What's his name?"

Mother set Thea in her basket and moved it into a sunbeam flooding in through the kitchen window. When she turned back towards me, she seemed intentional in her words. "Look here, Anna. Look what he brought me."

Mother lifted a flat brown paper sack from the counter and placed it on the table. She pulled out the edge of the fabric.

"Oh, Mother, it's beautiful." As I rubbed the edge of the blue flower-print fabric, it occurred to me it was the same deep shade of blue as the man's eyes.

Then she pulled out a new Simplicity pattern, two cards of buttons, and a spool of matching blue thread.

"Oh, my. You don't want Aunt Lo to see those buttons," I squealed. "She'll have to have them. You know how Aunt Lo loves buttons."

Mother chuckled. "Yes, she does."

She turned a card of buttons over in her hands, admiring them. "He told me these are called enameled openwork floral buttons." She'd intoned the words, savoring the sound of them. "I've seen nothing quite like them. When he visited me last, I mentioned I needed to make myself a new dress or two, that my dresses were old and worn. Keeping up with the family's clothes takes a lot of time."

I nodded. Mother made Gem and me beautiful dresses for school, but she never took the time to make herself something new.

"He said when he saw this remnant of fabric, he thought of me," Mother continued. "I told him I didn't take charity, but he insisted it wasn't anything of the kind, just a leftover from a textile mill somewhere in North Carolina... High Point, I think. He said I'd have to be careful to cut the pattern just right to avoid the flaws."

Mother had taken to using the condition of her dresses as an excuse not to go out. She used to love window shopping at Thrashers with Gem and me. (If she saw a dress, she could make it.) Gem and I loved those precious moments when nothing else mattered except being together. When she had extra coins, Mother would take us into Dirty Dan's, the ice cream parlor on the square. Dan offered three or four different flavors of handmade ice cream every day! Orange sherbet was my favorite, but I loved peach, too. After Thea was born, we stopped going.

"When was the last time he was here?" I asked.

Mother thought for a moment. "Last autumn, I think. October."

October?

"Mother, could he be the man who pulled me and Pauline out of the creek when we fell through the ice in January?"

She shook her head slowly. "No, Anna, I don't think so. Today, he mentioned he hadn't been this way this year because the Depression made it more difficult for him to have the money to travel. I'd ordered several spools of thread when he was here last. He sent those to me by mail."

Mother was adamant.

"Okay, young lady. You haven't told me why you're home from school so early. Please don't tell me you got expelled this late in the school year." She laughed. I loved Mother's laugh. I didn't hear it enough.

"No, Mother. I came home to tell you Charlie and I want to play kickball after school. All the children are playing! Please don't say no."

"That's fine, but don't stay too late. I need you here to set the table for supper."

"We won't. I promise." I turned to leave, knowing Charlie was waiting for me.

"Anna." Mother's voice was serious now. "Please let's keep the notions man's visit here today between us. He's been a friend since I lived on the farm in Mulberry. He's so nice to bring me little things like thread and buttons and chalk, but your father doesn't like it. He wouldn't like it if he knew the notions man gave me this beautiful fabric. If you don't mind, please don't mention you saw him to Popo... or anyone else."

I looked at Mother, confused. Finally I said, "I won't."

"Promise me, Anna. Promise to keep this secret."

"I promise."

***

I thought about that first beautiful spring day and that conversation with mother for as long as I could stay awake. Finally closing my eyes, I settled back into the cool of the early morning, drifting off again, wondering if he really was the man who pulled Pauline and me from the icy creek in January. Or could the man who stepped into the creek to save us be the hobo they called Jimbo? Finally, my notion that the man who saved us was an angel lulled me back into a peaceful sleep.

"Annie, Annie, wake up." Gem stood in our bedroom doorway, hand on her hip. The excitement in her voice pierced my early morning sleep with the most beautiful words I'd ever heard.

"Come quick! The boys are home!"

Act II

Chapter 15

"Where's Charlie?"

"Come give your Aunt Rachel a kiss, and I'll tell you."

I fell into my aunt's outstretched arms. She pulled out a chair from the kitchen table and sat down, drawing me face-to-face with her. "Your Mother tells me you've had an exciting week, Annie." My aunt smoothed my tangled hair, then pulled me in for another hug.

I nodded, my words of explanation caught in my throat.

"Your Uncle Maddy and I are spending the night to give Rosie a rest. I'm sure you'll tell us all about it."

"Where's Charlie?" My voice was soft, but insistent.

"He's out with his father, tending to Rosie and unloading the wagon. We arrived early to avoid the heat of the day, but Maddy wanted to get Rosie brushed down and in the barn before the sun gets overhead. Old Barney will have to share his home with his cousin." Aunt Rachel laughed at her little joke. It occurred to me she laughed a lot compared to her older sister. Mother rarely laughed anymore.

"Go on, now," she said, as she released me from her arms.

I ran through the kitchen and out the back door. Standing on the top step of our back porch, I watched the chaotic activity around our small barn.

My uncle, Madison Caldwell, who folks in Jeffries referred to as the gentleman farmer from Mulberry, managed the scene. His large farm wagon sat next to our barn door facing the path to South Street. The west side of the barn abutted the trees that lined Prairie Creek, giving the barn much-needed shade on hot days. Our chicken coop rested against the side of the barn that faced Mother's garden and our small apple orchard. We also had a cherry tree and apricot tree behind our house. The chicken coop opened to a large pen, where the hens strutted around their patch of the world, mimicking the level of activity around them.

I watched as my brothers, Gus and Blinn, unloaded several bales of hay and bags of chicken feed, and carried them into the barn on their shoulders. When they came out for another load, Gus spotted me and waved. His skin tanned, his hair lighter from the sun, my brothers shoulders stretched against the cotton fabric of his worn shirt. Physically, he didn't seem the same brother who'd left for the country three weeks ago. He'd somehow broken away from the confines of the deliberate pace of growing up, and sprinted into the realm of adulthood.

Uncle Maddy's voice was music to my ears. "Let's get the chicken wire unloaded, boys." He pointed to a spot in front of the chicken coop. "Too many tree roots on the other side for the goat pen. It would take us all day to dig the post holes there, but I think we're good here." My uncle pushed his spectacles up on his face before jumping up into the wagon.

I ran down the porch steps and over to the wagon. "Uncle Maddy! Uncle Maddy!" I called.

"Hello, sleepyhead." My uncle looked down at me from the wagon. His brown eyes seemed big and round through his spectacles.

"Uncle Maddy, why are you building a goat pen?"

"Go see for yourself." He pointed toward the open barn door before turning back to his work. "Watch where you're stepping."

Heeding my uncle's warning, I stood to the side of the open barn door, looking in. Cory worked to settle Rosie into the stall next to Old Barney. The barn on my aunt and uncle's farm was four times the size of ours, so whenever the Caldwells came for a visit, Rosie spent a few minutes showing her dislike for her cramped quarters. Cory caressed between her ears, easily talking her into her unwanted situation, soothing her as he backed her into the stall.

"That's good, Rosie girl." My brother petted her mane and scratched an ear, giving the horse her due attention. "How about an apple?"

As Rosie chomped on her dried apple, Cory climbed over the side of her stall into Old Barney's. "How ya doing, old boy? Did you miss me?" The horse's neck bobbed up and down. Cory stroked his side, happy to see his friend. When the horse settled, Cory called out, "Okay, Charlie, let's introduce them."

I walked into the barn as Charlie and Gem emerged from the shadows. Charlie held a rope tied around a young goat's neck. She was as white as a ball of cotton with black spots down her back. She had a long white beard and mischief in her eyes. Charlie opened the stall gate and handed the rope off to Cory.

"Meet Belva," said my brother. "She's your new stall mate."

Gem and Charlie stepped up on the bottom slat of the gate for a better view of the goat inside the stall. I ran over and climbed up next to Gem. The goat leaped about around Old Barney's hooves for a moment before Cory reined her in with the rope and calmed her.

She immediately settled down. Cory praised her. "You're a good girl, Belva."

"Belva?"

Charlie jumped down and pulled me from the gate. He wrapped his arms around me and held me tight in his arms.

"Did you miss me, Annie?"

"Maybe." I didn't want to say it was the first time I felt normal since I discovered the Corpse in the Creek.

***

With the help of MaMaw Ghere in Aunt Lo's usual place in the kitchen, Mother put on a to-do for breakfast—eggs, biscuits and gravy, fried chicken, apple popovers—to everyone's delight. Once Bernard helped his father get Cooter hitched up and off on his Saturday route, our friend joined us, almost as happy to see my brothers and Charlie as I was. The adults ate in the dining room where there was plenty of room. The rest of us crowded around the kitchen table, enjoying the family reunion, hearing all about the boys' days in the country helping Uncle Madison prepare the farm for the upcoming harvest.

"Once the fall harvest begins, that's all he does, eighteen hours a day, until the harvest goes to market," Gus explained. "Uncle Maddy wants everything shipshape going into the harvest because he doesn't have time to do or fix anything until the harvest is in. We mended fences, patched a couple leaky rain barrels, helped Aunt Rachel clear patches of her garden that quit producing... that sort of thing."

"And sharpen blades." Blinn held up a bandaged finger that resulted from the task.

"What about Belva," I asked. "Why did she come to town with you?"

"That goat is a pest," explained Gus. "The other goats on the farm didn't cotton to her, particularly Ethel. Belva got her so roiled up that she stoped producing milk. Uncle Maddy thought he might have to put her down, but Cory calmed her down."

Charlie added, "Cory has a way with animals."

"That's for shore," added Bernard. "I reckon Cooter favors him better than me, even though I feeds 'im, brushes 'im, and cleans his hooves." Bernard shrugged.

"Uncle Maddy and Aunt Rachel said that Cory could have the goat if Mother would allow it," Gus added.

Cory piped up. "I thought she'd be good company for Old Barney when we're off at school. Horses and goats get on pretty well."

When the boys were all talked out about their time on the farm, we fell silent as Gem began gathering the dishes and carrying them to the sink.

"Anything interesting happen around here while we were away?" asked Blinn.

Bernard's eyes widened. Gem, who was standing at the sink, laughed. "Oh, you boys will not believe what happened here last Saturday. Go ahead, Annie. Tell them what you found."

I looked up at Bernard sitting across the table. He gave me one quick wink.

"What did you find, Annie?" Gus urged.

"I found a dead man in Prairie Creek."

***

For the rest of the day, talk of my discovery dominated the conversation. Popo, Gem, Bernard, and I answered questions as best we could, filling in the details of what we knew about the sheriff's investigation. Popo gently worked our trip to the rock near the Interurban tracks into the telling, but I knew Gem and I would face Mother's wrath after my aunt and uncle returned home to Mulberry in the morning.

While the adults took after-supper tea in the parlor, the rest of us gathered in the yard in front of our house to enjoy the crisp cool air settling in, diluting the day's burdensome heat. Pauline and Helen came over to see Charlie, joining us on our sunset vigil after Mother called their mothers, promising Gus would walk them home later. Gem's friend, Evelyn, stopped by, too. Gem spread an old quilt in our front yard for us to sit on and retrieved a large bowl of popcorn and a plate of fudge she and Mother had made earlier in the day. I wasn't hungry, but I ate a piece of fudge anyway.

"Was that the first dead person you've ever seen?" Leave it to my friend, Helen, to get to the heart of the matter.

"Yes."

Gem elbowed me. "Annie, you were at PaPaw's wake and funeral." Gem pointed toward the Ghere house on the other side of Prairie Creek.

"I don't remember much about that, but I'll remember the Corpse in the Creek forever."

The fact I didn't remember the funeral of Augustus J. Ghere, Sr. disturbed me. I was too young when he died, though through Gem's sharing of her vivid memories of our grandfather, it seemed I'd gotten to know him. Once in a while, I get a memory flash of his open coffin in MaMaw Ghere's parlor, the room shadowed in black and white, dim and dreary, as people milled about talking in low tones. That seemed the only memory of my own I had of my father's father.

Gem adored PaPaw Ghere, and he adored his first-born grand-daughter. He died on June 29, 1926, Gem's sixth birthday. Gem remembered every detail of the wake and the funeral that followed.

I laid on the edge of the quilt and looked up at the stars, thinking about all Gem had told me about PaPaw and his funeral.

***

Miriam Ghere sat on a wooden stool next to the coffin as her husband's many friends paid their final respects. Clad in a plain black full-length dress that matched her stoic demeanor, she thanked people for coming. Her tears had dried up for the wake, but her red-rimmed eyes revealed her pain at the loss of her beloved husband.

The president and co-founder of the Ghere-Douglass Company, wholesaler of eggs, milk, cheese and butter, Augustus J. Ghere, Sr. had been an important man in both Jeffries and Indiana, having served a term in the state senate. At the time of his sudden death, he still held seats on several prestigious boards, including that of Culver Military Academy.

When the line of guests ended, Miriam slipped from her stool and headed into the kitchen to check on the final preparations for the late afternoon meal to follow the wake. Gem climbed up on MaMaw's stool for a better look at her grandfather inside his silk-lined coffin. Popo stepped behind his daughter and put his arms around her.

"Can I touch him, Popo?"

"Yes, honey, you can touch him."

Gem drew a gentle finger across his cool cheek to his lips. "He looks like he's sleeping."

Popo chuckled. "And having a pleasant dream. Your grandfather was perpetually pleasant."

"He always kissed me right here," she said, a finger touching the middle of her forehead.

"That's where PaPaw kissed all the people he loved the most."

"I never saw him kiss MaMaw there."

"Your PaPaw loved your MaMaw more than life itself, but you held a special place in his heart. Never forget that, Gem. Never forget him."

"I won't. I promise."

Popo leaned in and kissed his daughter on the forehead.

"Just like PaPaw's kisses?" he asked her.

"Just like PaPaw's," she assured him.

Maggie had spent three days preparing the food for the dinner per her mother-in-law's explicit instructions. Since they were dining in their backyard, Miriam selected a picnic menu to showcase the foods Ghere-Douglass Company wholesaled—side plates of deviled eggs, topped with a decorative sprinkling of paprika, two huge silver platters of vegetable crudités that served as both French appetizers and table decor, MaMaw's special-recipe potato salad, a secret she'd finally shared with Maggie, cold fried chicken, and crispy-top macaroni and cheese casseroles that were pulled from four neighbors' ovens along South Street at the same precise moment. Miriam looked at the clock on the wall and announced. "Only two more hours."

"Two more hours of what?" asked her daughter, LoRetta.

"Two more hours that I have to wear this brave face." With that, she turned to the two maids she'd hired to assist with the somber occasion and issued her last-minute instructions. Then she slipped into the backyard for her last inspection of the tables before inviting her guests to sit down for an early supper.

While the menu was anything but chic, the presentation befitted a king and his court. MaMaw's spotless starched linens draped a long succession of tables to accommodate thirty-four people that included family and close friends. Per MaMaw's instructions, the maids set the tables with an unlikely duo of patterns, mixing the flower-rimmed Limoges French porcelain MaMaw inherited from her mother with the Bridgwood and Son with royal blue butterflies, snails, and other doohickeys she received from her beloved husband many Christmases before. (Such an indulgence," she'd exclaimed, when she opened the first of many perfectly wrapped boxes. MaMaw adored her china's slightly scalloped rims edged in gold. PaPaw knew her oh, so well.)

"Oh, MaMaw," complained LoRetta when her mother pulled both patterns of china from her cabinet. "I know you're grieving, but need I remind you, the Brits and the French don't always get along." LoRetta waved a hand over the two sets of china. "That combination will likely incite an international incident."

"Piffle, dear," replied MaMaw, unarguable determination in her voice. "Our esteemed British friends and our esteemed French friends will feel equally honored."

Aunt Lo rolled her eyes.

Miriam alternated the two patterns to disguise her lack of enough of either pattern to accommodate all her guests. The massive flower arrangement at the center of the tables pulled colors from both sets of china. Fortunately, she had enough fine linen napkins embroidered with a royal blue and white flower with a pink center that she'd folded and placed on top of the plate stack that miraculously pulled the two opposing sets of china together perfectly. The two sterling silver candelabras, also from her mother's estate, defied the slight breeze that wafted through the backyard, keeping the oppressive July heat at bay.

The serve-yourself dessert table included Maggie's delicious butter cookies, made with heaps of farm-fresh butter, and her own pineapple-drop cookies she'd topped with royal icing. Also on the table were slices of Maggie's special honey-poached quince pie she made from the quince pie filling she'd canned the previous autumn, and a pound cake with fresh strawberries and whipped cream for toppings.

After all the guests had reluctantly departed, Aunt Lo said she'd personally witnessed Old Man Gregory enjoy *three* pieces of quince pie.

"I wish I could help clean up," Miriam told her daughter, daughter-in-law, and maids, "but I'm exhausted. At least I can rest knowing that we sent our guests home full of compliments... and food... before the funeral service tomorrow at Holy Cross Church. By noon tomorrow, it will all be over." The sadness in her voice brought tears to her daughter's eyes.

The next day, Miriam's life in Jeffries' high society was dead and buried in Bunnell Cemetery, along with the lifeless body of her beloved husband.

***

With joy and trepidation mingling in the star-lit night, we settled into the quietude that comes easily amongst those we love.

"Do you hear the owl?" Charlie's breath tickled my ear. "A Great Horned Owl, I think. We spied a family of them in our copse of bur oaks last spring. My father says they eat the rodents that threatened our crops."

I'd seen that owl before... in my dreams.

"Hey, it's nice out here." Popo walked onto the porch, Uncle Maddy right behind him. "It's a lot cooler out here than in the dining room. Do you mind if we join you?"

Without an answer, Popo sat down on the top step of the porch, then stretched out his legs. Uncle Maddy wandered about in the front yard, mostly looking at the sky.

"Maggie and Rachel are finishing up in the kitchen."

Gem stood up. "I should go help them.

"MaMaw is drying the dishes. They'll have it done in short order without your help."

"I could get Thea ready for bed," Gem offered.

"Honey, your mother and Aunt Rachel stuffed the baby full of food. Then Thea went from your mother's hip to Rachel's lap, to being sound asleep in her basket. Stay here and enjoy the evening."

Gem settled back on the old quilt next to Evelyn. "We were just talking about dead people."

"I should have known." A corner of Popo's lips turned up, but his eyes looked sad.

"Gem, did you see the face of the dead man Popo pulled from the creek?" Charlie asked Gem.

"Yes, we all did. I walked right up to him and looked down into his face. I wanted to see if I recognized him, but I didn't."

"Did he look as peaceful as PaPaw did when he died?"

Gem thought for a moment. "PaPaw looked content." My sister took a deep breath and closed her eyes. "The stranger looked everything but content."

I moved from where I'd been sitting between Charlie and Pauline to my father's side. His arm instinctively curled around me as I pressed my face into his side and sobbed. If was as if a dam had broken inside me, releasing my feelings about the man who died outside my home.

There in front of family and friends, I cried for the stranger, for his family, and for myself struggling to understand death.

I'd prayed that the return of Charlie and my brothers would comfort me, pull me away from my thoughts about the plight of a stranger whose death had entwined itself with my life. I hoped that being surrounded once again by the people I loved would make me feel safe, impervious to the inevitable outcome of every life. Instead, I felt the discontent of the dead man stirring in me. I believed the only one who truly understood how I felt was my father.

When I was all cried out, Popo pulled his handkerchief from his pants pocket and dried my tears.

"Popo, please tell us the story about the time you found Mrs. Barner dead in the woods?" Gem had her diary on her lap, open to a blank page.

"On a pleasant evening like this, maybe we should turn our attention to more up-lifting topics."

"I'd like to hear it," Charlie piped up.

"Me too." Pauline loved listening to my father tell his stories as much as I did.

Uncle Maddy added, "I'd be interested in hearing that story myself, Augie."

All cried out, I went back to sit with Charlie and my friends. My cousin took my hand. He didn't understand all that happened in his absence, but I felt grounded for the first time in days.

"We're all eager to hear it." My uncle sat down in the grass next to his son. "How did you stumble upon a dead woman in Barner's Woods?"

Popo looked at me. I nodded my approval. "It didn't happen quite like that."

"Then tell us how it happened," Uncle Maddy urged.

With one deep breath, Popo gathered his thoughts and everyone's attention, and told us what he remembered about that day.

***

It was cold that day. I remember thinking my fingers were frostbitten, despite wearing my gloves. My hands shook holding the reins as I took Isaak Walton Road north out of Jeffries. Calvin, my horse, reared back his head, letting me know he was none too please with our adventure out to Barner Farm that morning, his huffing and snorting visible in the vapor of the cold mist.

When I pulled up to the Barner's barn, I spotted Joshua Barner coming off the steps of the main house. "Let one of my boys pull Calvin into the barn to warm up a bit while we talk."

"I'm sure he'd be mighty grateful."

"Hurry on inside, Augie. We've got fresh coffee brewing. We can go over the numbers in my den."

Joshua turned and called out, "Hey Bert, can you get this horse inside for a spell? I got some business to do with Mr. Ghere."

"Sure thing, boss. Is it okay if I let the dogs out?"

"Go ahead. They won't be out long in this cold, that's for sure."

I followed Joshua up the porch steps.

"Come to think of it, Augie, I might get a better deal from you if I leave you out here to freeze." The man laughed heartily, reminding me of the way his mother laughs. He pulled the door open and stepped aside to allow me to enter first. That's when I heard him gasp and run off the porch toward the barn yelling, "Bert, Bert!"

I turned and followed my friend to the barn. Two other farmhands came running when they heard Joshua yelling.

"What is it, boss?" a panicked Bert asked.

Joshua turned and pointed. "That dog! Where did he come from?"

Bert turned and squinted his eyes. "Can't say that I know."

One of the other farmhands spoke up. "He was with the others when we fed them last evening. Knowing it was going to be a cold one, we put their food in the barn so they'd be out of the weather. We threw some of those old wool horse blankets on the hay back there." The farmhand pointed to the back of the barn. "I counted six dogs, just to be sure they were all inside." Bert pointed a gloved finger as he counted the dogs. "Seven. I must have under-counted by one last evening."

Both of Joshua's hands went to his face. "Oh, dear God, no," he whispered. Then he turned to the south, toward the trees along the creek. "That's Mother's dog, Cannon. He never leaves her side."

When Joshua pointed upward. I immediately knew what pierced his mind like a sharpened blade.

No smoke.

"Saddle up my horse, Bert. Get the other boys to hitch up the wagon. Something's not right out at Mother's place."

"I'm coming too," I insisted. "My rig is ready to go. Let's take it."

Joshua was in no mood to argue. "Let's do it, boys."

Attuned to our urgency, Calvin trotted along the well-worn path between Barner Farm and Mrs. Barner's cottage in the woods, making quick time on the mile-and-a-half-long journey. Two of Joshua Barner's farmhands soon caught up on horseback.

When we arrived in the clearing, Joshua jumped down from the wagon before Calvin stopped, and pointed toward the small porch. "It's open. The door... it's open."

I dropped the reigns, jumped down from my rig and followed Joshua into the cottage.

"Mother, are you here?" he called out. No answer.

The open door allowed a beam of morning light into the one-room cottage. Joshua walked slowly to the feather bed where he and his brothers used to pile onto their mother for her goodnight hugs and kisses.

Sarah lay there in peace, covered to her chin in a stack of quilts. He touched her beautiful face with the back of his hand, stroking her cheek. "She's gone," he whispered, tears streaming down his face.

I choked back a sob that had unexpectedly welled up in my throat, then turned and walked back out into the winter cold, seeing beyond its crystal blue skies, recognizing this place for what it truly was.

God's handiwork at its finest.

Chapter 16

"Elijah and Sarah Barner were fine people." MaMaw Ghere stood in the front doorway. I didn't know how long she'd been there, but from the sadness on her face, she had relived the death of her friend.

"They were, indeed," agreed Popo. He stood up and held his hand out to his mother. "Please come join us, MaMaw. It's a pleasant evening. It might help us all overcome the recent unpleasantness."

MaMaw took her son's arm and walked across the porch to the steps. Uncle Maddy pulled the wooden rocking chair from the porch, placed it at the foot of the steps and invited MaMaw to sit down.

I found it odd for MaMaw to assume the role of the old matriarch. Only in her mid-sixties, she was the youngest of the two couples, and the only survivor of what was once the center of Jeffries' social circle. While her daughter, LoRetta, epitomized fashion in our little town, MaMaw still wore the Victorian-era dresses of her generation. This evening she wore a square neck, blue floral print with a ruffled hem, short puff sleeves, and a hand-smocked waist. Aunt Lo referred to her mother's taste as homey, but with her silver hair piled on her head, her leather button shoes always polished to perfection, and the stately way she carried herself, I imagined she could add an element of grandness to any queen's court.

As MaMaw settled into the rocking chair, Gem implored her grandmother. "Please tell us what you remember about the Barners."

MaMaw rocked back and forth, thinking for a few moments. Then, in her grand style, she unraveled the colorful tapestry of a few of her fondest memories.

***

Elijah Barner inherited the vast tract of Barner land from his father, who had inherited it from his father. Elijah was a jovial man with a knack for coaxing and carving a wee bit more out of the farmland each year. To protect his farming dynasty from the inevitable natural disasters that plague north-central Indiana, over time he added chickens and dairy cattle to his family's operation.

Elijah Barner and Augustus Ghere, Sr. developed a relationship through their respective businesses. Elijah produced the eggs and raw milk, and PaPaw wholesaled the products. Through their businesses, they became fast friends. Miriam Ghere and Sarah Barner often exchanged letters and got their families together for annual picnics on the farm and Christmas celebrations at the Ghere house.

Sarah Barner was a wonderful woman... kind, humble, spirited. She was also a loner who was comfortable in her own thoughts. MaMaw remembers one year when Sarah, Elijah and their four boys visited the Ghere's house for Christmas Eve when Augustus, Jr., LoRetta, and Karl were young. Miriam went to great lengths to curate the decor and the holiday meal to perfection. It was the first time Miriam recognized her friend's contrary natures, as if exquisitely engaged in a cooperative ballet, of sorts... two distinct Sarahs whirling about in unison.

Slipping easily from a role as hostess into one as a guest, Sarah epitomized both the grand dame of the respected (and highly profitable) Barner dynasty *and* the humble visitor. The money and prestige never seemed to turn her head as did the details of life's incredible adventure.

Helping her children add a string of popcorn to the Christmas tree, Sarah seemed completely present in the moment. In the next moment, she seemed to slip away to a place all her own. Her sacred place... that's what Elijah called it. Sarah's beloved husband wanted to go there, to be there with her, but she kept it to herself.

Elijah and Sarah met in Chicago when Elijah's brother, David, graduated from medical school. Sarah Oliver had taken a job in the ticket booth at Dearborn Station, an unusual position for a young woman, though no one argued about her efficiency, nor her ability to soothe even the most frazzled passengers. When she looked up and saw Elijah smiling at her on the other side of her ticket window, she was immediately smitten with the strapping young man. She watched as he walked away, nonplussed by the chaos of the train station. When she could no longer spot him in the crowd, she sighed and returned her focus to the line of travelers needing tickets to New York, St. Louis, New Orleans, and beyond, all places Sarah dreamed of visiting one day.

An hour later, after calling out "next," she looked up as Elijah stepped forward, his winning smile and sparkling green eyes causing Sarah's mouth to drop open in amazement.

"You forgot something, miss."

Once she caught her breath, she asked, "Is that right, sir? What exactly did I forget?"

"You forgot to put your name and address on the back of my ticket, so I might write to you about the rewards and travails of being a farmer in the heartland of our great nation."

"Is that so?"

"It is, indeed." Elijah slid his ticket into the opening in the glass window and pointed. "Write it there."

"But you'll have to surrender your ticket when you board the train, sir."

"I'll have every detail memorized by then, miss." Elijah pointed a finger at his forehead. "It will be safe right here. I'll never forget."

Her hand trembling, Sarah wrote her name and address with her pencil, and gave the ticket back to him.

Nodding once, he turned to walk away.

"Hey, mister. What is your name?"

Elijah smiled. "You'll find out soon enough."

When Sarah arrived home that evening, she helped her mother finish preparing supper for her father and younger brothers. Then she kissed her mother's cheek and went upstairs to her room. "Don't you want to play Rummy with your brothers and me, dear?" her mother called up to her.

"Not tonight, Mummy. I've something to do, but I promise I'll play tomorrow."

After her bath, Sarah sat at the writing desk in her room and composed her first letter to the stranger she'd met in Dearborn Station. She tucked the envelope under her mattress and waited. Amidst the hustle and bustle of the hectic train station, imagining the man provided the girl a great escape. But after two weeks had passed without a letter, she'd almost given up on hearing from the young man.

After a grueling day, she arrived home one evening to discover he hadn't forgotten her.

"Hello, Mummy. Give me a moment to hang up my coat, and I'll help you with supper."

"Sarah, dear, a letter arrived for you today."

The young woman turned and looked at her mother. "What letter is that?" she asked, a slight tremble in her voice.

The older woman pulled the envelope from her apron pocket and handed it to her daughter. "It's from an Elijah Barner of Jeffries, Indiana."

"Elijah," she muttered. The name was music to Sarah's ears.

"The Barner family owns half the state of Indiana!" her mother added. "Have you met this man?"

"Yes. He's a boy I met at the station. I asked him to

send me advice on growing my flowers," she replied, hoping her answer satisfied her mother. She didn't want to admit she'd given her name to a stranger.

"The last thing you need, dear, is advice on growing your flowers. You have the knack."

After reading Elijah's letter ten times, she pulled the letter she'd written to him from under her mattress, wrote his name and address on the front in her perfect script, memorizing the details as she went, and tucked it into her small handbag. Then she pulled it out and wrote on the back of the envelope, "Please send me advice on growing flowers."

When Elijah received her letter, the note on the back was all he needed to know for certain. He was in love... madly in love.

After a year of letter-writing and several visits to the city to visit, Elijah popped the question. Within weeks, the two were married in a huge Chicago wedding paid for by Geoffrey and Ida Barner, Elijah's parents and the proprietors of the farm. On her only visit to the farm before the nuptials, the peace and beauty of the Indiana countryside overwhelmed Sarah. That's when Elijah got the idea of building his future wife a cottage in the woods, so she'd have a place of her own away from the hectic pace of farm life and the demands on all who lived there.

To Sarah, life on the farm seemed a mighty contrast with her life in the city. "Listen," she whispered to Elijah as they sat on the front porch swing during her visit.

"What is it, darling?" Elijah asked his bride-to-be.

"The sound of a country evening is fraught with moments of silence, glorious silence. If you listen closely, you can hear God speaking to your soul and see His miracles unfold right before your eyes."

"Thank you for reminding me of that, Sarah... my sweet Sarah. But life on the farm isn't as serene as it seems at the moment. Mother worked very hard to make your visit special. She wanted nothing to change your mind."

Sarah laughed. "Nothing will change my mind."

"My mother works just as hard as anyone else around here, including my father and me. In fact, in some ways, she works harder. One day, you will fill her role as the matriarch of this farm and family.

"Every season is different," he continued. "Every day is different, and every moment is different. Most people are aware of the changes of seasons, but I'm intimately immersed in the day-to-day changes of my surroundings. Even the subtleties impact this small patch of land on this vast earth. When you learn to recognize that, you realize you're always on the edge of something new, something unexpected. There is nothing static on a farm, nothing regular, nothing mundane. I never ask, Where's God? I'm fully aware that He's right here."

"My dear Elijah, that's the lesson you first taught me." Sarah gripped his hand with both of hers. "I never expected the most wonderful man in America would walk into Dearborn Station on a spring day and steal my heart away. Since then, I promised myself to live every day as you do, expecting the unexpected. To be honest, I never expected to see God's fingerprints everywhere I look, as I do here. His creation takes my breath away."

"In America?" Elijah looked at Sarah, his eyes twinkling.

Sarah's confusion quickly gave way to understanding. "What I meant to say was, the most wonderful man in the *world*."

"Now, that's my girl."

Elijah looked towards his fields and the woods beyond. Then he took a deep breath, his head leaning back, taking in the fading evening light. "You'll probably never see all those exotic places you've dreamed of visiting, darling. But when you find a place you truly fit, when you embrace God's plan for you, nothing else matters except the driving desire to quench your daily curiosity about what exactly He has in store for you next. The gift of this life is delirious faith, the excitement to see what blessings God will reveal to me next. I'll always be a visitor elsewhere, and I'll always be at home here. I want you to be at home here, too."

Sarah took his hand. "I already am."

When Elijah Barner built his young wife, Sarah, the cottage in the woods about a mile and a half downstream from Barner Farm, he found what he believed to be the most beautiful spot on all of Prairie Creek. It was a place where the creek widened to the size of a small pond, capturing the sunlight and spilling it over onto the patch of land he had cleared for his wife's homestead. He used the wood he'd cut to build the cottage, tucking it partially into the trees to blend into its surroundings.

The willful Sarah Barner, her hair piled high on her head, her cheeks the perfect shade of rose from the sun, never shied away from engaging a trespasser on her patch of paradise. It seemed the more children she had, the more protective of her little "summer house" (as Elijah called it) she became.

Her youngest son, Joshua, often told of a particular traveler who happened upon the cottage one early summer afternoon. Somehow aware of his approach, Sarah flung open the door and sat down on the top porch step with a shotgun across her lap, its walnut stock worn smooth by generations of us. Stoic determination to protect what was hers, set as stone across her beautiful face.

Young Joshua Barner huddled inside the cottage with his older brothers watching the encounter between his mother and that "dirty, rotten trespasser." Through the open window, they saw the man emerge from the trees and walk into the clearing in front of the cottage. Sarah didn't so much as twitch.

"Howdy, ma'am. Beautiful day, ain't it?" His face lit with a broad smile as he held out his arms, palms up, and turned around slowly, taking in his surroundings. "You alone out here, miss?"

"You seem an educated sort, so I'm assuming you can read." With the barrel of her shotgun, Sarah pointed at the no trespassing sign posted along the edge of the clearing near the creek.

The man laughed. "Why don't you come out here and read it to me?"

"Mister, if you know what's good for you, you'll get off my property. The quickest way to do that is to cross over the creek, then walk straight ahead into those woods on the other side. About 100 yards in, you'll find a path that takes you to a road that goes directly into Jeffries. Consider this your one and only warning."

"You got a shell in that barrel?"

"Locked and loaded when you were half a mile out. Our conversation is now over. Get off my property."

The man spread his legs apart and planted his feet.

BOOM!

A split second later, buck shot rained down, some pelleting the roof of the cottage.

The woods fell silent, but for the gasp of the stranger. Before he could recover from the sudden blast, Sarah broke open the barrel with a satisfying click, and slid another shell home with a soft thud. The metallic snap signaled her readiness.

"If you listen carefully, mister, you'll hear a pack of hounds coming down that trail over there." Sarah's voice remained steady. She did the man the courtesy of pointing to the trail with her gun barrel. "Those hounds are leading a posse on horseback. They'll arrive just in time to watch you bleed out, or to see me preparing supper for my husband and children. Your choice."

"The creek's deep here! I can't swim!" he bellowed.

"Seems to me this is as good a day as any to learn."

As the sounds of men hooting and hollering made their approach known, the trespasser's predicament went from bad to worse.

"Help me, help me!" he screamed. "I'm drowning."

Unable to maintain their silence a moment longer, the four Barner boys burst through the door and ran to the creek-side, laughing and pointing at the man flailing about.

"Put your legs underneath you and stand up, mister. That spot's only waist deep." Thomas Barner had a knack for saying the obvious.

By the time the stranger had the sense to walk out of the water, paws and hooves were pounding up the well-worn trail next to Sarah's hide-away.

"Ma'am, did this man threaten you?" One of farmhands asked Sarah.

"He's a pest. I know how to handle pests. If the sheriff sees fit, I hope he'll provide this pest with a map out of the area. Next time I lay eyes on him, I'm shooting first and asking questions later."

When it was all said and done, the man spent five days in the jailhouse. The last sheriff wasn't as accommodating to prisoners as Sheriff Boggs.

***

The Barners' large family was the pride and joy of Elijah. "Farming is a complex business," he'd often tell his first born, Adam, whom he believed would take over the operation one day.

Adam had a head for business and was eager to learn. By the time he was fourteen, he kept the farm's books to the penny. By the time he was sixteen, he could negotiate deals with suppliers and wholesalers that brought tears of joy to his father's eyes. That's when Elijah made his big mistake… he sent Adam upstate to Lake Maxinkuckee to attend Culver Military Academy. Adam returned "a leader of men," according to his mother, Sarah, and "too big for his britches," according to his father, Elijah. Adam soon "felt the calling" and promptly left the farm to take a management position in the burgeoning American Steel Company in Gary. Following the declaration that Titus J. Vandercook, the founder's son was missing in action—another tragic loss in the Great War—Adam was there to fill the void. Through his competence, dedication and sheer determination, the eldest Barner son rose above all the other executives at American Steel to replace Cletus E. Vandercook's missing son as his right-hand man. Elijah scoffed at his son's success, but Sarah beamed with pride. Eventually, Elijah marched off to his lawyer's office to change his will.

The responsibility to carry on the farm then fell to Thomas, who had an aversion to manual labor, and often sneaked off with Clyde Boggs and Augie Ghere to enjoy the pleasures of the bars, restaurants and especially the movie theaters in Indianapolis. Clyde and Augie preferred the smoky atmosphere at the Ritz Theater, but the Rivoli over on 10th Street on Indianapolis' east side enraptured Thomas. After his two buddies hopped on the last Interurban back to Jeffries, Thomas often stayed over to watch the latest film playing at the Rivoli. One day, Thomas returned to the farm after a foray into the city and announced that he planned to attend the Indiana University Maurer School of Law in Bloomington. When Elijah asked why he'd give up the farm life in favor of being a lawyer, Thomas proclaimed, "Being a lawyer is the only way I'll be able to marry a motion picture star!" Just out of law school, Thomas did, indeed, marry a low-level starlet. When Elijah set out again to change his will, he didn't call his son.

David was a shoo-in to take over the family farm... why hadn't Elijah realized it before? Not only kind and attentive to his family and the farmhands, he was a hard worker and eager to please his father. When it came to the health of the farm animals, David really shined. Every time one of their dairy cows labored to give birth, David was there with calming words of comfort. He seemed to know naturally what to do when a cow was in distress during delivery. Elijah admired his son. Not only did he look the most like his mother of all his sons, he had her disposition. One day, when Bert fell out of the barn loft and broke his leg, David took charge. He instructed his mother, Sarah, to call Doc Becker. Then David moved Bert to his bed, tended the farmhand's cuts and bruises, and got him as comfortable as possible until the doctor arrived. David watched attentively as Doc Becker set his leg, then tended Bert until he was back on his feet. Months later, when another farmhand fell and broke his arm, David set it himself.

"Have you ever thought about going to medical school?" Doc Becker asked one day. "Yes, sir," answered David. "My Uncle Jonah is a doctor over in Columbus and does well. I thought maybe I could get my education and join his practice." That's exactly what David did, to the chagrin of his father.

"Now what?" Elijah asked Sarah. "I suggest you talk to the son meant to have this farm all along." Before Elijah marched off to his attorney's office yet again, he looked into Joshua's face. "Son," he said, "are you going to stick around and run this farm like a proper Barner, or are you going to become a city boy like your brothers."

"Sir, I'm planning to stick around until the day I die."

Chapter 17

With the beginning of the school year just a couple weeks away, Mother sent us off with her mad money to select fabric for new dresses. "Check the Woolworth's remnant table first," she suggested.

"But mother," Gem argued. "If it's a remnant, that means some other girl at school might have a dress exactly like mine."

"If you get something from a fresh bolt," Mother pointed out, "that doesn't mean someone else will not buy from it, too. Besides, I have loads of ric-rac and ruffles and ribbon and pretty buttons to make your dress special. Plus, I have my own patterns. No one will have a dress exactly like yours, Gem. I promise."

The enameled openwork floral buttons Mother received from the notions man crossed my mind. I wondered where Mother had hidden them.

"I suppose," Gem sighed.

"Don't leave without Charlie and Bernard," called Mother. "And don't lose that money."

"She's trying to distract us from that dead man," Gem grumbled to me when Mother was out of earshot.

"Oh, well."

Half and hour later, Gem and I stood with our noses pressed to the glass of Woolworths. "I'm pretty sure that's her," Gem whispered. My sister leaned back and wiped the fog from the window with her hand.

"That's who?" Charlie stepped up beside me and looked in. "Is that Alma Mae Butler?"

"Exactly!" Gem exhaled loudly, her exasperation enveloping the four of us. "That's who we're trying to avoid."

Charlie shrugged.

While Sheriff Boggs believed his beloved wife, Martha, was the town gossip, and Popo insisted it was Sally, the operator at the Bell Telephone Company, everyone else in town attributed the title to Alma Mae. The town grapevine began and ended on her doorstep.

Gem stood on her tiptoes and peeked in the window again. "Looks like she's having quite the conversation with one of the store clerks."

"Hit 'pears to me, ef I ain't mistook, that pore clerk can't hardly git a single word a-spoke." Bernard rolled his eyes, which was the extent of his criticism of another human being.

"Why are you avoiding Mrs. Butler?"

I took hold of my cousin's arm and pulled him away from the window. "Because she'll ask us about the Corpse in the Creek. Mother doesn't want us talking about that with other people any more because it will make her telephone ring. She's ready to move on."

"Aren't we all?" huffed Gem.

I shook my head. "NO!" I insisted. "Not until we know his name and where he came from. Not until Sheriff Boggs can inform his family of his death."

"I reckon I'm of the same mind as Annie." Bernard turned and stared at the courthouse in the center of the public square. "Hit's the Christian thing to do, to let kin know, an' all. So's they kin give 'im a proper layin' to rest."

"If we want to avoid Mrs. Butler, perhaps we should go somewhere else for a while, somewhere she won't spot us."

"Good idea, Charlie." Gem looked up and down Main Street.

Bernard piped up. I got me a notion. Let's go set at the table 'hind the Blue and White fer a few ticks. Then we kin come on back. Look," he said, pulling a few coins from his pocket. "I'll fetch us each a glass o' lemonade while we're a-waitin'."

I'd seen the back of the Blue and White Café through the diner's backdoor but never sat at the old wooden table behind the building. Years of wear and weather had rubbed the chair's wood smooth, but the years of exposure showed on the rough-hewn table's boards. I scooted back into a chair, then ran a finger through the letters carved by those who once sat there and wanted to be remembered. A jagged heart, bleached and faded, read, BB LOVES LO. Could that be a young Boggy Boggs professing his eternal love for my Aunt Lo? Or was it commemorating the love between two people from long ago, unknown to me? As I sat there, my feet dangling, I wondered if the mysterious hobo, Jimbo, had sat in this very place after begging a meal from the Lockwoods.

"Why don't you go see to that lemonade, Bernard," my sister urged. "I can feel the sun coming on."

With a quick nod, Bernard stood up and reached into his jeans pocket for his coins. I watched as the boy looked around.

"Try the backdoor." Reading Bernard's mind, Gem pointed toward the door near where the table hugged the building. "No sense walking all the way around to the front door. People use the backdoor all the time."

With the words barely out of Gem's mouth, the door burst open. Loaded down with boxes and other trash, Paul Lockwood walked to the burn barrel along the alley and stuffed them in.

When he turned back toward the door, his eyes widened as he spotted us. "Well, hello." His voice was pleasant and kind. "I didn't see you there. What can I do you for?"

Charlie stood up and offered our explanation. "We came downtown so my cousins could pick out fabric for their new school dresses. When we got to Woolworth, Mrs. Butler was in there carrying on quite the conversation with the clerk, so we came here for a few minutes to sit out of sight until she moves on."

"Perfectly understandable."

"Popo and Aunt Maggie prefer Gem and Annie not talk about the dead man anymore," Charlie added to further explain our presence.

"I can't say that I blame them. A sad situation that's had this town in a tangle of gossip for days. Not that anyone cares what the cook thinks... except my wife, of course... but this unfortunate death is in the excellent hands of Sheriff Boggs. He'll sort out this mystery. In the meantime, the living need to go on living."

My hand resting on the table, I closed my eyes as my finger traced the BB carved into the wood. I thought that if I closed my eyes long enough, the answers to the questions that plagued me might reveal themselves. What was his name? Why was he here? How did his body get into Prairie Creek? In that moment, I realized there was one question I wanted answered more than any other: Who pulled Pauline and me from the icy creek last winter?

"Open your eyes, Annie. Open your eyes."

"What?"

My sister was staring into my face. "Mr. Lockwood asked you if you'd like to try a piece of fudge with your lemonade."

"A woman from the west side of town lost her husband recently and is trying to make a few dollars so she doesn't lose her house," Paul explained. "You know my wife... she wants to help her out. I'm sure Roxy would appreciate your opinions."

Bernard opened his hand and looked at his coins. Paul smiled at the boy. "Now you know, Bernard, if you tell me what you think of the fudge, the lemonade will be on the house."

We clapped and cheered as the man went back inside.

We sat in silence for a while, all four of us engaged in our own thoughts. From my chair near the door, I looked out toward the alley. To my left, someone had piled up a few more old chairs and other clutter. Beyond that, a short wooden fence that had seen better days ran along the property line between the Blue and White and the Clinton Theater. Paul Lockwood's burn barrel sat near the alley, as far away from the building as possible.

"The only good view from here is straight up," pointed out Charlie. We all looked up at the greenish-blue sky devoid of clouds. "It's going to be another hot day."

"We could haul our settin' chairs yonder." Bernard stood and walked to the old shed that stood to the right next to the burn barrel.

"What is that building?" I asked.

Charlie piped up. "It looks like an old horse shed. I bet someone used it to keep their horse and carriage in there."

"Miss Roxy's parents, I suppose," Gem offered. "The Blue and White Café belonged to them before they died and Miss Roxy took over."

"I give Mr. Lockwood a hand cleanin' it out a spell back. Says he's savin' to buy one o' them motorcars fer his missus and keep it in here, but don't you go blabbin'. That there's a secret." Bernard got up and circled the shed. We followed. "It's still shut up tighter'n a tick, jest like we left it."

"So no one can get in without the key?" I asked, knowing the answer. I lifted the heavy black lock that hung from its hasp and pushed aside the keyhole cover with my thumb. The lock reminded me of the one on Aunt Lo's cedar chest, only bigger.

"Not 'less they climbs in through the winder on t'other side."

Gem, Charlie, and I followed Bernard to the window. Charlie climbed up on a wooden bench to get a look inside. I climbed up next to him. Someone had painted the panes black, so we couldn't see inside. Charlie put his hands on the top frame and pushed, but the window only gave about an inch.

My nose twitched at the stale smell of old hay mingling with a faint musty odor and a whiff of gasoline that drifted out of the small opening. I stood there a moment imaging the fancy motorcar, spit-polished to perfection, that would one day be inside.

"Maybe Mr. Lockwood will take us for a ride someday," I said.

"Come on," Charlie urged. "Mr. Lockwood will be back soon. Let's pull our chairs under the eaves there..." Charlie pointed. "...so we can stay in the shade a while longer. I don't want my fudge to melt."

Chapter 18

I awoke pressed against my sister's back beneath bedcovers. My sister had covered us with a light blanket in the night. To me, the contrast between the blazing heat of the previous August day and the cool of the night was stark. That's when I realized I hadn't been vigilant since discovering the Corpse in the Creek. Had the edge of summer arrived early this year? Tears welled in my eyes. Had I missed savoring the music of its anticipated arrival at Aunt Lo's side?

"Do you want to come in? Maggie is making coffee." Popo's whispered voice drifted up the staircase. I pulled myself up to look out the window above our bed into the still-dark sky.

"Nah. To be honest, my friend, what I need right now is this cool air to clear my head. I shouldn't have come here so early, but this thing is keeping me awake at night. I need someone to bounce the facts off of because I have this niggling in the back of my mind that I'm missing something."

Like a moth to a flame, I slid quietly from bed, padded barefoot down the staircase and looked out the open front door. Popo sat on the top step of our porch while Sheriff Boggs paced back and forth in front of him. I stepped out onto the porch.

"What are you doing up? It's still early."

I sat down next to my father. "I overheard you talking."

"I'm sorry we woke you, Angel. You should go back to bed."

"I want to stay with you, Popo."

Sheriff Boggs came to my rescue. "Let her stay, Augie. She's as much a part of this as anyone. Somehow, your daughter sees things I miss."

He resumed pacing, his head down. Finally, Popo spoke up. "Let's go through it all again, Boggy. What do we know so far?"

The sheriff planted his feet, took a deep breath and reviewed the facts to date. "Annie discovered the body of a stranger in the creek last Saturday, and you pulled him out. Dead as a doornail." He turned and looked at the spot where the man had lain in our yard alongside the creek.

After a long moment, he continued. "A circus ensued, complete with that clown from the *Morning Times* asking his ridiculous questions, a mere boy who, thanks to my wife and the miracle of the Bell Telephone Company, figured out something was going on here and beat me to the punch."

"Maggie's telephone call to you tipped off Sally." My father's words seemed matter-of-fact, not as full of accusations as they had before. "Folks got wind something was up and started showing up and seeing for themselves. Isn't that right, Annie?"

I nodded. "Only that reporter and a couple other people from town got here before you. That's all."

"She's right, Boggy. You were only five minutes behind them, and those five minutes didn't amount to a hill of beans. The reporter was doing his job. Besides, you got your favorite rump roast out of the deal, though I'm not so sure Martha owed you the whole thing."

The sheriff rubbed his belly. "Regardless, I got it. With all the belt tightening going on because of that stock market crash in '29, I'm never sure when I'll get another one."

"What else?" Popo prompted.

"Despite all the people who gathered here, no one in town knew who that fellow was. A week later, no one has stepped up and provided an identity, or even a clue to his identity. Biddy sent telegrams to the surrounding counties inquiring about reports of any missing people, but so far, we've gotten nothing. It's time I expanded my circle of inquiry out to a hundred miles, especially into Indianapolis. Someone somewhere knows this man. I've just got to find out who that is."

Sheriff Boggs rubbed his hands over his face. I could tell he was tired, unshaven, brow furrowed with worry lines. As he resumed his pacing, the first light of the morning sun revealed dark circles under his chestnut-colored eyes. Popo sat motionless, allowing him time to collect his thoughts.

"Where'd you leave off, Boggy?" Popo finally prompted.

The sheriff took a deep breath. He continued, "Then Annie and Gem got me on the trail of the Interurban engineer, Hector Toops, which is still the best lead I've had." He leaned down and patted my head. "According to Hector's account, I learned our stranger was ailing from a hurt head, but he was still among the living when the engineer made a special stop to talk to him last Saturday morning. Most people would have sped on by to keep on schedule, but he stopped. That Hector is a good man."

"He is, indeed." Popo stood up and stretched. "Okay, keep going."

"Later that day, when I stopped by to talk to Doc Becker, he told me something interesting. The Friday night before Annie found him, Doc told me he'd had a hectic day with office visits, house calls and the like. So he turned in early, about eight o'clock. He said he woke up in the night to find his wife sitting on the edge of the bed. He asked if everything was alright. Mrs. Becker said she'd heard an animal rooting around out back. She told me it was about eleven-thirty when she heard the ruckus, too late for the Interurban."

"Probably a raccoon?" Doc Becker had offered.

Mrs. Becker conceded, saying he was likely correct. "But it was one big raccoon."

"Even if Hector had dropped the man off late, he would have remembered and told you when you talked to him," noted Popo.

"Exactly right, Augie. Perhaps someone else pointed the stranger to Doc Becker's place before Hector did. And that raccoon rooting around behind Doc Becker's place on Friday night wasn't a raccoon after all. Could it be the man was disoriented, lost in a strange town at night, and was looking for help?"

"Could be."

Sheriff Boggs paused again, his eyes upward, searching his memory.

"After Doc Becker examined the man's body at the morgue, did he find anything else?" asked Popo.

"There was the head injury." Sheriff Boggs rubbed the left side of his head over his ear to indicate the injury we saw last Saturday when I discovered him in the creek. "He also found a crescent-moon shaped scar at the edge of his right eyebrow." He traced the location with his index finger, then paused. "Doc Becker said that at some point, probably during his youth, he broke his right leg pretty bad, though it appeared to have healed just fine. He suggested I could ship the body down to Indianapolis, where the coroner could get his leg X-rayed to be certain, but what's the point? Doc Becker was certain those injuries had nothing to do with his death, but mentioned them to me because they might help with identification."

Popo rubbed his bare arms, chasing away the chill. Then he turned and looked at the crest of the rising sun, its red glow reflecting off the gathering clouds. "A storm's coming," he muttered. I stood up and grabbed my father's arm, pulling it around my shoulders as I stared at the dawning day, another day filled with talk of the dead man.

Finally, Pop turned back to his friend. "Keep going, Boggy. What else?"

"After we took our ride on the Interurban with Hector, we stopped to talk to Mrs. Parlett. Dear woman... I can't image such loneliness. Of course, I live with the town gossip, so the occasional quiet sounds good to me."

"Be careful what you wish for, Boggy."

Without further comment about Martha, the sheriff continued. "Mrs. Parlett gave me confirmation of what I was already mulling around in my head based about Roxy's comment. Mrs. Parlett saw Jimbo on South Street that morning, but he wasn't there begging for breakfast. My experience with the man is he doesn't come out into the open much. He avoids the townsfolk unless he's after something."

"Like a free meal."

"Staying in the shadows helps keep the hobos on the right side of the law, here and in other towns."

"Out of sight, out of mind?"

"Not exactly. I keep a good eye on those boys who do wander into town. I give them their due in terms of respect. Some of those men went through hell during the Great War and their suffering lingers to this day. They're all broken men, including Jimbo." The sheriff paused for a moment, then added, "Especially Jimbo."

"I can't fathom what they endured. The men I know who survived the Great War don't want to talk about it."

Sheriff Boggs nodded. "But I suspect when Mrs. Parlett spotted him on South Street that morning..." he pointed up the street... "he was after something."

"So maybe Jimbo talked to this fellow on Friday evening, told him where Doc Becker lived, and then followed up on Saturday morning to see if he made it?"

"That sounds like a stretch, but it has crossed my mind."

"What would a hobo have to do with a stranger-in-town? Do you think the stranger came to town to find Jimbo?"

"Nah," replied the sheriff. "The letter the children found leads me to believe he was looking for the woman he loved."

"You're right, of course," agreed Popo.

The silence that settled between the two men shattered when Mother opened the door, her best silver tray in hand.

"Good morning, Boggy. I thought you two..." Mother looked at me, but continued without questioning my presence. "...could use some coffee."

"That's exactly what I need to clear my head," said the sheriff. "Thank you, Maggie."

Mother stirred cream and sugar into both cups and handed them to the men. "I'll bring you a cup of hot cocoa, Anna." Mother turned and walked back inside.

Without prompting, the sheriff continued where he'd left off. "The next couple of days, I put the hunt on for Jimbo around town. I didn't want to make too big a deal about it since folks seemed to be settling into the truth, not because I said it, but because your incorrigible sister-in-law put it out on the town's high-minded grapevine that his death was an accident." I was relieved the sheriff omitted the role Gem, Bernard, and I played in getting that bit of truth out. "After our foray to the hobo camp, I'm getting the impression ole Jimbo isn't interested in talking to me."

"I can't imagine why not." Popo shook his head and chuckled. "An upstanding citizen such as yourself."

Sheriff Boggs ignored his friend.

"All I've worked out in my head about this case so far makes sense. I thought I was fitting the pieces of the puzzle together, and the complete picture was about to come into focus. But Jimbo's avoidance of a friendly conversation with an amiable fellow such as myself puts a sharp edge back on this case that keeps poking at me when I'm trying to sleep."

"You never told me why you thought Jimbo was still at the hobo camp when we went out there."

"First off, I could feel his eyes on us. That instinct is probably driven by the fact he loves apple season around here and stays until it's over. Mrs. Parlett said it, but I already knew it to be true. Jimbo makes his way out to the orchards and picks apples in exchange for whatever he can pick up off the ground. He's still around... I'd bet on it."

"So you believe he's still around, just avoiding you?"

"That is correct, my friend. Jimbo's not going anywhere until the first hard freeze. He's lurking about in plain site, it's just that I can't seem to put my finger on him."

"It's just a matter of time," Popo assured him.

"Then why do I feel like time is running out on this matter?" Sheriff Boggs resumed his pacing.

Finally, Popo interrupted the sheriff's thoughts. "Let's get back to it. What else?"

The sheriff recalled that the first person to point to Jimbo was Roxy Lockwood, the proprietor of the Blue and White Café. "I stopped in a couple days ago, mostly because meatloaf with mashed potatoes and onion gravy was the day's special, but also because I wanted to know why Roxy thought I should talk to Jimbo."

"What did she say?"

"She told me to talk to Paul. He feeds Jimbo out back from time to time, which I already knew. As a veteran of the Great War, Paul feels an obligation to help fellow warriors with the occasional meal. What is it about Paul and Roxy... thinking they can fix the plight of mankind with a few hot meals?"

"Says the man with the taste of meatloaf and mashed potatoes still on his lips."

The two men laughed. "Are you saying Maggie's pie hasn't helped you through a rough patch or two?"

"Not saying that at all. Now go on," Popo prompted. "Tell us what happened when you talked to Roxy and Paul."

Sheriff Boggs walked back to the porch and sat down. With his arms crossed over his chest, he recounted his recent visit to the Blue and White Café, starting at the beginning, as was his habit.

***

"You about ready to head home, Sheriff?" Biddy Ann stood in the doorway of her boss's office, her coat over her shoulders and her pocketbook in hand.

"Nah, Biddy. Not just yet." Sheriff Boggs stood up and stretched. "Martha called and said she had a sick headache, so I thought I'd go by the Blue and White for a bite."

"I hear Roxy's serving meatloaf tonight."

"You don't have to tell me. On nights like this, the aroma of whatever Roxy has on the menu wafts through my office window."

"Are you saying you're happy Martha's not feeling well so you have another excuse to stop by the Blue and White Café for supper?"

"Not saying that at all, Biddy. I've got official business to conduct there regarding my investigation."

"You'll be investigating with your mouth full of meatloaf." It wasn't a question.

"Why don't you stop picking apart my investigating style and get on home. Maybe even hold on to your job."

Biddy Ann smiled. "Sure thing. See you tomorrow."

Sheriff Boggs walked over to the Blue and White Café and settled into a chair at a table near the front—the only table available. He noticed the restaurant was unusually busy for that time of the evening. Old Man Gregory stopped by his table for a moment on his way out and explained that the Nickel Plate's train number 42 from Lima had arrived late because of a minor truck accident that resulted in a load of lumber being dumped on the tracks at Red Key crossing, putting the train behind schedule over an hour.

More tired and grumpy than usual, the railroaders seemed to find their repose in a slab of meatloaf and a piece of peach pie topped with a scoop of Roxy's handmade vanilla ice cream. Sheriff Boggs feared the meatloaf he craved would be gone before Roxy had the time to take his order. He perused the café's limited menu for another alternative. After settling on beef stew, he pushed aside his menu and propped an elbow on the table. A moment later, Roxy slid a plate in front of him.

"You read my mind." His face lit up as he eyed the meatloaf and mashed potatoes with a double portion of onion gravy, just the way he liked it.

"I hate to be the one to tell you this, Sheriff, but your mind isn't hard to read." A tight smile on her face, Roxy winked at him as she made her way back to the window to pick up another order.

The next time she got close when his mouth wasn't full, the sheriff said, "When things slow down, I'd like to know more about why you think I should talk to Jimbo about my case."

"Talk to Paul." Roxy pointed at the kitchen with her pencil stub. "He knows Jimbo about as well as anybody around here, though that isn't much."

"When is a good time?"

"You ever done dishes, Sheriff? You can have as long a conversation with Paul as you want, provided it's in the kitchen." She nodded a head toward the serving window, where Paul placed two plates.

"Order up," he called.

Boggy held up both hands and wriggled his fingers. "Nope. I hear all that hot water might chafe my trigger-pulling finger. I wouldn't be much of a sheriff if that happened."

Roxy rolled her eyes. "Tell you what. I'll bring you a piece of pie..."

"With ice cream."

"I'll bring you a piece of pie with ice cream to help you kill a little more time. When things slow down, you can mosey back to the kitchen and talk to my beloved husband all you want. Things should slow down here shortly. How many more railroaders could there be to feed tonight?"

The sheriff looked over his shoulder at train number 42's conductor as he scooped mouthfuls of pie and ice cream off his plate with a spoon.

"Deal."

Twenty minutes later, the sheriff pushed through the kitchen door. Leaning against the sink full of dishes, he said, "Let's talk about Jimbo."

"I wondered when you'd get around to asking me about that 'bo."

While the pace in the dining room had slowed, Paul hustled around the kitchen, cleaning and tidying up as he talked. "Sure, I fed Jimbo and some of the other veterans from time to time. Mostly leftovers. A dab of this and a dab of that. They're always grateful for a meal, especially from someone who's been through the same horror they've been through."

"Paul, by chance, did you see Jimbo Friday, a week ago?"

"I did." Paul picked up a dishrag and wiped off a pan. "On hot days, I keep the backdoor open to let the heat out of the kitchen." Paul nodded his head toward the door. "Late Friday evening, I spotted Jimbo sitting there at that old table where I like to sit to get a moment of peace between busy spells."

"That table out back against the wall?" asked Sheriff Boggs.

"Yep, that's the one." Paul turned and placed a clean pan on a shelf above his stove. "Jimbo was smoking a cigarette," he continued. "I thought it odd, so I walked out there and asked him, 'Since when did you take up smoking, Jimbo?' The man replied, 'I guess a piece of my former self shows up once in a while. At least this time, it's my old smoking self, not my old skirt-chasing self. Let me tell you, that old boy got me into a world of trouble.'"

Paul said Jimbo laughed at his own joke, which made him chuckle, too.

"Then I asked him, 'Jimbo, where'd you get the money for tobacco?' Jimbo took his time with his exhale before answering me. 'I did a stranger a favor earlier this evening, and he paid me handsomely for it.'"

"Friday evening? The Friday before last?"

"Yep."

"Please continued," urged the sheriff.

"Here's where it gets interesting... Jimbo laid two Liberty half dollars on the table."

"You don't say," replied the sheriff. "The Ghere sisters and Bernard Thompson found two shiny Liberty half dollars out near the creek behind Doc Becker's house the other day. An odd coincidence, wouldn't you say?"

"That's interesting," said Paul before continuing. "Jimbo said to bring him the evening's special—full portions—and a piece of Roxy's peach pie with a scoop of handmade ice cream. I'd have to scrape to get a full scoop. 'Extra gravy, if you please,' he added. Then he looked at his half-smoked cigarette and snuffed it out. 'I better hang on to this. I've a hankering to complete my evening meal with a smoke.'"

"I told him I'd see what I had left, as it was getting on to closing time. Then I said, 'Tell you what. I've got a half bag of tobacco stashed in the kitchen that I've been meaning to get rid of it. Roxy won't kiss me when I smoke. It's yours if you want it.' From the size of his smile, you'd have thought I'd offered him the Taj Mahal. Then Jimbo settled back into his chair. 'One more thing,' he said. 'I'll take my change.'"

***

"Annie, come down here and look at this."

The sheriff pointed to the east. I walked down the steps of the porch and into the dewy grass that sent a chill up my spine, making me shiver. I turned to see the sunrise above the streetscape. "You know what they say, Annie? Red sky at night, shepherd's delight. Red sky in morning, shepherd's warning."

"Warning of what?"

"Of bad weather ahead, just like your father said."

Popo joined us in the yard, picking me up in his arms as he looked at the sunrise on another summer day. As my father held me, I listened intently for the symphony, scanning Prairie Creek for white mist, sniffing the air for the faint fragrance of musk melons now eager to be picked from their vines. Oh, how I longed for all the signs of the edge of summer. More than that, I longed for the reassurances of my Aunt Lo that through the fog of this tragedy, all the pleasures of the edge of summer still awaited us.

My father set me on the ground and turned back to his friend.

"I've got to find Jimbo," pronounced Sheriff Boggs. "He's a key to me solving this thing, to figuring out the identity of the dead man. I just know it."

I tugged on the lawman's sleeve.

"What is it, Annie?"

"I know where Jimbo is."

Sheriff Boggs looked at me. In the faint light of early morning, I could see the confusion on his face.

"Where is he, Annie? Where's Jimbo?"

I pointed over his shoulder to the north, to the faint wisp of dark gray smoke rising over the creek in the distance.

"He's there. I'm sure of it."

Chapter 19

"Can I warm up your coffee?"

"Thanks, Maggie. That sounds great." The sheriff pushed his empty plate to the center of the table and moved his cup toward Mother.

She topped off his coffee, set the pot on the table, and sat down. "I was hoping you'd shed some light on that letter Bernard and my girls found over by the Interurban tracks."

"Oh, boy," I muttered under my breath.

"What would you like to know, Maggie?"

"It seems I'm only getting bits and pieces of the truth of how three children gained a critical piece of evidence in an ongoing sheriff's investigation."

"Sounds like a sheriff not doing his job. Is that what you're saying?"

Mother smiled. "You're sitting at my table with a belly-full of my breakfast..."

"And a fine breakfast it was."

"I expect the courtesy of the truth, Boggy. You can give it to me straight or I can get on the telephone with my dear friend Martha and get it from her."

"No need to go to extremes."

Sheriff Boggs recounted how he'd come into possession of the letter.

"Gem and Annie swore to me they'd stay away from those tracks. And that Bernard Thompson, whom I feed regularly and sometimes clothe, went along with their nonsense!"

The sheriff held up his right hand, as if he'd swear to it on a Bible. "They're good girls. They found that letter at least a dozen feet from those tracks. Besides, I'm sure you understand that finding a body in the creek right outside their front door means they're involved in this matter up to their eyeballs... whether or not you or I like it or not."

"So I've been told on numerous occasions. I just don't want their impulses to overwhelm their good sense. I want them to be safe."

"I assure you, they're safe. No bogeyman is going to jump out and harm them." Sheriff Boggs turned to me. "The truth is, your girls have given me my best leads in this case. I'm about to find out if Annie's correct again, though I suspect she is."

I smiled. Though Popo did a good bit of hand-wringing and pacing after I pointed out the smoke coming from Mrs. Barner's old cottage, it was good to know Sheriff Boggs thought I was correct.

Mother stood up, then turned to face the sheriff, a hand on her hip. "You're changing the subject again, Boggy. What does the letter say?"

The sheriff felt his breast and pants pockets as if he were searching for it. "I don't have it on me at the moment. Biddy put it in the safe. It's locked up tight as a drum."

I smiled at the expression, thinking about how Bernard had used those exact words regarding the old shed behind the Blue and White Café.

"I didn't know you had a safe at the sheriff's office," Mother commented.

"We don't go around telling folks about it. That way, it's extra safe." The sheriff flashed Mother his full grin.

Mother stared at the sheriff. "What does the letter say?"

Sheriff Boggs looked embarrassed. "It's a man pouring out his heart to the woman he loves. He asks her to run away with him... to marry him. That kind of thing." The sheriff looked sheepishly at my mother. "Does that answer your question?"

"I suggest you bring that letter over for me to read. It might give me an idea of who wrote it, or to whom the man wrote it."

"Yes, ma'am."

The sheriff stood up. "If Augie would skip the pomade, we could get on with it. I want nothing alerting Jimbo to the fact we're coming, if he is, indeed, in that old cottage in Barner's Woods." He looked at me and winked.

"Are you taking your gun?" asked Gem, who'd stumbled her way to the kitchen table, still wearing her nightgown.

"What is it with this family and their questions about my gun?"

My hand flew to my mouth to muffle a giggle.

"No, I am not taking my gun. As I've said at least a hundred times in the last few days, Jimbo is harmless. He's also smart, and he doesn't want to risk his freedom."

Popo walked into the kitchen, tugging on his shirt sleeves. "We should probably get on with this so we can both get back to business as usual. I've got several calls to make this morning and still have a dead man to identify so my family can get back to normal."

I stood up. "Where do you think you're going?" Mother asked.

"I'm going with them."

After the two men decided they wanted to wait until it was full light before trekking through the woods to the abandoned cottage, I'd gone upstairs and dressed so I'd be ready when my father and the sheriff started off through Barner's Woods.

"You heard the sheriff. He needs me."

"I don't recall him saying that, Anna." Mother planted both hands on her hips.

"Well, he does." I walked through the kitchen to the back porch before I turned and called out, "Let's go, gentleman. We're burning daylight."

As the screen door slammed behind us, I heard my mother call out, "Wear your boots, Annie."

I did as Mother said.

***

Sheriff Boggs took the lead, as we made our way through a familiar portion of the woods to the path that ran along the creek. Few houses had been built on this side of the creek beyond ours. The houses on the other side of Prairie Creek diminished in number the farther north we walked.

Just beyond Washington Street, the sheriff veered to the left into the thick of the trees. I knew the woods here were an extension of those lining the creek alongside our house, though thicker... mostly unchanged through centuries of the region's history. Sheriff Boggs moved nimbly through the growth, as a fox navigates its territory, his old water-stained boots seeming to grip the terrain beneath him, as he led us deeper into the sylvan thicket.

But for the crunching of our feet and our labored breathing, I was aware that the forest was suddenly still... no birds chirping, no squirrels scampering limb-to-limb, no breeze blowing. I looked overhead at the gathering storm.

"Follow in his footsteps, Angel," Popo whispered as I tripped and stumbled over tree roots, fallen branches and rocks. At one point, Popo and I lost sight of the sheriff, but soon came upon him leaned against a pine tree. That's when he picked me up and carried me piggyback for a few minutes, moving gracefully through the thick trees, ducking branches and sidestepping obstacles as if he'd walked that exact route a thousand times.

Finally, he slowed and pointed. "Lights ahead." I looked up over his left shoulder. But for the darkening skies, the faint glow would have been undetectable.

Sheriff Boggs stopped. As Popo came up behind us, the sheriff whispered, "Take a rest, but don't talk." His words were barely audible. "I want to check things out before we approach."

I opened my mouth to ask if he could see the cottage, but thought better of it. He set me down on a fallen log, put a finger to his lips, then moved off through the trees for a better view.

I stretched out my legs. That's when I spotted the debris that clung to my red boots. I wiped off one of them with my hand to make sure they'd made the journey without being damaged.

Popo sat down beside me, wrapping his arm around me for a quick hug. I nodded, wordlessly assuring him I was fine. We both dripped with the sweat. Thinking about my boots, my mind drifted back to the day after my friend and I had fallen through the ice on Prairie Creek.

***

Pauline's parents had come early to collect her. Although Mother had washed and ironed all her clothing, she told Mrs. Kimmel that Pauline's wool coat was still damp. It hung in our basement until it stopped dripping, then Mother had done her best to clean it and reshape it before hanging it near our furnace to finish drying out. That morning, Mother had taken her iron to it, but even after her best efforts, she'd pronounced it damp and unfit to wear of such a wintry day.

"Up and at 'um, girls," Mother urged, rousing Pauline and me from our sleep. "Pauline's parents are here. Mr. Kimmel hitched up the horse and buggy, and is taking his beautiful girls to the Blue and White Café for breakfast, then going over to the rummage sale to see if they can find another wool coat."

"What will I wear in the meantime?" asked my friend.

"Your mother is bringing your coat from last year."

"But it's too small!"

"Pauline, in situations such as this, we must learn to make do." With that, Mother tapped her on the nose. "Both of you, get cleaned up and ready for the day. Pauline, I've left your clothes in the bathroom. Now scoot."

After Pauline's parents picked her up, I found Gem at the kitchen table, bouncing Thea on her knee. The baby smiled at me when I approached the table and said, "Sissy, sissy." I kissed her on the head and took my seat next to Gem at the round table.

Popo sat next to me, reading the *Morning Times* and stirring his coffee. "It says here that Charlie Chaplin's new film, 'City Lights,' is premiering in Los Angeles at the end of the month. How long will it take for it to show down at the Clinton Theater?"

"I don't know, Augie," Mother answered. "It rarely takes very long."

"Look here," Popo continued. "It says here that Thomas Edison died."

"Charlie, will you go tell the boys to come in for breakfast?" Mother asked. "They're out in the barn tending to Old Barney and my chickens."

A few moments later, we heard the stampede of feet... Gus, Blinn, Cory and Charlie in a race to get to the table. After they settled in, Mother placed the food on the table and sat down.

"Hey, Annie," Cory said, as he scooped gravy onto his biscuits. "Don't leave your stupid boots on the porch steps. I tripped on them in the dark this morning and nearly fell down."

"That's right," added Blinn. "If I hadn't grabbed hold of his arm, he would have landed on his butt at the bottom of the steps."

"Better his butt than his head," muttered Gus. The three brothers chuckled.

"What boots?" I asked my brother.

"Those stupid red ones that Aunt Lo bought at the rummage sale awhile back. Those are yours, right?"

The newspaper dropped from in front of Popo's face. Without a word, he pushed away from the table and walked through the kitchen to the back porch. A moment later, he returned carrying my red rubber boots.

"Annie, are these the boots you were wearing when you fell through the ice yesterday?"

My eyes widened as I nodded.

"How did they get on the back steps? I went over to the other side of the creek and found the exact place where you tried to cut across the creek, but I didn't see any sign of your boots. I figured we'd fish them out of the creek in the spring when the ice melted."

I shrugged.

We ate our breakfast in silence.

***

Popo and I had caught our breath before Sheriff Boggs returned. I looked down at his water-stained lace-up boots and couldn't help but wonder if he'd rescued Pauline and me... and my boots last winter.

"Someone is definitely in that cottage," Sheriff Boggs told us in a hushed tone. "Look, you can see it right through there. The door is open."

I made my way to a giant bur oak that stood beside the clearing that edged the shoreline where Prairie Creek widened. The creek was deeper here, more active than the stretch that ran alongside of our house.

"Where's the cottage?" I whispered to Popo.

"There," he said, pointing across the clearing to where the forest began again. At first glance, anyone traveling along the creek had to follow the clues... the clearing, the garden patch, the outhouse, the woodpile, the sign that read, "Private Property. TRESPASSERS WILL BE SHOT." Finally, my eyes settled on the little cottage that blended into the trees. Built of rough-hewn oak, it seemed a clever wind had gathered up the remnants from the forest floor and gave it form. Even the stone fireplace that rose on the creekside of the cottage befit God's original design.

"It's rustic," Popo muttered in my ear. Popo then turned to Sheriff Boggs. "Now what?"

"Let's get this over with before it rains."

Chapter 20

"Hello, Sheriff. I've been expecting you."

"Is that a fact?"

The hobo turned toward the sheriff, an old tin mug in his hand. "I see you've brought an entourage. Come in, come in. All are welcome."

The law man stepped into the small cottage, Popo and me on his heels. Before my eyes had adjusted to the dim light, the sheriff's words broke my gaze from Jimbo to another figure standing in the room.

"Long time, no see, Adam. How are you doing?" Neutral in its tone, the sheriff's voice lacked enthusiasm for the unexpected occupant. He held out his hand to the man who immediately shook it.

"It has been a while, Clyde. I don't get down this way to visit my brother as often as I'd like." The man then turned to my father. "And Augie Ghere, my brother's friend and business associate. Good to see you, too. How's your brother?"

"Same old Karl."

The two men chuckled. "This must be your youngest. Anna, if I recall correctly."

I stepped forward and pulled Popo's arm around me, a safe place where I could get a better look at the man. Dressed in the clothing of a farmhand, he resembled his brother, Joshua. At a glance, he could be mistaken for his youngest brother, but the lines of his face were sharper, his haircut that of a businessman. I wondered if he'd wore the wide-brimmed straw hat hooked over the spool of a chair to confuse anyone who spotted him.

"Actually, she's not my youngest anymore," Popo corrected. "I have a ten-month-old, Thea."

Adam's face lit up with a smile. "Of course. Joshua told me about your tiny baby girl some months back. How could I have forgotten? How's she doing?"

"Better than most who arrive in this world as early as she did. The day little Thea was born, Maggie pronounced her to be fine, and went about making it so. Maggie is quite a mother."

"What brings you out here to the woods this morning, Adam?" The sheriff's investigator's voice interrupted the friendly banter, making clear to his accidental host that answering his question was non-negotiable.

"I could ask you the same question."

The smile on Adam's face disappeared, the conversation taking its expected serious turn. Sheriff Boggs waited.

"Joshua spotted smoke coming out of the chimney. He keeps a close eye on this place the same way he did when Mother was still with us. He was helping load a truck bound for your place, Augie—it's a shame you won't be there to receive it—so I volunteered to walk out here to check on things. I found this hobo, encroaching on Barner property. I was just negotiating his departure when you folks showed up."

I noticed an open padlock hanging on the hasp by the door when we entered. "Who unlocked it?" I wondered.

I looked at the fireplace. The wood rack near the old stone hearth was empty, but a bucket of coal sat in front of it. The flame that had blazed in the fireplace earlier had died down to a pile of hot coals. A kettle sat on an iron grid above it, whistling gently.

Adam turned back to face Sheriff Boggs square on, his feet apart as if facing a bully. "Now that you know why I'm here, I think the more important question is, what brings you folks to Barner property this morning? Looks like we're in for a downpour. You don't want to get caught out in a storm."

"Truth be told," replied the sheriff, his face giving away nothing "I expected to find Jimbo squatting on Barner property. I didn't expect to find you with him."

"Both of our good fortunes, then." Jimbo smiled, but his eyes betrayed his expression.

Adam lifted his hand toward the big table where his parents and brothers used to sit and share their meals so many years ago. "Please, Sheriff, have a seat. Tell me the real reason you've come all the way out here to my mother's abandoned cottage on a day like this."

Sheriff Boggs and my father pulled out chairs. "Are you going to join us, Jimbo? It's you I'm here to talk to."

"How did you know Jimbo was here?" asked Adam. "I just discovered him here myself."

"The smoke, same as you. Had a hunch since Jimbo's been eluding me the better part of a week."

Before sitting in the chair next to Popo, I looked into the hobo's still blue eyes. The man I saw reflected there wasn't the same man dressed in rags with the unkept hair and beard, standing before us. He was someone else.

"Forgive my manners, but I've nothing to offer unexpected guests," a sweetness in the hobo's voice. "Made this coffee this morning from yesterday's grounds. It's weak, as you can image." The man held out his mug as if to toast us, then took a sip.

The sheriff glanced at the second tin mug that sat on the table, but said nothing.

"We won't be long." Sheriff Boggs nodded toward the chair across the table from him, a silent invitation for the hobo to have a seat, to engage in a conversation on the same level. Jimbo pulled out the chair and sat down. Adam sat in the chair at the head of the table, where I imagined his father used to sit.

The sheriff cut to the chase. "What do you know about the dead man found in Prairie Creek last week?"

"So much for any further pleasantries." Jimbo smiled broadly and brushed a piece of wild hair from his face. Then he ran his thumb and index finger along either side of his mouth, smoothing his unkept beard. "What makes you think I know anything at all about that..." Jimbo considered his next words. "...unfortunate incident?"

"Jimbo, we've got a storm bearing down on us, and a mile and a half to go on foot to get out of it. If you'd like to beat around the bush, the best place for us to have a long conversation would be in my office. Then we could take all the time in the world. Or you can answer my questions now so we can get to town ahead of the storm. Your choice."

Jimbo paused again to consider his options. "Is this the child who found that poor fellow?"

"Yes, it is. Again, if you want to go on a fact finding mission of your own, I'd be happy to tell you everything I know. But I'd prefer to do that back at my office, where I can put my feet up and drink some coffee myself. I hear Roxy's serving chicken and dumplings today, so you might have to wait in one of my jail cells while I'm over at the Blue and White Café enjoying my lunch since I never miss going there on dumpling day. Or you can answer my questions now so we can all get on with our days, including Mr. Barner here, who I'm sure has more important things to do than chitchat with us."

Jimbo threw his head back again and laughed. "You think your jail cell can hold me?"

Sheriff Bogg's stoic face never cracked, never moved. His mind seemed fixed on the hunt for the truth he'd been chasing for more than a week.

"You win, Sheriff."

That's when Jimbo told us about his encounter with the man I found dead in Prairie Creek.

***

According to Jimbo, Friday afternoon gently dissolved into a tepid evening, with this region of Indiana finally getting a small measure of welcome relief from the onerous August heat.

"I was resting in my idyllic setting in the woods." Jimbo's voice reflected his restful state, as if his mind had returned him to that moment. "The hobo camp stinks more than usual this time of year—the stench of wet wool and unwashed bodies mingling with the blood, sweat and tears of the downtrodden."

He paused as if his thoughts stalled from their telling.

"Go on," urged the sheriff.

"So much penury, so much hopelessness," he muttered. The hobo closed his eyes and shook his head, the travails of his friends heavy on his heart. "Thank God for the generosity of Paul Lockwood and other kind souls."

The sheriff agreed. "Yes, Paul's a kind man."

"I was feeling rather peckish for the sweetness of strawberry-rhubarb pie with just a hint of clover honey on my tongue, so I cast caution to the wind... decided to trust dumb luck. The triumph of hope over experience, I suppose." Jimbo lifted his chin and raised a hand, the gesture a child with the correct answer might use to get his teacher's attention. With a plan to resolve his hunger pangs, Jimbo waited until dusk to begin his brief journey into town.

"No offense, Sheriff, but we travelers avoid drawing the eye of the law, your sort being suspicious by nature. If you ask me, it's a sad way to look at life... questioning everyone's motives but your own."

Sheriff Boggs pursed his lips, offering no objection to the man's observation.

"Of course, it takes longer to get from the camp into town when you travel in the shadows. I was in no hurry... enjoying the time spent with my own thoughts."

When he arrived in town, he found his way to the table behind the Blue and White Café, aware that Friday evening wasn't his best option for a handout. But he hoped the Lockwoods would share whatever they had left at the end of their busy supper shift.

"Though eager for that pie—too much to expect, I suppose—I waited patiently. I remember sitting there, minding my own business, thinking about nothing in particular. (Oh, the pleasures of an empty mind.) In my vague state of consciousness, I became an entranced witness to the breeze's stealth invasion of the spirit-breaking humidity. Such a delight." He sighed heavily. "The alley behind the diner catches the breezes that linger above that old table there. In the winter, the effect is pure hell."

Jimbo took a deep breath and paused again. As the hobo pulled together his thoughts, I glanced around the cottage for any dishes or other evidence he had eaten there. Then I sniffed the air. No lingering aroma of bacon or biscuits, but it also lacked any hint of musty air. I wondered how long the door had been open, how long Jimbo had been inside? Had it been days?

"I figured my first foray into conversation would be with Paul Lockwood, who pops out the back door of the restaurant from time to time to escape the incessant chaos inflicted upon him by the steady stream of loud, hungry widowers, railroaders and sundry other miscreants. Poor man, being married to his job like that."

The hobo said he sat there, his back to the wall of the building, looking out over the alley that cut the city block in two. With most of the downtown businesses closed for the night, Jimbo expected to see no one but for the glimpses of the passersby in the public square, dressed in their Sunday best, streaming toward the Clinton Theater for its evening showing of "A Free Soul."

"I stewed in my thoughts, wondering if the *yokels*..." He spat out the word as he would a bitter herb from his tongue. "...had a glimmer of understanding of Lionel Barrymore's brilliant portrayal of Stephen Ashe, or Clark Gable's exquisite performance as Ace Wilfong... a character for the ages."

Lulled away from his usual vigilance, Jimbo said he suddenly spotted a stranger stumbling up the alley. The man, carrying a leather overnight case in one hand and a walking stick in the other, stepped forward with great difficulty.

"A cane?" questioned the sheriff.

Jimbo's eyes widened a bit and his head snapped back slightly, reminding me of Cory when he shares a detail of one of his shenanigans that he wished he'd left to shrivel away in the dark. Once it passed from Jimbo's lips, there was no recalling it. He simply nodded once and continued his story. "I don't think he saw me at first, hidden in the shadows. But when he drew closer, I asked him the most obvious question: Are you okay, mister?"

The man came to a stop, struggling to stay upright.

"'I've got the worst headache,' he muttered. Then he raised a shoulder toward his head."

I closed my eyes and raised my shoulder to my ear in sympathy with the man. The gesture seemed natural, though it seemed an odd detail for the hobo to include in his telling.

"I couldn't make out his face in the dim light, but I imagined it taut with pain. My first impression was that he had imbibed too much, not unlike our hero, Stephen Ashe, in the film, '*A Free Soul.*'"

Sheriff Boggs rolled his eyes. "Would you mind moving this epic along, please?"

"*Ahh*, you're a man who doesn't appreciate a cliff-hanger. Understood."

"I'm a man who doesn't appreciate getting caught in a downpour."

After an easy chuckle, the hobo continued.

Jimbo invited the man to come take a load off. When the stranger didn't move, he pressed. "Have a seat. I promise not to bite." He pointed to the chair across the table from him.

Once he realized Jimbo wasn't one of Jeffries' upstanding citizens, the stranger hesitated.

"Sit," he insisted, gesturing with his hand.

The man stumbled forward, propped his cane against the table, dropped his overnight case, and pulled out the chair. Then the man fell straight to the ground. Jimbo hurried around the table to help him up, settling him into the chair. The stranger put his head down on the table and groaned.

Jimbo sat back down across from him and waited. A few minutes later, he lifted it and looked over at the hobo. "He thanked me, saying he needed a few minutes to clear his head, and that with a good night's rest, he'd be ready to carry on with his business in the morning."

"What about his cane?" prompted the sheriff. "Do you remember anything about it?"

"Indeed, I do," gushed Jimbo, now eager to reveal the details. "It was an exquisite ebony cane topped by a Niello-inlaid silver crutch handle. Oh, that handle... a work of art, so beautifully ornamented with swirling floral motifs. The cane hailed from the Caucasus region, if I'm not mistaken."

"Okay, I get it... the cane was nice. Do you recall what the man was wearing?"

"Of course I do! One would have to be dead or daft to not marvel at his three-piece herringbone suit and his olive Truman paisley cravat. A rather audacious fashion statement for a hick town such as Jeffries."

Sheriff Boggs pursed his lips and stared at the hobo.

Jimbo beamed with his own humor. "Now, where was I? Oh yes... I said to the gentleman, 'If you don't mind my asking, what business do you have in Jeffries?' He said, 'I've come in search of the most beautiful woman in the world.'" Jimbo added a hand flourish to his story. "The words put a faint smile on his face. 'I let her slip away, thinking someone else could fill my life with love and affection. I was wrong, so I came here to make things right in my life, to find my one true love and convince her to marry me.'"

Jimbo noticed an indentation on his finger that once bore a wedding band. "Did your wife die, mister? Jimbo asked. "The man replied, 'She is quite dead... to me, sir.'"

The man rubbed his head again, then dragged his hand over his left eye, trying to clear his vision.

"Did you hurt your head, mister?"

He replied, "'I fell and hit it on a rock.'" Jimbo emphasized the words. "'Poor judgment on my part. These things happen when you're in a tizzy, realizing that you're madly in love and that love could slip away forever if you don't act. I've been such a fool.'"

"Whence did you originate, sir?" Jimbo asked the man. "He wiped a tear from his eye and answered, 'Hyde Park. Came in on the Wanatah line. The rocking of the train sure whipped my headache into a frenzy. Couldn't wait to get off.'"

"I assume he arrived on a private pullman," Jimbo offered. "A man like that doesn't travel with commoners."

"If you say so." The sheriff's voice sounded sarcastic.

With a satisfied look on his face, Jimbo continued, "I hate to say it, mister, but maybe you ought to have a doctor check you out. I understand Jeffries has an excellent physician. Doc Becker is his name. He fixed up one of my fellow travelers when the poor sot fell out of a tree (drunk, of course) and broke an arm not too many weeks ago. I'm sure Doc Becker will take a look at that bump on your head, maybe give you something to ease your headache." Jimbo gave the man directions to Doc's house and office. "It's not far. Just a couple of blocks past the public square."

"He asked me where the Little Palmer House was located."

The hobo laughed. "That's an easy one. Just follow the delicious aroma of chocolate. They serve a mighty fine dessert there."

Then the man asked Jimbo if he would deliver his overnight case to the hotel? "He requested I let the manager know he'd be checking in after he saw the doctor. Then he said the magic words. 'I'll pay you to do it.'" The hobo's face lit up recalling the offer of payment.

Jimbo agreed to deliver the man's baggage for two dollars. "A small fortune, but I accepted the man's first offer, as my tongue still begged for the sweet taste of strawberries and honey. Oh, how I prayed Mrs. Lockwood hadn't sold her last piece."

With some difficulty, the stranger fished four silver half dollars out of a pouch in his bag. As he staggered away, Jimbo called out to him. "Hey, mister. Who should I tell the manager to expect? The man looked back at me. 'My friends call me Smitty' is all he said."

Jimbo said he waited until the man was well out of sight before retrieving the overnight bag from under the table. He walked to where the alleys crossed mid-block and turned toward the rear entrance to the hotel, checking for passersby where the alley ended in the public square.

"When I got close to the back door of the Little Palmer House, I stayed in the shadows, waiting silently. Finally, that lazy bellhop I often see back there sneaked out, lit a cigarette, leaned his back against the wall, and puffed away. When I was sure he wasn't being joined by any other slackards, I stepped into sight. Surprised to see me, he almost swallowed his cigarette." Jimbo chuckled at the memory.

Jimbo could tell he was about to make a run for the backdoor of the hotel and stepped into his path.

"I need a small favor, brother."

"Nah, nah. I ain't doing a favor for the likes of you." He straightened his brimless cap and squared his shoulders.

Jimbo ignored his comment. "A man named Mr. Smitty will check into your fine establishment in about an hour. He asked me to deliver his overnight case to you for safekeeping. If you take it inside and place it in your cloak room until he arrives, there's a tip in it for you."

"How much of a tip?"

Jimbo pulled one of the silver half dollar pieces from his pocket and flipped it into the air, catching a beam of the streetlight that shone from the end of the alley.

"Sure, mister. I'll take the overnight case inside to the cloakroom. I'll be on the lookout for Mr. Smitty, too."

"He's an important man from Hyde Park. If he finds his overnight case safe and sound with all his belongings intact, there'll be another tip in it for you."

"Thanks, mister. I'll be right back for that tip."

"Good man."

Five minutes later, the bellhop reappeared in the alley. Jimbo pulled one of the silver coins from his pocket and flipped it to him. The bellhop caught it and placed it in his pocket.

"Thanks, mister."

Jimbo slipped into the shadows and made his way back to the table behind the Blue and White Café. "After doing a fellow traveler a favor, my thoughts returned to my hankering for that heavenly taste of strawberry-rhubarb pie. I worried that my distraction denied me of the pleasure of the delicacy, that delightful contrast of flavors between the tartness of the rhubarb with the sweetness of the strawberries and honey. But God answered my prayers."

Sheriff Boggs rolled his eyes.

After enjoying his full meal, including a generous piece of strawberry-rhubarb pie (it was his lucky night) and saying his goodbyes to Paul Lockwood, Jimbo strolled through the alleys to the back of the hotel. Sure enough, within a few minutes, the bellhop made an appearance.

"Did our guest arrive safely?" Jimbo asked him.

"Not yet. I thought he'd be here by now."

"So did I."

Suddenly, the backdoor of the hotel burst open, and the manager called out to the bellhop. "Are you out here again, Bertie? Our guests are calling for you and you're nowhere to be found. Now get back in here and do your job."

Jimbo figured one of two things had happened to Smitty. He either got lost and was stumbling around somewhere between the Blue and White Café and Doc Becker's place, or Doc Becker had taken him in for the night to keep an eye on him.

"Now that it was dark, I could move more openly. I walked the way I'd told the man to go, looking for any sign of him. When I got to Doc Becker's, I didn't see any lights on in his office or in the rest of his place. So I meandered back to the camp, hoping for a spirited night around the campfire. The 'bos didn't disappoint me."

***

After taking a deep breath, the hobo settled back into his chair and took a sip from his mug. I felt the nudge of the hobo's foot as he shifted in the old chair, then glanced under the table to see it tapping nervously.

"Are you satisfied, Sheriff?" Adam appeared impatient with Jimbo's story and our presence.

Breaking his gaze from the face of the hobo, Sheriff Boggs turned his steady eyes on the man. "Now hold your horses just a minute, Adam. Jimbo is filling in a few of the missing details of my case. We won't be much longer."

Adam stood up and walked to the doorway, where he leaned against the frame, his arms folded tightly across his chest. Was he showing us out? The sheriff ignored him.

"Someone spotted you over on South Street on the morning Annie discovered Mr. Smith's body in the creek. Explain that, if you will."

"Ah, my poor Angelina. Discovering such a horror." His sympathetic voice didn't match his playful eyes. I leaned against Popo.

"Let's move this along, Jimbo," Sheriff Boggs urged. "Tell me what you were doing on South Street Saturday morning."

"You have a way of cutting to the chase. Honestly, there's not much more to tell."

When he awoke in his lean-to in the hobo camp, the air was moist and leaning toward chilly. The birds were just warming up for their sunrise concert, calling to each other. With the campfire long burnt out, Jimbo could still see the moon and even the shadows of a few stars in the breaking dawn.

"The first thing on my mind was Smitty, that poor fellow. I imaged he was snug in his bed at the Little Palmer House, sleeping off the hangover that often follows a headache such as his. Being the compassionate man that I am, I wanted to know for sure. So I got myself all gussied up..." Jimbo threw his head back and guffawed. "...and walked toward town. There, near your warehouse, Mr. Ghere, a man has a little shop where he repairs farm equipment, sharpens blades for them when they don't have the time, that sort of thing."

"That's Ralph Edwards," Popo said. "He's been there for as long as I can remember. My father knew him well. He repairs equipment for Ghere-Douglass. A real curmudgeon, but competent and fast. If he's got work, he's in his shop doing it."

"That's the man," said Jimbo. "He's got a telephone on the wall right inside his back door. Seems he had it mounted where the telephone line came into the shop. He has a standup desk there below the telephone where he writes orders with his pencil right on the desktop. When he's completed the job, he spits on his finger and wipes the order away. I've seen him do it."

"I can vouch for that," Popo chimed in. "He's got a nice counter up front, but his regular customers drop off items for repair in the back there. He writes everything on his desktop, just like you said."

"I rapped lightly on the backdoor and heard him grumble, 'Who is it?' I nudged the door open a crack. Once my eyes adjusted to the change of light, I spied Mr. Edwards sitting at his workbench, a double-barreled shotgun propped against the wall... well within his reach. I suspected a shell rested in one of those barrels."

"What can I do ya for?" he asked without looking up.

"Mind if I use your telephone?" I held up my nickel.

He gave me a sideways glance. "Leave it on the desk there."

"I turned my back to the man, so he couldn't hear me."

"Hello, Mr. Edwards," came the pleasant voice of the operator.

"Little Palmer House." I said as little as possible, wanting her to believe I was Mr. Edwards.

When the desk clerk picked up, Jimbo told him he wanted to leave a message for Smitty, who had checked in the night before.

"One moment, sir." After a pause, the clerk informed me that no one named Smitty had checked in.

"Something must have delayed his arrival. I'll call back at a later time."

The sun was coming up, but I walked into town and by Doc Becker's place to see if I could spot Smitty. Curiosity, mostly. I'm a nosy man... I admit it. I found a pleasant spot in that little patch of trees across from his place. Stayed there just long enough to smoke a cigarette and to see the doctor leave with his medical bag. No sign of any doings in his office there, so I figured Smitty didn't make it, or was there the night before and left. By that time, I was ready for my morning nap, so I slipped into the shadows and made my way back to camp."

"I'm confused, Jimbo. Your story seems to be pretty straightforward. I can follow-up and get a few things confirmed. One thing confuses me... why have you been hiding out from me, just as you did when Augie and I visited the hobo camp?"

"Because I don't want the 'bos to think I'm too friendly with the law. They stay crossways with the law, and like it that way. You walked into their jungle, big as life, and they didn't like that even though you left without causing a stink. They feel threatened by you, by any man with a badge."

Sheriff Boggs' face remained expressionless. "Why did you come way out here to this abandon cottage to stay clear of me? Especially since your boys have your back."

"I sneaked out here to get a little peace and quiet."

I glanced at Adam, who didn't react to Jimbo's confession that he sneaks onto his brother's property and sleeps in his dead mother's bed.

"Skeeter was snoring to the beat of his own drummer, and to be frank, Sheriff, I've sensed trouble brewing in those woods the last few days. Something's got the 'bos riled up. They were pointing an accusatory figure toward each other, and I wanted to stay out of their trouble."

Sheriff Boggs stood and straightened himself to his full height. "Thanks for the tip, Jimbo. I'll keep a keen eye out for any trouble out there."

Popo stood and pulled me to my feet. I felt the hobo's eyes on me.

"Sir," I said, "my sister said the man's suit reminded her of a sparrow's feathers."

"Oh, Angelina, you have an astute sister."

"She saw a sparrow on a branch over the place the man lay dead."

The hobo smiled. "Have you ever heard the Legend of the Sparrow?"

The thunder rumbled outside. Popo guided me toward the door.

"Wait! Just another moment, please! I want to hear the Legend of the Sparrow."

Chapter 21

Huge drops of rain chased us along the path through the trees swaying in the wind. Sheriff Boggs led the way, followed by me and Popo. The only words the he spoke as he made the way before us were, "Hurry, Annie. Let's beat the downpour."

I hurried, almost running to keep up with the sheriff, my father close at my heels. I saw the flash of lightning and heard the crack of thunder in the distance, foretelling the summer storm to follow. By the time Popo pushed me up the steps of our back porch, the rain was coming down hard. I panted from our near-run, though goosebumps covered my arms.

Mother stood just inside the kitchen door, handing us towels as we passed through.

"Glad you're home."

Mother draped another towel over my shoulders, then used an end of it to dry my hair. "Was it worth all this?" she asked.

I looked up at her and smiled. "I met Jimbo."

"Well, come on, then. I'll make coffee and cocoa. Gem, Charlie and Bernard have been pacing the floor in the green room, waiting for you to get back... to find out if you learned anything new."

"Bernard's here?" I asked Mother.

"Oh, yes, he's here. As soon as I told Charlie where you'd gone, he dashed across the street to tell Bernard. Once his father headed out on his route, Bernard came directly over to wait with your sister and cousin. He's been part of this from the beginning."

Mother put on a fresh pot of coffee and filled the sugar bowl with cubes. "By the way, Augie, your brother telephoned a while ago, asking where you were. I told him you had to visit the Barner Farm. I hope that wasn't a lie."

"The fact is, we had an interesting visit with Mr. Barner. It just wasn't Joshua Barner."

Before he could elaborate, Gem, Charlie, and Bernard ran into the kitchen. "You're back, you're back!" shouted Charlie.

"Did you get to meet Jimbo?" asked Gem.

"Everyone, just settle down," Mother instructed. "Give them a chance to dry off and take a breath, then they'll fill us in. Now sit!"

As we settled around the table, Gus and the twins joined us. I was certain Gus and Blinn were interested in our adventure to Mrs. Barner's old cottage, although I suspected Cory was more interested in the cocoa Mother was preparing.

Sheriff Boggs gave a rundown on who we found in the cottage, with plenty of *oohs* and *ahhs* coming from around the table. Once he finished, everyone fell silent for a moment, absorbing all he'd said, fitting a few new pieces into the puzzle, confirming a few more, about the Corpse in the Creek.

Mother freshened the men's coffee and sat down.

"Well, Boggy, was Jimbo telling the truth about this Smitty fellow?" She dropped a cube of sugar into her cup and stirred her coffee.

"When you've been sheriff for as long as I have, you develop a sixth sense about these things. My gut tells me Jimbo was telling the truth about having an encounter with that man. The letter the children found confirms much of his story. Did Jimbo tell me the entire truth? That I don't know. It's whatever else that was going on in that cottage today that has my hackles up."

He let that idea settle in.

"Much of what Jimbo told us I already knew." The sheriff's eyes rolled upward, reviewing the facts, putting the pieces together in his head.

"Did you learn his name from the letter?"

Sheriff Boggs looked into Mother's face and nodded once. "I apologize, Maggie, but I didn't want that information out for speculation, by you or anyone else. I suspect Smitty is a nickname for Smith, a common name in this part of the country. The more common the name, the more speculation that can go into it. I didn't need the cud chewing by the locals muddying up my investigation, or my mind." He pointed at his forehead. "I apologize for keeping that letter from you, Maggie."

"What about now? Can I see it? Everyone in this kitchen deserves to know exactly what that letter says."

"I'll bring it over later. I promise."

The sheriff sipped his coffee, at least one burden off his shoulders.

"Jimbo offered a few insights into this mystery that are easily verifiable," he finally added.

"Tell you what, Boggy, once the rain stops and I head over to my office, I'll pay Ralph Edwards a visit to make sure Jimbo's story lines up with what he remembers."

"I'd appreciate that, but wait until we're face-to-face to tell me what you found out. Let's not fuel the grapevine anymore than we have to.

"Mum's the word." Popo touched a finger to his lips.

"That goes for everyone in this room. Sally puts one of her twists on what she hears, and the next thing I know, I'll have a citizen's posse out there at the hobo camp causing a ruckus. I'm close to wrapping-up my investigation. I just have to put my feelers out at the Wanatah Depot and wait. Unfortunately, I've grown impatient waiting for the last pieces of this case to come together."

"Seems to me when a man arrives in one of those fancy Pullman cars, someone at the depot is bound to notice."

"You're right, Maggie. Someone knows who that man was. I just gotta ask the right person the right question. I'm heading to the Wanatah Depot when I leave here."

"If that man was there, Oscar Klopfer will know," Mother added. "He keeps a close eye on everything there."

"He's an attentive station master," agreed the sheriff. "He's been at it a long time. After I speak to Oscar, I'll stop by the Little Palmer House to chat with Arnold Grayson." He grinned ear-to-ear. "I'm looking forward that conversation almost as much as I look forward to your pie, Maggie. Almost."

"Annie, what did you think of Jimbo?" Charlie asked me. "Was he scary?"

"No, he wasn't scary. Mr. Barner was a little scary, but not Jimbo. He looks like a hobo on the outside, but when you look into his eyes, he seems to be somebody else."

"Isn't that true of all these hobos?" asked Mother. "Prior to their Great War involvement, they were all different people. I can't image being surrounded by war with your friends dying around you and not coming out a changed man."

What Sheriff Boggs said next shocked everyone. "If I were a betting man, I'd bet Jimbo hasn't seen a single day of war." Then he stood to leave. "The rain is letting up. I want to get on over to the Wanatah Depot."

"I'll walk with you." Popo turned to Mother. "I've got a stack on my desk to review, so don't hold supper for me."

Then Popo turned back to Sheriff Boggs. "Just something else to add to the stew... Joshua is too busy this time of year to entertain company. He's scrambling to get everything in order before the harvest."

"Like Uncle Maddy?" I asked.

"Exactly, except Joshua's farm is about four times the size of your uncle's. One of his men told me last week that Joshua was expanding his main pastures and building a mill on top of the regular maintenance he does. He's in no mind for his big city brother to drop by for a visit."

"That begs the next question: Would Joshua send his brother out there to the cottaged unarmed to investigate? At the very least, he would have spared one of his farmhands to go along."

"You're right, Boggy."

"Adam's presence in that cottage with our hobo is a mystery for another day. Let's get going before it pours again."

***

Gem and I dried and put away the breakfast dishes. I waited impatiently as my sister swept the kitchen floor. On most late summer days, Mother would send us out to the garden to pick vegetables for supper, but the heavy rain kept us indoors.

My brothers, Charlie and Bernard, left to feed Old Barney, Belva, and the chickens, and to clean up the barn. As Gem put away the last pan, Mother stepped back into the kitchen. "This rain has cooled down the upstairs. I'm going to put Thea down for a nap and work in my sewing room for a while. I've got a pile of mending to do, and I want to get the patterns for your new school dresses laid out. The first day of school is just around the corner. When the boys come in, tell them to stay inside until this storm passes."

"We're going to play games in the green room," replied Gem.

Mother nodded her approval.

The coolness of the green room struck me when I opened the door. Rather than get the checkerboard and Rook cards out, I sat in the window seat, watching the rain pick up and the wind rattling the treetops. I thought about Gem's sparrow and hoped it found shelter.

Just as Gem returned with her diary and pencil, the boys thunder into our enclosed back porch, stomping their feet to shake the water from their heads and clothing absent their usual verbal commotion. When they filed into the green room, Gus turned on the big Zenith radio, but too much static made it impossible to tune in to WLS out of Chicago.

"Sheriff Boggs should be able to put a name to the Corpse in the Creek before long, don't you think?" asked Charlie.

"Smitty." I pulled my legs onto the window seat and wrapped my arms around my knees. My cousin came over and sat next to me.

"Sheriff Boggs thinks it's a nickname for Smith." My brother smiled at me. "The sheriff is going to find out who he was."

"Do you think the sheriff had enough time to get to the Wanatah Depot before the downpour?" I asked.

"I doubt it. He and Popo probably got wet if they didn't hitch a ride with someone."

"Lawzy me. Pops an' ol' Cooter, they's out yonder in it, too!" Bernard gazed out the window where he could get a glimpse of South Street. Branches from some trees were scraping the windows and the side of the house.

"Annie, how it is you got to go with Sheriff Boggs and Popo to the cottage this morning?" asked Charlie.

I thought for a moment. "I heard Popo and Sheriff Boggs talking early this morning, so I went outside. When I saw the smoke rising from the direction of the Barner Farm, I just knew that's where Jimbo was hiding from Sheriff Boggs. I don't know why he and Popo let me go with them, but they did. I would have followed them if they'd left me behind."

Cory paced back and forth a couple of time before asking me, "What was it like, Annie? Finding those men in that old cottage?"

"Jimbo didn't seem too surprised to see us, but Adam Barner sure did. He was dressed like a farmhand, but he's not nice like his brother. Jimbo might look like a hobo, but he talks all uppity."

"Uppity?"

"Yeah, like Mr. Grayson at the Little Palmer House. Aunt Lo taught me that word." I sighed, wishing my aunt was here.

Gus ignored his younger brother. "What else, Annie?"

"Jimbo called me Angelina. I remember thinking it was a pretty name and wished it was my real name."

Charlie smiled at me. "Your name is part of it. The A and N at the beginning, and the N and A at the end. Popo calls you Angel, so it's like your name."

"When we got there, Jimbo was drinking coffee from a tin mug, and there was another mug on the table. There was a bucket of coal by the fireplace."

"What fer would they be a-keepin' a pail o' coal in that there forsaken shack?" asked Bernard. "'Less'n it ain't forsook, after all."

"Oh, and he told me the Legend of the Sparrow."

Gem, who had stretched out on her belly on the floor to write in her diary, sat straight up. "What legend?"

I told Gem everything Jimbo had told me.

Chapter 22

The Legend of the Sparrow

In the vast expanse of the Indiana prairie during the 18th century, where the grass whispered secrets to the wind and the sky stretched endlessly above, there lived a man of the Miami tribe, who was known among his people for his wisdom and kindness. His name was Awan, which meant, "He Who Speaks to the Wind." Awan was revered not only for his wisdom but also for his attire, which mirrored the colors of the earth and sky. His garments were adorned with intricate patterns that reflected the hues of the prairie—deep browns, vibrant greens, and the brilliant blue of the sky at dawn. But most striking of all was his cloak, which bore the colors of the sparrow's feathers: a rich brown like the earth, streaks of black like the shadows cast by the clouds, and a pure white breast that gleamed like the first snow of winter.

One day, as the sun dipped below the horizon, painting the sky in shades of orange and purple, Awan did not return to his village. His people searched for him, calling his name into the twilight, but he was nowhere to be found. It was only as the first star appeared in the night sky that they found him, lying still upon the prairie, his spirit having departed for the sky world.

The people of the village mourned deeply, for Awan had been a guiding light in their lives. As they prepared him for his journey to the ancestors, something miraculous occurred. A sparrow, its feathers mirroring the colors of Awan's cloak, appeared from nowhere. It circled above the mourning crowd, its white breast gleaming under the moonlight, before descending to perch upon Awan's chest.

The appearance of the sparrow was no coincidence. In many cultures, sparrows are seen as symbols of hope, community, and the resilience of the spirit. They are known for their hardiness, their ability to thrive in a variety of environments, and their cheerful song, which brings joy to those who hear it. The sparrow, with its white breast and feathers that mirrored Awan's clothing, was recognized as a sign that Awan's spirit lived on, watching over his people and offering them comfort in their time of grief.

The legend of the sparrow and Awan spread throughout the land, a tale of enduring love and the unbreakable bonds between the earthly and the spiritual worlds. It was said that the sparrow had been sent by the Creator as a reminder that even in death, we are never truly parted from those we love. The sparrow's presence reassured the people of the village that Awan's wisdom and kindness would always be with them, like the whisper of the wind through the grass and the warmth of the sun upon their faces.

And so, the Legend of the Sparrow became a cherished story among the Miami people, a story of loss, love, and the eternal cycle of life. It reminded them that in every ending, there is a new beginning, and that the spirits of their ancestors are always close, guiding them with the wisdom of the ages.

The sparrow, with its simple beauty and its song of hope, became a symbol of the enduring connection between the physical and spiritual worlds, a reminder that love and wisdom transcend the boundaries of life and death.

Chapter 23

My scream shattered the peaceful rest of my family. "Who are you? Who are you?" I demanded.

I felt Gem's arms around me, keeping me from falling out of bed in the fog of my nightmare.

"*Shh, shh, shh,*" she whispered, her face buried in my neck now wet with her tears.

"Anna, sweet Anna," Mother uttered as she rushed into our bedroom. "My baby girl, carrying the worries of the world on her shoulders."

Mother lifted me into her arms and sat down on the edge of our bed. Bits of reality slipped into my thoughts... Gem crying into her pillow, Popo's hand on my back, Gus standing in the doorway... though I couldn't shake my confusion.

"Who are you?" I screamed again.

Popo's gentle voice broke through the fog. "Tell me who you're talking to, Angel."

"The man who pulled me from the creek, the man who was dead in the creek!"

"They're not the same, Angel. They're two different men."

I raised my face toward my father's voice. "Different?"

"I'll stay with Annie until she goes back to sleep. Go back to bed, Maggie, and get some rest while you still can. Something tells me we're rushing headlong into one hell of a day."

***

I awoke to a light rap on our front door. Gem sat up next to me. We both pulled ourselves up on our knees and looked out the window. In the glow from the first crest of sunlight, I could tell the clouds had rained themselves out, and the day promised to be a beautiful one.

Gem jumped out of bed, ran across the hallway and down the stairs. I wasn't far behind her.

"Good morning, Maggie. I saw the lights on. I hope you don't mind me stopping by."

"Good morning to you, Boggy. It seems my daughter had to discover a dead man in the creek to rate such a high calibre visitor, especially this early in the morning."

Mother pulled the door open, an invitation for the sheriff to come in.

"I've got a pot of coffee on. Are you interested?"

"You know I am. And see here, two of my favorite girls are up and at 'um."

Gem and I gave Sheriff Boggs a hug.

"Come on, the coffee's almost ready. Augie should be down in a few minutes. You two can walk into town together."

Mother set a cup and saucer in front of the sheriff and poured his coffee. Then she pulled out a chair and sat down.

"So tell us. What brings you to our street this time of morning?"

He eyed Gem and me for a moment.

"In answer to your question, Maggie, the reason I'm here so early is to deliver Gerald home in time to start his route. That's when I thought I'd stop by, seeing the lights on, and all."

"Gem and Annie will keep their mouths shut, if that's what you're worried about. Isn't that right, girls?"

We both nodded.

"Your girls are special, Maggie. You know that."

"If you're having breakfast with my beautiful Ghere girls, you might enjoy the entire set." Popo stood in the doorway with Thea in his arms.

"Now that you mention it..."

The men exchanged greetings that included kisses on Thea's cheeks. After Popo sat down, he handed my baby sister to Gem. Mother got up and retrieved another cup and saucer from the shelf, placed it in front of Popo, and filled it with steaming hot coffee.

"Boggy was about to tell us why he's here this morning," Mother smirked.

"I hope it has nothing to do with that creek," groaned Popo.

"Not today, Augie."

Sheriff Boggs dropped a cube of sugar into his coffee and stirred it, adding a full pour of cream.

"Best I give you a quick rundown on last night's events. Gerald Thompson got into a scuffle at the Sleepy Owl Saloon. Tempers were already hot over Jeffries being without its ice because of equipment problems at the icehouse... again. And the iceman happened to be sitting right there to take the heat."

"Warm beer does that to a man," quipped Popo.

"Does Bernard know?"

"Yes, Maggie, he knows. He was sitting on their porch step when we walked up. I turned Gerald over to his son since Bernard seems to be the only adult in that household."

Then the sheriff gave us a rundown of evening's events.

***

Last evening Biddy Ann hadn't been gone five minutes when the bartender from the Sleepy Owl Saloon burst through the door at the sheriff's office.

"Come quick, Sheriff. A fight's about to break out!"

When the two men stepped out of the sheriff's office, the loud voice of a man in a one-sided argument echoed across the public square, the cheers of a crowd egging him on. The bartender took off running for the saloon, with the sheriff right behind him.

Sheriff Boggs' eyes hadn't quite adjusted to the dim saloon when he spotted who he thought was Gerald Thompson sitting at the end of the bar. Then a ranting man, scrawny as a beanpole, stepped into view, spewing insults at Gerald while poking a spindly finger in his chest. Gerald looked down at the irksome finger, his silence misinterpreted as a sweet and kind demeanor, though the sheriff had learned in his few encounters with Gerald that the giant-of-a-man simply found it easier to get through life by ignoring the perpetually caustic condition of mankind. Thinking he had the advantage, Beanpole escalated his dissatisfaction about the icehouse equipment failure and its delete-rious effect on the temperature of his beer by peppering his mount-ing verbal attack with some rather off-color language... the kind that would have made Attila the Hun's wife blush. Then Beanpole did the unthinkable... he gave big ole Gerald Thompson a big ole push on the chest. When Gerald stood up, his barstool tipped over, and his beer glass crashed to the floor. "That was the moment I wished I'd taken Biddy's advice and gone home early for some much needed rest. But don't tell her I said so.

"In this life, you see what you want to see," continued the sheriff. "In that moment, I saw a drunken gasbag and wouldn't have been surprised if that's was Gerald's exact view of the situation."

"It didn't stop you none from drinking your fair share," Gerald offered, a feeble consolation.

All of Gerald's composure flew out the window when Beanpole yelled, "Not only can't you do your job, Iceman, your wife's a *hussy*." He'd spat out the word hussy as if he were trying to get a dry fur ball off his tongue. That lit up Gerald like a firecracker. He didn't cotton to anyone besmirching his wife's reputation, although he hadn't spoken a word to her for going on three years. No point, in Gerald's mind, since he often found himself on the wrong side of reason.

Gerald puffed himself up to his full stature. In the dim light, he looked like a grizzly, which caused the rest of the saloon patrons to gasp and step back.

"Say it again," growled Gerald.

Any man in his right mind would have recognized the threat, understood a pummeling was in the cards for him. But being a drunkard, Beanpole took a step back, due more to his unstable state than any good sense. When he opened his mouth to meet Gerald's challenge, he'd forgotten the word.

That's when the sheriff entered the fray, stepping smack dab between the two drunks. The possibility drifted across his mind that he may soon have the second dead man in two weeks on his hands. He wasn't sure which one of the three men it would be, though he figured the odds favored Beanpole.

"Good evening, gentlemen." The sheriff spoke slowly, hoping for a moment of calm to evaluate his tenuous position. "Take a breath, Gerald. He's not worth the time you'll spend in jail." The sheriff held a calming hand out toward the big man's chest, but didn't dare touch it for fear it would be confused in the heat of the moment as Beanpole's.

That was precisely when Beanpole remembered what he was going to say. Standing on his tiptoes, he looked over the sheriff's left shoulder and hissed, "Hussy."

Reacting in self-defense, the sheriff raised his left arm to protect his face. Gerald's punch winged his elbow, causing the sheriff's open hand to smack his own nose, but the result of the blow didn't end there. The punch landed slightly off target, thank God, but clipped Beanpole's nose and knocked him to the floor.

"Two bloody noses with one punch," someone called out. A cheer rose from all corners of the saloon.

"Go get 'em, Gerald!" his friends cheered.

That's when Beanpole got to his feet. A bit more sober now, he drew his sleeve across his nose, reevaluated his odds and chose flight over fight. He turned to run out of the saloon, but discovered an arc of regulars—all friends of Gerald Thompson— surrounding him.

"He's been trouble since he walked in here this evening. What do you want us to do with him, Sheriff?"

"Well, Willie, I'm thinking they both need to cool off in a jail cell for the night so they don't take up their quarrel outside after I go home. It just so happens I have two cells."

The sheriff took Gerald by the arm. "If a couple of you boys will escort Beanpole over to the jail, I'd be mighty appreciative."

Two men grabbed him and led the way through the saloon to the door. The sheriff followed with Gerald. Then he turned and said in his loudest, authoritative voice, "If you boys would spend a little less time drinking and a little more time at home on your knees praying, maybe your lives wouldn't be such a living hell."

"Said the man who's married to the most beautiful woman in Jeffries," shouted a voice in the back. "Hey Sheriff, wanna sit down and discuss that over a warm beer?"

All his friends laughed.

"Shut up, Homer, before I lock you up for being stupid."

***

"That's quite a story, Boggy." Mother crossed her arms over her chest.

The sheriff grinned. "That was my first telling of it," he chuckled. "I promise it will get better as the day goes on."

Mother pursed her lips. "I still believe Gerald is a sweet and kind man." Mother looked at Gem, then at me.

"What happened to Beanpole?" asked Gem. "Did you walk him home, too?"

"Nope." Sheriff Boggs shook his head. "Beanpole is a farmhand out at Barner Farm."

"Dean Poole." Popo corrected.

The sheriff looked at his friend. "How do you know Dean Poole?"

"I bump into him now and again when I'm out at Barner Farm on business. Nice fellow, when he's sober."

The sheriff pursed his lips. "Makes sense." Then he picked up where he left off. "After getting Gerald tucked in for the night, I got to work cleaning up Dean's nose, as well as my own. We decided I'd lost the most blood. Then we had a friendly conversation. I convinced him to let this thing go, not to pursue any further recrimination, legal or otherwise, against Gerald, because if he did, I'd tagged him as the reason the town and Barner Farm was without their iceman, suffering in the heat in the coming days."

"Oh, boy. That was some threat."

"About two o'clock this morning, Dean got that look in his eye."

"What look is that, Boggy?"

"The look that told me he was about to puke all over Biddy's nice, clean jail cell. So I unlock his cell real fast and sent him out the door toward the Little Palmer House." A broad smile crossed his face. Mother chuckled. "By then, Gerald was sleeping like a baby, except for the snoring. I left him be, knowing he had to be out early this morning delivering ice. I walked home, got cleaned up, and took a nap, and headed back to the office before sunup."

"What a night!" sighed Popo. "If it's not one thing, it's another."

***

"Girls, go upstairs and get ready for your day," instructed Mother. "Take Thea and get her washed up and dressed, too. Then wake up the boys. I want them to get their chores out of the way before it gets too hot."

As Gem dressed Thea in our room, she told me to wake the boys. When I stepped into the hallway, I heard the voices of Sheriff Boggs and Popo, below me. I paused at the top of the staircase to listen.

"...so Ralph Edwards confirmed Jimbo's story. He visited Edwards' shop, just like he said, and called the Little Palmer House to check on this Smitty fellow."

"I'm glad that checks out. Before I go, I wanted to pass on something else. You can share it with the others later."

"What's that, Boggy?"

"Yesterday, I retrieved Smitty's overnight case from the Little Palmer House. Boy, I'll tell you, that took some doing, with Arnold Grayson still nursing his grudge against me for not throwing Paul Lockwood and those railroad rascals in jail and throwing away the key."

"It's early. I've got time for another story." Popo prompted.

Chapter 24

After the conversation with Jimbo in the old cottage in Barner's Wood, Sheriff Boggs returned to his office. Wet to the bone from the rain, he arrived to find Biddy Ann on the telephone. Taking one look at her boss, she pulled a rag from her desk drawer and handed it to him as he walked through to his private office in back.

There, he dried his face and hair the best he could, then pulled off his boots and sat down for a good long think.

Finally, noticing a break in the downpour, he put on his boots and walked out of his private office.

"Anything new I should know about, Biddy?"

"You up for the story of how the Myers' dog ate one of Widow Winslow's prized chickens?"

"They're prized chickens now, huh?"

"You want the story or not?"

"Nope. I'll be over at the Little Palmer House if you need me."

"Bring me a brownie when you come back."

Mrs. Thompson had her hands full trying to keep the hotel's lobby clean and dry. When the sheriff strode into the hotel, Mr. Grayson ran about, shouting orders and pointing to this and that. His staff appeared too busy trying to take care of all the previous tasks their boss had assigned to notice his latest tantrum.

When Grayson spotted the sheriff blocking his doorway, he composed himself, crossed his arms across his chest and stood, legs apart, as a sentry refusing to allow the lawman to take a step further into his castle.

In his most condescending voice, he said, "Good afternoon, Sheriff. To what do I owe this most unexpected and unwelcome visit? Perhaps you're interest in dining with that foul Lockwood fellow, or a couple of raucous railroaders in my fine establishment."

"I believe, Mr. Grayson, you possess something I want."

"And what might that be, Sheriff?"

"Evidence in the Corpse in the Creek case."

The chaos in the hotel lobby came to an immediate standstill.

"While I assure you, sir, I am not in possession of any evidence, perhaps we should take this conversation into my office, away from prying ears."

The hotel manager led Sheriff Boggs through a door behind the counter to his small office. It was meticulous. Stacks of squared-up paper lined his desk, and a row of sharpened pencils lay within easy reach. He pointed to the only guest chair in the room where Sheriff Boggs sat down.

"I must say, you smell a bit like wet wool this afternoon." Mr Grayson sniffed dramatically and lifted his nose into a higher altitude.

"My socks got wet chasing down some criminals to keep the town... and your hotel... safe."

"I sincerely doubt that. Your reputation for arresting criminals in this town appears lackluster... or rather, nonexistent."

"I run a tight ship." Sheriff Boggs crossed his legs, placing one foot on his knee where the aroma provided a more immediate impact on the manager's senses.

With a finger to his nose, the manager asked, "Now what's all this talk about evidence?"

The sheriff told him that someone gave the bellhop who worked last Friday evening the dead man's leather overnight case to store in the cloakroom before he checked in.

"That bum. I fired him for sneaking out the back door to smoke too many times. That young man was poor-mouthing when he came in here begging for a job, yet I suspect he spent every dime he made from his tips on tobacco and rolling papers. With that stock market crash of October last, you'd think he'd find a better way to spend his money."

The sheriff nodded. He allowed the lengthy silence to settle over the small office. The sheriff pulled on the heel of his boot to give his wet sock a little breathing room.

Finally, the sheriff insisted, "Let's have a look in the cloakroom, Mr. Grayson. You can wait me out all day, if you like, in which case I'll need to take off my boots and dry out my socks on your desk." The sheriff leaned forward and patted a clear corner.

The manager took a deep breath and immediately regretted it. "Certainly," he coughed. Turning his head to catch his breath, he continued, "I have nothing to hide. As I've said, this upstanding establishment is not harboring any of your so-called evidence."

The sheriff stood up, opened the door, and led the way back to the lobby.

Arnold Grayson pulled a key from his pocket and unlocked the door to the cloakroom. "We are very serious about protecting our clientele's belongings here at the Little Palmer House, as you can see," huffed the manager.

Coat racks lined both sides of the small room. Sheriff Boggs inspected the floor under the clothes, dragging a hand along their hems. "Who does this belong to?" he asked, pointing to a leather satchel.

"That belongs to a gentleman who is enjoying his lunch in our dining room while he awaits his train's departure."

"And that one?" The sheriff pointed to another lone travel case.

"We are holding that for a woman who went off with her sister. She'll be checking into her room a bit later."

He pointed to a third bag under the coats near the door.

"That one belongs to..." Mr. Grayson paused. "To be honest, Sheriff, I don't know who that one belongs to."

"How long has it been here?"

"A day or two, maybe," guessed Mr. Grayson.

"I'm betting more than a week, sir." Sheriff Boggs knelt on the floor and pulled the overnight case into full view and opened it.

Mr. Grayson looked shocked. "I didn't know it was here."

"You disappoint me, Arnold. I thought you knew everything."

"Perhaps you can leave the hotel's name out of this."

"Perhaps you can stop storming over to my office on a whim to complain about whatever's got your goat. Pettiness doesn't become a gentleman, Arnold."

After Sheriff Boggs opened the overnight case, he examined the contents. He looked at the tags on the clothing. "I'd hire that bellhop back, if I were you."

"Why's that?"

Sheriff Boggs pulled a wad of cash from the inside pocket. "Because this is still in here. This amount of cash could have changed that boy's life."

Arnold Grayson pursed his lips and nodded. "That amount of cash could change anyone's life."

"Sometimes a little compassion goes a long way, Arnold."

"Like with Paul Lockwood and those two boys from the Nickel Plate?"

"Something like that."

Sheriff Boggs pulled a small box from the bottom of the case. He stood up and opened it.

"Dear God in heaven!" Mr. Grayson exclaimed. "Whomever that ring was for must be one special lady."

"I need to find that special lady, Arnold. Anyone come to mind?"

The two men talked about the case and the ring for several minutes.

"How are the Ghere girls doing?" Mr. Grayson asked.

"Gem, the oldest, seems fine. Between you and me, little Annie has me concerned. She's keen on being involved, and frankly, able to put pieces together that the rest of us miss. But not knowing who the man is tears her apart inside. Her sheriff needs to get this case solved so Annie Ghere can be a child again."

The hotel manager placed a hand on the sheriff's arm. "I apologize for being a horse's behind," he said. "If I can be of any further help to you, please let me know."

The sheriff closed the ring box, tucked it back into the overnight case, then picked it up.

"If someone comes looking for that..." The hotel manager pointed at the overnight case. "...what should I tell them?"

"Tell them to come see me. In fact, that might be a good time to walk that person over to my office yourself. Biddy and I will be happy to see you."

The sheriff walked out of the cloakroom, then turned back to the hotel manager. "Speaking of Biddy, she could sure use one of your brownies."

"Coming right up. It's on the house. In fact, I'll make it two."

"Much appreciated, Arnold. Much appreciated."

Chapter 25

"Are you sure you want to do all this, Maggie?" Popo placed his fork on his plate and pushed it away.

"I'm sure." Mother pulled out her chair opposite Popo's at the kitchen table, sat down, and picked up her pencil. "It is your mother's birthday, and I think a little celebration is just what the doctor ordered. I've heard enough talk about death. It's time to bring some joy and laughter back into this house, don't you agree?"

Gem and Charlie nodded enthusiastically. "Annie, Charlie and I get to go downtown to Thrasher's to buy MaMaw a birthday gift!" Gem noted.

"When your chores are done," Mother insisted.

"When our chores are done." Gem sighed and looked into her plate.

"Is my beloved mother going along with this plan of yours?"

"She is." Mother nodded as she tapped her pencil on the list she'd made.

"I hope you're the one dealing with my sister when she returns from Wheaton." Popo pulled the spoon from his coffee and took a sip. "She doesn't like missing any celebration she can be the center of."

Mother chuckled. "In this circumstance, LoRetta will understand. Besides, she and MaMaw plan to take their usual foray to Indianapolis when she returns. They spend the day window shopping..."

"...because my sister is flat broke after spending two weeks with her cousin."

"Exactly," continued Mother. "While they're there, two of MaMaw's old friends are joining them for late afternoon tea at some French café over on Illinois Street."

"My old stomping grounds," interjected Popo.

Mother ignored his comment. "They're returning that evening on the last train out of Indianapolis."

"Their trip used to be big doings, before the stock market crashed."

"They make the best of things. That's what we all do... make the best of things." Mother sighed.

"I'm sorry I won't be here today to help you with the preparations. I know it's a lot of work, but things at the office are tight and this *is* a workday."

Mother pursed her lips. "It seems every day is a workday anymore. Don't worry, the children and I will get everything done..." Mother waved her list. "Just be sure you and Karl arrive here by six o'clock."

"Oh, good. I get to spend the entire day with my dear brother, and the entire evening, as well."

Mother smiled. "And don't forget your beloved sister-in-law, Iris. I'm holding the party in the garden, picnic-style."

"Reminiscent of PaPaw's funeral?"

"Not exactly." Mother ran her finger down her list. "No fine china. No candelabras. My flowers speak for themselves from their places in my garden, so no grand arrangements on the tables."

Mother reviewed her menu... ham salad and chicken salad sandwiches, MaMaw's potato salad, wilted lettuce salad. "Tomatoes are out of season, but I think I'll mix a couple of jars I put up earlier in the summer with the last of my cucumbers. We'll see."

"What kind of pie?" Popo asked, his eyes lit up.

"No pie."

"What? No pie?"

"Augie, your mother requested chocolate cake, which reminds me..." Mother looked up at the clock. "I need to get busy making that cake before it gets too hot in here."

"Where are the boys?"

"Gus and the twins are cleaning up the barn and chicken coop. I don't want this party ruined by any unsavory odors."

My mother flipped over her list to review her guest list. "At about half-past five, Gus is going to go down and escort Mrs. Parlett back here. She was delighted to be invited but insists on bringing her five-bean salad. As I recall, it's delicious."

"What's Iris bringing?" Popo teased, his eyes shining.

"Her charming personality and perhaps a large dish of horehound candy."

Gem, Charlie and I groaned.

"I've sent word to Old Man Gregory to come... he appreciates my cooking. I haven't heard back, but I feel certain he'll be here."

"He'd come if you were serving pie."

Mother shook her head. "No pie." Then she added, "Augie, please go by Doc Becker's house and invite him and his wife? Also, would you stop by the sheriff's office on your way to Ghere-Douglass and invite the sheriff?"

"Certainly, Maggie. Should I ask him to bring Martha?"

"Yes, of course. It's been a while since I've seen Martha. And tell the sheriff to bring something else."

"What's that, Maggie?"

"The letter."

With that, Mother began her preparations to bake MaMaw's birthday cake.

"I like cake better, too," whispered Gem.

"You're strange," I whispered back.

***

"Mother, I'm finished cleaning the barn and chicken coop." Gus ran over to Mother, who was assessing her flower beds, and tickled Thea.

"What about the goat pen?"

"Cory is finishing that up now. He and Blinn are going to pull the sheets of plywood out of the loft for the tables. Bernard has extra sawhorses in his barn, if you need them."

"Do you want us to water the garden again today?" Gus asked.

Mother handed Thea to her oldest brother and knelt down next to her largest flower bed, filled to overflowing with a veritable symphony of color and fragrance. She checked the soil for moisture, then gently held one of the papery heads of a cornflower between the fingers of her open hand. The brilliant blue flower with a pink ray in the center... so perfect that it reminded me of the images I viewed through the kaleidoscope in my classroom.

Mother smiled. "I think they're fine for now. You boys did a good job watering yesterday. You've other things to do today to get ready for MaMaw's birthday celebration."

She walked along the stone edge of her flower garden, breathing in its beauty. Then she stopped. "You missed a few there, girls." She pointed to a handful of withered flower heads. Mother tasked Gem and me with dead-heading the entire garden, a job she often did herself.

"We couldn't reach those without stepping on some flowers," I grumbled.

"I think I can reach them," offered Gus. Mother sat down in the grass and reached for her youngest daughter.

I sat down next to her. "See how many I got." I held my basket so she could see the bottom covered with dead blooms.

"I got more." Gem plopped down on the other side of Mother, holding out her basket. "See."

"You both did a wonderful job." She leaned over and kissed Gem's head. "This garden will be the floral centerpiece of this evening's celebration." Then she turned and kissed my head.

My father wore his affection for his six children on his sleeve. He was quick with a hug and a kiss, a compliment, and a word of encouragement. Since my discovery of the Corpse in the Creek, Popo had helped me carry that burden of finding a dead stranger outside our home. He wanted to know the man's name, where he lived, if he had a family. He wanted all those things for me. In that moment of resolution he so craved, he wanted something more, something for himself. He wanted the happy-go-lucky Augustus J. Ghere, Jr. back. He wanted to go about making deals with the local farmers, then letting his brother Karl handle the rest of the business. Being my strength during this time of trouble seemed his saving grace.

Mother was her husband's opposite. Aunt Lo once described her as stoic. She went about the arduous task of rearing her children without complaint. She allowed herself only one indulgence... her flower garden. I didn't understand how Mother, joyful in its presence, failed to recognize it as God's handiwork. I didn't understand why she had so little faith.

"Tell us again, Mother," urged Gem. "What do the cornflowers symbolize?"

"They symbolize hope," she replied. "Cornflowers are so courageous, their star-like blossoms stand up to all the elements of nature."

"There," Gem pointed. "What about the Black-Eyed Susans?"

"I've told you a thousand times," Mother replied. "They symbolize justice, encouragement and motivation. Geraniums are associated with love, peace, joy, and health. Look at the asters! Aren't they beautiful? They symbolize love, wisdom, faith, valor, patience, and elegance. I remember my mother saying that, according to the Greeks, stardust falling to earth created the asters. I understand why they believed that."

Then we sat there in the grass, Gem, Thea and me uttering not a sound for fear of shattering the only genuine moment of peace we'd known for nearly two weeks. Mother and her flowers stilled us when nothing else earthly could. I took a deep breath, my mind drifting to the celebration ahead, to Aunt Lo's return in a few days, and to the onset of the edge of summer, with all its miracles. I wondered if there'd be any new children in my class at school this year and if the new dress my mother was making for the first day would be the prettiest one in my room again. I looked at the deadheads in the bottom of my baskets, then at the magnificent flowers in Mother's garden. The stranger's death was his, not mine.

"My cake should be cool by now. I need to get back to it." Mother stood up with Thea in her arms. Her dress worn, hands red and rough from work, and strands of hair that slipped from her hairpins framing her face. I looked at her standing in the rays of the mid-morning sun, her flower garden behind her. She was the most beautiful woman I'd ever seen.

"You girls finish up here and get cleaned up before you go downtown. I need you to pick up a few things from the grocer on your way back, so take Charlie or one of your brothers with you to carry the bag."

"Charlie!" I shouted, joyfully raising both my arms to the cloudless azure sky. "Let's go." I felt joy for the first time in many days.

Chapter 26

Charlie led the troop of Ghere children up the back porch steps and into the kitchen, each of us glowing in the wake of MaMaw's birthday celebration. Cory held the door as we slid past him with stacks of plates, bowls, and silverware.

"There's not much food leftover," growled Cory. "I could sure use more of Mother's potato salad about now."

"When I walked Mrs. Parlett home, she commented that everyone enjoyed her bean salad," noted Gus. "She seemed as happy as I've seen her in quite some time."

Gem and I headed straight to the basement, me carrying a basket filled with Mother's linen napkins, my sister's arms draped with Mother's best table clothes. "Annie, are you sure you counted those?" questioned Gem. "Mother will need every napkin for Thanksgiving."

"They're all here, I promise."

After dropping off the laundry, Gem and I dashed back upstairs. Our family milled around the kitchen table, not yet ready to let go of the joy and excitement sparked by Mother's last-minute celebration.

"Do you think MaMaw liked the pin we got her?" asked Gem.

"She said it was beautiful, that she felt like a queen wearing it." Mother smiled at her daughter, as she filled the kitchen sink with soapy water. "You and Anna picked the perfect gift for your grandmother."

"That's for sure." Popo walked into the kitchen, a smile on his face. "She couldn't stop talking about it when I walked her home." My father pulled out a chair and sank into it. "It's been a long day."

Mother's blue eyes reflected the happiness that had been missing from her face for quite some time. "Let's get these dishes done and put away," she said. "Then we can all sleep late tomorrow morning."

"Hooray!"

Suddenly, her attention shifted to the doorway, her eyes immediately losing their life.

"Sheriff."

"The front door was open. I hope you don't mind."

"No, no... of course not. I just put water on for tea. Please join us." She turned and looked at the teakettle. Turning back, she asked, "Did you get Martha home safely?"

"I did. She asked me to thank you again. It was a wonderful treat to be included in Mrs. Ghere's birthday celebration."

I looked from Mother to Sheriff Boggs and back to Mother. Both stood motionless, their eyes locked for a long moment. The room fell silent.

Finally, Mother held out a soapy hand. "Boggy, please sit down."

The sheriff patted his breast pocket of his jacket. "You wanted to see this."

The letter.

"It's about time." Mother wiped her hands on her apron, then held one out to receive the letter.

Sheriff Boggs hesitated.

"It just doesn't feel right revealing the man's personal thoughts. I've read it at least ten times and other than learning his name was Smitty, I've come away with nothing else. I do have a new theory about this man's presence in Jeffries, though. Because of his head injury and his disorientation, maybe he got off the train at the wrong stop."

"I hadn't thought of that, but it makes sense," offered Popo with a nod.

"According to Jimbo, the man arrived in a private Pullman car, but I haven't been able to track that down. I spoke to the trainmaster at the Wanatah Depot and he can't find a record of it. So he put out the word on both their Chicago to Louisville and Chicago to Cincinnati lines to locate our mysterious Pullman car."

"What about the Nickel Plate?" asked Mother.

"That's another can of worms." The sheriff shrugged and shook his head. "But regarding the Pullman car, there's another possibility."

"What's that, Boggy?" Popo leaned forward.

"Jimbo was mistaken."

"Or he lied." Suddenly, all eyes were on me again.

"Anna, why in the world do you believe Jimbo lied to the sheriff?" Mother stared at me, a hand on her hip.

"He's an uppity talker."

"No argument here," confirmed the sheriff. "Sometimes he talks like a hobo and sometimes he talks like he's from the most prestigious family in New England. But that doesn't mean he's lying."

I looked down at my feet. "Jimbo uses his hobo words to fool you and his uppity words to let you know he's better than you."

The sheriff's head jerked back. "Annie, why do you think that?"

With my eyes now staring directly into the sheriff's, I answered, "The same way you do, Sheriff."

"The man Jimbo once was, and the man he is, talking out of the same mouth." The sheriff muttered. Of course, he understood what was obvious to a child.

"He's a liar, plain and simple!" I shouted the words.

The tension rose in the room and held us prisoners. From the moment of my discovery, the unknown had poked and prodded at us until all our emotions lay on the surface, raw and bloodied. Despite our brief respite, we still chased the same demons that haunted our unanswered questions since I discovered a dead man in Prairie Creek.

"Anna." I looked at my mother, tears streaming down her face. "Anna, please..."

"No!" My word came from Popo's lips. He held up his hand, stopping Mother from continuing. Then, in his gentlest voice, he urged me, "Angel, tell us why you believe the man was lying."

With my eyes glued on the sheriff, I spoke the words that only made sense to him, Popo, and me.

"It was all a lie... the lock hanging from its hasp, the pot of coal by the fireplace, the extra coffee mug sitting on the table. Mr. Barner's clothing was a lie, and it didn't look as if he was in any hurry to get rid of Jimbo."

My father stood up. "If Jimbo was trespassing, why wouldn't Adam Barner appreciate the county sheriff showing up to handle a squatter in his beloved mother's cottage?"

I nodded once, my eyes glued to my father's. "His boots."

"What about his boots, Annie?" questioned the sheriff.

"I looked under the table and saw his old stained work boots there. He had on a pair of brand new boots... fancy boots, not like the ones they sell at Thrasher's or Woolworth's or the rummage sale." Like mine.

"Adam brought him new boots?" asked Popo.

"The strawberry-rhubarb pie was a lie, too." I continued.

"What?"

"Mr. Lockwood served Jimbo peach pie with ice cream the evening that Smitty came to town." I let that notion settle in. "Even that makes little sense, since his favorite is apple. Miss Roxy always has apple pie. MaMaw told me once that Mrs. Lawrence, who bakes pies for the Blue and White Café, works her fingers to the bone during apple season. She cans hundreds of jars of filling for her Dutch apple pies, her speciality. Miss Roxy always has it. Every day." My voice trailed off. "It's Jimbo's favorite."

"Much of what Jimbo told us has checked out," Sheriff Boggs insisted, his voice now defensive. "What difference does a piece of pie make to this investigation?"

"Jimbo was killing time," Popo muttered softly. "He knew a storm was coming, and every second he talked about what didn't matter ate up the time to talk about what did matter."

"But..." the sheriff paused and closed his eyes.

"You didn't ask him the most important question of all, Sheriff," my voice filled with accusation. "You didn't ask him his real name."

"All the hobos are running from something, running from the truth." The sheriff paced in a small circle. "When I ask for names, they get nervous and usually shut down... don't tell me anything worth knowing. So what if he sprinkled in a few lies with the truth?"

"Or maybe he sprinkled a bit of truth into his lies, just to keep you happy," Popo offered matter-of-factly. "Annie's right, Boggy. When Jimbo ran into your investigation of the Corpse in the Creek, the time for running from the truth was over."

"I don't know the name of the man who pulled Pauline and me out of the creek last winter. I don't know the name of the man I found dead in that creek. I don't know the name of the man who stayed in that cottage on the creek for more days than Mr. Barner cares to admit. It seems to me, Sheriff, if you knew one of those names, maybe the others would be easier to figure out."

I walked over to the sheriff and took his hand. "Did you pull me and Pauline out of the creek last winter?"

"No, Annie, I did not." His eyes moist, his voice strained, he added, "I wish I had so you could put that behind you, but I didn't."

I turned and looked at my mother. "Do you know who pulled us out of the creek, Mother?"

Her eyes locked on mine. Did her head shake subtly? She took a step backwards. "No, Anna, I swear to you I don't know."

I took a deep breath. "My name is Anna Marie Ghere," I thought. It was the only thing I knew for sure.

Chapter 27

"I think it is what it is... a love letter from a forlorn man named Smitty to his beloved. Maybe the keen eyes of the Ghere girls will see it differently."

"What was Biddy Ann's impression of the letter?"

"About the same as mine. Biddy's pretty sharp." The sheriff grinned.

"Biddy is sharp, but seeing things the same as you may not be something she'd brag about."

"That's for sure, Maggie," agreed the sheriff. "That's for sure."

With that, Sheriff Boggs pulled the letter from his pocket, slipped it out of its envelope and handed it to Mother, who read it aloud to us.

My Darling Tee Tee,

I waited at our usual spot in the park, as you requested. You never arrived, though a million times over I envisioned the sway of your perfect walk as you moved toward me where I sat on our bench, my hands quaking, my heart pounding.

At dusk, the air chilly, I called out to you. "Come to me, my love. I have much to say." But you never came, you never sat next to me, your lively and loving eyes never beheld me, never saw the man I'd become since our last meeting. I finally left the park, a broken man.

I was told you'd left, gone home to avoid me and another heartbreak. You didn't know that I'd gone to the park to tell you I love you, that I'm free to be with you now. It could have been a perfect day in your perfect season, with supper at the little café you so adore. We would have laughed and talked about all the worldly things about which you read, and the market crash of last October. (I remember you telling me I need not worry a moment longer about the uncertainties of the world, that I hold the future in the palm of my hand.) Then, as our delightful evening concluded, I would have knelt before everyone in the café and requested your hand in marriage.

I'm here to beg you to be my wife. Your love, your faith in me, that's all I need to be a happy man. Yes, I come from riches and power and influence, but those pale to having you at my side for the rest of my life.

Oh, my darling Tee Tee, don't turn your back on me for keeping a part of myself from you. My life is complicated, and finding you was unexpected. Now I crave the simplicity of loving you for the rest of my life. I never expected to fall in love with you, darling... to love you the way I do. I was wrong to keep my secrets from you, but I promise to make it all up to you.

I imagine awakening in the cool of late summer with you snuggled against my back. I long to sit next to you on a bench in Shakespeare Garden watching you as you marvel at the Vs of Canada Geese overhead making their way south for the winter, and to wander the outdoor market on Maxwell Street in search of your favorite reminders of home.

I was a fool not to realize that from the first moment we meet, you were the one. You have always been the one. Please come to me in the lobby of the Little Palmer House and allow me one last chance to win you over.

With all my love and devotion,

Smitty

As Mother ended her narration of the private letter from the dead stranger to the woman he loved, I choked back a sob that had welled up in my throat. I stepped to my father's side. "Oh, Popo," I whispered as I fell into him.

"What is it, Angel? What is it?" His arms fell around me in a tight embrace.

As he held me close, I looked up into his face, my cheeks wet with my grief.

"Dear child, what's the matter? What is it?"

I whispered the answer. "Aunt Lo."

"What? What do you mean?"

"The woman... it's Aunt Lo."

"What? What makes you think that, Anna?"

I could only squeak out three words.

"Edge of summer."

Chapter 28

On the morning of Aunt Lo's return to Jeffries, the anticipation of the new school year seemed the farthest thing from our minds. A couple days after our conversation with Sheriff Boggs, Mother told Gem and me she needed to pin the hems on the new dresses she'd made us, so we'd be ready to start school on Monday. The task slipped her mind amidst the revelations discovered in Smitty's letter.

The evening after MaMaw's birthday celebration, everyone agreed that LoRetta Ghere was indeed the woman Smitty had sought before an unfortunate accident had resulted in his death. Mother insisted Sheriff Boggs not contact Aunt Lo before she left Wheaton, as she may become too overwrought to travel home after learning of Smitty's death.

"We've waited this long to find out who the man was," insisted Mother. "We can wait two more days. Let LoRetta have her peace, as there won't be much of that when she gets back to Jeffries."

Before leaving for work that morning, Popo instructed his sons to have the carriage hitched up and ready to go to the Wanatah Depot to meet the 4:20 train. He wanted to be there waiting when Aunt Lo arrived. Then Popo left without breakfast. Did he know we planned to be there, too?

Gem picked at her breakfast, though Thea eagerly ate the bits of egg and toast Gem offered her. When our baby sister seemed satisfied, Mother lifted her from Gem's arms.

"I'm going up to my sewing room to finish my mending. I'd appreciate it if you girls would clean up the kitchen before going about your business."

"Yes, ma'am." Gem's voice sounded as if she hadn't slept in weeks.

"I left a note for MaMaw on my desk, asking her to come for supper. Please take it over to her when you've finished in here. If Iris isn't snooping around, let MaMaw know it's important for her to be here when LoRetta arrives. I want to fill her in on what we've learned, so she's not blindsided if an item appears on the front page of the *Morning Times* tomorrow."

Charlie stepped into the kitchen doorway. "Good morning," he grumbled. He pulled out a chair from the table and sat down.

Mother turned back to us. "While you're all together, I want to remind you what Sheriff Boggs asked you yesterday not to breathe a word of what we've discovered about the dead man these last few days to anyone."

Gem, Charlie, and I nodded our heads.

"I hope that by the end of today, our good sheriff will be well on his way to solving this mystery once and for all, and we can *finally* put this tragedy behind us... get on with the school year and our lives."

"Aunt Maggie, can we tell Bernard what happened yesterday?"

Mother thought for a moment. "I suppose so, but remind him that what we've learned needs to stay close to the vest until Sheriff Boggs can get to the bottom of this tragic death."

"Thank you, Aunt Maggie. I felt funny not telling Bernard."

"I didn't see him yesterday. Where was he?"

Charlie looked down at the table before answering. After the sheriff escorted his father home from jail, Bernard decided to join his father on his ice delivery route. After arriving home and settling in Cooter for the night, Bernard is tired. He says the heat exhausts him, so he goes straight to bed. In this heat, he's been sleeping in their barn."

Mother blinked back tears. "Bernard is a good boy, and wise beyond his years."

***

After we washed the breakfast dishes and straightened the kitchen, Gem, Charlie, and I headed next door to MaMaw Ghere's house. Gem rapped lightly, not wanting to raise the ire of Aunt Iris. A moment later, MaMaw opened the front door. "Oh, my goodness," she exclaimed. "To what do I owe the pleasure of this visit from my beautiful grandchildren?"

Charlie wasn't really her grandson, but MaMaw never made the distinction.

Gem hugged our grandmother before handing her the note from Mother. "It's important that you come," Gem whispered.

MaMaw nodded her understanding.

Just as we turned to leave the porch, Iris's voice boomed from the hallway. "What's all this? A little early for a social visit, isn't it?"

MaMaw didn't miss a beat. "Good morning, dear. My grandchildren were just telling me about Maggie hosting a big supper tonight to celebrate LoRetta's return. Doesn't that sound divine?"

"Actually, no. Please give your mother my regards, but Karl and I won't be attending."

"I will tell her." With a wink at MaMaw and a peck on her cheek, Gem turned to leave. "See you soon, Aunt Iris," she called behind her.

With a growl, our aunt closed the door.

***

"Where's my diary?" Gem looked around frantically.

"It's right thar." Bernard pointed at the floor of the barn.

"I hope Cooter didn't leave his calling card down there."

"Gem," Bernard said calmly. "Fust off, ol' Cooter ain't got no hankerin' fer doin' his bizness under that thar bench, no siree! An' second-like, I keeps this here barn neat as a pin."

It was, indeed, neat as a pin. Bernard had slid the big door of the Thompson's barn open. The sunlight streamed in, but the barn, which was shaded by large bur oaks and maples, remained cool. On hot days like this, Charlie, our brothers, and the other neighborhood boys often gathered in the Thompson's barn to pass the time until their families needed them. Today, Bernard invited Gem and me into their sacred place, where we huddled around our mutual secret to nurture our certainty that once Aunt Lo returned, Sheriff Boggs would finally put the mystery of the Corpse in the Creek to rest, once and for all.

While Gem called out the facts she'd recorded in her diary, the seven of us mulled over the what-ifs and wherefores of every aspect of this mystery one last time. Once Aunt Lo returned, we would know who the man was, Sheriff Boggs would notify his family, and the case would be closed.

Except in my mind, there were still other mysteries to solve. Who was Jimbo? Why was he in the Barner's abandoned cottage? What was his connection to the Barners? No one else seemed interested in Jimbo and his past except me... although I was almost certain that our most recent conversation with the sheriff had stiffened his backbone, as well as his resolution, to find out everything he could about the hobo who'd gotten the best of him.

At least, I hoped that was the case.

Act III

Chapter 29

My aunt, LoRetta Ghere, stepped from the passenger car of the 4:20 arriving late from Chicago. Breathless at the sight of her, I gripped Gem's arm for balance. My sister's eyes, wide with amazement, meet mine, then looked back at our aunt.

She wore a simple pink A-line dress with one panel of pink polka dotted fabric sown into the skirt. Otherwise ordinary, the dress bore one of Aunt Lo's typical flourishes... rows of three pink pearl buttons she had insisted Mother sew onto the shoulder seam just above the short set-in sleeves. Aunt Lo added a touch of elegance to her ensemble with a new brimmed flax hat with a bowknot positioned above her right eye.

But what shocked Gem and me was her hair. Our aunt had *always* worn her hair "wound." Some years before, Cuba Spaulding, the owner of Huffer's Beauty School, persuaded Aunt Lo to be her guinea pig for a hairstyle she'd seen in a fashion magazine. As her beauty school students looked on, Miss Spaulding wound thick stands of Aunt Lo's hair, then affixed them to her head in pin curls. What amazed anyone who watched was that when Miss Spaulding completed the "do," not a single bobby pin showed. The hairstyle delighted Aunt Lo so much, she'd returned to the skilled hair dresser every other week since to have her hair washed and wound. Without Miss Spaulding's styling skills for two weeks, Aunt Lo pulled her long brown wavy hair over her right shoulder. Its color complemented the bright red-orange lipstick she had undoubtedly borrowed from her red-headed cousin.

The porter followed the subject of our undivided attention down the metal steps to the platform, struggling with her various bags and boxes. He seemed flustered and out of sorts at her powerful suggestions to be careful with her items. She was the epitome of calmness, an air of cool sophistication enveloping her... until she saw the crowd gathered to welcome her home.

"What in the world?"

As Aunt Lo stepped forward, cautious now, the Ghere clan encircled her. Me, Popo, Gem, Gus, Blinn, Charlie, (Cory remained on the street near the station with Old Barney and our carriage) Bernard Thompson, and of course, Sheriff Clyde Boggs.

"This is quite the reception." Aunt Lo's voice remained calm, controlled. "Well, well, well, even the good sheriff has seen fit to welcome home one of Jeffries' outstanding citizens."

"I have, indeed, Miss Ghere. I hope your trip back to town was enjoyable."

"Quite."

Popo called out instructions to his sons. "Gus, Blinn, load up your aunt's baggage and tell Cory to get it home."

Aunt Lo looked confused for a moment. Then she turned to face Sheriff Boggs, looking up into his emotionless face.

"To what do I owe the pleasure of your presence here today?"

"Miss Ghere, it seems we have a situation that requires your immediate attention."

"I see."

"If you don't mind, Miss Ghere, I'd prefer we talk in private, away from the listening ears and gossiping mouths of the good citizens of Jeffries." With that, Sheriff Boggs extended his arm, which Aunt Lo immediately took.

As the two departed the Wanatah Depot, they said nothing. We followed in silence. Once on the street, Popo gave Cory instructions to take his sister's belongings upstairs to her room, regardless of what his Aunt Iris has to say about it.

"I telephoned MaMaw and told her you were coming. She said she'd be on the porch waiting for you and would shoo away Aunt Iris if she became a nuisance." Then my father turned to Bernard. "Are you going along to help Cory?"

"Nah." That was all he said.

As Old Barney pulled away from the Wanatah Depot with the loaded carriage, Sheriff Boggs resumed his walk up Jackson Street toward the courthouse, Aunt Lo still on his arm.

"Tell me, Sheriff, how is Martha? Beautiful as ever?"

"That she is."

"You never told me how you came to run off with the daughter of the piano player at the Ritz Theater?" Aunt Lo's smile revealed her mischievous nature.

"When the lovely LoRetta Ghere rebuffs you, what's a man to do?"

Aunt Lo chuckled. "I do see your point."

We walked on toward the courthouse and the sheriff's office inside. "Do you want to tell me what this is all about? I must say, you act as if someone died."

"That is the case, Miss Ghere, though it's not anyone in your immediate family."

"Ahh, it's a relief to know that. Am I a suspect in the death of whomever has died?" She threw her head back and laughed at the notion.

Sheriff Boggs smiled. "I hadn't given that any thought, but perhaps I've missed something. To hear your niece tell it, I have missed a few things during my investigation. I've sworn to do better."

Biddy Ann had a fresh pot of coffee brewing when the entourage arrived at the sheriff's office. She stood behind the counter, a faint smiled pressed into her lips as the small crowed followed her boss and Aunt Lo into her little sanctuary. As she poured mugs of coffee for the adults, she looked at the rest of us and said, "Sorry I can't serve you pop and *petits fours* but the sheriff cut my entertainment budget."

"The county cut your entertainment budget, Biddy. Take it up with the mayor."

"The county cut his budget, too." With that, she returned to her desk behind the counter.

The sheriff pulled one of the old wooden chairs that sat along the wall into the center of the room. Gem and I took our places on the bench where we sat with the fan on us not so many days ago when we presented Sheriff Boggs with the letter we found by the big rock down near the Interurban tracks.

"Before I begin my interrogation of this witness..."

"Interrogation?" my aunt muttered, a hand flying to her throat. "Oh, my."

"I wish to remind my deputies..." the sheriff pointed to all of us. "...that allowing you to be here during this conversation is extraordinary. I'm only allowing it because you've been in this with me from the start. LoRetta, do you have any objection to letting your brother and the rest of these yahoos stay while we have a little chat?"

"I want them to stay. I would like to get on with whatever this is so I can go home. It's been a long day."

"In due time, LoRetta." Turning to us, the sheriff pointed a finger and slowly waved it across the lot of us. "Everyone of you must put a lock on your lips. If any of you say a word while I'm questioning Miss Ghere, Biddy will show you the door."

"Or a jail cell," added Biddy Ann from behind the counter.

"Or a jail cell," the sheriff reiterated. "Biddy has been itching all summer to toss someone in the slammer with the rats and throw away the key."

"The sheriff had me a couple of overnighters, but they got away before I got here the next morning," Biddy Ann grinned. I looked at Bernard's face, but he didn't react. "I've been hoping we could take advantage of that special on pickled eggs they're running over at the Airport Diner. Something our prisoners might enjoy, though I'm sure the rats won't have anything to do with those eggs."

"That'd be cruel and unusual punishment, Biddy. Cruel and unusual. Is anyone here up for a stay in our jail with the Airport Diner's pickled eggs on the menu?"

"No, sir." Charlie spoke for all of us.

"Good. This shouldn't take long." The sheriff pulled a chair from along the wall, placed it facing Aunt Lo and sat down. "Gus, would you do me a favor?"

"Yes, sir?"

"Stand by the door. If you see anyone headed this direction, let Biddy know. She'll handle the situation until I'm available." With that, the sheriff turned his attention to my Aunt LoRetta.

"Are you ready to proceed, LoRetta?"

"To tell the truth, Sheriff Boggs, at the moment, I feel like I'm sitting in the wrong pew at church. But proceed, if you must."

"Saturday before last, your nieces were out for an early morning walk, only to discover a body in Prairie Creek there at the South Street bridge."

"Oh, my." My aunt's open hand thumped her chest right below her neck. "That's horrible."

The sheriff pulled the newspaper article from his breast pocket and unfolded it. "No one in Jeffries seems to know who the man is, but I believe you do."

"Me?"

Sheriff Boggs turned the newspaper clipping toward my aunt so she could get a look at his face. As she stared in disbelief at the photo, tears welled up in her eyes and ran down her cheeks. Then her head fell into her hands and she wept. Gem and Charlie were at her side immediately. I stood up, unable to move for a long moment, then ran to her, fell on my knees in front of her and sobbed into her lap. A moment later, Popo pulled me into his arms. "That's it, Angel," he whispered. "Let it out. Let it all out. It's almost over."

Sheriff Boggs gave everyone a few moments to calm down before continuing. Then he instructed Gem and Charlie to return to their seats.

"LoRetta, I'm sorry to put you through this." The sheriff reached over and patted her hand. "Who is this man? What's his name?"

My aunt sniffed and dabbed her eyes with her lace hankie. "His name is Harrison Smith MacDonell."

Sheriff Boggs sat quietly, mulling over her simple answer to the question that had plagued him—had plagued us all—for days.

The sheriff's eyes widened. "The Harrison Smith MacDonell of the Smith Foods conglomerate?"

Aunt Lo nodded. "I'm ashamed to say that for the past five years, I've known him as Harry Smith, or simply Smitty. I met him at the Morton Arboretum five years ago. We have been friends ever since, someone I'd often seen during my visits to my cousin's home each summer. We corresponded through the years."

As Aunt Lo searched her memories, Sheriff Boggs waited patiently. None of the rest of us dared make a sound. Finally, she continued.

"His letters were always friendly. I never understood why he sent them. Perhaps to keep himself on my mind. Our relationship was..."

"It was what, LoRetta?"

"Pure emotion, I suppose. It became a fantasy I enjoyed playing out once a year. I'm ashamed to admit I'm that shallow... that needy. Come winter, when I shivered alone in my bed, thoughts of him drifted away. I was always grateful when I could finally bury the fantasy of an aging spinster in a cold grave. But as I thawed through the summer, I wanted to see him again. I prayed he'd be there in Wheaton to make me feel like a schoolgirl again. The anticipation of seeing Smitty reminded me to savor the sweetness of summer before it was gone."

"Did you see him this year?"

"Yes, I did... the day after I arrived. A couple days later, my cousin's husband, Jean-Claude, learned Smitty's true identity... saw his photograph in the *Chicago Tribune*. He is... was... a socialite, an heir to the MacDonell Food empire, as I said. He was also married and had a son. I thought... nevermind what I thought. When I learned his true identity, I refused to see him again. I insisted Jean-Claude tell him I knew his secret and that I'd gone home."

Sheriff Boggs told LoRetta what he'd learned over the course of his investigation with her filling in the blanks for the better part of an hour.

"Did Smitty ever use a cane?"

"Yes, of course. He told me he'd fallen from a horse when he was seventeen. He cut his forehead and broke his leg. It was a bad break... it left his right leg a little shorter than his left, so he used a walking stick when he was out. He'd often joke about being a bit wobbly."

"Did his cane have a silver handle?"

"Yes, it was lovely. I take it you haven't found it."

"No, LoRetta, that seems one of the unsolved mysteries surrounding this case."

"I assure you, Smitty would not have been down by Prairie Creek without his cane."

"I'll check back with Arnold Grayson. Perhaps we missed it when we searched the hotel's baggage room."

"What about his motorcar?"

The question thunderstruck the sheriff.

My aunt continued, "I know little about such things, but he was quite proud of it. It was a Ford sports coupe of some sort."

"This is the first I've heard of a motorcar," he finally said. "I have a witness who says Smitty arrived by train, perhaps in a private Pullman car."

"That's certainly possible."

I wanted to shout that Jimbo was a liar, but with the threat of being tossed into Miss Biddy Ann's jail cell with the rats with only pickled eggs to eat caused me to hold my tongue.

"Sheriff, I need to go home." Aunt Lo stood up and turned toward the door. "We can resume this conversation another time. I'm tired and want to be with my family now, if you don't mind."

"One more thing, LoRetta." The sheriff handed her the letter Smitty had written her. She read it, blinking back tears, then folded it and placed it in her pocket.

Aunt Lo straightened her back and held her head up, though the sadness in her eyes gave her away. "I did not strike him down, but I must come to terms with my culpability in Smitty's death all the same."

Popo held out his arm to his sister. She took it and leaned into him.

As they approached the door, Sheriff Boggs called out his last question. "Did you love him, LoRetta?"

The personal question stopped her in her tracks. She turned and looked into the sheriff's unblinking face.

"I'm sorry, LoRetta. I had no right to ask you that question."

"You asked me a question, and I will answer it." Her words were soft, measured. "Did I love Smitty? Yes, I did. But I loved the idea of loving him even more. If I could do it all over again, would I change the last five summers, choose a different path? Knowing what this led to, absolutely. I think the important question is, what was I willing to sacrifice for a permanent relationship with Smitty under perfect circumstances? The answer to that is nothing. Absolutely nothing. Does that answer all your questions?"

Their eyes locked. Sheriff Boggs nodded his head ever so slightly.

"If I were twenty years old and still full of adventure, I might have run off with a divorced man," admitted Aunt Lo. "But time, and the love of my family, have created bonds I cannot break now. Marrying Smitty was just a fantasy, one that is now sadly dead." She smiled weakly. "On lonely nights, I still have this." She patted her pocket that held the letter from a man who loved her deeply.

Sheriff Boggs' face reflected my aunt's despair as she contemplated what was, and what might have been. I wondered if he had loved the idea of loving Martha and of her loving him, but it had never blossomed into anything more than a wistful fantasy wrapped in a marriage. Was he sad for Aunt Lo, or for the decisions he'd made in life? Or both?

"If you'd like a little something for the town grapevine, tell Sally this: Smitty's kisses were sweet and gentle, and oh, so polite."

A tear trickled down Sheriff Boggs' cheek.

"Good day. I wish I could say it's been a pleasure." With that, LoRetta Ghere took her brother's arm, and together, they left the sheriff's office.

As we walked toward home in silence, I watched an undulating ribbon of grackles overhead making their way south. I longed for the mundane rut of autumn, and the stillness of winter that would follow.

Chapter 30

"LoRetta, perhaps this is a conversation we need to have after the girls go to bed."

"No, no, Maggie. It's fine. I've nothing to hide from my nieces... or anyone else, for that matter." Aunt Lo dropped a cube of sugar into the tea Mother had poured for her.

Gem and I hadn't left her side since Sheriff Boggs told her everything he'd discovered in his investigation regarding the identity of the Corpse in the Creek. Aunt Lo took in every word, then filled in the blanks with what she knew about the man, and it had been plenty.

Mother sat down at the table next to MaMaw Ghere. We were all eager for details of what transpired during her stay in Wheaton.

"LoRetta, we can do this another time. You look exhausted."

"No, Maggie, I need to get all these conflicting emotions out of me so I can move on. If I'd known what I was coming home to, I think I would have stayed in Wheaton with my cousin."

"Now, now, dear daughter." MaMaw patted LoRetta's hand that rested on the table. "The truth will come out. It always does."

"Sheriff Boggs will see to it," insisted my mother.

"That's what I'm afraid of," muttered Aunt Lo.

"Start at the beginning, dear."

That's when Aunt Lo told us the story she'd kept from Sheriff Boggs.

***

Every summer just before school started, LoRetta Ghere packed her bags with her finest clothing and hopped aboard the Wanatah headed north to Chicago. Just two stops before Chicago, she got off the train at the college town of Wheaton, Illinois. There she spent two luxurious weeks being pampered and spoiled by her beloved second cousin, Louisa Rousseau, also a librarian.

The two became inseparable in second grade, when Louisa's family returned to Jeffries to take over the modest millinery business after the death of Louisa's grandfather. Her family soon discovered Beatrice Augh had a knack for the business. Her unique designs, especially her hand-embroidered wool flower berets, delighted the residents of Jeffries. All the women in town had to have one... or two.

Louisa's appearance at school that autumn was a godsend to LoRetta, who had spent the first five years of her life with her brothers, Augustus, Jr. and Karl. Of course, Miriam Ghere doted on her only daughter, but having three children less than three years apart meant she had her hands full taking care of all her babies. Augustus, Sr. also depended on his wife to nurture their social standing in the community. After founding the wholesale business with his partner, Ernest Douglass, in Marion, Indiana, the two soon moved Ghere-Douglass to Jeffries to be closer to the wholesaler's main customers and to be near the intersection of three major railroad lines. The move meant Augustus depended on Miriam to entertain business associates in their home. That meant the Ghere children's only real playmates were each other.

That is, until Louisa arrived at school only to discover that LoRetta was family. Louisa fit right in with the Ghere clan, and quickly became their beautiful and beloved "red-headed stepchild." Even as a child, Louisa added zest and excitement to their lives. LoRetta learned early on not to linger too long in Louisa's shadow, to step forward and cast her own.

After marrying Jean-Claude Rousseau a decade ago, Louisa moved with her new husband to Wheaton, Illinois, where he had accepted a position teaching literature at the college. Louisa loved the school, which was founded as Wheaton Female Seminary, a pioneering women's college built as a living monument by Judge Laban Wheaton to his beloved deceased daughter. Though Louisa married the name Rousseau, French for redhead, she epitomized the flamboyant implication of her new surname.

Wearing her lush, ginger hair piled loosely on top of her head, strands falling in perfect ringlets to frame her oval face, Louisa turned heads in every room into which she strolled. As she was anything but the quiet, stoic librarian, people eagerly sought her out for intellectual and passionate conversation.

Jeffries, Indiana, was certainly not the place for flamboyant librarians. But during those two short weeks near the edge of summer, LoRetta Ghere left the staid strata of her small town behind to absorbed the intellectual atmosphere of the college campus and expand her very being to become her cousin's reflection, though LoRetta thought herself a slightly dimmer counterpart to the dazzling Louisa Rousseau.

During the first week of LoRetta's stay with her cousin in Wheaton, two of their mutual friends, also librarians, joined them for fun and relaxation before the official start of the new school year.

Stella Deering, of Springfield, Illinois, and Lillian Cox of Indianapolis, added another dimension to their discussions. Like Louisa, Stella and Lillian were married without children. That meant that on those fabulous carefree days they spent together, the foursome spent exactly no time talking about children. That was the one thing about their time together that LoRetta thought sad. She longed to find a husband and have a house-full of children together. She and her friends talked insatiably about finding LoRetta a handsome man to marry, but the topic of children never came up.

"I want a man like Jean-Claude," declared Aunt Lo one day with longing in her voice. "He's kind and brilliant and handsome. Most importantly, he lets his wife be herself."

One evening when Jean-Claude served his wife and their three houseguests hors d'oeuvre from a silver platter, Louisa was expounding on her most fantastical dream. "Imagine, my friends, running off to Paris, living in a quaint chalet on the edge of the art district, taking all your meals at cafes. *Ahh*, that would be the life."

"What about you, Jean-Claude?" asked Stella. "Do you want to run off to Paris as well?"

"No, I'm happy to stay here in Wheaton. I'm developing an exciting course in modern literature on C. S. Lewis and his magnificent works. That's all the excitement I need... besides Louisa, of course."

"Then I'll have to run off without you, darling." Louisa held her head high, pressed her lips together, and showed us her most adorable smirk.

"You would never let her go, would you Jean-Claude?" Stella insisted. "Never in a million years."

"If my beloved wife wants to run off to Paris, who am I to stop her?"

Louisa chuckled. "What would you do without me, dear husband?"

Jean-Claude's face became placid. "I'd simply find someone prettier and marry her."

"You wouldn't dare."

"Try me."

With that, Louisa's houseguests laughed politely, breaking the moment of tension—the only moment of tension Aunt Lo ever witnessed between her cousin and her husband. But the conversation gave my aunt an entirely different perspective on the couple's relationship. Louisa may be confident in herself, but so was her husband.

The day following the women's arrival, Louisa always planned their annual trip to the Morton Arboretum. Soon after Louisa moved to Wheaton, she heard about the plans of Joy Morton to open his seventeen-hundred acres of tree-filled landscapes to the public to enjoy the beauty of plants and nature that inspire the arts. As a surprise to her guests, Louisa hired a motorcar to take them there for the day. The four loved the arboretum so much, they made it an annual event.

For Morton Arboretum's fifth anniversary, Louisa arranged a private tour of the vast library in the Thornhill Mansion, the Morton's private residence. After the tour, the women enjoyed afternoon tea on the home's vast patio with other select guests. As they sat there taking in their magnificent surroundings, they marveled at the changes that had occurred at the arboretum since their first visit.

When their conversation lulled, LoRetta caught sight of four men emerging from a path in the tree line near the edge of the mansion's lush lawn. It appeared one man had fallen. The others laughed and joked as they helped him up, dusted him off, and handed him his walking stick. As they stepped onto the patio, LoRetta heard the man who'd fallen say, "I'm such a klutz."

One of his friends replied, "A stiff cocktail might help you stay upright." They all laughed. The men then sat down at a table on the patio and continued their jovial conversation.

Although there were several people enjoying the day, the man who had fallen set his attention on LoRetta. "Look there, Lo," said Lilian, nudging her friend's arm gently. "See that man over there? He has his eye on you." When LoRetta looked over, the man smiled and waved. After a few moments, he got up from his table, walked over to their table, and introduced himself.

"Good afternoon, ladies." A mischievous smile lit up his brown eyes. "Lovely day, isn't it?"

"Delightful, indeed," offered Louisa.

LoRetta looked past the gentleman at his friends, all smiling with rapt attention on him. She wondered if he'd come over to talk to her and her friends on a dare.

"Please join us... I'm sorry, but what is your name?"

"Smith," he offered. "Harry Smith. My friends call me Smitty." With that, he held out his hand to LoRetta.

"Nice to meet you, Mr. Smith," replied LoRetta. "Would you care to join us?" He readily accepted. Once he settled into a chair next to her, LoRetta made formal introductions.

"These are my dear friends, Stella Deering, Lillian Cox, and Louisa Rousseau. We're all librarians. Louisa is also my cousin."

"Are you ladies from Lisle?" He pointed toward the nearby town.

"Louisa lives in Wheaton. Her husband is a professor of literature at the college."

"Is your husband also a professor, Miss... I'm sorry, I didn't catch your name."

"My name is LoRetta Ghere. I don't have a husband."

"Very good, Miss Ghere. Is your first name L-O-R-E-T-A?"

"No, it's spelled the traditional way, with two Ts," she quipped. "My mother did have the audacity to capitalize the R, although she's never gotten around to telling me why."

Everyone laughed.

"Let me make sure I have this correct. It's L-O-R-E-T-T-A. With two Ts? And is your last name spelled the traditional way?"

"It is, indeed, if your tradition spells it G-H-E-R-E."

"Just the one R then?" he teased.

"That is correct, Mr. Smith. Just the one R."

The witty and charming Smitty immediately enchanted the four women, especially LoRetta Ghere.

By the end of their afternoon conversation, Smitty knew everything about the women, but they learned next to nothing about him. As the time approached for the women to depart for Wheaton, Louisa turned to Smitty and extended an invitation.

"'Tomorrow evening, my husband and I will host a little gathering at our home on campus. We're kicking off a new season of our monthly gatherings just as classes are about to get underway for the year. We talk politic and religion, mostly, the forbidden topics, if you will. Mostly those from campus—professors and administrators—attend these little functions. (Only two women attend regularly, and we earned our way into their inner circle.)" Louisa delivered the word *earned* with the verbal jab of a woman knowledgeable about the forbidden topics. "I schedule the first gathering each year so my friends..." she waved her hand at her companions... "can be part of that conversation and help me give the men attending a run for their money. Oh," my cousin squealed, "I think I just mentioned another of those forbidden topics." The three women joined Louisa's chuckling at her little joke.

"That is a gracious invitation. How could I decline?"

"Wonderful. Your friends are invited, as well." Louisa pulled a scrap of paper and pencil from her pocketbook, jotted down the time and place, and handed it to the near-stranger. "It's been a pleasure, Mr. Smith."

"Likewise, Mrs. Rousseau."

As the women walked away, LoRetta turned for one last look. He was leaning on his walking stick, his right hand up in a wave, smiling.

LoRetta Ghere was immediately smitten.

"That visit to the arboretum will always be my most memorable." Aunt Lo sighed deeply and looked into her cup of tea. "That was the year I meet Harrison Smith MacDonell, though I didn't learn his full name until this summer. That man was so handsome, so debonair, I could hardly take my eyes off him, could barely utter an intelligible sentence." She blew the steam from her tea and shook her head somberly.

"Did he attend Louisa's gathering?"

"He did indeed. That year, he became part of our social circle for the entire two weeks I was there. He fit like a glove, always bringing a fresh perspective to our conversations. He told us he worked in his family business in Chicago, but never elaborated much."

Aunt Lo sighed deeply. "Once a fool, always a fool, I suppose."

After they met, Smitty wrote her letters. "He sent them to me through Louisa, who forwarded them wrapped in her usual missives to me. I'd given him my address, but I thought he'd lost it."

"Did you write him back?" Mother asked.

"I reciprocated by sending my reply to the Hyde Park post office address listed on his envelope. I addressed the letter to Mr. Harry Smith and included my address once more. Despite this, he persisted in sending his correspondence through Louisa. At the time, I couldn't fathom his reasoning for this indirect approach, but now I believe I understand his motives."

Over the next few years, the two always got together when LoRetta went to Wheaton in August to visit Louisa. "We'd have dinner together at some romantic out-of-the-way café, or meet for a stroll through the college campus, talking about anything and everything. He became a fixture at the gatherings held at Louisa and Jean-Claude's in late August, dazzling one and all with his knowledge and wit. I read everything I could that came into the library throughout the year just to keep up with him at our next meeting." Fond memories of Harry Smith took Aunt Lo's breath away. "This year was different."

"Oh, you saw him on your visit to Louisa's this year?" asked Mother.

"I did indeed."

The day after Aunt Lo arrived, Smitty called and invited her to a quaint café in Wheaton, where they enjoyed a delightful lunch together. "He talked of things he'd never mentioned before."

"Such as...?" Mother prompted.

"How I felt about having children. His question came out of the blue, and it shocked me so much that I didn't know what to say."

"Oh, Tee Tee, darling. You don't want children?"

"Yes, of course. I'd have a dozen children if I could. But you know my age."

"Not too old to have children."

"Maybe not, but I am too told to have a dozen."

He chuckled, then patted her hand.

"He asked me if I had a fellow back in Jeffries, if I'd ever consider leaving my family and my hometown. That sort of thing. It was all too out of character of our usual conversations, that I found it difficult to give him straight answers. Was he going to ask for my hand in marriage? I didn't know.

"Smitty seemed to recognize my discomfort. Finally, he changed the subject, returned to our usual exchange on the state of the world and the continuing signs of economic depression. When he dropped me off at the Rousseau's door, he said, 'I'll see you day after tomorrow at the gathering.'"

"Yes, Smitty, you will."

Aunt Lo looked around the table. "That was the last time I saw him until I looked at his dead face in the horrible photo Boggy shoved under my nose."

"What happened next during your stay at Louisa's?" asked MaMaw.

On the afternoon of the big gathering, the houseguests in the Rousseau home were in the kitchen, helping Louisa get ready for the event. LoRetta stood behind the ironing board, pressing the hostess's best linens when Jean-Claude rushed in.

"Louisa, may I speak with you a moment?" he asked his wife.

"Right now? I must finish icing my lemon cake so I can move on to preparing the raspberry tartlets. You know how much your friends love my tartlets."

"Now." Jean-Claude left the room, leaving the swinging door to the kitchen swaying back and forth.

When Louisa returned a few moments later, she looked just as stricken as her husband had earlier. "Dear cousin, I must show you something." She held a newspaper in her hand. "Perhaps we should do this in private."

"Nonsense," LoRetta retorted. "Stella and Lillian will stay."

With the three gathered around Louisa, she handed the newspaper folded open to the social page to her cousin. The headline read, "Socialite Harrison Smith MacDonell Makes Rare Appearance at Company's Annual Meeting and Banquet." The article included a photo of Smitty, smiling for the camera with wife Eva on his arm.

"Would you like to sit down, dear?"

"I think that would be wise."

While Lillian rushed to the stove to put on water for tea, Stella and Louisa helped LoRetta to the table.

"I'm so sorry, Lo, but I felt I had to show you this since we're expecting him to show up here this evening."

The tears were already streaming down LoRetta's cheeks.

"I am truly speechless," she finally choked out. "I actually thought I might entertain a marriage proposal this evening. What a fool I've been."

"What a deceitful cad our Mr. Smith has been. We were all deceived by him, including my beloved husband. What are you going to do?"

"I don't ever want to see him again. If he shows up tonight, please send him away."

Jean-Claude stood in the doorway, his face dark with anger. "I'll handle that for you, my dear LoRetta. Leave it to me."

Louisa rushed over and hugged her husband. "Thank you, my love." Turning to her cousin, she said, "Now you listen to me, LoRetta Ghere. I have a lively few days planned for you, Stella and Lillian. Tonight is just the beginning. Because I am your hostess who went to great effort to plan your stay, I expect each of you to dab on a little rouge, don your finest dresses, and be everything I promised my other guests you would be... charming, engaging, and above all else, brilliant."

"We appreciate all you do for us every year, Louisa. I know my few days here are the highlight of my year," offered Lillian.

"I totally agree," added Stella.

"Lo, we know you are hurting, but there's plenty of time for tears later. I want you to enjoy the rest of your stay here. Did I mention we have tickets for a live performance of Bob Hope at Blackstone Theater on Friday night? I hear he is marvelous."

As LoRetta prepared for the gathering that night, Jean-Claude tapped on her bedroom door. "I'm sorry, dear cousin, but Smitty is begging for you to speak with him. What shall I tell him?"

LoRetta felt the pain of her loss rising in her chest. "Tell him if he'll go away quietly, I'll meet him at our favorite bench in Wheaton Park in the morning at ten o'clock."

"But you'll be on the train to Chicago at ten o'clock," Jean-Claude pointed out.

"Just tell him."

"What if he comes back here looking for you tomorrow?"

Now angry, LoRetta replied, "Tell him I've gone home to Jeffries... that I never want to see him again."

***

Just before dawn, I awoke pressed into the warmth of Gem's back. The air had changed, now heavy and cold on my skin. I slipped from bed and padded silently downstairs to the green room, where I turned Popo's chair toward a window overlooking the still-lush trees and the creek beyond. After curling up there, inhaling the comforting fragrance of my father, to await the sunrise, I considered all that had happened the past few days, an improbable prelude to the edge of summer. Suddenly, something caught my eye through the window. I leaned forward. By the light of the moon, I saw footsteps moving through the rising white mist from the water. I swear I heard my beloved Aunt Lo wailing, her grief echoing along Prairie Creek, where I'd discovered the man she loved dead.

Chapter 31

"Mother, it's beautiful." I twirled around, the skirt of my new dress swirling about my legs.

"Stand still, Anna. I want to get this pinned up so I can stitch the hem this morning. School starts on Monday."

I saw a small stack of clothing, mended, washed, and pressed, on the table next to Popo's chair.

"Are those for Bernard?" I asked.

"They're not much, but better than nothing. Bernard must've grown three inches this summer and his pants look a might too short. Those are a few things the twins outgrew. Charlie can take them over to him later.

I looked down at my mother as she worked. Her pin cushion on her wrist, she measured the length of my dress with her yardstick, skillfully marking the hem with straight pins as I turned on her command.

"Once you get that dress hung up, I'll need you to look after Thea for a few minutes while I pin up Gem's dress."

"Mother." Gem was standing in the doorway of the green room holding Thea.

"What is it, Gem?"

"Sheriff Boggs is on the telephone. He wants to speak to you."

Mother got up from the floor and sighed. "What now?"

"Gem, put on your dress. I'll pin it up when I come back."

Mother returned a few minutes later. "Annie, go get Charlie and your brothers. We need to sit together for a few minutes so I can tell you what's going on. I only want to say this once... I am so eager to get this entire episode behind us."

I handed Thea back to Gem and ran to get Charlie. "Tell the boys Mother wants them in the green room now." I added the now because I couldn't wait to hear what Mother had to say.

Mother sat on the edge of Popo's chair—I'd never seen her sit there before—with Thea wriggling in her arms. We gathered around.

"Something is going to happen today that I want you to be aware of," she began. "At one o'clock, Sheriff Boggs is making an announcement regarding the death of the man that Annie discovered in Prairie Creek three weeks ago. He's invited the reporter from the *Morning Times* and anyone else who wants to find out from the horse's mouth the outcome of his investigation. Then he will officially close the case."

"Did he tell you any of the details?"

"No, Gem, he didn't. I believe the purpose of his call was to get this announcement out on the grapevine so people will show up and hear for themselves. He said that after his announcement, he's taking Martha to Indianapolis to visit her folks. He hopes that by Monday, with school starting, everyone will move on from this case and so town can return to normal."

"Mother, can we go to town for Sheriff Boggs' announcement? Please?"

Mother looked at Gus. "If your brother will take you."

"Will you, Gus?" asked Gem.

"Sounds like a fun way to spend our last Friday of summer."

"What about Aunt Lo?" Charlie's face looked somber.

"She's at the library preparing for the new school year. They're short-handed because the county let go a couple more of the librarians. There's a lot to do before Monday, but frankly, I'm glad LoRetta is busy. You can stop by and tell her what's happening, but I doubt she'll want to be there. In fact, she needs to stay away."

"Will the sheriff bring up that the man loved Aunt Lo?" I asked.

Mother's answer unsettled me. "Sheriff Clyde Boggs isn't one to hide the truth."

***

We arrived at the public square just before one o'clock. When we heard the noise from the people gathering, we ran the last block to the square to discover a crowd the likes of which we hadn't seen since the circus came to town the summer before last. Gus gripped my hand, and I gripped Gem's as our eldest brother pulled us through the throng of spectators, Charlie, Blinn, Cory, and Bernard trailing close behind us.

Suddenly, Gus stopped. Standing on his tip-toes, he spotted a horse-drawn wagon parked in the road near the front of the court-house. "Come on," he said, pulling us forward. When we got to the side of the wagon, Gus dropped my hand.

"Hey, Sam," he called to the driver, a boy about Gus's age.

The boy raised a hand. "Hey, Gus."

"Do you mind?" Gus nodded at me and Gem.

"No problem."

"Up and over, little sister."

Next thing I knew, Gus hoisted me over the side of the wagon. Gem was next. One by one, the boys landed in the wagon next to us. Then Gus walked around the horse and climbed up on the bench seat next to his friend.

From our higher advantage, we had a better view of the crowd. Gem counted thirteen horse-drawn wagons and carriages, and four motorcars pulled along the curbs surrounding the courthouse. After spying us in the back of Sam's wagon, children began filling two other wagons to better see the event about to unfold.

"Look," shouted Blinn. "That's Bill Goodman and his mother in that Stutz Bearcat." Mr. Goodman was a classmate of our mother's, and now the town's undertaker. He took over the family business after his father passed away. Blinn didn't know the folks in the other two motorcars, although Charlie suggested they were press from out of town, maybe the *Chicago Tribune,* since Harrison Smith McDonell was a big shot from that area.

"People are coming from all over," Blinn muttered.

I searched the crowd but saw no sign of Popo. Mother said he planned to visit Barner Farm today, along with a few stops at Ghere-Douglass' smaller suppliers in the area.

A moment after the big clock on the courthouse struck one o'clock, the door to the sheriff's office swung open and Sheriff Boggs, his wife Martha, on his arm, stepped out. I saw Biddy Ann standing in the doorway.

"Good afternoon," said the sheriff in a loud voice. "Please quiet down so everyone can hear. Let me tell you what I'm here to tell you, then I'll take a few questions."

I saw Biddy Ann step back to make way for a man rushing out with a soapbox in his hands. He placed it on the ground near the sheriff, who gave it a skeptical look before stepping up. The sheriff nodded his thanks to the man who retreated back into the courthouse.

Sheriff Clyde Boggs raised his hands into the air. "If you'll settle down, I'll get started."

As the chatter in the crowd dissipated, all eyes were on the sheriff.

"A few weeks ago, the Ghere sisters discovered a dead man in Prairie Creek by the South Street bridge near their house. The man was not a fellow resident of Jeffries, nor was he someone anyone in town could identify at the scene. In those first few hours after the discovery of the man..."

"The Corpse in the Creek," someone shouted from the crowd.

Sheriff gave the man a wry smile. "Would you like to tell the story, or shall I?"

"Go right ahead, Sheriff."

"Thank you. In those first few hours after the discovery of the dead man, my assistant and I went to work figuring out who he was and how he died. We had plenty of help from the good citizens of Jeffries, particularly the Ghere family. I'm here today to report those findings to all of you."

The sheriff let that sink in before continuing.

"The man's name was Harrison Smith MacDonell, known to his friends as Smitty. His family owns the Smith Foods Company in Chicago."

I looked at Charlie, who simply shrugged.

"Late last week, I sent a telegram to the sheriff in Chicago. He replied to me immediately. He then informed the family, who confirmed the man had gone missing. His father said it wasn't unusual for him to disappear for a few days, that Smitty loved to go on impromptu adventures from time to time. But he acknowledged his son had been gone longer than usual."

"What caused his death?" The reporter from the *Morning Times* looked at the sheriff, his pencil posed over his small tablet.

"Mr. MacDonell died from a head injury, likely due to a fall. That's according to Doc Becker, who isn't sure when or where the accident happened. At first, we thought he traveled to Jeffries on the Wanatah in a private Pullman car, but now believe he may have driven here in his motorcar, a Ford Model A Sports Coupe. Someone told me he passed such a motorcar out on the county road just north of here early Friday afternoon, but he couldn't pinpoint exactly where. I checked out the man's story but didn't find any sign of the motorcar, and his family doesn't know where it is. If anyone knows anything about that motorcar, please call my office."

The sheriff paused a moment to collect his thoughts. "Mr. Mac-Donell died from his head injury here in Jeffries. I have a witness who saw him near the creek early that morning, before the Ghere sisters discovered his body in Prairie Creek."

"Hector Toops?" I whispered to Gem.

"Yep."

"We believe the man was looking for Doc Becker's place when he died and fell into the creek. Doc Becker says that if the man had made it to his office, it was likely there was nothing he could have done to save him at that point. Head injuries like that don't happen often, but when they do, they are often fatal."

"Yesterday, I received a telephone call from the sheriff in Chicago. He said that Mr. MacDonell had driven to Wheaton College the day before he went missing. He returned home from that visit and seemed fine. Next thing the family realized, over two weeks had passed without seeing hide nor hair of the man. Unfortunately, we solved the mystery of his disappearance for that family.

Then the reporter shouted, "Was he married? Any children?"

"I understand he and his wife had irreconcilable differences and were in the throes of an ugly divorce. They have one son."

Murmurs spread across the crowd. The sheriff waited for them to die down before continuing, "Today, Biddy Ann mailed the newspaper clipping from the *Morning Times* to the sheriff in Chicago, along with specifics about where he's buried. I suspect the family will want to move him to a more appropriate grave on their family estate in Hyde Park."

I cringed when Gem told me they had buried Mr. MacDonell in a pauper's grave next to the poorhouse.

"Why did he come to Jeffries?"

The sheriff cleared his throat. "To ask the woman he loved to marry him once his divorce was final."

"Where did you find his overnight case?"

"In the cloakroom at the Little Palmer House... the overnight case of a man who never checked in."

"Tell us the name of this mystery woman who this man came to sweep off her feet."

Sheriff Boggs took a deep breath. "LoRetta Ghere."

The crowd lit up with *oohs* and *ahhs*, and mercy-mes and say-it-ain't-sos. Then somewhere in the crowd shouted, "That home-wrecker!"

I happened to be looking at the crowd when I saw poor old Mrs. Alma Mae Butler's hand fly to her forehead. Then she swooned and fainted. Fortunately, her two sons were flanking her in that critical moment and caught her before she hit the ground. Their quick-wittedness and grace made it appear they had caught her mid-swoon before.

"Now you listen to me," the sheriff shouted. "The people of this town are aware LoRetta Ghere is a fine, upstanding member of this community. Many of you attend Holy Cross Church with her, stand next to her on Sunday mornings to praise God Almighty. The fact is, LoRetta, her cousin, Louisa, and their friends at Wheaton knew the man by another name, Harry Smith. They did not know he was an heir to the Smith Foods fortune and they did not know he was married. As I understand it, Mr. MacDonell hoped to start a new life with his son and Miss Ghere. Apparently, money can buy you a new life, if you've got enough of it. I believe he wanted LoRetta to be part of that new life, although she has assured me that once she found out the truth about Mr. MacDonell, she would not have accepted his offer. Her life is here in Jeffries... with all of you."

"How long did Miss Ghere know this fellow?"

"Five years, as I recall." The sheriff's eyes looked up, searching his memories. "Miss Ghere said her cousin, Louisa Rousseau, takes her and two of their other friends to the Morton Arboretum every summer during their visit to Wheaton. Five years ago when they were enjoying refreshments on the patio of the Thornhill Mansion, Mr. MacDonell joined their conversation. LoRetta said he was an intellectual—he added an interesting perspective to their conversation—as well as charming. Louisa invited him to a gathering she and her husband were hosting to kick off the new school year at Wheaton College. Smitty became a fixture at these gatherings every year since, until this year. Mr. Rousseau saw a photograph of Mr. MacDonell in a Chicago newspaper, recognized him as the liar he was and banned him from attending this year's gathering. That's it, the end of the story."

"How did you find out about his overnight case at the Little Palmer House?"

Sheriff Boggs looked as if he hadn't expected that question. He paused a moment, then smiled for the first time since mounting the soapbox in front of the courthouse. "That's called good sheriff-ing.

Now, if you'll excuse me, my lovely wife and I have a train to catch." He stepped down from the wooden box and extended his arm to Martha, who took it.

"One more question, if you don't mind."

The sheriff turned to the reporter.

"Where's Mr. MacDonell's overnight case now?"

"Locked up tight in my safe. I have informed the sheriff in Chicago that I will turn it over to the MacDonell family upon his request, after he closes the matter on his end. Now, if you don't mind..."

Biddy handed the sheriff his own overnight case. The crowd parted as the couple strode down the steps of the courthouse toward the Wanatah Depot, Mrs. Clyde Boggs' sashay, every bit as alluring as LoRetta Ghere's.

Chapter 32

When school resumed in north-central Indiana, the waning summer slipped by, bit by bit, on the first hint of the autumn breezes. That year, the gentle edge of summer lingered into mid-September. Though school had started anew, nudging us into our rote autumn routines, thoughts of Harrison Smith MacDonell continued to dance along the edges of my dreams, still bright and alive. Yet in the bright daylight, he was a man whose life had been cut short in a final desperate act of winning over the woman he loved. Did that kind of love come around but once in a lifetime? Or would my aunt have a second chance at that all-consuming bliss?

I witnessed summer's impending demise in the night sky, as the moon and stars seemed to linger in their transit to a predestined autumn array. I could see the subtlety in the trees as they offered their first telltale signs of turning leaves, adding a hint of color to the summer's green-dominated landscape. I could see it in the thickening morning mist as the hot air of the day willingly succumbed to the cooler water flowing in the creek at night. Most of all, I could see it in the behavior of the people who inhabited our little town, their bodies enjoying the last cooler days of summer, but their minds having already moved on in anticipation of a new season, an old routine.

Mother aired out the stifling heat from the green room earlier than usual, insisting that all the windows stay open throughout the night to capture the late summer's cooling breezes. I longed for the autumn days ahead when I'd sit in the window seat, wrapped in a blanket, leaning against Charlie as he read to me. I imaged lying on my belly, stretched out on the floor of the green room, playing checkers with Pauline while listening to Abbott and Costello on WLS out of Chicago on Father Blinn's old Zenith radio. I thought about the days just ahead when Gem and I would gather up the first of the falling leaves of gold and orange and red that we'd iron between sheets of wax paper and tape to the walls of our bedroom. I thought about the season to follow, that grand finale of the year that promises a new beginning in spring. For now, our once-sacred edge of summer was an enigma. I prayed for autumn to blow in quickly, and for the winter that followed, hoping to find a respite from my thoughts.

As summer made its transit to autumn, Mother changed, too. The first days after school resumed seemed her best, as she, with Thea on her hip, puttered in her garden, plucking the last of her harvest from the stems and vines of the vegetable plants that had responded to her coaxing to come forth and produce food for her family throughout the summer. When we returned home from school in the afternoon, we often found her in her small sewing room, singing the songs she'd heard on WLS, as she tackled the perpetual stack of mending, or sewed a new garment for one of her brood. In the days before autumn's official takeover, Mother smiled more, finding her contentment in her hours of near seclusion.

All talk of the Corpse in the Creek ceased at the beginning of the school year. Pauline and Helen, my two best friends besides Charlie, quickly regained their status as the center of my universe, as we settled into our new classroom during those first few days of September.

Sheriff Boggs' frequent visits to our home stopped. Now, with the case of the Corpse in the Creek behind him, he turned his focus back to the day-to-day affairs of a small-town sheriff.

But for the waning speculation of Aunt Lo's role in the matter, the townspeople seemed satisfied that Harrison Smith MacDonell's death was a closed chapter in Jeffries' history. From time to time, I spotted Gem gazing at the tree limbs where she'd first spied her sparrow. One time when I asked her about it, she told me she wondered about the things that had happened. So did I. But I mostly wondered about Jimbo. Did the hobo depart Indiana for the Alabama sunsets he professed to adore? I was certain he wasn't the man who pulled Pauline and me out of the creek last winter, but I'd decided that if I ever saw him again, I would ask.

***

"Popo... Popo."

My father lowered his newspaper and looked around the table at his family.

"Popo."

Gem's fingers went to her lips hiding a smile her eyes gave away. Then she pointed toward the floor.

"What's this?" he asked as he folded his paper and laid it next to his plate.

"I believe your daughter has outgrown her basket." Mother peeked under the kitchen table. "Yes, I'm quite sure of it."

"Popo."

"What can I do for you, Little Bit?"

"Hode me," pleaded Thea.

My father reached down and pulled his youngest daughter into a bear hug. Thea giggled with delight.

"When did you learn to crawl?"

"I taught her." Cory slathered apple butter on his biscuit, then stuffed half of it into his mouth.

Popo looked at Mother who nodded. "He had a little help."

"Everyone treats her like a baby," Cory said with a mouthful.

"That's because she *is* a baby," Gem pointed out. Cory ignored the comment.

"She squalls and someone picks her up and gives her what she wants. All of you." He pointed around the table with his butter knife. "Add Aunt Lo, MaMaw Ghere and Bernard, it's no wonder Thea is spoiled. I figured it was time for her to strike out on her own."

Cory returned his full attention to his biscuit.

"Why do I have the feeling there's more to this story?"

"Go ahead, Cory," prompted Mother. "Finish your story."

"Blinn and I were playing checkers on the floor in the green room yesterday," continued Cory. "I was about to beat his pants of..."

"Were not!" Blinn's face turned red.

"Was to... and Thea started squalling. I told her if she wanted something, she'd have to come to us."

"Cory got on his hands and knees and crawled over to her," Blinn added to his twin's story.

"Pardon the interruption." Gus stood in the doorway of the kitchen. "Popo, someone is at the door who needs to speak with you."

My father's smile slipped from his face as he pushed back his chair from the table and stood up. "I wonder what this is about," he huffed. A few moments later, he returned to the kitchen, a note in his hand.

Mother moved Popo's plate to the sink, then refilled his coffee cup. She filled a second one for herself and sat down next to Gem.

Popo eyed Gem and then me, then looked at the note. "Boggy received a telegram yesterday from the sheriff in Chicago announcing that Mrs. Harrison Smith MacDonell would arrive at the Wanatah Depot this morning on the 9:10 to collect her husband's overnight case. Mrs. MacDonell insists upon visiting her husband's grave." Popo took a breath, then focused his eyes on Mother's. "She wants to meet the girls who discovered his body."

"Why in the world would she want to do that?" Mother pulled her spoon from her coffee and rested it on her saucer with a clink.

"Boggy says the woman is having difficulty moving past her husband's unexpected death and believes meeting the girls will help her do that. He asked me to accompany them to the gravesite this afternoon. You are welcome to come with us, Maggie."

"Are we welcome to refuse a visit to that hideous hellhole where society has cast aside its unwanted?" Mother's face tightened with anger.

Popo shook his head subtly but didn't speak.

"What about your work, Augie?" Mother asked. Our family had been tightening its belt the last few weeks. The economic depression seemed to hang in the air as a pall over everything.

"I'll get my calls finished this morning," Popo replied. "I may have to go in tomorrow to finish my orders and bills for the week."

"Sunday is the only day you have with your family." Mother's disappointment showed on her face.

"In these difficult times, we do what we have to do." Popo stood up from the table. "I'd better leave now. Gus, please have Old Barney hitched to the carriage by one o'clock. It will take us half an hour or more to get there. At least it looks like we have a beautiful day for a carriage ride."

***

After lunch—a fried egg sandwich with pickled beets—Mother insisted that Gem and I take a bath and put on our best dresses. Pulling the tangles from my hair with her brush, she instructed us to be on our best behavior.

"Please come with us, Mother."

"No, I need to stay here to take care of Thea and do my chores."

"The poorhouse is creepy," I added, hoping to influence her to change her mind.

"That place gives me the willies," shuttered Gem.

"You girls don't have to go." Mother's gentle voice put us at ease. "I won't make you. In fact, I wish you wouldn't stir up this incident all over again."

"I'm going," I insisted.

"Me, too." Gem paced in a half-circle around Mother and me.

"Fine."

"Can Charlie come with us?" I always felt safer when my cousin was with me.

"There's not room in the carriage for another person," Mother said. "Gus told me Cory was riding upfront on the bench with him to keep Old Barney calm. That leaves barely enough room inside the carriage for you, Gem, and your father. I just hope going out there today will finally put an end to this matter, once and for all."

"But Mother, we still don't know..."

"Anna, enough!" Mother squatted down in front of me and took my face in her hands. "Sweet, sweet child," she cooed. "You're right. There are questions that remain unanswered. The answers may come tomorrow, or they may never come."

My eyes fill with tears.

Mother kissed my cheek, then continued, "You're a seven-year-old child. That's who you are... a child who stumbled into an unfortunate adult situation. Sweet girl, I need you to understand that what you think about grows, and that poor man you found seems to be all you think about these days."

"But I..."

"You don't have to talk about what you discovered, but I see it on you face, in your eyes. Anna, it's better to think about your family... about your friends. Think about what you have right here, in this moment, because it will slip away faster than you can image. The happy memories you make now will help get you through the tough times later in life. Learn, laugh, play. Let *him* go! Put this matter to rest and move on. It's time. Promise me, Anna, that after your trip to the graveyard today, you'll try to do that. Do you promise?"

"I promise." I hoped it wasn't a lie.

Chapter 33

Gem and I stood on the curb next to our carriage and waited. We didn't pace, we didn't fidget, we didn't talk. We simply waited, consumed by our thoughts that crowded out everything but what lay ahead.

At five minutes past one o'clock, I spied Popo on top of the bridge crossing over Prairie Creek, the place where the most grievous season of my young life began just a few weeks before. I wanted to call out to him, to scream, "Don't look down!" but I knew that every member of my family would forever cast their gaze downward, a prayer drifting upward, in search of that assurance that the Angel of Death had moved on to disrupt the lives of others. I imagined the rush of the creek swirling over the gravestones, forever bearing the memory of Harrison Smith MacDonell.

Without a word, Popo lifted me into the carriage, scooted in beside me, then reached out and pulled Gem in on his other side. Gus climbed up on the bench seat next to Cory and took the reins.

"Giddy up, boy," he called.

I watched as Cory reached out and patted Old Barney's rump. With a swish of the horse's tail, we rolled forward, the *click-a-de-clack* of wooden wheels on the pavement a soothing antidote to the internal howl of our collective trepidation. With me tucked under one of our father's arms and Gem under his other, we rode in silence, Popo oblivious to anything other than his own thoughts.

"Just ahead on the left," announced Gus, his words more the timbre of the ice man singing out his wares than a young man on a resolute mission to a potter's field.

Old Barney stopped abruptly and snorted, his head nodding back and forth. Cory jumped to the ground, grabbed the horse's harness, and pulled his head to the side, obscuring his view of the Clinton County Poorhouse.

Gus climbed down from the bench seat and circled around to the side of the carriage.

"It's best you walk in from here, Popo. Old Barney is having none of this."

Popo nodded. "Let's get this over with, girls."

Taking ahold of Gus's hand, Gem climbed down. Popo and I followed.

"We're going to walk Old Barney past the poorhouse grounds." Gus turned and pointed. "There's a shady spot just past the house. Cory brought a few dried apples to feed him, and a little braid of Belva's hair he made. He swears the smell of Belva comforts that horse." Gus shrugged. "Who knows?"

"Don't look at me," Popo muttered, rolling his eyes. Cory had a way of befuddling Popo.

"It looks like they're standing in the graveyard about twenty feet from the main house." Gus pointed in that direction with his chin.

"You'll see them when we pull away. I'll keep an eye out. When I see you walking back, Cory and I will meet you here with the carriage."

"Thanks, Gus." Popo patted his son's shoulder. "I appreciate you and Cory bringing us out here today."

"Okay, Cory. Let's give Old Barney a change of scenery.

As the carriage slowly moved forward, we stood on the road staring across at the poorhouse. A mansion once owned by the county's richest farmer, the two-story red brick home, with north and south wings, had fallen into disarray after the death of the childless proprietor. His wife, unable to keep up with the demands of the enterprise, soon followed her husband to the grave. A decade passed without distant heirs stepping up to claim it, to bring it back to life. Finally, the county took it over to house the poor and the debtors.

From a distance, the house looked innocuous enough, with rows of trees lining the long walkway to the oak front door, now dry and cracked from years of neglect. It was the desolate graveyard that stretched along the south side of the building, cluttered with haphazard rows of worn wooden crosses, that spoke to the human misery that had flourished at the poorhouse for decades.

A gust of wind out of the north swirled the skirts of our dresses. Gem and I wrapped our arms around ourselves against the chill, grateful that Mother had insisted we wear our sweaters. The notion of autumn flitted across my mind. I wanted to think about autumn, to make it grow into its own splendor, and heal the wounds of the last few weeks, but I couldn't. One more open door lay ahead. It had to be closed.

Sheriff Boggs stood at the graveside, a woman and boy next to him. I spied the white A&P paneled truck parked a few feet away in the poorhouse's shadow. The truck seemed a familiar detail in an otherwise surreal scene, with bold red letters spelling out FRIENDLY SERVICE above the windshield, and HOME DELIVERY below.

Gem pointed to the truck. "Look, Popo!"

"The good sheriff must have borrowed the truck so the *poor wido w...*" Popo spat the two words off his tongue. "...didn't have to ride in a carriage like us commoners."

Sheriff Boggs held up a hand and waved.

With Popo still gripping a hand of both of us, he pulled us through the sea of graves, the dust of fallow ground clinging to the fresh polish of our patent leather shoes. In the distance, I beheld rich, black fields still holding their autumn harvests, giving me hope that one day even this potters' field could be overrun with life. I wondered what would grow out of this tragedy... and this gathering.

Popo called out, "Hello, Boggy."

My hand slipped from my father's. I planted my feet as he and Gem moved closer to the grave of Harrison Smith MacDonell.

"I hope you haven't been waiting long," the tone of my father's voice betraying his feelings.

I stopped... and waited for the wind.

***

"This is Gemma Ghere." As Sheriff Boggs pointed to her, my sister held out her hand to the woman dressed in a full-length black dress. She wore black gloves and a mourning hat with a veil.

"This is her sister, Anna." I, too, held out my hand to the black glove. "And their father, Augustus Ghere, my long-time friend." Then the sheriff turned to his visitors to introduce them to us. "This is

Eva MacDonell and her son, Mackie. We were just discussing Mr. MacDonell's missing cane and motorcar."

As I took in the haphazardly made cross bound with thin twine, the word, "Unknown" and the date of death etched into the wood, I shuttered at the thought that the man whom my Aunt Lo loved was in this place and forgotten as so many others. I tried to count the days since the sheriff informed the family of his passing, but couldn't recall the number.

I suddenly realized I didn't belong there. I wanted to go home. I wanted to hear Thea squall. I wanted to taste Mother's sweet apple pie on my tongue. I wanted to sit in the window seat and drift into a daydream, the sound of Charlie's voice in my ear. My eyes slipped from the familiar face of Sheriff Boggs to the peculiar figure in black, to the boy with red-rimmed hazel eyes. I finally found comfort in the single dandelion growing on the mound of loose dirt at their feet. The lowly flower, unfit for Mother's garden, raised its splendid yellow head above the pall of death. God's inexplicable thumbprint.

After the uncomfortable formalities, Mrs. MacDonell got down to business. "I'm sorry I asked you to come all the way out here today. I didn't realize it was such a dreadful place."

Her voice was sweet, though I couldn't read her face behind the veil.

"It's a shame anyone ends up here, let alone my beloved husband."

I looked up at her son, Mackie, who stood next to his mother. His expression surprised me. As the wind tousled his hair, his eyes widened in surprise.

None of us knew how to respond to Mrs. MacDonell, so we allowed a gulf of silence to grow between us. I took hold of Popo's hand again as I looked at the cross, thinking about the pauper's grave beneath it that held the remains of the heir to the Smith Foods empire.

"I understand you discovered my husband's body in a creek."

I said nothing.

"Yes," Gem finally nodded. "Prairie Creek. It runs by our house in Jeffries. We were walking our baby sister. When we crossed over the bridge, Annie saw him below in the creek. That's when she ran to our house to get our father."

I had nothing to add.

"I am so sorry you young girls had to be the ones to find him. We need to put the death of my husband to rest, for your sakes."

For *our* sakes? I saw Mackie shake his head as Mrs. MacDonell dabbed her nose with her lace hankie. "He was an important man in Chicago, you know," she added, a trace of indignation in her voice. "Very important. Mackie will take his place one day, won't you, dear?"

The boy stood motionless.

Mrs. MacDonell then stated that she intended to have her husband's body exhumed from his pauper's grave and properly buried in the family plot in Hyde Park. That would all happen as soon as the sheriff completed the paperwork, and she could arrange for a proper hearse and a proper wake and a proper priest to officiate a proper service. I pressed my hands to my face.

"Tell me, Mr. Ghere, what role did your sister, LoRetta, play in all of this?" She waved her hand over the grave.

I felt the bolt of shock course through my father's body. I dropped his hand, now understanding why Mrs. MacDonell asked us to the graveyard.

My father took a step forward and planted his feet. "Sheriff Boggs can speak to the integrity of my sister," huffed Popo. "I assure you, she is blameless for the unfortunate death of your husband."

"That's not what I understand of the matter," Mrs. MacDonell replied coolly. "I'd rather hear from your sister directly."

"Your are sadly misinformed. I am speaking on behalf of my sister."

As the temperature at the scene heated up, I stepped back out of the fray. I turned to see Gem staring out toward a copse of trees near the edge of the farmland. I realized she was watching Mackie meandering toward the trees. Then something else caught my eye.

"Gem," I whispered. "Look." I pointed to the bird perched on the top of a wooden marker midway across the graveyard. "It's your sparrow."

My sister gasped. As if it knew she had finally spotted it, the bird took flight toward the trees. Gem didn't hesitate... she ran after the bird, me right behind her.

We stopped at the edge of the thicket next to Mackie, Gem turning about beneath a fragile limb to get a look at the sparrow. "It's him," she muttered. "My sparrow."

"Hello, Mackie," I said to the boy. "I'm sorry about your father." I was also sorry I'd found him, but I didn't say that.

"Please don't think ill of him," pleaded the boy. "He was a good man." Mackie looked down at his hands. I took in his copper-colored hair, a spray of freckles across his nose and his sad hazel eyes. Beyond his boyish features, I could see his father in him.

"They named me after my father," he said. "I loved him very much."

Gem nodded almost imperceptibly, her eyes still glued to the sparrow that sat on the branch above Mackie's head.

"Your father never told our Aunt Lo he was married. She didn't even know his real name until just before he died."

"I know."

"You know?" I asked, surprised that a boy so young would know his father's business.

"Father told me about your aunt. He told me how much he loved her, how much he wanted to make a life with her and me."

Gem turned her face to Mackie, wide-eyed.

"My father was determined to get a divorce from my mother," he continued. "She spent most of her time in Europe with her friends. She only returned home for major events covered by the newspaper. Nothing about Mother ever seems real."

"But she's here now," Gem offered.

"She plans to leave on another around-the-world adventure with her friends as soon as we return to Chicago," Mackie scoffed.

"Will you go with her?" I asked.

"Oh, no. I've got to get back to school. I'll stay with my grandfather in Hyde Park, where I belong. Father and I lived with him on the family estate. Mother was rarely there." Mackie took a breath. "Grandfather had finally arranged for their divorce. Mother wasn't happy about it, so Father wanted to take us to live in New York for a while, until she settled down. Grandfather wouldn't hear of us leaving. He insisted we stay in Chicago so Father could learn to run the company he would inherit one day. My grandfather realized his son was miserable married to my mother and hoped that, once he was free of her and building a new life with your aunt, he could concentrate on learning the business."

"Aunt Lo would have nothing to do with him after she learned he was married," I muttered.

"He told me. He wanted a chance to change her mind, to make things right."

Tears rolled down Mackie's face. The sparrow overhead ruffled its wings.

The boy choked back a sob. "When I return home, I must buckle down on my studies. When I turn twenty-one, that's ten years from now, I will own the majority interest in Smith Foods. I don't want to disappoint my grandfather, lose what he's spent a lifetime building.

I'm scared, but Grandfather said we'd get through it together. I just hope he lives long enough to do that."

"Gem, Annie, let's go home." I turned to see Popo standing halfway between the grave of Harrison Smith MacDonell and the trees. "Come on, girls."

I raised my hand in a wave.

"Will you write to me and let us know when your mother plans to move your father's body to Chicago... and how you're doing?"

"Yes, if you promise to write back with any news. Tell me your address. I'll remember."

Gem told him. "Our best to you, Mackie." Gem gave the boy a quick hug, then ran toward Popo. I followed. As I drew near, my father leaned down and scooped me into his arms and carried me out of the graveyard. I sensed it was the last time a father would hug his little girl.

As we rode home, I felt the autumn breeze drifting through our carriage lift the burden of the Corpse in the Creek from my shoulders. I wanted to be a child again, yet I knew I couldn't. That was the secret I must keep from my mother.

Chapter 34

We rolled into the house, a benevolent thunderclap, stealing away Mother's peaceful day with Thea. Though rare, that day the entire school-going Ghere clan plus Charlie had converged on the sidewalk near Mrs. Parlett's house to complete the brief journey home together.

Mother seemed breathless, a hand pressed to her chest, as we filled the house with the clatter of our feet and the chatter of our day. The day was no longer hers.

After we changed out of our school clothes, Charlie and I trailed Gem into the kitchen, where Mother had already begun her late afternoon routine of preparing the kitchen for cooking supper.

"You received mail today?" Mother pulled an envelope from her apron pocket.

"Who's it for?"

Mother studied the face of the envelope for a moment. "It appears to be for all of you. Anna, run get your brothers. Then we'll open it together."

Once we were all gathered around the kitchen table, Mother handed the envelope to Gem. She opened it and waved the carefully handwritten note around, pointing to the large script letters at the top that read, "It's a surprise!"

We all clapped, even Gus. Gem cleared her throat and loudly read the rest.

You are cordially invited to celebrate
the birthday of
Bernard Thompson
next Saturday, September 26,
in the basement at the Blue and White Café.
The party begins promptly at two o'clock in the afternoon.
Don't be late!
Remember, mum's the word.

Love,
Paul and Roxy Lockwood

Hurrah! A party!

***

On the day of the party, we arrived at the Blue and White Café at a quarter before two o'clock. With Miss Roxy pointing towards the door to the basement at the back, we trailed through the narrow aisle between the chairs at the counter and the single row of tables, two with lingering customers. Miss Roxy smiled at us as we traipsed past.

"There's already a crowd downstairs. As soon as I finish up with these last customers, Paul and I will be down to get the party started."

Gus opened the door and headed down, trailed by Blinn, Cory, Charlie, Gem, and me.

"Annie, a moment, please."

I turned to our hostess. "Yes, Miss Roxy?"

"Your father stopped by a few minutes ago. He wanted me to tell you he was running over to Woolworth to pick up a gift for Bernard."

I thought about the gift Gem and I had made for our friend. My sister found a scrape of Aida cloth from a basket in Mother's sewing room. She cut two pieces for a bookmark for his Bible, then carefully stitched a cross on one of them. Gem wanted to include a Bible verse, but decided the only one that would fit was, "Jesus wept." Gem also decided the verse was inappropriate for a party.

"Annie, would you stand here at the door and watch for your father? We're also expecting a few more children, and Sheriff Boggs said he'd stop by. I've got things to do in the kitchen to get ready, not to mention, get rid of..." Miss Roxy tipped her head toward the row of tables where her last customers had planted themselves for the duration.

"What do you want me to do?"

"I've got the door locked, so you'll have to unlock it to let your father and any other party guests in. I'll let the last few customers out once they've finished up." Roxy looked over her shoulder. "I may have to give them a shove, if you know what I mean."

"What if someone else wants to come in to eat?"

Miss Roxy pointed at the sign she'd hand-lettered and taped up in the window. It read, "Closed for a special event. Reopening at four o'clock."

"Tell them to come back later. If they give you any guff, I'll be around, or you can call out to Paul..." Roxy pointed to the window behind the counter where Paul passed the food he'd prepared through to his wife. "...and Paul will come out and punch them right in the nose."

Miss Roxy tapped my nose with a knuckle, which made me giggle. "No, he won't."

"Yes, I will," Mr. Lockwood called out from the kitchen. Then he stuck his fist out through the window, which made me laugh. Miss Roxy laughed, too.

"Are we all set here, Annie? It shouldn't be more than five minutes before we can get downstairs to the party. I'm surprised your father isn't back yet."

"He probably ran into someone he knew. Popo always has something to say."

"You're right."

I took up a place in the large front window where I had a good view of the door. Miss Roxy disappeared into the kitchen, but not for long.

"Can I get a refill on this coffee?"

I noticed Cornelius Higginbothan tapping his finger on the edge of his coffee cup. When that didn't get the proprietor's attention, he tapped his spoon on the inside of his cup. *Clink, clink, clink.*

Miss Roxy boiled out of the kitchen. "Fresh out," she stated. With that, Miss Roxy slapped his bill down on the table, rattling the empty dishes.

"Make a fresh pot. I'll wait." Mr. Higginbothan turned back to his friend. "... and that blasted sheriff of ours wouldn't do a thing about it."

"Pay up and get out." Miss Roxy's voice was calm.

"Hon, do you need my help?" Paul Lockwood's face appear in the serving window.

"No, hon. I think I can take these two without a problem."

Miss Roxy slid the bill in front of Mr. Higginbothan. "And what, pray tell, is this?" he demanded as he glared at the back of his bill.

"That's a little map I drew for you." she said, pointing to her drawing. "It shows you the way to the Airport Diner. They serve coffee there all day."

Mr. Higginbothan's eyes widened. "They serve pickled eggs left over from the Great War there!"

"I hear they're a delicacy. You boys need to pay up and get on over there before they're all gone."

"Roxy Carter, I hate it when you get like this." Mr. Higginbothan pushed back from the table and stood up.

"It's Roxy *Lockwood*, and I hate it when you don't tip a girl for her hard work."

Miss Roxy marched to the counter and stuck out her hand. Both men paid their bills. The four railroaders at the other table took the hint and filed over to where Miss Roxy now stood behind the counter.

"Are you going to let us out of here?" demanded Mr. Higginbothan.

"Not another word out of your mouth unless, of course, you want me to ban you from my fine establishment... for life."

After all six men paid their bills, Miss Roxy escorted them to the door. I turned the lock so they could get out.

She leaned out of the door and took a quick look around. "A crowd is gathering in front of the Clinton Theater to get tickets for the matinee showing of 'Dr. Jekyll and Mr. Hyde.' Do you want to see that film?"

"It's scary." I wasn't fond of scary films, but Gem loved them. "I don't want to see it."

"Smart girl. Life can be scary enough. No sense adding to it." With that, Miss Roxy headed for the kitchen. "I'll call over to Woolworth to find out if your father is still there. Don't forget to lock that door, Annie Ghere."

"I won't."

Just as I was about to turn the lock, I spotted Emerson Keller, one of Bernard's classmates, on the other side of the street. I watched as he crossed over, but instead of walking straight toward the Blue and White Café and the party, he slipped into the crowd in front of the Clinton Theater. I stepped outside to see what he was up to. Before long, I saw him emerge from the crowd and walk toward the restaurant. Then he turned back. Suddenly, I heard Alma Mae Butler squeal, then rub her backside with her hand. Her sons turned to search the crowd. Emerson had somehow vanished.

I stepped back into the Blue and White. "Mr. Lockwood," I called out. "Emerson Keller has a bean shooter."

"Is that a fact?"

"Pretty sure. Mrs. Butler just got popped in the backside, and then Emerson disappeared into the crowd instead of coming here. I think he slipped it into his back pocket under his jacket."

A moment later, Emerson appeared in front of me. "Annie, what are you doing here?"

"Guarding the door."

"You can tell Mr. and Mrs. Lockwood I'm here so they can start the party now." Emerson laughed at his little joke.

"You tell them yourself."

As Emerson walked through, Paul Lockwood stood next to the basement door.

"Well, look who it is, the life of the party." With that, Mr. Lockwood stuck out his hand to shake Emerson's. "Good man, good man, glad you're here," he said as he patted his shoulder. "Will you please tell our guests that we'll be down in a minute or two to get the party started?"

"Yes, sir."

Paul Lockwood leaned back against the wall next to the stairs to the basement, a big smile on his face. Then he pulled Emerson's bean shooter out of his sleeve and held it up. "Our little secret, Annie."

I nodded. "Yes, sir."

"By the way, Roxy talked to the clerk over at Woolworth, and she assured my lovely wife that Popo had just left. Do you mind waiting another minute or two by the door?"

"No, not at all."

I turned to lock the door, and there stood Earlynn Musgrove, the sworn enemy of my best friend, Pauline Kimmel.

"Hello, Annie. How are you?"

"Fine."

I wasn't sure why Pauline had taken a dislike to Earlynn, other than she was the most beautiful girl we'd ever seen. She had thick, dark hair that fell to her waist, and sparkling blue eyes. My clothes were as nice as hers, though mine were homemade and hers were store-bought. Her mother always placed a ribbon or bow or clip in her hair with exact artistry to give her a finished look. (That's how my Aunt Lo described it.)

Today, a blue bow held a ponytail near the top of her head. The gift box for Bernard had an identical bow on top.

"Where should I go, Annie?"

I pointed to the back of the diner. "Through that door and down the stairs."

Earlynn turned to wave at her mother, who stood on the sidewalk beside a carriage. Mrs. Musgrove held up one hand and wriggled her fingers. "I'll be right here at four o'clock. See you then, dear."

Before pulling the door closed and locking it again, I turned toward the public square to look for Popo. He should be here by now, but was nowhere in sight.

With my eyes focused on the street corner next to the National Bank Building, I almost missed him. He stepped out of the shadows and cut catty-corner across the street to the courthouse. Without thinking, I let go of the door and ran after the man who once lurked in my dreams, spoiling my sleep. As I approached the door to the sheriff's office, the name I hadn't spoken in weeks slipped from my lips.

"Jimbo."

Chapter 35

I reached the street corner in time to see Jimbo amble through the open door of the sheriff's office. I hesitated a moment, then ran across the street. The sun had begun its grand transit to the west, its rays now broken by a scud of clouds, causing erratic shadows to dance along the side of the courthouse.

I hesitated again... took a breath.

As I crept forward, passing through the door, I noticed the wedge of wood Sheriff Boggs used to prop it open. After a thousand kicks, it still held the weight of the marred pine door with the brass mortise lock.

Inside, cooler air had cleared the stifling heat of summer, along with the raw emotions exposed there during the investigation into the death of the Corpse in the Creek—Harrison Smith MacDonell—some weeks ago. Someone had pushed the old fan over next to the peachy-orange WAKE ALL clock, its electrical cord now hanging down the face of the counter.

I walked across the waiting area, aware of the sound of my shoes clacking against the pine floors. As I neared the counter, I heard the distinctive voice of Jimbo, whom I'd first set eyes upon that stormy August morning at Mrs. Barner's old cottage in the woods.

"Word around camp has it you wanted to talk to me. Here I am. Talk."

After a long silence, Sheriff Boggs spoke. "How's your good friend, Skeeter, doing these days?"

"*Ahh*, a social visit, is it? At least you aren't planning to lock me up and throw away the key."

"Not at the moment."

"Could we get on with whatever this is? Let's not allow your inability to get to the point cause me to miss my deadhead to Alabama."

"Sunsets." The sheriff said it matter-of-factly, the answer to a question no one asked.

"Indeed. The most beautiful sunsets I've ever set my two eyes upon."

"Is Skeeter dead-heading to the Yellowhammer state with you?"

Jimbo chuckle. "I adore those sunsets, but ole Skeeter is more of a moonshine man."

"When is the last time you saw Skeeter?"

Jimbo said nothing.

"Answer the question so I can get on with my day," urged the sheriff. "I have a birthday party to attend."

"I believe you know more about the whereabouts of my friend than you're letting on."

I felt my heart beating in my chest. What did Sheriff Boggs know?

"Skeeter's from around these parts and never wanders far, not even in winter," continued Jimbo. "He told me one evening when the camp was particularly pungent how he savors the earthy fragrance of the growing fields here in Indiana. In context, I understand his preference for the stink of this place, the smell of life over the lingering stench of explosive gunpowder and poisonous gases mingling with the putrid odor of rotting flesh next to him in the trenches."

I cringed.

"You're sure about that?" The sheriff paused, his question sullying the air as a whiff of gunpowder.

"If memory serves, when I was dreaming of sunsets, Skeeter was sucking on a fresh bottle that had arrived on the Pennsy from his favorite still over near Logansport. When Skeeter drinks, he gets a bit loquacious."

"Did your friend ever mention *Muncie*?"

Jimbo chuckled again. "Nah. He never mentioned it. Last I saw that 'bo, he was carrying his bundle stick and headed out to catch a cannonball. Said he'd flopped here long enough. He drug up and left, but I'm sure he didn't go far. As I recall, he was heading up to Kokomo."

"I'm told your good friend, Skeeter... one Lester Robinson of Logansport, turned up in Muncie about a week ago. They found him dead in an empty boxcar. According to the Delaware County Sheriff, the putrid odor of *his* rotting flesh is so bad that the trainmaster is threatening to set fire to that boxcar."

"Poetic justice, perhaps. Skeeter was no angel."

"Something the two of you had in common."

"Yes, I suppose that's true."

An uncomfortable silence fell between the two men. I stood motionless at the counter, my hand on the swinging wooden gate, holding my breath, listening, afraid that if I moved, I'd give myself away as I had when listening to Mother and Aunt Lo's conversations through the cold air return over the sofa in our parlor.

"I wouldn't know anything about that, Sheriff," Jimbo finally said. Then the hobo did the oddest thing. He laughed heartily.

"Rumor around town is that *you* killed Mr. Robinson in the Nickel Plate train yard over a difference of opinion. Do you recall that?"

"It appears my friends have stabbed me in the back, dismantled my clever façade of virtue, brick-by-brick."

"It appears so," agreed the sheriff, his tone pleasant.

Then the hobo told his story easily, pridefully. "It seems dear ole Skeeter hadn't the least bit of regard for my passion for the poetry of Ezra Pound. 'Sing we for love and idleness, Naught else is worth the having. Though I have been in many a land, there is naught else in living.' Magnificent, of course, but poor Skeeter preferred the nonsense of Ralph Waldo Emerson... the sage of Concord indeed!" Jimbo spit the last words off his tongue, a pill too bitter to swallow.

"So you beat a little *poetic* sense into his skull with a railroad spike?"

"I'd say that's a fair portrayal of events."

"I also heard that a couple of your 'bos helped you toss his lifeless body into the boxcar that's been stinking up the Muncie train yard."

"I admit, they did the heavy lifting. I prefer to give credit where credit is due."

In the long silence that settled between the law man and the murderer... my encounter with him at Mrs. Barner's old cottage whirling through my head... until his soft voice dragged me back into the moment.

"What is it, Sheriff? The smile on your face seems... well, a bit out of context with the serious nature of our conversation."

"I am simply marveling at the arrogance of your truth-telling."

"Some are worthy of arrogance."

"And yet, Jimbo..." Sheriff Boggs prompted.

"As honesty is the best policy for the moment, I implore you to say what's on your mind."

"And yet, your involvement in the death of Mr. Robinson isn't all there is to this intriguing tale, is it? One hobo killing another. No one really cares. However, a hobo being murdered by the missing and presumed dead, Titus J. Vandercook, will hit the newspaper headlines from Chicago to your beloved Alabama, New York City to Los Angeles. What do you think?"

"It seems you're the man with all the answers."

"Even a simpleton such as myself sees through the veil of arrogance you hide behind."

My head spun. Should I run for the door or hold my breath and continue to eavesdrop? The WAKE ALL ticked, my heart beating out of rhythm with its monotony.

"Sir, is your name Titus James Vandercook?" the sheriff insistent.

Jimbo sniffed and muttered but finally found his voice.

"I used to be Titus."

Chapter 36

That scorching Friday in August 1931, before all hell broke loose in Jeffries, dissolved into an almost tepid late afternoon, with the region getting a small helping of relief from the onerous heat. The gentle breeze that tickled the tree branches high overhead reminded the townsfolk that the weather in central Indiana in August always kept them guessing.

Jimbo waited until dusk to begin his short journey into town, his sights set upon the generosity of Paul Lockwood, who had a soft spot in his head and heart for the war veterans who perpetually battled their demons in their squalid camp at the edge of town. But a fantastical sense of excitement, a driving impulse, pulled him from his makeshift lean-to early. Jimbo patted his belly, an acknowledgement that he'd received the message. After years on the road, the hobo had learned to trust his gut.

With the sun lingering in the western sky, Jimbo made his way down the alley to sit at the old wooden table behind the Blue and White Café, his back to the wall of the building, a position that overlooked the dirt path that cut the city block in half. With most of the town's businesses closing for the night, Jimbo listened to the sounds of locks turning in doors, polite farewells between neighbors, and the rhythmic shuffling of shoes against the sidewalk.

The man closed his eyes, a picturesque image of Jeffries drifting across his mind. He relaxed into the fleeting moment of peace and quiet that would soon succumb to the sounds of a crowd of movie-goers, dressed in their Sunday best, streaming toward the Clinton Theater next door for its evening showing. Any minute, Jimbo expected Paul Lockwood to burst through the backdoor of the Blue and White Café to enjoy a smoke ahead of the supper rush of lonely widowers and ravenous railroaders. Much like that old Mrs. Parlett, Paul was an easy target for a handout. His wife, Roxy... not so much.

Jimbo leaned his head back against the wall. A thin grin crept across his lips, as he pondered for the thousandth time the titular character, Elmer Gantry, in Sinclair Lewis's infamous novel by the same name. He recalled the moment he discovered the book on a sidewalk in Chicago, its back broken, its pages moist from the evening dew. He imagined a pious reader had chucked the book from a window in disgust. Jimbo viewed his unexpected discovery as a stroke of luck at a time he felt luckless. When the book dried enough that he could turn the pages, he read it cover to cover in one day. The hobo admired, even identified with, the deeply flawed preacher who rose to prominence despite his greedy, shallow, and philandering ways.

And yet.

Jimbo couldn't rectify the fiction that was Gantry with the reality of the Shining One. For a long moment, his thoughts bobbed and weaved in the twilight, as his mind darted from one vivid memory to another of that early spring evening in 1928, now indelibly imprinted into his memory.

After fleeing another preposterous proposition from his father's henchmen men to return to Gary and assume his rightful place at the top of the American Steel Company and the Vandercook dynasty, Jimbo had hopped aboard the first Pennsylvania Railroad train out of Cincinnati, headed west. As Fate would have it, the tracks paralleled the Ohio River for several miles. The scenic landscape, coupled with the soothing sway of the boxcar, lulled him into a heightened state of peace.

As the miles passed outside the boxcar's open sliding door, Jimbo reverted to brooding again over his father's audacity, the patriarch's insistence that his money could buy his son anything. Laying aside what his father's money had already bought him, Jimbo remained resolute in his delusion that, by God, his father couldn't buy him!

As the train eased into Prospect Station, Kentucky, the hobo swore he heard the song of the angels in the distance. Captivated by the music, he quietly left the boxcar and strolled up to the first person he saw, an old man with a small dog in a basket.

"What's that singing?" asked Jimbo. The dog yapped twice before curling up for a nap.

"Revival." The notion oft stands alone.

"Revival, you say?" Jimbo thought about the grifters and charlatans Lewis wrote about in his book and wondered if his 'bos back at the camp outside Jeffries had kept his book safe and dry. He resolved to look for it the moment he arrived back there.

"Can you tell me where to find this revival of which you speak?"

The old man turned slowly on his stiff legs and pointed south. "Tent out by Putney's Pond. Not far."

"Thank you, sir." Jimbo patted the little dog, careful not to disturb its sleep, then drifted along the road out of Prospect Station, allowing the angelic music to pull him forward. Remarkably, it relieved the burden of being a wretch of his own making. "Was his current plight out of spite for his father and his damn money?" he wondered for the millionth time.

The last rays of the setting sun reflecting off the still face of Putney's Pond, Jimbo again acquiesced to the pull of revival drawing him for th... out of himself. He felt giddy when he finally laid eyes on the big tent staked near the water, swaying with energy.

With the canvas door of the tent tied to the side with a cotton cord, the hobo slipped into the last row next to a young woman dressed in her Sunday best, her gloved hands clutching her worn pocketbook. When the singing ended, the crowd sat down on the wooden benches in unison. The makeshift sanctuary fell silent.

"Where's the preacher?" Jimbo finally asked the woman next to him.

She leaned to one side, then the other, to see around the rows of heads in front of her.

"There," she whispered, pointing. "He's still praying at the altar."

"Shhhhhh."

The preacher stood slowly and turned to face the crowd.

The *oohs* and *ahhs* rose to a breathy cadence, until the preacher, his hands raised over his head, recited the watchwords of believers.

"Let us pray."

The congregants bowed their heads, all but Jimbo.

The words of Psalms 23 flowed from the preacher's mouth with power and certainty. "The LORD is my shepherd; I shall not want. He maketh me to lie down in green pastures: he leadeth me beside the still waters. He restoreth my soul."

Jimbo leaned into the aisle to get a better view of the preacher. Finally, he nudged the woman next to him. "What is that?"

Without opening her eyes, she whispered, "He's got the shine."

"What does that mean?" he questioned.

"His cup runneth over."

Jimbo scratched at his beard and shook his head. "I don't understand."

The woman opened one eye. "He's so filled with the Holy Spirit that it spills out of him," she explained. "So he shines."

"Who told you that?" the hobo insisted.

"No one told me." The innocence of her youth struck Jimbo with each staccato word. "I've come here the last four evenings and figured it out my own self. You'll see."

"NO! NO, I WON'T SEE!" Jimbo was on his feet. "He a trickster, a hoaxster, a charlatan! Where's his bag of snakes? Where's the fake cripples he will certainly heal? Where's his collection plate to gather the last coins you people possess?"

"Shhhhhh."

"No snakes. No collection plate," the woman assured him. "Just the gift of salvation."

"NO, NO, NO!" Then under his breath, "This can't be right."

Jimbo stepped into the aisle to face the preacher, his heart pounding.

Their eyes met, the hobo's filled with anger, the preacher's filled with love. Then the preacher did what Jimbo never expected... he reached out a hand to the lost soul.

"Brother, do you want to meet the Lord?" he asked in a soothing voice. "He already knows you."

Jimbo took a step back.

"Brother, take my hand and I'll show you the truth."

The hobo turned and ran out of the tent, his heart pounding, his head spinning. Then he heard the voice of the preacher reaching out to him. "Yea, though I walk through the valley of the shadow of death,

I will fear no evil: for thou art with me, thy rod and thy staff, they comfort me."

"Those words won't protect you!" Jimbo shouted back. "That God of yours won't protect you!"

Once outside, the hobo stopped. He reached into his pocket and pulled out his last Ohio Blue Tip matchstick and flicked it with his thumbnail. It ignited instantly. Then he held the flame out in front of his face a moment before lighting the end of the cotton cord that held the canvas door flap open. One second. Two seconds. Three seconds.

Then he threw the match to the ground and ran. He ran as he hadn't since his youth spent on the athletic field at Culver Military Academy. Odd, he would think of that place in the aftermath of his first major criminal act.

Just as he reached the tree-line, Jimbo tripped on a protruding root and fell on his face, bloodying his nose. He screamed, trying to rid his mind of the shining face of the man whose name he'd never know, whose face he'd never forget. He lay there, hoping any survivors of the fire would come for him in a demonstration of their true angry and hate-filled selves. No one came. He finally rolled over, hesitant to behold the carnage he'd created.

No fire in the distance. Just the faint echo of the angels' song drifting over Putney's Pond.

***

Suddenly, Jimbo's eyes popped open, and fell upon a well-dressed man striding toward him, his head held high, an air of determination in his step. The man carried an overnight case in one hand and a walking stick in the other.

At first glance, Jimbo could have sworn the man's face shone in the falling dusk. Certainly his thoughts of the Shining One just moments before cast its illusion upon this stranger in the alley. He struggled to rectify the two, though his moral failings never allowed him to do so.

"A delightful evening we're sharing, is it not?" commented the stranger.

"It is, indeed."

"Sir, I'm wondering if you might point me to the Little Palmer House." The man set his bag on the table and leaned his walking stick against it.

"Certainly," replied Jimbo, now fully engaged with the man. "Just a few more yards that way." He pointed up the alley. "You'll see the entrance on your left. But perhaps you should rest for a moment. You look worn out."

"That I am." The stranger took a breath. "I'm embarrassed to say that I was so eager to get here, I forgot to fill up my motorcar with gasoline when I had the chance. Ran out on the county road to the north of here just past the creek. A kindly old farmer took pity on me and helped me push it off the road up near his barn. Said he'd run out of gasoline a month back, but agreed to look after my motorcar until I returned. I gave him a silver half dollar for his trouble. Told him I'd be back in a day or two and would bring him gasoline, as well."

Jimbo nodded. "That was quite a walk."

"Yes, it was. I should get over to the hotel." The stranger collected his bag from the table. "Thank you for the directions."

"If I might ask, sir, what brings you to our fair town?"

The stranger smiled. "Love. I'm madly in love with a wonderful woman who lives here in Jeffries. I've come to sweep her off her feet. If she says yes, I'll marry her at my first opportunity and take her back home to live. She'll be the talk of the town."

"Where might that be, sir?"

"Hyde Park. Are you familiar with it? I've lived there my entire life. Of course, I went to boarding school at Culver Military Academy."

"Of course."

The two men's eyes met. In the most neutral tone he could muster, Jimbo spoke the truth disguised as whimsy. "I believe you're living my life, sir."

Not knowing how to respond to the odd comment, the stranger nodded politely. "Thank you, again, for your help. I'm much in need of rest."

As he turned, he bumped his walking stick with his foot, and it fell to the ground.

Jimbo jumped to his feet, driven by an unexpected anger churning in his gut. "Let me help you with that, sir."

The hobo moved around the table, reached down and gripped the end of the walking stick. Instead of pressing it into its owner's out-stretched hand, he swung it as hard as he could, catching the stranger on the left side of his skull. The stranger fell to the ground.

Laughter from the street caught Jimbo's attention. The Clinton Theater's box office must have opened. Without hesitation, Jimbo dragged the man by his feet to a spot in the shadows behind the Lockwood's shed. With his heart still pounding in his chest, the hobo returned to his place at the table, just in time for Paul Lockwood to push open the door with a stack of boxes.

After tossing them into his burn barrel, he turned back toward the door.

"Good evening."

"Jimbo, you startled me."

"So sorry, my friend. I've hit upon a bit of luck and have come for supper. I'll have a full serving of tonight's special, and a generous slice of peach pie with a scoop of homemade ice cream, if you please."

"What? You don't want apple?" Paul teased.

Jimbo's faced beamed. "I'm feeling a bit adventurous this evening."

"A full serving of tonight's special with peach pie and ice cream... coming right up."

Chapter 37

My hand flew to my mouth. I couldn't believe what I'd just heard right from Jimbo's own mouth. He had murdered Harrison Smith MacDonell for no reason. My heart beat so hard in my chest, I feared the two men could hear it.

"You lied to me at Mrs. Barner's cottage that day."

"Perhaps you're not the simpleton I thought you were." Jimbo sniffed loudly. I imagined the smug look on his face. "People mix the best lies with a healthy dose of truth. Tell me you haven't done it yourself."

"Since we're now sifting the truth from the lies, please explain how Mr. MacDonell's overnight case ended up in the cloakroom at the Little Palmer House, and how he ended up in Prairie Creek."

"That last part would require of bit of speculation on my part."

"Give it your best shot, Jimbo."

"When Paul went back inside the Blue and White Café to retrieve my supper, I looked around for the man's overnight case. My luck held. During my tussle dragging the man out of sight, the overnight case was pushed under the table. I grabbed it and carried it behind that old shed and dropped it next to Mr. MacDonell. Figuring I had a bit of time before Paul returned, I pilfered a few coins from a side pocket of the overnight bag—enough to pay for my extravagant evening—then returned to the table and waited. Just as my heart beat returned to normal, but before I had time to contemplate what I'd done, Paul appeared and presented me the most delicious meal I'd eaten in a long time. I closed my eyes and imagined myself dining on the roof garden at Hotel Astor in New York City. The food was somewhat pedestrian, I admit, but the enjoyment was equal to any meal I've eaten."

"Keep going."

"After I'd eaten, and Paul and I had settled up, I walked to the alley behind the Little Palmer House and gave the bellhop the man's overnight case, just as I told you the day at the cottage."

"A bit of truth sprinkled amidst the lies."

"Exactly." Jimbo paused for a moment before continuing. "As I strolled back to camp, one minor aspect of my deed befuddled me."

"Only the one?"

Jimbo continued without regard to the sheriff's question. "Dare I leave the body there, only steps from where Paul Lockwood encountered me?"

"But he wasn't dead, was he?"

"Again, you impress me with your dullard intellect." Jimbo chuckled. "I waited until the camp became quiet... I'm sure it was past midnight... then slipped back into town. That's when I discovered the man was gone, but surmised that if someone had found his body, it would have caused a commotion."

"Chalk one up to my dullard intellect, but I'm curious... how did Mr. MacDonell end up on Prairie Creek behind Doc Becker's house? Who told him to go there?"

Jimbo laughed. "I don't think he went over to South Street seeking a doctor. I assume a man on the edge of death went in search of the woman he loved. You fail to grasp the strength of a man's will when fueled by undying love for a woman... which is an unfortunate circumstance of the human condition."

Sheriff Boggs sounded confused. "After you discovered the man wasn't dead, you went..."

"I went in search of LoRetta Ghere."

I gasped at the mention of my aunt's name from the lips of a murderer.

"Where else would the man go?," Jimbo continued. "I apologize for failing to tell you that Mr. MacDonell told me all about his beloved, her name and where she lived. I also remembered hearing her name from Mrs. Parlett, her neighbor."

"That's quite a tale."

Jimbo remained silent.

"Your military service during the Great War... that was a lie, too."

"Ah, you have done your homework, Sheriff Boggs. Impressive. In my defense, I could not escape the bonds of Daddy's money. You don't think America's pre-eminent steel magnet, Cletus E. Vandercook, would allow his only son to fight in the trenches during a needless war with the rest of the rabble, do you? I sat behind a desk in Chaumont for several months. After an unfortunate incident involving a bottle of cheap whiskey and a couple of well-worn trollops, I was no longer welcome there and returned state-side. Though he was none too pleased with me, my father greased a few palms to remove the incident from my military record. I had some time to kill before I could return home as the honorable battle-worn soldier described in my discharge papers. After hobnobbing around New York awhile under an assumed name, of course, I joined my band of brothers in the real trenches here in

America to learn the stories of our warriors. Let's just say I took to the lifestyle."

"I assume you'll take to the prison lifestyle as easily."

"We both know that will never happen." Jimbo sounded confident, unaffected by the threat. "Lock the cell door and throw away the key if you must, but I assure you, it won't hold me for long. If my fingers can't beat the lock, I assure you my daddy's money can. Money can buy anything, my friend, including a bit of favor with that pretty young wife of yours."

I heard the rustling of clothing, followed by two slaps on the sheriff's desktop, then silence. That's when I heard my name, faint at first, yet full of concern. "Annie. Annie! Where are you, Angel?"

I counted to three, then slipped behind the counter and ran through the door of the sheriff's small office. "Sheriff, you're missing Bernard's party." My voice sounded frantic. My eyes met his, then drifted down to the two thick stacks of bills on the desk in front of him.

"Angelina," Jimbo hissed. "What an unexpected pleasure."

"Annie!" The voice was closer.

"I was looking for Sheriff Boggs," I stammered. "Miss Roxy is ready to serve Bernard's birthday cake."

"I've been keeping your sheriff busy with tales of my past, haven't I?"

Sheriff Boggs didn't react.

I looked at the hobo sitting in the chair in front of the sheriff's desk. It wasn't the time for questions, but I had to know something for sure. I took a deep breath. "Did you pull me and my friend out of the creek last winter when we fell through the ice?" Already certain of the answer, I wanted to hear it from the man's own mouth. I wanted any idea that he was my hero put to rest, once and for all.

At first, he looked confused. Then the sparkle returned to his eyes. His words as sweet as honey, yet drawn with the swiftness of a sword, "Angelina, I wouldn't get my boots wet for the likes of you."

Suddenly, Jimbo's hand shot out, grabbing my wrist and pulling me to him. I screamed. "Let go of me! Let go of me!" I struggled against his powerful grip. Terrified, I looked at Sheriff Boggs.

"She goes with me as far as the camp," Jimbo hissed.

In one swift motion, the sheriff swept the cash into his desk drawer and drew his gun.

"Nope," he replied, his voice calm, the click of his gun startling.

"At last, I've discovered your line-in-the-sand." Jimbo laughed, but his grip on my wrist tightened.

I expected Sheriff Boggs to spring from behind his desk and pull me away from the hobo. Instead, he sat, cool as a cucumber.

Finally, he spoke. "My Uncle Spunks not only took this Lugar off a German soldier he killed..." The sheriff waved the gun a bit. "...but he taught me how to use it. I can blow a fly off the side of your head without so much as grazing you. Right between your eyes seems a better option, though."

The sheriff raised his gun... adjusted his aim. I trembled.

"Is that a fact?"

"It is, indeed, a fact, Jimbo. It seems to me your death would resolve a load of my current problems."

"Or bring on a whole slough of other problems." Jimbo stared at Sheriff Boggs.

"Let her go. I will not say it again."

"Angel, are you in here?" The voice of my father.

I jerked my arm again, and Jimbo let go of my wrist. "Popo," I cried, as I ran out of the sheriff's office to where he stood in front of the counter. I climbed up his body and felt his arms wrap around me.

Sheriff Boggs strode out from his office, followed by Jimbo. "My apologies, Augie." he offered calmly. "I'm afraid Jimbo frightened Annie. After Bernard's party, I'll explain everything to you."

Popo took a deep breath to control his fury. Before he could reply, Adam Barner, followed by his brother Joshua, stormed through the door of the sheriff's office.

"What's going on here?" demanded Adam.

"*Ahh*, my chauffeur has arrived in the nick of time," chuckled Jimbo as he pushed past the sheriff. "I've just worn out my welcome here."

Adam's right eye twitched. "Let's go, Jimbo."

"One last thing, Mr. Vandercook. If I ever see the likes of you in my town again, I'll shoot first and ask questions later."

"I thought we had a deal, Sheriff."

"No deal." Then Sheriff Boggs looked straight into Adam's face and repeated his emphatic words. "No deal."

"No honor among thieves." Jimbo glared at the sheriff.

"This is *my* town. You're no longer welcome in *my* town. If I get wind that you're lurking about the hobo camp, or within a hundred miles of Mrs. Parlett, I'll put you down like a rapid dog and bury you so deep that *your daddy back in Gary* will never know what happened to you. Did I made myself clear enough to get through that pompous head of yours?"

Jimbo looked down. Adam backed up a step.

"Did I make myself clear?" shouted the sheriff.

"Clear as crystal."

Adam stepped forward and took Jimbo's arm.

"One last thing, Titus. Take a bath. You smell like the garbage that you are."

Chapter 38

I felt like dead weight in my father's arms as he carried me out of the sheriff's office. The short walk to South Street now seemed a long journey home. My father shook, not under the burden of my weight, but with anger... I was certain of it. Popo didn't understand all that had happened in the sheriff's private office, but Sheriff Boggs would tell him what he wanted his friend to know. I would never tell my father anything about my recent encounter with Jimbo... Titus.

Gus walked beside us, his hand never leaving my arm. "Aunt Lo is on her porch," he said as we approached the bridge. My brother nodded to where our aunt sat on a swing, swaying gently back and forth in a steady rhythm. "We have seen little of her since she returned from Wheaton, but I know Charlie and Bernard go sit in the library after school while she's working. She keeps busy, but she's sad."

My father turned his head toward his sister. "Leave her be. Your aunt has been through enough."

After Popo climbed the steps to our house, he set me down on my feet just as Mother opened the door.

"I got a telephone call from Roxy..."

"Call her back and tell her everything is fine, that Annie is here with us."

Mother nodded and stepped back into the house. She'd wait for Popo's explanation.

"I'm going to Aunt Lo's." My voice sounded weak, though I was as determined as I'd ever been in my life. "She needs me."

I expected Popo to try to stop me, but he said nothing as I walked across our yard and up over the bridge, pausing only for a moment to check the stones below where the water swirled over them. When I climbed the steps to the porch, Aunt Lo put down her foot to stop the motion of the swing and looked at me.

Her eyes were puffy and rimmed in red. She wore no rouge on her cheeks, nor lipstick on her lips. Since she hadn't yet faced the gossip at Huffer's Beauty School, she'd piled her hair loosely on top of her head, though several wavy strands had escaped and fell around her face, softening her features. She looked real, vulnerable, beautiful.

Aunt Lo opened her shawl as I fell into her warmth, her arms enfolding me. We sat in silence for a long while, watching the colorful leaves fluttering in the late summer breeze. The silence I shared with my beloved aunt was the kind that signified there was nothing left to say.

Now I was certain Jimbo hadn't pulled Pauline and me out of the icy winter water, yet I'd known that deep down all along. Sheriff Boggs hadn't pulled us out either. Why would he investigate for my father if he had? Then there was my Mother's answer. She told me she didn't know who pulled us out. I believed her, though I suspected she knew something she wasn't telling me. As I lay on Aunt Lo's lap, I resolved the matter in my own mind.

I remembered my aunt saying, "Secrets are burdens far too heavy for seven-year-olds to bear." She was wrong. I shared a secret with Mother that was her burden more than mine. Then I thought about the stacks of cash I saw on Sheriff Boggs' desk earlier, knowing Jimbo paid off the sheriff of Clinton County to overlook his crimes. I vowed never to tell Aunt Lo about the money. God had already put the truth about Clyde Boggs on her heart years ago, and I would never add to her pain.

I held two secrets that I would never reveal to anyone while the person I shared them with was still alive. I knew them both to be good people who loved me. Better the burden of a secret than the burden of the ugly truth destroying their lives.

The back-and-forth motion of the swing soon lulled me into a trance, and finally into a light sleep in which I dreamed of the black-and-whiteness of the poorhouse, and the shadows of its debtors who toiled against time and their own souls in search of a way out of their hell on earth. The rows of wooden crosses reminded me that many never did.

The faint sound of light footsteps on the porch steps drifted into my thoughts. My head was on my aunt's lap, eyes still closed, when the sheriff spoke. "May I have a word, LoRetta?" His words were a whisper on the breeze.

"Certainly, Sheriff. How can I help you?"

"Can you identify this?"

My aunt drew in a long breath. "Most certainly," she answered. "That's the silver handle of Smitty's walking cane, though it appears worse for the wear. I believe you'll discover a swirling floral motif under all that soot. Where did you find it?"

"At the bottom of the Lockwoods' burn barrel."

Aunt Lo must have had a hundred questions, but she asked none of them.

"LoRetta." One word. "There's something else."

I opened one eye and focused it on the sheriff.

He reached into his coat pocket and pulled out a diamond ring. "Smitty meant this for you, LoRetta."

I opened my other eye and set both on his face as a tear slid silently down his cheek.

Her hand shot to her mouth. I looked up at my aunt's face, her eyes closed as she held back a flood of emotions. "I couldn't possibly," she whispered, her head nodding back and forth.

"The man died trying to give this ring to the woman he loved. I'm certain his dying wish was for you to have it." Then sheriff looked over his shoulder toward the creek where the man had taken his last breath. When he turned back, he lifted my aunt's left hand from her lap and slipped the ring on her finger.

"It's a perfect fit," he whispered. "Wear it today, then do with it as you please."

"I told you, Boggy, I wouldn't have accepted his proposal."

"Yes, you would have, LoRetta. He was everything you deserved. Kind, rich, handsome. And Mackie, the son you never had... such a sweet boy, hungry for the love of a mother. The perfect family... everything you've ever wanted."

Tears steaming down her face, she held up her left hand and looked at the ring. "Sheriff," she finally said. "I owe you an apology."

"For what, LoRetta?"

"This whole mess was my fault."

"No, it wasn't. Stop blaming yourself."

"But it was. When I found out Smitty was married, I insisted Jean-Claude tell him I had gone home. That was a lie. Hurt and angry, I wanted nothing more than to hurt him back. But more than that, I wanted to stay with Louisa and my friends in Wheaton, to *enjoy myself*. How petty and selfish of me. If only I'd had the courage to face him when he came to see to me, none of this would have happened. He would still be alive today."

"Stop, LoRetta. Please stop! Have you forgotten Smitty came here to rectify his lies of omission?"

"We both know that one lie doesn't justify another." Aunt Lo sighed deeply and closed her eyes again. "Oh, those dank angry spaces between your heart and your head, so full of what ifs," she finally muttered. "I've always considered myself a pious woman, Boggy. I can always spot the faults in others. Then one little white lie came out of my mouth so easily, and we know what happened because of it."

"God knows your heart. He will forgive you."

"That He will. I just don't foresee how I'll ever forgive myself. There will always be those what ifs disturbing my sleep."

Sheriff Boggs looked at his feet, then back at Aunt Lo. "Forgiving oneself... that's the hardest thing of all."

The tension between the two drifted away, and simple comfort settled in. They had been there before, I was sure of it.

"For what it's worth, LoRetta. I think you're courageous. You've faced the gossip and criticism from the entire town, held your head up and did your work at the library."

My aunt chuckled bitterly. "There's no comfort in courage, now is there, Sheriff Boggs?"

He shook his head. "No, there is not. Before I go, I have a question for Annie."

My aunt patted my arm. I nodded once.

"Deputy, do you have any idea where I might find Smitty's motor-car?"

Visions of the open lock on Mrs. Barner's cottage and the heavy black lock on Paul Lockwood's shed fluttered across my mind. I remembered Jimbo's comment about how a prison cell couldn't hold him. Then I recalled the stale smell of old hay mingled with a faint musty odor and a whiff of gasoline.

I raised up to lean against my aunt. "It's in Paul Lockwood's shed."

The sheriff's eyes widened. "Who would put it there?"

"Jimbo. He can pick locks, you know."

"I guess I do, now that you mention it." The sheriff sniffed with satisfaction as the last piece of the puzzle fell into place. Then the man reached into his pants pocket and opened his hand in front of me. "These are for my deputies. You earned them."

I looked at the two shiny Walking Liberty half dollars Bernard discovered in the crack of the black walnut tree near the Interurban tracks. "Don't they belong to Mrs. MacDonell?"

"Finder's keepers. That's the law of the land."

I closed my hand around the coins. I decided I'd give one to Gem and the other to Bernard. I didn't want any reminders of the Corpse in the Creek. I wanted to bury that memory with the secrets I kept.

The sheriff stepped a moment longer, as if he had something else to say. Then he stepped off the porch. "I appreciate your time. Good afternoon, ladies."

My aunt and I swayed back and forth in the swing, the slow passing of time expressed in blessed silence, uninterrupted, except when MaMaw opened the door to peer out to check on her two girls. Finally, I asked Aunt Lo the question that had been on my mind for a while.

"What's it like to fall in love?"

The woman chuckled softly. "Perhaps you should ask someone who fell in love but didn't get her heart broken."

I waited, knowing she would say more in her own time.

"I loved him so very much." Aunt Lo sighed deeply.

"How did you feel when he married Martha?"

Aunt Lo choked back a sob. "I've never gotten over it."

She put her arm around me and pulled me closer. We cried together, her tears of grief for the man she truly loved but could never have... my tears of grief for my beloved aunt.

I glanced at the sore spot on the underside of my wrist. A bruise was already forming where the hobo had gripped my arm. Jimbo's thumbprint... a reminder of all that happened in Jeffries in the last few weeks. I promised myself to keep my wrist hidden from Popo until the bruise faded, the memory of the hobo along with it.

As the sun faded, I heard Charlie calling me from the other side of Prairie Creek. "Annie! Supper!"

I wasn't ready to go home just yet. I had one more question for Aunt Lo.

"What were Sheriff Boggs' kisses like?"

She threw back her head. One word slipped from her lips, but I heard its faint echo on the breeze.

"Fire."

With that utterance, the edge of summer slipped away without fanfare, and autumn's welcome normalcy set in.

Epilogue

"Aunt Lo, do you believe in angels?"

"Of course I do, Annie."

"Pauline and I believe an angel pulled us out of the creek last January. Nothing else makes any sense to us."

Aunt Lo thought about what I'd said for a long moment. She finally nodded. "I think you and Pauline are right. But you know what that means, don't you?"

"What does it mean, Aunt Lo?"

"It means God saved you for a reason."

About the Author

Born and reared n Lima, Ohio, Patra Ann Taylor loved listening to her mother opine about her life growing up in Frankfort, Indiana during the early 20th century. Inspired by her mother's memories, Taylor wrote "Christmas Angels," a classic "happy ending" holiday novel that paints a detailed picture of life during a bygone era in the American Midwest. "Edge of Summer," the first novel in her Anna Ghere Mysteries series, is based on the same characters.

Patra spent her lengthy professional career as an editor, freelance writer, and newspaper columnist. Today, she focuses on writing historical mysteries and other books. She lives in Mount Pleasant, South Carolina with her husband, Stephen Bucher, and their Australian terrier, Olive.

If you'd like to keep up with the latest in Patra's upcoming Anna Ghere Mysteries series, please sign-up for her newsletter, *Charlie's Word,* by visiting her website at https://patraanntaylor.com/.

www.ingramcontent.com/pod-product-compliance
Lightning Source LLC
Chambersburg PA
CBHW071747110726
47908CB00006B/1722